THE HO

Jane felt the thin gold chains slither across her naked belly and thighs, through the cleft of her buttocks, and then she gasped in surprise and ticklish delight as her anus was strocked by a single feather. The harness was completed by Henry's looping the chains up to her nipples and fastening them with two tight golden clasps.

'There!' he said. 'Now look in the mirror.'

Jane did so, and saw a criss-cross of gold across her belly and fesses, looped in a sensuous pattern. The fan which was secured inside her sex stood up from the curving clasp; she felt the other nestle against the cleft of her buttocks.

'To open the fans,' said Henry, with the air of a conjuror performing a trick, 'simply press the clasps with the muscle of your lovely sphincter, and hey presto! You're the belle of the ball.

A NEXUS CLASSIC

THE HOUSE OF MALDONA

Yolanda Celbridge

This book is a work of fiction.
In real life, make sure you practise safe sex.

First published in 1994 by
Nexus
Thames Wharf Studios
Rainville Road
London W6 9HA

This Nexus Classic edition 2002

www.nexus-books.co.uk

ISBN 0 352 33740 0

Typeset by TW Typesetting, Plymouth, Devon
Printed and bound by
Clays Ltd, St Ives PLC

Contents

1

A Thief Caned

Jane Ardenne threw off the green silk coverlet and yawned, smiled at the prospect of another lovely day in lovely London, then went to the window, stretching her naked body. Outside, Cheyne Walk hummed with traffic, and the river flowed still and grey under a fresh spring sun. The trees in Battersea Park were bright with new leaves. Jane thought, there is nothing so nice as to stand naked at my window and look out on my city. It was Saturday, her day for Portobello Market, and, doubly yummy, Henry Gordon Playste was her date that evening.

'I've got a date, I've got a date tonight,' she sang, feeling silly, because Henry was more than a date, he was her super lover, not that all her lovers weren't super – they had to be, or they wouldn't be allowed to love her! – he was a friend, he was a kiss-smooth body under his adorable power-striped suit, he was a briefcase stuffed with papers that had lots and lots of dollar signs on them, he was always working and never seeing her as much as she wanted, he was adorably cute and maddeningly rich! Or perhaps the other way around.

She looked at herself in the mirror on the ceiling, then in the mirror over the fireplace, then tried to look at both at once, trying to find a flaw in her body, something she could have a good worry about, and failing, as she knew she would. Feeling naughty, she pressed her bare breasts to the window, misty from the night's breath. The few passers-by showed no astonishment at the sight of a nineteen-year-old heiress pressing her naked teats to her window. Out of their gaze lay the lush forest of blonde curls that

1

prettily garlanded her pubis; but the full, ripe young breasts, with their big soft nipples like apricots in a dish of honey, were nakedly, radiantly visible. She felt quite delicious and naughty, then put her fingers over her nipples as though from modesty, but really to give them a little stroking, because the act of showing herself nude to strangers made her quite tingly with excitement. She wished that all the millions of London's people could look at her at once, and the idea made her sex moisten a little.

She wished Cassie were here, sweet Cassandra, her friend who was more than a friend, so that they could stand naked together, and look out at Chelsea, and giggle and stroke each other and have a little cuddle, and then maybe ... Oh, what was the use? Cassie was in Spain, her last letter from Marbella answered eagerly, then followed up, then followed by a plea for contact, and no further letter had come. She must do something about it ... One of these days. Go to damn Spain herself, maybe, and find her, for Cassie was too special to lose for ever, and when she had found her, give her a good telling-off, and be really, really cross, and pull her jeans down and give her a darn good spanking on her bare bottom – well, it would be her bare bottom, wouldn't it, since Cassie didn't usually bother to wear panties – and then when her bottom was all red and smarting, they would have a stupendous cuddle and kisses, then put their arms round each other and ...

Every time she thought of Cassie, she ended up the same way, all wet and fluttery in her sex! Damn! She grinned ruefully. One of these days! Yet, as she padded into the kitchen to make breakfast, not bothering to slip on a robe, she wondered why she had thought of actually spanking Cassie. She was so mad at Cassie's flightiness, her neglect – ooh, she was so horrid and selfish! – that it seemed right she should be punished. Tears, hurt looks, a shouting match, would have no effect, Cassie would just laugh.

'Cassandra,' she would say, 'do you wish to break my heart, you neglectful temptress?'

'Yes,' Cassie would say, with a rich smile. She knew Cassie. Yes, a good spanking, that was the thing. Make her bottom squirm – her bare bottom, mind, those lovely globes all twitchy and pink and hot under my bare palm!

God, she thought, I'm dripping wet down there! What gave me the idea of spanking her? I've never thought of that before. And then she remembered that curious book she had bought the day before in the Charing Cross Road. She took it for the binding, really, in sumptuous white Morocco, which would look nice on her groaning bookshelf alongside all the other white Morocco bindings. And she had felt so ... sexy as she bought it! Books as furniture, indeed, that was in the bookseller's disapproving eye.

'I do read all my books, you know,' she said severely, and he grinned.

'You'll read that one, Miss, and be back for more. I know by your eyes.' The cheek of the man!

The book lay on the coffee table, awaiting transfer to the shelf, alongside all the things in French and Spanish and German which she felt obliged to plough through – how she could enthral a dinner party with her tales from eighteenth-century travellers in the Caucasus, or tickle their palates with recipies as served to Louis XIV! But a quick glance had told her this book was not about cookery or travel, except by the kinkiest of definitions.

De Artibus Castigationis, by one Parfaite Cecilia of Ubrique – a nun from some mysterious Spanish convent? – printed in Amsterdam in the seventeenth century, and evidently a translation from some monkish Latin. The English title was *The Fine Arts of Chastisement*, and she could see why it had to be published in Amsterdam. The frontispiece was an engraving, showing a naked girl strapped to a flogging frame, with four vicious whip-thongs frozen in mid-air on their way to stroking her writhing back. She was being whipped by another woman, wearing a strangely exciting costume of tight chains and feathers, and Jane wondered what was going through the mind of each woman as they conspired in their savage ritual.

In the kitchen, she prepared coffee and eggs and juice, and brought her meal to the coffee table. She ate lazily, forcing herself not to look at the book until she could relax

3

with a cigarette, but still she wolfed the food, without admitting she was hurrying to open it. It was a quarter past seven; annoyed at her impatience to look at the silly thing, she told herself to make sure her kit was ready for her market stall before sitting down to relax. She would open the book, of course, but only to kill time before going off in her Range Rover about nine. It would probably be a disappointment.

She went into her workroom, where her moulds and turning-wheels and kilns lay cool from the night, and inspected the shelves full of gaudy wax candles. She began to work, though it was scarcely arduous, filling boxes with the bright wax ornaments, for she considered them works of art, really, although happily her customers burnt them at dinner parties in Hampstead and Islington, and had to come back for more. There were even nice chocolate candles, which you couldn't burn, but you could eat them, and every single candle was modelled from a man's erect penis.

'A girl has to have a trade,' she would say, 'and my great-something grandfather made his fortune up in my native turf, which is rainy old Northumberland, by making candles, and all sorts of other things too, and that is why his lovely little great-something granddaughter happens to own a flat in Chelsea as well as big chunks of said Northumberland, and why is it so strange to make a fortune selling candles, anyway it's sort of in my blood, you know? and yes, they are all modelled from life . . .'

Her work complete, she returned to the table, sat down and poured herself another cup of black coffee, lit a Gauloise, then nonchalantly yawned again, and reached for the book with fingers that she wished were not trembling. Being naked made reading it seem somehow naughty, and she put her feet up on the coffee table with her thighs apart, which seemed naughtier still.

The book was copiously illustrated, and she studied the pictures with increasing, horrified fascination. The text was solemn, po-faced even, with detailed descriptions of punishments, tortures, and the equipment used to inflict them.

4

She saw torments she would not have thought bearable, with metal clamps, rods, and harnesses merciless in their caress of naked flesh. The majority of the illustrations, however, showed floggings in all their terrible forms. Naked men and women were lashed with a variety of horrid implements – cane, tawse, scourge or birch – and as she scrutinised the loving detail of the punishments, Jane realised that the fingers holding her cigarette had unconsciously strayed to her quim, which was quite tingly and wet as she stroked. She put the cigarette out, and, swallowing, put her hand back between her legs and, as she read on, rubbed her stiffening clitoris with the tips of her fingers. She thought of herself lashed by those fearsome whips, and shuddered. What must it be like? Then she thought of being dressed in that curious gaudy harness, and flogging Cassie's naked bottom with a long birch or cane, and shut her eyes as she felt her quim gushing with hot love-juice. What, oh what, must it be like?

This is crazy! she thought, and opened her eyes. Trembling, she made her way to the bathroom for a shower, but once there, she could not help looking at her buttocks in the mirror and wondering what they would look like after a naked spanking, or *zurrado* as Parfaite Cecilia quaintly called it. On impulse, she picked up one of her silver hairbrushes and slapped herself gingerly on her bottom, but it hardly hurt at all. She spanked herself again, harder, and saw a pretty crimson flush where her naked skin had received the blow. Another slap made her bottom nice and crimson, and it did hurt, now. She began to spank herself as hard as she could, feeling the hot smart suffuse her body with a giddy glow that was pain and pleasure at the same time. She looked at herself in the mirror, and saw her eyes heavy with desire, her lips slack and red. On and on she spanked herself, not counting the blows.

'Naughty girl! Silly girl!' she hissed with mock severity. She thought through her stinging pain, my poor bare bottom is glowing now, like the furnace for my candle moulds, and she thought then of all those cocks somehow inside her at once, fucking her soaking quim as her naked bottom

squirmed under a spanking; then it was more than a spanking, a heavy four-thonged whip lashing her without pity,
making her helpless naked body writhe under her caress,
as her cunt-petals now writhed pink and glistening at the
caress of her fingers, waving and swelling like some beautiful sea-flower.

The silver hairbrush descended without ceasing on
Jane's bare nates; her hand was on her clit, throbbing and
hard, sending shock waves of pain and desire through her
nipples and spine. Her cunt-petals lapped the waters that
flowed from her gushing sex, and as her bottom smarted
and glowed with fiery pain, Jane Ardenne cried out in the
savage sweetness of her orgasm.

The Portobello Market was cheerful with the gusto of
spring and the crackle of folding money. Jane set up her
table and her bright display, and right from the start there
was a steady stream of customers. They were, as usual,
mostly women, with naughty glints in their eyes, helped by
Jane's offer of 'Free Glass of Champagne with Every Purchase'. She figured that, at fifteen pounds a throw for her
intricate designs, she could afford this little marketing device. Men tended to look furtive, pay and hurry away, but
the women liked to chat, curious how the candles were
made, who Jane was, and how she got such splendid
models.

Jane nursed her own glass of champagne, just to look
sociable, for her lady customers who bought their candles
in fours or sixes expected, with the thriftiness of the well-
heeled, to get a glass for every single candle. It was a nice
way to spend Saturday morning, although she was still a
little dazed from the unexpected intensity of her masturbation, and the smarting of her still-glowing spanked bottom.
She thought of Henry, could scarcely wait for his arrival
that evening. How she wished it could have been Henry
who spanked her! Maybe he would; but he would be too
gentle, perhaps, not wanting to hurt her. That wouldn't be
good, but then, if he were rough, and hurt her too much,
that wouldn't be good either. The flogged girls in that

strange book would surely not complain that their lacings were too gentle.

And yet, some of them had had a dreamy, faraway look in their eyes, as though they were actually enjoying their punishment, as though it were akin to some weird sexual ecstasy! A spanking was one thing, a bit of harmless fun. She recalled, now, that Henry had once or twice threatened playfully to spank her as 'punishment' for some flirtation or other, and she had made it firmly clear that he was out of order. Perhaps she shouldn't have; perhaps, now, she could provoke him into really spanking her, just for fun, nicely. Not seriously, of course. To see what it was like. Yes, a gentle spanking might be a naughty thrill for both of them, not like the proper floggings in those pictures . . . it was so confusing!

As she talked to her customers over their champagne, she found herself looking at their bottoms and wondering if they were spanked by their men, how they would look with their panties down and their bums all pink and squirming, and she found that those thoughts made her quim seep with wetness again. Suddenly she needed to pee! Her market kit was designed for just that: she wore a brief leather mini-skirt, and a rather low-cut silk blouse, both red, with a lot of gold chains nestling between her breasts, which was meant to be, and was, a rather deliciously tarty complement to her risqué merchandise. You had to look the part at Portobello, and she had learned that the most successful traders were precisely those with all the patter, who looked like charming, unscrupulous flash gits.

Taking a moment between customers, she moved discreetly to the side of her car and opened her thighs to pee, smiling with relief as the little pool formed between her calfskin thigh-boots. Then she noticed a young girl, rather embarrassed, hovering around her display, as though she didn't dare to touch or enquire. The girl took advantage of Jane's absence to move closer, absent-mindedly, as though she were really looking for something else. She was maybe seventeen, pale, and beautiful in an elfin way, with soft blonde locks like Jane's own, framing a narrow, pretty face and a skin of translucent gentleness. She wore a light grey raincoat, and under it some kind of dark blue school uniform. Well, she did not look like someone with fifteen pounds to spend on an erotic candle, so Jane politely approached her.

'Like anything?' she said. 'They're fifteen pounds each, and a free glass of champagne with every purchase.' The girl's answer surprised her.

'What kind of champagne?' she asked.

'Why, Taittinger,' said Jane.

'That's nice,' said the girl. 'But fifteen pounds is an awful lot of pocket money. They are lovely things, though.' And she blushed heartily. Jane warmed towards her.

'Still in school uniform, on Saturday?' she said.

'I go to a boarding school, the Rosebush School, actually.' She named one of the most exclusive, and expensive, schools in London. 'My name's Sarah Pennington,' she added, though Jane hadn't asked.

'Well, Sarah, I'm not sure the Rosebush School would appreciate your bringing back one of my candles,' said Jane in a kindly tone. 'Perhaps they might think you are too young for such things.'

'Yes, I suppose so,' said the girl ruefully. 'Would you mind if . . . if I touched one?' Jane laughed.

'Touch as many as you like, Sarah,' she replied. 'Rather bewitching, aren't they?' Jane reached out and began to stroke a big pink candle; decorated with roses, which Jane had modelled from Henry's own cock.

'Are these all real?' asked Sarah, blushing again. 'I mean . . .'

'I know what you mean. Yes, they are real, every single one.'

'Gosh, Miss, you must know a lot of boys.'

'Boys? Yes, you could say I know a lot of boys.'

'Have you one special one?'

'I suppose the one you are stroking with such evident pleasure, Sarah.'

'He must be very handsome. What's his name?'

'Why, his name is Henry.'

'That's a nice name.' Jane's heart melted. She imagined all the thoughts and dreams and desires that must surge in the young girl's breast, and was on the point of telling her she could keep the candle, when Sarah turned and said that she had better go. At that moment Jane saw something peeping from the pocket of her raincoat. It was the pink tip of a candle, a 'Henry'! It was so artlessly concealed that she must have filched it in a hurry, while Jane was distracted by her peeing. At once Jane seized the girl's arm with the speed and severity of a hunter.

'Just a minute,' she said, and retrieved the candle from Sarah's pocket. Rage welled up inside her. She had been about to give her Henry's cock as a present, and this little angel had pinched it!

'So you are a thief, Sarah Pennington,' she said harshly. 'Well, I don't suppose they'll be impressed at Rosebush to see you arrive back at school in a police car.' Sarah's face blushed an angry red, then changed abruptly to the paleness of terror.

'Oh, God!' she blurted. 'Please, don't call the police! Daddy would be so angry, and the Sisters at school, and I might be expelled, and then I'd never get to finishing school! Oh, I do so want to go to finishing school! I'm just eighteen, I can go very soon. I've never done anything like this before, honestly, truly, oh please don't call the police!'

All this was blurted in a terrified rush of anguish, and Jane almost, but not quite, felt sorry for the poor girl with the angel's face. Her voice was soft and melodious, with the ease of wealth, and Jane realised that the Burberry concealed no common tea-leaf from across the river – but a tea-leaf none the less. There were inquisitive stares from the other stalls.

'We don't take kindly to thieves, here,' said Jane.

'I'm not a thief!'

Jane waved the wax penis in her face.

'This says you are!'

And Sarah blushed deep red, whether from shame at her crime or embarrassment at the succulent cock only an inch from her rosebud lips Jane wasn't sure. She hung her head, and began to sob gently. Then she gasped, and swallowed, and took a deep breath, as though filling her slender frame with courage.

'Miss, I know I've done wrong, and I must be punished,' she sobbed, 'but I beg you, don't bring the police.' Jane felt awful. It was a wretched thing to see the girl cry. She put her arm round Sarah's shoulders, and gave her a little hug.

'Oh, Sarah, I have to,' she said gently. 'Everybody's watching – they can't see me let a thief go unpunished, or I'll be thrown out of the market.'

'You mean, like expelled?'

'That's it.'

Sarah looked up, and smiled through her tears.

'Well, Miss, I needn't go unpunished, need I?'

'How do you mean?'

'You could punish me yourself.'

'I can hardly send you to jail!' cried Jane.

'No . . . I mean, if you called the police and everything, I'd be punished at school, I'd get a caning, certainly, and it would be on my school record for ever and ever, and I would never be admitted to finishing school!' And the tears threatened to well up again.

'Are you suggesting that I should cane you?'

'Well . . . yes, Miss. Not hard, I mean, but, well, you know, that could be my punishment, couldn't it?' Jane stared at Sarah in gaping astonishment, and yet she felt her heart pound with a strange excitement at the thought of caning the girl's bottom, of making her squeal and sob as she flogged her, and then, Jane knew, she wouldn't mind those sobs at all.

'Please, Miss, I beg you, punish me yourself – I'll go home with you, if you like, and you can cane my bottom and I promise I'll take whatever you decide. I'll hate it, I know, and the pain will be absolutely horrid, but then I'll have been properly punished to your satisfaction, won't I?'

Jane found that her inner thighs, pantyless, were beginning to feel wet from the liquid that now seeped quite copiously from her tingling slit. Her eyes were misty, her breath harsh as she looked at the sweet elfin face of this girl who

10

was pleading to be beaten! What was happening to her? Instead of dismissing the request as ridiculous and possibly dangerous, she was longing to accede to it! Well, the girl was eighteen, legally an adult in most things. Jane frowned.

'Look, I don't like this mess any more than you do,' she said. She wished she could send the girl away, but she could not deny the surging of her body, the wetness in her quim at the thought of that girl naked under her lash!

'I know I've been foolish! I must pay for it!' cried Sarah passionately.

'But a caning? One girl caning another, people might think that a little bizarre.'

Now it was Sarah's turn to frown in puzzlement. 'Why, we are often caned at school. It is the normal punishment. Sometimes, Miss, on our bare bottoms. We have to kneel over a flogging-stool, and lift our skirts, and pull our panties down to our knees, and then we get the cane all bare. How it smarts! It is awful. Oh, I hope you won't cane me on my bare bottom, Miss!'

'I haven't said I will,' answered Jane, fighting to control her rising swell of desire to make the naked body of the girl squirm. It was as though Sarah's very innocence were a tool of devilish seduction; as if – but no, it couldn't be – as if she knew exactly what she was doing, and had known right from the start.

'Oh, please, Miss,' repeated Sarah. 'Miss, if I deserve it, yes, I'll take it on the bare bum!' Jane's resistance broke.

'Sarah, I wouldn't be so cruel! You can take it on your skirt, it's all right! I'll make you sting, but . . .' She paused, and blushed furiously, realising what she had said.

'Thank you, Miss,' cried Sarah Pennington, and put her arms around Jane's waist, and kissed her so that her tears moistened Jane's cheek, as wet desire flowed from her helpless, throbbing, cunt-lips.

On the way back to Cheyne Walk, Jane was in such a turmoil of fear and tremulous anticipation that she could scarcely concentrate on her driving. Of course, she insisted to herself, the girl deserved to be punished for her moment

11

of foolishness – if foolishness it was – and of course a caning was the logical, supremely sensible solution. Henry had a theory about it: like all men, he had a theory about everything. He said being caned on the sensitive buttocks was a ritual which reinforced upper-class solidarity. The recipient of a beating at Henry's public school accepted his punishment wholeheartedly, chatting civilly to the chastiser before, after and even during the flogging, eager, even grateful, to show a stiff upper lip. They would discuss the finer points of the beating, dispassionately, as though it were a cricket match, and shake hands afterwards.

An added *frisson* was that boys sentenced to 'six of the best', normally delivered on the trousers, could elect to take the beating from either matron or the headmaster's wife, a woman's delivery being thought weaker: but in that case, they were obliged to take the cane on the naked buttocks, to compensate. Either way, a beating coolly given and received was a reminder that maintenance of the gentleman's code was well worth the momentary discomfort of an individual. A gentleman, Henry had always chosen to be beaten by the women.

So, Jane told herself, what she was about to do was quite normal, even salutary: a girl with Sarah's accent could scarcely suffer the indignity of a police station! And yet, she was afraid: not for the comfort of Sarah's presumably experienced bottom, but of her own new and disturbing emotions.

Sarah, in contrast, behaved as though a caning from a stranger were the most natural thing in the world.

'By the way, Miss,' she said, as they drove through South Kensington, 'what are you going to beat me with? I expect it'll be pretty tight. You were so cross with me! I'm keen to get it over with – the waiting's the most painful part, really.'

'I hadn't thought,' replied Jane. 'It's not every day I cane juvenile delinquents.' She did not add that this was the first time in her life she was going to cane a girl's naked buttocks, for, yes, she shall take it naked, thought Jane, and my quim is sopping wet and my heart's pounding, and I don't know what's got into me.

'You must have a riding crop around your house, or something,' stated Sarah.

'Cheyne Walk isn't the best place to keep polo ponies,' said Jane drily.

'I suppose not. A cane, then, a quirt, or a nice whippy birch?'

'Why, of course not,' said Jane in astonishment.

'We'll have to buy one, then,' said Sarah briskly, as though it were she in charge. 'Look, if you can find a place to stop – Walton Street's your best – I'll pop into Harrod's and get something.' Numbly, Jane agreed, and did manage to find a parking space. She sat nervously with the motor running, her body on fire with anticipation, until the younger girl scampered merrily back from the shop with a long slender object wrapped in the distinctive shopping bag. Jane wondered if Harrod's did a special size of bag specially for canes, and gunned the motor just in time to avoid an approaching traffic warden. Sarah bubbled with enthusiasm as though she had bought herself a fluffy toy, not an instrument of punishment.

'I got you a lovely one, Miss. It's yew, a four-footer, with a splayed tip, and I bet it'll hurt dreadfully!' Jane nodded, and wondered why her heart leapt with desire at the innocent froth of Sarah's words.

'Actually, I don't know much about canes,' she said.

'Oh, I do, Miss,' said Sarah. 'When you go to Rosebush, you know all about canes.'

'What a lovely flat!' cried Sarah as they entered Jane's home. 'Do you live here all alone?'

'Yes, I do, as it happens,' said Jane curtly. 'And I don't think you need to know any more than that, young lady. You had better be thinking about what my cane is going to do to your bottom.'

'I'm thinking of that, all right,' said Sarah brightly, so brightly in fact that any hesitation Jane felt about the punishment was quite gone. Sarah removed her Burberry, and folded it neatly on the sofa. Jane looked at her slender frame, crisply encased in her uniform, yet with the breasts

13

and bottom of a ripe woman blossoming under the sober skirt and blouse. Jane's belly trembled with a desire to punish this elfin thief for her insolent beauty.

'Well, I suppose the civilised thing is to offer you a glass of champagne before we proceed to business,' she said. 'I could do with one myself. Taittinger all right?'

'Yes, please,' said Sarah. 'I hope you're not nervous, Miss.' Jane fetched glasses, and they toasted each other with mock gravity.

'Here's to your beating, Sarah,' said Jane. Sarah's eyes shone with a fierce sparkle that was not just from wine.

'Here's to my learning my lesson,' she said gravely. 'But you haven't told me how many I'm to get.' Jane took a deep breath. Now was the moment of truth. Could she go through with it?

'It'll be a full six, Sarah,' she said quickly.

'Yes, I deserve it, don't I? This champagne is scrumptious.'

'Bare bum, I've decided.'

'Thought you would,' replied Sarah, draining her glass and grinning impishly. 'Well, we had better get on with it, Miss.'

'Right,' said Jane, businesslike now, 'over the sofa, please, with your skirt well up, and your panties round your knees.'

Sarah obeyed, bending over the sofa and raising her skirt to reveal a delicious pair of blue silken panties embroidered with butterflies in gold thread. Over these stretched a white lace garter belt with straps holding up the sheerest white silk stockings. She undid her garter straps and pulled down her panties to her knees, and Jane had a stifle a gasp of admiration at the perfect roundness of her smooth bare fesses.

'Pretty panties,' she said.

'Thank you, Miss. Actually, I'm glad it's bare bum, because then they won't get spoiled. Would you like to take me on tiptoe, Miss? It hurts more that way, because I can't wriggle so much to ease the smarting. I'll slip my shoes off if you like.'

14

'Yes,' said Jane, faint with desire. 'Yes, I'll take you on tiptoe. I . . . I want to make you smart.'

When Sarah was correctly positioned, her thighs straining as she perched on her delicate pointed toes, Jane raised her cane to her arm's full height, and stood, heart racing, over those naked white buttocks, tempting her beyond endurance with their innocent nudity. She felt a crazy desire to stop and kiss them, before they were flayed: they were so utterly, gorgeously pure.

'Well,' she blurted, trying to sound jovial, 'I dare say you won't be so glad when I begin your punishment, Sarah, for I've decided to give that bare bum of yours a really tight skinning. It'll be six juicy whistling cuts, and you will remember your lesson, all right.'

'Mmm,' said Sarah.

'No flinching, Sarah, and no silly squirming or girly wriggling, or the stroke's repeated. Understand?'

'Mmm,' said Sarah again, as though she were about to lick a bowl of cream.

'One!' Jane brought the cane down as hard as she could on Sarah Pennington's trembling, naked, and utterly adorable bottom.

As the cane whipped across her bare flesh, Sarah clenched the cheeks of her bottom, but made no sound other than a sharp drawing of breath. Her legs, stretched taut on tiptoes, shivered slightly. Jane waited for long seconds before lifting her cane to deliver the second stroke, and when that fell viciously on Sarah's fesses, the girl shut her eyes and pursed her lips tight, with a little catching sob at the back of her throat. Thereafter the beating took place in total silence, except for the crack of the cane on the blushing skin of Sarah's bared nates.

The cane felt quite heavy, and Jane wondered how the girl could take it with such apparent calm. Each stroke made her clenched buttocks quiver like two lovely white blancmanges, now prettily adorned with pink, and shook the garter straps, unfastened to permit the lowering of her precious panties, which dangled over the tops of her stockings. Jane felt herself becoming wet between her thighs as

15

she gazed at the flogged bottom of her victim, framed by the swaying garter straps. She felt a crazy desire to kiss that smarting croup, to have it for herself and feel the lash descend upon her naked body. And she felt an anger, that Sarah was experiencing a private intensity, which she could, or would not, share. What thoughts passed behind those tightly closed eyes?

Jane was panting hard, and sweating well, when she finally lowered the cane after the sixth cut.

'There!' she gasped. 'That's it. You've taken six.'

Sarah did not move, except to open her eyes, and shake her head as though it had been immersed in water. She opened her mouth, and now she made a sound, a long, low moan that seemed to come from the very pit of her belly.

'Aaaah,' she rasped. And now her bottom began to squirm crazily, shuddering and dancing with all the pent-up pain of her beating.

'Oh, oh,' she cried, through clenched teeth. 'Gosh, Miss, that was tight. Oh, how tight it was! My bottom feels on fire! I've never taken such a beautiful tight lacing, I think!'

'Beautiful?' said Jane. 'Well, if you think it thus.' And in truth, the sight of those bare fesses dancing for her was indeed beautiful. Was it possible that the victim of her lacing could feel that beauty too?

'I mean in the sense that something done expertly and with grace is beautiful. Daddy laces me sometimes, when I'm naughty – I suppose I shouldn't tell you this, but it's at home in Dorset, you know? I mean, it doesn't really count, does it? And it hurts horribly, but it's beautiful in a way because he is so good at it, and so strong and tender at the same time, and makes me feel I never want to upset him again. He takes me in my nightie, and makes me lift it up, and gives me twenty-one beats with his silver hairbrush on my bare bottom. Always twenty-one, I don't know why. It smarts awfully, though it doesn't hurt half as much as the cane. Especially your cane. Oh, I am prattling like a little girl, I suppose you think I'm a silly.'

'Well, you can get up now,' said Jane. 'That wasn't really so bad, was it? And no ... I don't think you're silly.'

Sarah swallowed and gasped for breath. She looked around; her face was as crimson as her bottom, and her eyes brimmed with tears, but she grinned fiercely.

'Oh, Miss,' she said, 'it was much worse. I don't think I shall ever be naughty again! I must look – may I please go to your bathroom?'

'Of course. You may pull your panties up now, Sarah.'

'No . . . I'll take them right off, please. You see, I don't know how to say it, well, I'm all . . . naughty.'

Jane looked and saw that the inside of Sarah's thighs glistened with moisture.

'Yes, I see,' she said. 'Well, leave your panties and run to the bathroom and take a good look at yourself. I hope the sight will teach you a lesson, for your bum's well blushing, girl.'

Sarah stood up, and skipped out of her panties, then, holding her skirt carefully up, she hurried to the bathroom. Jane was intrigued to see that this virginal convent girl, as well as possessing a pair of quite unvirginal panties, had shaved her mink so that the lips and inner thighs were completely naked, right up to the top of her prepuce, and the hairs above were sculpted into the shape of a butterfly that seemed to flutter up towards her belly. She thought it awfully pretty and, as Sarah made bathroom noises, she went to get another glass of champagne and sat down with a cigarette.

'Everything OK, Sarah?' she called after what seemed quite a long time.

'Oh, yes,' said Sarah rather faintly. 'I'm fine. You've made my bottom so red, Miss!'

'It had to be done, Sarah, you know that. There is some ointment in the cupboard, if you need it.'

'Thanks. I'm just . . . looking at myself, actually. I hope you don't mind?' Jane laughed.

'No, I don't mind. There is a glass of champagne for you, if you like.'

'Thanks awfully, but I must rush. And I don't want to be squiffy at Rosebush, or I'll get another lacing.'

Jane finished her cigarette, and thought that Sarah gave

17

little sign of rushing. The bathroom door was slightly open; she padded quietly, and glanced through. Sarah had arranged the folding mirrors of the bathroom cabinet so that she could look at her behind. With one foot on the carpet, and the other perched on the side of the bathtub, she gazed at her red bare buttocks, writhing slightly as her hand caressed them. Her skirt up, and her fingers between the shaven lips of her quim, Sarah Pennington masturbated.

Sarah finally departed, saying that the cane that had flogged her was a gift, to make up for her crime. She insisted on having the precious Harrod's shopping bag, though. Her face was flushed as she donned her Burberry, and her eyes glistened with innocent satisfaction. Jane had to suppress her own desire to take the girl's wet quim against her own lips, to find that throbbing little virgin's clit and tongue it to the sweetest of orgasms. But something told her to beware of Sarah Pennington, virginal though she might seem.

'I must rush, Miss. I'm expected at Daddy's for luncheon, and then back at Rosebush by teatime.'

'Do you have far to go? I can call a cab.'

'Oh, no, it's just off Walton Street, actually. Wait – before I go . . .'

To Jane's astonishment, she took the yew cane and knelt at Jane's knees, then kissed the cane which had so recently whipped her bare bottom, and handed it reverently to the woman who had punished her.

'Thank you, Miss, for my chastisement,' she said gravely, and left without another word.

Jane thought of taking a shower, but decided not to. Henry was coming later: he wouldn't want that. And when she lifted her arms to smell herself underneath there, and bent her head to sniff the aroma of her moistened sex, she thought that there was something different about her scent. It was as though giving the tight beating to Sarah's naked and compliant arse had awakened a new power, a new knowledge in her. The events of early morning, too, the way her own arse had glowed so pleasantly at the slightest of slaps, the suddenness of her urge to masturbate . . .

She made herself some lunch, prawns and bits of lobster and salady stuff from the fridge; she could not eat much. All the time, she wondered if Sarah Pennington had been using her, if she had arranged their little scene precisely in order to receive a beating for her absurdly obvious theft. But why? And why had Jane herself become wet and trembling in her belly as she whipped the girl?

She forgot about all the things she had planned for the afternoon, and curled up in her chair to spend the rest of the day engrossed in the strange enchantments of Parfaite Cecilia's *De Artibus Castigationis*.

It was only much later, when she got up to do some tidying for Henry Gordon Playste's visit, that she noticed one of the wax models of his penis had disappeared from the bathroom along with her prized set of silver hairbrushes.

2

The Golden Harness

Jane looked out the window and saw a silver-grey Mercedes pull into the underground garage. She knew it must be Henry, although she had never seen that car before. Henry changed cars as often as he changed neckties, which was pretty often. He had a key to the garage and access to one of the three parking spaces that went with Jane's very large flat. Henry was her boyfriend, but she had not seen him for over three months. And she had made many new candles in those months. Jane thought their relationship cool; she called it an open boyfriendage.

She had the champagne in an ice bucket, and wore just her little black silk number, the one that hung on her breasts like gossamer with the thinnest of straps on her bare shoulders, and nothing on underneath. She was barefoot, nails and lips painted fiery red, and in the bathroom she had carefully shaved her legs and armpits, then, on a sudden impulse, shaped her mink into a butterfly. She wore no perfume and no jewellery, and, most important, she hadn't showered. She sniffed her armpits, and smiled, for they were ripe with the smell Henry liked. More accurately, the smell of her drove him wild.

'I want Jane to smell fruity and rank, and like Jane,' he would say, 'not like some essence of French tart out of a bottle.' He loved to have his face clamped beneath her arm, or to press his lips and nose to her lush mink, breathing in the aroma of her with great contented sighs. Henry was awfully sweet.

She was excited at his visit, and felt all warm and fluttery inside, and, she had to admit, her quim was just a little bit liquid. It was not just the thought of Henry's arms around her, and the smell of his maleness, and her hands on his trim, muscled bum as he thrust so hard inside her, and . . . Oh, all those yummy things! She was getting wet just thinking of it. But also, the book of punishments, studied so soon after Sarah's bare-bum caning, had thrilled her more than she wanted to admit. She was not sure if Parfaite Cecilia's scholarly tone masked a secret exuberance as she detailed the floggings, scourgings, *bastinados*, and even the humble *zurrado*, the bare-bum spanking, all accompanied by meticulous woodcut illustrations.

And she was not sure what to make of her own reaction, the excitement as she studied the impossibly serene faces of those naked men and women who bared their bodies to the lash. The book rested on her top shelf with the other Morocco volumes, and she didn't think Henry would spot it there. And then she wondered why she was embarrassed: the very fact of being embarrassed was strange!

She was ready to cook them a cosy supper, if that was what Henry wanted, but she felt somehow edgy, and she hoped he would take her out instead. Either way, she knew, she would have a delicious sleepless night, with the freshness of a new love, or a love rekindled; then a traditional snuggly Sunday of newspapers (she loved being sent out to get them for him!), breakfast in bed, a walk to the Cross Keys for lunchtime pints, then a lazy vinous lunch, and, well, more bed.

Henry came in and put down the bulky package he was carrying. Jane raised her lips for a kiss, and put her arms round him. To her surprise, he was not wearing his usual silk or cashmere suit, but a tight black jacket of soft thick calfskin, black boots to match, and jeans. Admittedly, the jeans were razor-pressed, and probably had a fabulously expensive Italian label, but they were still jeans. And his soft, silky locks had been replaced by a bristling crewcut!

Without saying a word, his face stony, he put his hand on the front hem of her dress and jerked it up to her belly, revealing her naked pubis. Then his hand forced itself between her thighs and clamped the lips of her sex very hard.

He kissed her brutally, his tongue caressing hers with the harsh voracity of a serpent. He pressed her to him, and she knew that he had put on weight: a lot of weight. There was a whipcord in those arms, and iron in his chest. As his mouth pumped hers in a long, wet kiss, she whimpered softly, and clung to him, her nipples stiffening as they felt the metal buckles of his blouson scratch her through the thin silk of her dress.

She felt his fingers on the tingling lips of her quim, then sighed as he put in two, three, then four fingers, driving them with startling force all the way inside her, and, with the heel of his hand clamped against her pubic bone, he held her like a vice. After kissing her for an age, until she could hardly breathe, he released her, and smiled for the first time, the cruel knowing smile of a predatory beast. Flushed and gasping, she automatically smoothed down the front of her dress, her face radiant with surprised delight. Eyeing her, he slowly licked the glistening fingers that had penetrated her slit.

'Well . . . hi!' she said, flustered. 'You . . . you've put on weight, Henry!'

'You were all wet,' he said. 'Your cunt was all wet and oily.'

'You make me feel naughty!' she blurted happily.

'I mean, you were wet before I got here. You were wet from thinking about fucking.'

'From thinking about you, Henry. But you've changed. You're all, sort of, hard. Leather and jeans! And your hair. I like it! Is that the thing in Leadenhall Street now, the butch look?'

'I haven't really changed, Jane, sweet. Nobody ever changes. A person is like a diamond, sometimes the light shines on different facets. Here, I brought you a birthday present.'

'It isn't my birthday, silly.'

'Ever hear this: "Today is the first day of the rest of your life"? Go on, open it.'

'Yes . . . yes, of course. But don't you want to . . . you know?'

She giggled, and felt so silly at this sudden attack of coyness! Almost bashfully, she lifted her dress up high, revealing her naked breasts, and put her fingers in her mink, to part the shining pink lips of her sex.

'You want to,' said Henry.

'Of course I want to, dummy! You can't sweep me off my feet and . . . and fingerfuck me like that, and not expect me to feel as horny as a goat.'

'I'll sweep you off your feet,' said Henry simply, and with a swift movement, he bent down and scooped her up, wriggling with delight in his arms, pleased that he was so strong.

'I want you to open your present,' he said, 'but since you are such an insatiable little fox . . . why, you've even shaved your mink for me.'

'Oh,' she answered, blushing, 'it's supposed to be a butterfly. Do you like it?'

'I love it.'

He was holding her so that the opening of her glistening red slit was just an inch from his lips, and abruptly he lowered his head and buried his teeth in her sculpted mink-hairs. Gently, he kneaded her mons with his lips, and then allowed his teeth to chew the plump flesh of her mound, just above the hood of her clitoris. She moaned and wriggled, and his arms clutched her like granite pillars, and then he sank his nose and lips between her thighs, parting them a little, so that his mouth could fasten on her swollen labia, and his darting tongue tingle against her naked clitoris. Jane closed her eyes, unable to stop herself writhing as the man feasted on her; she heard him greedily sucking at the juices which flowed now so copiously from her swollen cunt-lips, and swallowing as he drank, all the while mercilessly caressing her clit with his stiff, flickering tongue, and making her shudder with electric pleasure. He held her body like a cup, and she felt like a sacrificial chalice.

Her hand clutched the back of his neck, pressing him against her cunt, and with her free fingertips she stroked her stiff nipples, squeezing them and pinching them hard

23

between thumb and index until her body pulsed with the sweetness of harpstrings. She longed to throw off her dress, and be naked with him, his flesh to eat. Her chin was wet; saliva trickled helplessly from the corner of her lips parted in a silent scream. Her cunt was a hot fountain, and she swam helplessly in its gushing oil, her whole body reduced to the searing point of white light that was her throbbing, tongued clitoris; then the spasm of her climax shook her, and she writhed in her man's arms, and her scream was no longer silent.

Tenderly, Henry carried her to the sofa, and sat her down. Her dress was still around her neck; she looked down and saw that her mink and inner thighs were gleaming with her liquid, and the lips of her sex shone red and swollen. He stood before her, hands on his hips, and smiled. She lay back and lifted her thighs, drawing her sex-lips apart with her fingers so that he could see the glistening flesh inside.

'Henry,' she gasped hoarsely, 'come inside me, please, sweet Henry, fuck me with your cock.' Still he smiled; she focused, and saw that there was no swelling at his crotch.

'Oh!' she cried in alarm, 'Oh, darling Henry, let me . . .'

Frantically, she scrabbled at the zipper of his jeans, and drew the garment down. He was not wearing panties, and his cock hung there, almost cherubic in its innocent softness. To her surprise, his penis and balls were completely bare, shaved of the silky mink she loved so much. She pressed her lips to the flaccid penis, flicking the tip with her tongue and sucking his glans like a sweet, but the shaft did not stir. Hands on his bare buttocks, she bent under him and opened her mouth as wide as she could, then slipped her lips around his ball-sac and drew his whole manhood, penis and balls, into her mouth. It was too big for her to swallow the whole shaft, but she had the peehole tickling the back of her throat, and her lips almost covering his soft balls. She wasn't sure what to do: she had never known a man to be completely soft in such circumstances! So she delicately tongued the balls, massaging them very gently with her palate, while she sucked on the shaft of the cock.

24

Had she not been worried, she would have found the sensation adorable, like having a sweet little baby in her mouth, all to herself.

She sat on the bed and apprehensively slipped out of her dress, folding it neatly, of course, because a rich girl respects rich things. Henry undressed slowly, peeling off his jeans and boots, then the leather blouson, his purple silk shirt, and finally, with a ceremonial flourish, his gold Rolex. He stood still and naked, his cock soft, watching her. She saw that the soft, downy body she loved so much had changed somehow; he was harder, stronger, and his chest and arms swelled with taut muscle over a slabbed belly and thick, rippling thighs. The tender swelling of his naked pubic mound seemed almost menacing.

'Like what you see?' he said.

'Henry . . . yes, I like. You've changed, all right.' It was as though Henry were an entirely new lover, and that thought excited her still more, except that with his penis soft as a baby, he was not yet a lover. She swallowed, panting; her tender glow had given way to a new, fiercer, desire. She stretched out on the bed and parted her thighs, then began to caress her stiff clit with her fingertips, writhing her hips at the same time; she knew that men were turned on by the sight of a woman masturbating.

'Come on, Henry,' she sighed, 'can't you see how wet I am for that lovely sweet cock? Get him hard for me, please, fuck my cunt, Henry, fuck me please, fuck your woman.' Henry said nothing, and she moaned in rising desire mingled with frustration as her tingling clit made her radiant.

Suddenly, Henry's penis was erect, and monstrous in his shaven nudity. She scarcely saw his cock quiver or stiffen, but all at once, in a trice, he stood like an oak, her blurred eyes seeing the shaft thicker and stiffer than she could ever remember, the bulb swollen a fiery, gleaming crimson that mesmerised her as he came towards her – as that monstrous cock came towards her! – and he picked her up as though she were no more than a feather, then placed her on the bed so that she rested on her knees and elbows.

'I want to see your bottom,' he said.

Then she felt the tip of his tongue burrowing at her anus bud, sending thrilling tickles through her belly, and she wondered if he was going to take her there. He played and caressed at her bumhole for a long, gorgeous time, getting his tongue well inside her, and she squirmed to relax her tight sphincter and ease that sweet penetration.

His hands clasped her hips; moaning with delight, she buried her face in the pillow, and felt his tongue squirm out of her anus, and his fingers part the cheeks of her arse. The stiff cock nuzzled the cleft of her buttocks in a friendly kiss, then slid easily to her lips, which were dripping and swollen, and then she gasped with joy as with one hard, smooth thrust, Henry's penis plunged to the balls into her wet slit.

He fucked her slowly, deliberately, as though relishing every millimetre of wet, tingling pink flesh that his ramrod penis stroked, and relishing too, in stony silence, her moans and gasps and whimpers as she bit the pillow and thrust her buttocks to slap against the strange smoothness of his shaven mons.

Suddenly she heard a crack, and realised that, with both hands, he had slapped her naked buttocks. There was another crack, harsher, and another, and as he spanked her, soft fire seemed to spread through her bottom, and still that hard cock stabbed her so smooth and sweet with his trembling stiffness.

'Oh, yes, yes,' she moaned into the pillow, her conscious mind flooded by the fire in her body, and scarcely aware of her words. 'Mmmm, Henry, sweet Henry, spank me. Oh, spank my bare bum hard, hard as you can.'

Remorselessly, the stinging blows fell, and at each slap her bottom jerked at the pleasure of her smarting, and she shook her head.

'Oh, come, Henry, come inside me!' she cried. Henry's response was to continue her spanking with one hand, while the other delved savagely between her soaking thighs to find the throbbing button of her clit, which he flicked with his fingers, ruthlessly tantalising her, until she was soaring to a giddy plateau, and as her bottom bucked to the rhythm of his cock, she shuddered and howled into her pillow at the sweetness of her orgasm.

When her shudders had subsided to choking sobs of joy, she sank to the bedspread, with Henry's stiff cock still inside her glowing quim. He lowered his body on hers, and covered her, his lips pressed against her sweat-soaked hair. Her mind whirled, and gradually she realised she was still filled by that strong manhood, which lay inside her like a treetrunk, lapped by the waters of her love.

'Oh, God, you sweet man,' she gasped. 'You didn't come. Didn't I make you come?'

'You want me to come, Jane,' he said, and raised his body from hers so that his penis left her.

'Oh,' she cried, confused.

Henry took her shoulders and gently turned her onto her back, then made her lift and part her thighs. His cock filled her sex again, and this time he started to buck with fierce, rapid thrusts, slamming his hips hard against her, almost clinical in his stroking.

'Yes, fuck me, Henry,' she cried, 'fuck me, come inside me, give me your lovely hot spunk, please, oh please . . .'

At that moment, Henry's head fell on to hers and her lips were smothered in a clinging, brutal kiss as she heard him gasp, and felt his penis shudder inside her, and the seed spurt in a powerful jet to wash the neck of her womb. Then he sank slowly, and lay with his head on her breast, while she stroked his cropped hair, almost crying with happiness.

'Well,' he murmured, his lips against her big stiff nipple, 'I think a little champagne would be nice, Jane, and some dinner.'

'Oh, yes,' she said.

'And you must open your present.'

'Oh!' cried Jane. 'I'd forgotten. It looks super! What's in it?' The package was a box about the size of a case of wine, but when she picked it up, it was curiously light. The gift wrapping was a deep crimson, emblazoned with silver doves, and tied with a silver ribbon.

'Well, you have to open it,' said Henry. 'Be quick, I'm hungry.'

'Are we going out to eat? I can cook something here, if you like.'

27

'Yes, I'd like that.' Henry retrieved his watch. 'It's nearly eight. We'll eat here, and we can go out later, when you've opened your present. There's a couple of parties we might look at.' Jane loved the lofty way Henry referred to other people as though they were *objets d'art*.

'I'll do steak-frites-salade, Parisian style.'

'Super. Leave your present till later, Jane.' He put his arms around her and held her naked body to his, and kissed her on the mouth. 'Because, if I don't eat soon, I'm going to eat you up.'

'I'd like that,' she said.

She opened her wardrobe and took out the nice cotton shirt of Henry's that she liked to wear around the house. He put his hand on her bottom.

'No, don't wear anything,' he said softly. 'It's warm in here, and I want to feast my eyes on you. Let's eat nude. Remember Mykonos?'

'Of course – but you were a bit stuffy then.'

'Me? Stuffy? Never. What about that girl you met? She didn't find me stuffy.'

'That girl we met, Henry: Cassie. Don't tell me you didn't fancy her. I had a letter from her a while back. She's in Spain, it seems, in Marbella or somewhere. She was talking about going to some college or other; it's a bit vague.'

'Spain, eh? I'd like to read it.'

'So you do fancy her!'

'I fancy Spain.'

'I'll get the letter, it's stuck in the bookshelf somewhere.' Jane reached up to the top shelf, and found the letter wedged, logically, in the pages of her Spanish dictionary, beside her Morocco volumes. She stretched a bit more than was necessary, tantalising Henry with the view of her taut back and bottom.

'Mmm,' he said, and suddenly parted the cheeks of her croup to plant a full, clinging kiss on her anus.

'Oo!' she cried, delighted, and jumped with surprise, dislodging some of her books, which clattered to the floor. She blushed and giggled, and squatted to pick them up, but

Henry already held one: it was the book by Parfaite Cecilia.

'Oh,' said Jane, nervously.

'This is new,' he said, with a curious look.

'Yes, something I picked up in the Charing Cross Road. It looked quite amusing. Nice binding, too.'

'So you've read it?'

'Just bits,' she said cautiously. 'It's rather bizarre. I don't really know what to make of it.'

Henry took the book, and Cassie's letter, and wordlessly followed Jane into the kitchen, where she poured them champagne. They clinked glasses and drank. Henry made an 'mmm' of satisfaction.

'Henry, turn round.' Jane ordered, and he did so. 'Why, I thought there was something odd. Your bottom's all red.'

'Well, that was you,' he laughed. 'You were scratching the hell out of me just a while ago, don't you remember?'

'Henry, you were doing me from behind.'

'Some of the time. See, you forgot. That's what happens when a woman is inflamed with demonic pash.'

'Oh, you!' she turned to the stove, but she was sure those marks on Henry's bottom hadn't come from her nails.

'It's sort of cute, though,' she said absent-mindedly.

'What is?'

'Your bottom. All pink like that.'

'Oh.' He sat down at the table while Jane fussed with pans and oil, and began to read Cassie's letter.

'Looks like it was written on the hoof,' he said with a chuckle. 'Starts in blue ink, then red, then black. She is quite a kaleidoscope, your Cassie.' What about your bum, she said to herself.

'She's not my Cassie, she's . . . Cassie's Cassie. Anyway, you're just jealous you never made it with her, Henry.'

'Maybe so. Let's see. It seems that a French truck driver is the most fantastic lover – I can see why she chose to hitch-hike. No, wait, lecturers in sociology at the Sorbonne seem to be even more fantastic. Must be those wispy beards. She seems to be over the Pyrenees now, yes, for Spanish truck drivers are still more fantastic! And, wait for it, a certain waitress in Tarragona has the biggest, throb-bingest acorn she's ever tasted! Who's jealous now, then?'

'Not me,' lied Jane. 'Don't mock, Henry.'

'Anyway, she seems to have got herself well dug in on the Costa del Sol.' He read out loud: "It is one long party in Marbella, but I've kind of fallen for this particular boy." Fallen for, isn't that a gooey thing to say? "He's a student, not altogether Spanish – his name is sort of Mediterranean, and could be Greek, I guess, and I won't tell you what it is, for luck! Not that I don't trust you. Well, yes, I don't trust you, I don't trust that beautiful bod of yours, Jane. You'd have him away from me! Well, he says he's studying English – I'm so afraid he's just using me to practise irregular verbs!! – and it's up at some college in the mountains, called Maldona, or something, and it has something to do with England, I think. He's a bit vague, but he's promised to take me for a look. It sounds so romantic, all crags and dungeons! Well, this address, it's a little casita I've rented in the old town in Marbella, it's good until further notice, so do write, or better still, come and see me. Except I won't introduce you to my Student Body (!) for you'd nick him. Sometimes, when I'm doing it with him, I think of you, Jane darling, and that is how much I miss you. Millions of kisses in all the places you like most . . . Cassie."

'Yes,' said Henry, 'I remember her well. And yes, I do wish I'd made it with her. Have you written?' Jane nodded.

'She hasn't replied to any of my letters. And they haven't been returned by the Spanish post office, so I don't know what is going on.'

'Maybe this boyfriend has ravished her and whisked her away, his prisoner, to his haunted romantic castle. Hot-blooded Latins and so on.'

'If anything, it would be Cassie who ravished him,' said Jane. 'Come and help me chop potatoes.'

'Slavedriver.'

'If you like.'

'I like.'

Jane eyed the pink ripples on Henry's taut arse-globes, and wondered. When a brimming colander of potatoes was ready, Jane put the pot of oil to heat, and waited until it was smoky, before motioning Henry to stand back as she emptied them in. But as she upturned the colander, there was a sudden hiss, and a fizz of boiling oil that splattered smoking droplets on Henry's breast.

'Oh, shit!' shouted Jane. 'Oh, I'm sorry! I'll get some cold water!'

Henry's eyes were screwed shut; the oil gleamed as it trickled down his bare breast.

'No, Jane, are you OK?' he said.

'Yeah, sure. But get under a cold shower or something.'

'No, it's OK, honest,' he said grinning. 'I think the steaks are ready; let's eat while the chips fry.'

'You're not hurt?' she said, incredulous. 'I must have overheated the oil.'

'No, no.' Henry moved to take his place at table, standing to pour their claret and, as the wine sparkled into their glasses, Jane saw that Henry's penis was once more standing proudly erect.

'A very interesting woman, our Parfaite Cecilia,' said Henry, wiping the meat juices from his chin.

'You know her?' said Jane in surprise.

'I know of her. I've been taking an interest in things Spanish, funnily enough. Sun and shade, *sol y sombra*, all that sort of thing. Life in the raw, you know?'

Jane laughed.

'Well, we are in the raw now,' she said. 'How's your salad?'

'Excellent. The balsamic vinegar is essential, of course.'

'There's some Stilton, if you like, and grapes and walnuts.'

'You're fattening me up.'

'That's right,' she smiled, feeling outrageously happy and flushed with wine.

'Our friend Cecilia belonged to a rather exclusive and mysterious Order of . . . well, not exactly nuns, and not exactly Amazons, but somewhere between the two. I think she lived in the seventeenth century.'

'Yes, the book was printed in Amsterdam in sixteen fifty-seven. I haven't read all that much. It's spooky, yet fascinating . . . all those strange punishments. And inflicted by women!'

'And given to both men and women, with equal vigour. Were you excited by it?'

'Excited! That is not exactly the word.'

'I think it is, Jane. I think your heart beat a little faster, and your thighs became moist.'

'Oh . . . maybe a little. I . . . I can't deny it, Henry.'

'The Order was based in Spain, and her history is shrouded in hearsay. An order of women, attended by male slaves . . . there were rumours of strange, cruel rituals, some connection – a sort of sister Order – with the Knights Templar, who were crushed in England and France in the fourteenth century, but continued to be tolerated and to flourish in the Iberian peninsula. Cecilia, who must have been very important to have achieved the rank of Parfaite, was thought to be of English origin, a certain Cecily Pennington, of Essex. Anyway she came to a sticky end, our Cecily. The Inquisition got her when she passed through Salamanca on an alleged secret mission back to England, and she died a cruel death. Those were the times of the counter-reformation: suspicion of Catharism, of dealings with the Arabs of the Moroccon Caliphate – and the Spanish friars never believed that the Andalusians had really stopped feeling Arab – suspicion of anything remotely unorthodox, was universal.'

'A cruel death? How . . .?'

'Jane, she was whipped to death,' said Henry coolly. 'She was flogged very slowly, but without ceasing, with a four-thonged whip made of silken cords knotted tight. They wanted her to confess the secrets of her remote and forbidding Order, in the fastnesses of Andalusia, but she would not speak. And so, gradually, she was flayed alive, with the caress of a silken whip on her bare back.'

'My God,' said Jane. 'How awful.'

'Yes. But, Jane, you are flushed. The story has excited you.'

'Well, it's . . . it's intriguing. Such dark things that have happened in history! And we think the past is so romantic.'

'Why, as recently as the Napoleonic Wars, sailors of the Royal Navy were flogged to death, Jane. "Whipped round the fleet", they called it, and those men had no silken thongs to caress them.' Jane shivered, and took Henry's hand, and kissed his fingertips.

'Maybe we shouldn't go out at all,' she murmured. 'Stay in, watch some late night movie in bed . . . you know.'

'Oh, you'll want to go out when you see your present. A clue: I have in mind a fancy dress party, and not far, only in Lennox Gardens. We can walk, a good thing after all this wine.'

'But that's miles!'

'Isn't.'

'Is too!'

'All right, we'll cab it. But open your present. And you'll see why I wanted you naked.'

Eagerly, Jane unscrambled the wrapping paper, taking care not to tear its crackling lovely thickness; inside was a box, like a hatbox, and she opened it and peered inside.

'Well,' she said doubtfully. She could see gold glitter, and some sort of stick arrangements, and something like thin chains. 'What is it?'

'Take it out, you goose.'

Excited, she lifted out her present.

'Oh, it is lovely!' she cried. 'But I still don't know what it is! This is a gold chain, and these are gold clips, and these knobby things, curved like hunting horns, well, I don't know, they look naughty! These sticks, though –'

'Open them out, and you'll see. Push that little clasp at the base.'

Jane did so; each clasp released a swishing fan of brilliantly coloured feathers.

'They are peacock's feathers,' said Henry rather smugly, knowing how pleased she was. 'It's rather antique, actually.'

'Oh, it's gorgeous! But two fans! And these chains and things.'

'This is where I have to do some work,' said Henry, getting up, 'and I trust you will find it pleasurable. If you will please bend over? No need to shut your eyes.'

Jane felt the thin gold chains slither across her naked belly and thighs, through the cleft of her buttocks, and then she gasped in surprise and ticklish delight as her anus bud was stroked by a single feather, thin and stiff, and she giggled. Then Henry pressed hard, spreading her cheeks, and she relaxed her sphincter, so that the short feather slid deliciously all the way into her anus. It was followed by one of the little golden plugs, which was the clasp that bound the feathers of the fan together. Henry tightened the chains around her waist and across her sex-lips, so that they tickled her naked clitoris. Then the process was repeated from the other direction, with a feather inserted into Jane's very sex, right to the neck of her womb, and secured by the other golden plug. The harness was completed by Henry's looping the chains up to her nipples, which were by this time standing quite tingly and stiff, and fastening them there with two tight golden clasps.

'There!' he said. 'Now look in the mirror.'

Jane did so, and saw a criss-cross of gold across her belly and fesses, looped in a sensuous pattern. The fan which was secured inside her sex stood up from the curving clasp like a baton flush with her pubis and belly; she felt the other nestle against the cleft of her buttocks.

'To open your fans,' said Henry, with the air of a conjuror performing a trick, 'simply press on the clasps with the muscle of your lovely sphincter, and hey presto! You're the belle of the ball.'

Jane squeezed with her quim and her anus at the same time, and at the slightest of pressures, the two fans sprang into glorious rainbows, almost complete circles of dazzling colour, that swirled across her belly and fesses, caressing her with their softness, while the single feathers thrust into her anus and quim exerted a sweet tingling presure at her every step. Already, her slit was moistening the feather there, and she gasped, flushed, in the face, as she felt the tickle of the chain on her clitoris, almost maddening her with its delicate touch. She stared adoringly at her reflection; the two fans, or bouquets of feathers, were big enough to seem like a dress or short skirt, if seen from a distance. And if she slipped a top over her tingling breasts ... what an adorable costume!

'I look like a ballerina!' she cried. 'It's simply gorgeous!'

'Squeeze the clasps again,' Henry ordered. She did so, and the fans snapped shut.

'See? Closed position for when you are out and about, open for when you are at a *soirée intime*. Like tonight.' Jane practised opening and closing the peacock fans, and at each turn she felt a melting pleasure in her quim and anus, so that the lips of her sex were soon glistening with love-oil. She turned to Henry, wanting that cock to stand for her, and that he make her naked again and take her here, at once; but already his pink bottom and shiny bare pubis were disappearing into his jeans.

'I told you it was a fancy dress party,' he said. 'You will be quite a sensation, for I don't think there is another one like it in the world.'

'Is it very old, then?' said Jane, wondering at the beauty of her gift.

'Well, if you look at the illustration on, I think, page forty-two, of Parfaite Cecilia's book, you will see a girl strapped to a punishment frame, and taking a flogging from an older girl, apparently a Parfaite of the Order, quite probably Cecilia herself. And she is wearing a costume just like yours. What you now possess, Jane, is a Parfaite's ceremonial punishment dress.'

3

The Scene

Jane found herself blurting out the story of her caning of Sarah Pennington, and Henry, far from disapproving, seemed strangely excited.

'How lovely,' he said. 'In fact, you should meet Sarah tonight, at Netta and Caspar's party. She's a prefect at the Rosebush School, which Caspar owns, you know.'

'I thought it was run by nuns – she mentioned the Sisters.'

'They are sisters of a kind,' said Henry.

They walked hand in hand towards Lennox Gardens, Jane carrying presents for their hosts, Netta and Caspar, things which Henry said would 'amuse' them: the cane which she had got from Harrod's, and a wax model of her lover's penis. And, underneath her coat, she wore just the Parfaite's harness.

'It must be some fancy dress party,' she said. 'I'm all tingly!'

'You'll like Netta and Caspar,' said Henry. 'He's very rich, makes movies: always in Spain, or the Greek islands, anywhere the sun shines ripe on naked human bodies.'

'He makes porno movies?' giggled Jane. 'Maybe he has a part for me.'

'Not porno,' said Henry. 'Truthful movies. Netta and Caspar are into what we call the scene.' Jane did not understand.

'In fact, I'm going into business with Caspar,' said Henry. 'We're going to make movies in Spain, Jane, I want you to come with me.'

'Sounds fabulous. When do we leave?'

'I'm going tomorrow, Jane. I know it's a surprise, but, well, certain things have happened very quickly, and . . .'

'Because of Netta and Caspar, and this scene of theirs?'

'Yes. Tonight is by way of a test for me. Please come with me.'

'For how long?'

'For a long time, Jane.' He looked at her fiercely. 'Please think about it. I believe what you see at the party will . . . awaken you.'

Their hostess, Netta, was a handsome woman with cropped iron-grey hair, and she greeted Jane with a kiss full on the lips. She wore a beautiful black evening dress, a deep cleavage revealing most of her very large breasts, and to Jane's surprise it was made of sheer rubber. Her husband Caspar was a short, heavily-muscled man, his head was shaven and he sported a bushy moustache. He wore a scarlet silk tunic, like an ancient Greek, with a lovely frilly skirt that scarcely covered his manhood, which was very obviously naked underneath. He too greeted Jane with a kiss from rouged lips, and a murmur that Cecilia herself would be jealous of her beauty in that Parfaite's harness. Jane saw that semi-nudity, or androgynous costumes, as well as much leather, rubber and silver, were quite the norm among the guests. And there was a definite antique air. The conversations she overheard had a flavour unusual even in the smaller numbers of London SW.

'Your apodesmos must pinch your tits terribly, dear!' This to a young girl wearing only a thin strip of green satin, bound tightly round her breasts, and a leather thong, equally tight, that barely covered her pubis.

'Yes,' blushed the girl happily, 'it hurts like the furies! And the thong on my zona really chafes on my arse-bud! It's so super!'

But all eyed Jane's costume with envy, as she proudly swished her chains and feathers, and she thought that this 'scene' seemed quite exciting.

'Quite a caning you gave my slave Sarah this morning,' said Caspar, sneaking up beside her.

'Your slave!' Jane widened her eyes in surprise.

'Yes, she is a cheeky little thing: don't worry, you'll have your hairbrushes back. At Rosebush, we believe in the sanctity of discipline. A girl is better for having her naked bottom lashed, Jane. I am the custodian of Rosebush, the "scene" as Netta calls it here in London, but really it's a very old foundation. We adepts – my proper title – are a select few, but we are everywhere.'

'In Spain, too?' asked Jane nervously.

'Especially in Spain.'

Abruptly the mood of the gathering changed. There was an excited 'ooh'; the tinkly jazz which had been playing was replaced by a quiet but insistent drumbeat, like an African tomtom. Drinks were put aside, and there was an electric hum of excitement, as Caspar spoke.

'Our friend Henry is leaving us tomorrow for the shores of the Mediterranean, for Spain, the land of sun and shadow, of eternal clarity, of shrouded vice and naked pleasure, which is the spiritual home of us all. He has brought gifts, and he shall have a gift in return: the tender young cunt of my slave Sarah!' There was a round of de- lighted applause.

Netta stalked proudly into the room, leading Henry and Sarah behind her. She had changed from her rubber frock into a clinging catsuit of the same fabric, and had ex- changed her elegant slingbacks for a pair of impossibly tall stiletto heels. Her face was covered by a black rubber mask, with apertures for nose, mouth and eyes, that gave her the aspect of an avenging goddess. In her hand, she held the yew cane Jane had bought that morning.

Henry was nude, except for a pair of black leather pan- ties studded with silver nails. His lips were painted a bright scarlet, his cheeks powdered cream, and his eyes dark with mascara. From his head hung the beautiful tresses of a wig which exactly resembled Sarah's hair; Jane knew that those hairs had been shorn from Sarah's head. Sarah, too, was nude, but for the blue panties Jane had admired earlier. Both of them were tethered at their waists by a golden chain, which Netta held, flicking it to drive them on.

The drumbeat became louder. When they reached the

centre of the room, they knelt at Netta's instruction, and crouched beside each other, like dogs. Netta lifted her shining rubber forearm, and dealt first Henry, then Sarah, a single stroke of the cane on the buttocks. At the lash of the cane, Henry's leather parts began to bulge, and Jane marvelled that a single cane-stroke could evidently bring the man to erection. She felt her own sex begin to moisten.

Sarah stood up, head bowed, and slipped out of her panties, revealing her delicious butterfly mink glistening with her sweat and, Jane suspected, her seeping love-oil. She handed the panties to Netta and resumed her position, but this time she lay on her back with her feet on the floor and her thighs spread, showing the wet pink lips of her sex to the smiling assembly. Netta smoothly draped the panties over Henry's head, so that they encased him snugly, leaving his mouth and eyes to peek from the holes, his nose covered entirely by the gusset.

'Henry must prove that he can bring the slave Sarah to pleasure,' announced Netta, who had anchored her free hand casually on her rubber crotch. Jane's heart raced; she clenched her sphincter, gripping the feathers with her quim and anus, and writhed her hips slightly, so that her fans of plumage rustled. All round the circle of spectators, she saw hands caress breasts and lips and buttocks as they breathlessly awaited the spectacle. Netta bent down and rapidly unlaced Henry's leather thong. There was a gasp of admiration as the inside of his panties was revealed as sharp silver nailpoints, which had left their pink prickly imprint on his naked fesses. Kneeling, his face inches from Sarah's spread cunt-lips, Henry parted his buttocks to show his anus bud. Caspar moved forward and passed something to Netta.

'Henry shall receive a stroke of my cane on his bare bottom at the rate of one every three seconds, for as long as it takes him to bring Sarah to her pleasure,' said Netta. 'Only then will he be permitted to enter her. And to keep him mindful of his need for a stiff penis, he shall wear this, his thoughtful gift.' She held up the black waxen cock, and proceeded to slide it between Henry's cheeks, then plunge it with a smooth, easy motion, right up to the balls in his anus slit. Henry gasped once, then clenched his buttocks to hold the cock in place.

'You may commence, Henry, when you feel the first stroke of my cane on your naked croup,' said Netta, and lifted her caning arm, while, with her other hand, she began quite openly and deliberately to rub her own rubber-clad pubis. Jane was by now panting with excitement; she squirmed against her ticklish feathers, brimming with a strange moist longing to see Henry thoroughly flogged, and wishing that his cock could be inside her anus at that moment.

The cane fell with a crack across Henry's nates, and he groaned very softly, then plunged his tongue deep between the swollen folds of Sarah's labia. With a swift daring motion, he licked her with the whole flat of his tongue, making her moan and wriggle, and then found her clitoris with his flickering tip. Every three seconds, a cut of the cane blushed his trembling bare buttocks, but he made no sound except for a hoarse panting. The silence in the room was electric. Sarah's breath came in short mewling gasps now as Henry's tonguing brought her closer and closer to her plateau of orgasm. Netta, too, caressed her sex feverishly through her tight rubber pants, but her caning arm did not falter as she delivered one merciless stroke after another to Henry's squirming fesses.

At last, after eight cuts had been given, Sarah shrieked out loud and long, and followed her shriek with a series of staccato yelps, which gradually subsided into a soft, anguished moan, as Henry's tongue stabbed ever harder at her glistening clit.

'Oh,' she said at last. 'Oh, take me now, please.'

The flogging stopped: Henry had taken eight vicious cuts of the cane, without protest, without a quiver from his bared buttocks. Now he raised himself, still wearing the mask of Sarah's panties, damp from her juices.

'Wait!' cried Netta. 'The slut must be caned before she is fucked!' She handed the cane to Henry, who stood over Sarah as she crouched and presented her bottom to him.

'Six, and rapid strokes,' commanded Netta. Henry's arm was a blur as he lashed Sarah's bare croup with six savage cuts, delivered with all the force of his powerful muscles. The beating took no longer than four seconds! Jane's cunt was flowing wet as she watched that naked elfin body squirming silently at the force of the whipping.

Now, the spell was broken; the guests, in twos, threes, or even fours, became a writhing naked throng. Belts, chains and whips were raised to fall with passionate glee on willing bare flesh. Jane watched, mesmerised, feeling wetter and wetter in her quim as her lover Henry powerfully stroked the squirming body of the slave Sarah, as though he so superbly controlled his muscled body that he could pleasure her for ever without coming. Suddenly Jane felt a man's arm around her, his lips kissing hers as his naked body thrust against her, the penis stiff and throbbing on her belly. It was Caspar.

'Oh,' she moaned, and responded to his embrace. His Greek tunic was up around his neck; she looked and saw a cock monstrous in shaven nudity, and felt the gentle pressure of his hand on her neck. She knelt, and took the tip of the gigantic engine in her mouth, sucking and kissing it, then swallowed its entire length right to the balls, so that the throbbing glans tickled the back of her throat. Powerfully, she sucked on Caspar's cock, making him moan, and then she felt a pair of probing lips on her own slit, and a hard little tongue penetrate her cunt.

She looked down and saw Netta, squatting below her, her mouth already glistening with Jane's copious love-juice. Jane gasped as electric vibrations flowed from her stiffened clitoris, and bobbed her head up and down on Caspar's trembling penis. She could taste the first droplets of spunk at his peehole, when she jumped as a fiery streak of pain laced across her naked croup.

Startled, she saw that Caspar had taken a short cane, and was leaning forward over her back to stroke her buttocks. She groaned in protest, but he held her head to his throbbing cock, and the cane cracked again across her defenceless bare bottom. She worked faster and faster,

41

hoping to bring him off quickly and stop the dreadful pain, but his control was too great, and she took three stinging cuts while Netta still furiously tongued her moist, throbbing, clit, and at last Caspar's cock shuddered and he cried out, spurting his hot seed into Jane's throat, which swallowed every drop. Netta's tongue was busy, but Jane's approach to the plateau of orgasm suddenly made her tense and frightened rather than joyful. Caspar renewed his vigorous caning of her bare buttocks, and at that moment Jane felt a chill wash of fear engulf her. She broke away, trembling. Her mind and body whirled in confusion; she wanted to get out of there, out of that 'scene'.

'No!' she blurted. 'I . . . I'm not ready! Please! Let me go!'

Netta sat up, and with Caspar, watched Jane with a kindly expression.

'Of course you may go, Jane,' she said. 'Perhaps it is not yet time.'

Caspar reached out to stroke her hair, and kiss her tenderly on the cheek, and she felt such a fool, such a spoilsport! Henry was still fucking the slave Sarah, both bodies writhing in naked ecstasy.

'Henry cannot come with you,' said Caspar. 'He must fuck, you see, until all others are sated. Which may be hours. It is our way. He is the knight of our ceremony, so to speak – the whipping boy.'

'Henry!' cried Jane. 'Why . . . why didn't you tell me?' Henry stared at her, his expression far away.

'Don't go, Jane,' he panted. 'Stay with us. You are born to lead us, Jane. Can't you see how I adore you, by worshipping the body of this slave!'

All the guests were watching now, and Jane turned to go, quite unhindered. Caspar escorted her politely to the door. As she left the room, she heard, to her astonishment, the whole assembly murmur: 'We adore you, Mistress. We adore you, Jana.'

Crazy, she thought, when she had reached the safety of home. They got my name wrong! But why did I panic? I was enjoying it, really. I didn't want to be caned, damn it,

I didn't ask for it, and yet, it feels sort of nice and warm, now. Oh, I wish I'd stayed! I'll go back!

She realised she had not noted the number of the house in Lennox Gardens, and cursed herself for being so soppy. Yet Henry had sprung all this on her so suddenly. He had changed, under Caspar and Netta's influence – like Caspar, he had got so heavily muscled – and she was apprehensive. Yet still, watching his bare bum take that terrific caning had excited her, just like her own hard lacing of Sarah Pennington, and as for the pain of her own few strokes, well, it did leave a nice afterglow. She could maybe get used to it – but should she? Oh, damn again! Then, suddenly, she knew what to do.

Cassie, sweet Cassie, would sort things out, explain everything, as she always had. She would go to Spain after all, not with Henry but in quest of Cassie. And right away! Jane went to bed content and relieved, now that the agony of indecision was over. She drifted into an exhausted sleep, and dreamed of being naked with Cassie, on that sunny southern beach where they had met, and Cassie had a superb leather thong, and was whipping Jane's naked bottom without mercy.

Jane emerged from the Tunnel into France shortly after two the next morning. Her flat was secured, the keys left with friendly neighbours; in her bag were essentials, almost essentials, and a few keepsakes like her fan-harness and a penis candle of Henry's cock, for luck. She wanted to find Cassie first, though: Cassie was the mystery, and as her Range Rover ate up the kilometres down towards Spain and the Mediterranean, her thoughts dwelt on her absent friend, her teacher.

Outside Chartres she got stuck behind a truck with Greek number plates; suddenly, she longed to be in the south, near the soft Mediterranean where this child of the north knew her heart lay. She daydreamed of her first meeting with Cassie.

She had persuaded Henry to take her to Mykonos, the island where the beautiful people went. Henry was quite stuffy in those days, preoccupied with making his first, or second, million, but he agreed. They rented a villa over-looking the small whitewashed town, and Henry was content to sit with his portable phones and computers, spinning deals, until Jane learned of Paradise Beach, the beach for nudists.

A small boat piloted by a Zorba-the-Greek type took them there, a ten-minute ride as opposed to the forty-minute walk over the hilly island. Henry was initially surprised, but agreed to remove his boxer shorts, which he covered with a laptop computer, while Jane at once stripped and ran laughing into the turquoise sea.

There she met a smiling dark girl, tall, with a bewitching all-over tan: small, pert breasts, wreathed in long, lustrous black hair (Jane was instantly jealous) and a pear-shaped bottom to die for.

'English?' said the girl, splashing her playfully.

'Yes,' said Jane, splashing back and giggling.

'We English must stick together, it's all Germans here. But we Nordics all love the south, don't we? Although I'm a bit of a cheat, half Brazilian, half English, half Swedish.'

'That makes three halves,' said Jane.

'I suppose it does, doesn't it?' And they laughed conspiratorially.

Cassie gladly installed herself by Jane and Henry, and when she offered to rub her home-made sun oil into Jane's back, the offer was accepted with a thrilled pleasure. It stank, apparently a mixture of olive oil, orange juice and crushed garlic, but Jane adored the feel of Cassie's supple fingers as they massaged every inch of her tingling naked body, pausing tenderly on her nipples, and nonchalantly, thrillingly, brushing the lips of her quim as she worked on the soft inner thighs.

When it was Jane's turn to oil Cassie, she could hardly stop her fingers trembling at the feel of that smooth, velvety body squirming ever so slightly at her touch. She was aware of her sex moistening; she was sure Henry's penis was stiff as he slyly watched.

They passed a lazy afternoon, with frequent applications

of the home-made sun oil, and at each mutual massage, Jane's quim became wetter and her trembling more pronounced. Her belly tingled at the very touch of her new friend, and her fingers strayed quite openly into the lovely fat folds of the moist, open cunt-lips. She hoped, no, she was certain, Cassie felt the same way, so when the last boat was leaving, she gladly agreed to let Henry take it alone, while they walked back over the hills, to enjoy the sunset.

'Isn't it wonderful on a bare beach?' said Cassie, as they walked hand in hand up the rocky path.

'Yes! To feel free, not worrying about anything, not fussing with silly costumes or wondering if your mink is shaved properly. To feel the sun on your nude body, like a lover, it is so beautiful, isn't it? There is something bewitching about the south, the Mediterranean ...'

'We're all children of the Mediterranean,' said Cassie.

The two girls were still nude as they walked towards the hills. The track was steep and rocky, and thorns brushed their bare skins, but at last panting, they stood at the top of the hill. They looked back at the beach, glowing crimson in the sunset, and ahead of them at the sparkling lights of the twilit white town. The path was level now, taking them past stone walls and goatherds' shelters, and they strolled, in no hurry, holding hands.

'It is magic,' said Jane, 'as though we are all alone in the world.'

'That's right,' said Cassie, and, without warning, put her arms round Jane's shoulders and embraced her, pressing her lips to Jane's neck. Jane's face nuzzled Cassie's shoulder; the two girls stood in a motionless embrace, their breasts pressed together, until at last Jane whispered: 'Let's do it.'

Without a word, Cassie led her by the hand to a stone shelter. There was no door: inside, a couple of chairs, a table, and a straw palliasse. It smelled of animals; through the open window holes, they could see the velvet purple sky. They lay down on the palliasse and kissed each other on the mouth, their tongues darting, while trembling hands caressed naked buttocks, pressing their cunts together.

'I wanted you the moment I saw you,' said Cassie.

45

'I'm so glad. I'm so happy.'

'Shall I do this?'

'Oh, yes.'

Tenderly, Cassie masturbated Jane, parting the swollen lips of her cunt and finding the stiff clit, then sliding three easy fingers deep into her. Jane's pelvis writhed as her own fingers found Cassie's clit, and she gasped in astonishment as she felt it grow as big and hard as a thimble, then continued to swell until Jane was able to grasp the stiff wet member like the stem of a flower.

Cassie smoothly turned herself so that her mouth was on Jane's cunt. She was on top; her own sex was pressed to Jane's lips, and Jane took that distended wet clit between her teeth, sucking it into her.

Cassie's own tongue was busy at Jane's clit, flicking and darting and pausing to drive deep into the slit itself. Jane moaned in pleasure as she clutched Cassie's taut bare buttocks, pumping hard.

'God,' panted Cassie, 'how I'm going to come, Jane, I'm going to explode.'

She got up and stared at Jane through hooded eyes.

'My clit's never been so stiff, I think. You do things to me, Jane. And I'm going to fuck you properly, now.'

'Yes, oh, yes. Cassie ... I've never done it like this before. With another woman.'

Cassie's teeth flashed in a smile.

'I'm not another woman, Jane. I'm a woman's body that loves your woman's body. And when you suck my clit, you take my soul into your sweet mouth.'

'I'm so wet for you, sweet Cassie. Oh, do me.'

Cassie straddled her with the strength and grace of a mountain goat, their wet cunts pressed tight and slippery together, and Jane whimpered as she felt Cassie's swollen clit thrusting high in her slit so that the two clits rubbed hard and wet. Jane's arms were round her lover's bucking spine, and she whimpered, and heard Cassie cry, 'Ah, Jane, Jane, I'm coming,' and then Jane's whimper turned to a howl as her body became electric, and she shuddered with the force of her coming.

Dressed against the evening chill, they walked hand in hand down towards the town.

'It was lovely, wasn't it?' said Jane.

Cassie smiled.

'It's a pleasure to be taken sparingly, like fine wine,' she said. 'It is good for women to know each other and make each other come, taste the salty sea in our cunts. It makes us aware and alive, so that we may return to the necessary pleasure of the male cock all the more joyous in our womanhood.'

'You mean, women must love each other so that they may become . . . *more* female? Appreciate men's love the more? By that token, then, men should practise . . . Well, you know.'

'Greek love? No, Jane, that is a sterile practice, for a man is doing no more than make love to himself, to his image in a mirror. Women who kiss are making love to life itself.'

That evening, Henry took her to the taverna for a lobster dinner, to celebrate some coup he had arranged while Cassie and Jane were making love on their hilltop. Jane was radiant in her most daring strapless silk dress, and relished every stare, every lustful look. She let butter sauce dribble down her chin and breasts, rendering her dress transparent, and didn't care. She flirted outrageously with everybody, and tickled Henry's balls under the table to make him blush.

'You're in a good mood,' he said.

'I'm always in a good mood,' she replied.

'Not like this. What have you been up to with that Cassie girl?'

'Oh, nothing,' said Jane airily, and then put down her fork, gulped some wine and took Henry's hand as she stared him in the eyes.

'Actually, there was something,' she said, and told Henry what she and Cassie had done in every last detail.

'Why Henry,' she said when she had finished her story, 'you are as red as that lobster shell!'

But that night, Henry allowed Jane scarcely a wink of

sleep. And ever since then, Cassie had been part of Jane's life, thrilling her, exasperating her, and in a strange way loving her.

She smiled as the tender memories drifted in her imagination. Keen with the anticipation of seeing Cassie again, she reached the border at midnight. It was time to rest, in a soft French hotel bed, dreaming of Cassie and the bright morning which would take her into Spain.

4

Marbella

'Of course,' said the man at the next table, 'we all know we are going to die, but only the Spaniard knows he is going to be tortured to death.'

The accent was German; Jane looked up from her guide books. They sat on the terrace of the Cafe Marbella, overlooking the Alameda, the central square bustling with morning glamour. She saw a thin, youngish man, very straight long blond hair cascading over a leather jacket; jeans, sunglasses, and an open packet of German cigarettes. He raised his glass of beer.

'From England? Perhaps the north of England?'

'Well . . . how do you know?'

'The wonderful translucent skin, the high cheekbones, the wide, full mouth. I am a photographer by trade, you see, specialising in the mystic-erotic.' He said this very solemnly. She thought he was interesting.

'I've never met a mystic-erotic photographer before,' she said.

'I am in Spain because of the bright, spiritual light,' he added. 'But the Costa is not the real Spain. It is tacky. Up there –' he gestured vaguely towards the mountains '– is the real Spain, the dark places of shade and sunlight, the brooding lost villages, the peasants and lords with eyes burning with hatred and salvation; light and dark, and only blood between them.'

'Please join me,' said Jane. 'That sounds more like my kind of Spain. Or else you have a very efficient kind of German pick-up line.'

The man joined her, and waved to the waiter.

'Have a brandy with your coffee,' he said. 'That is the Spanish way. And I'm not trying to pick you up. Although, since you mention it, I invite you to luncheon with myself and my wife Greta. I am Harry Kuhl.'

'Jane Ardenne.'

'We have a villa up there, in the foothills of the mountains. It is the best way to see Marbella, Jane, that is, not being in it.' The waiter brought her brandy and coffee, and she sipped the fiery sweet liquid.

'Yes, please,' she said. 'But first I have something to do. I am here to look for a friend.' And she told him about Cassie, the address in the Calle Figueroa. Despite what he said, she liked it here: the sunshine made everything seem so easy and friendly. Even a simple pick-up, for she had no doubt that was what it was.

'You have modelled before?' said Harry.

'Not exactly,' she replied, with the natural unwillingness of any lady to admit she had not posed before a camera.

'Hmmm,' he said. 'Calle Figueroa is not far, but do not expect to find your friend. This is a very fluid society, the Costa del Sol. People come and go . . . drifters, nomads.'

Harry arranged to pick her up at one o'clock and drive her to his villa, on the grounds that the road was tricky, and her own car was safely put away in the garage of her hotel.

'Don't worry,' he said.

'I'm not worrying.' In fact, she was anything but worried; the idea that she might be invited to do some modelling work was enough to fuel her curiosity.

'Cassie Osorio,' said Harry, as he got up to leave.

'You know of her, then?' she cried eagerly.

He shook his head.

No. I think there is no one on the Costa called Cassie Osorio,' he said, with a lopsided smile.

Calle Figueroa was in Spain. A narrow street bedecked with washing lines, chattering with the screech of gossip and the buzz-saw roar of unmuffled motor-cycles; dazzling beams of dusty sunlight caressing dark shadows. Jane had no trouble finding the house from which Cassie had written; but it was closed and shuttered. She peered through the letter-box and saw that the house was empty, and her dreams of a surprise greeting melted. She clicked her tongue in annoyance.

There was a sound from the house next door. A window had snapped shut, indicating that, quite reasonably, she was being spied on. She rapped on the neighbour's door, and got no answer. She rapped harder, and there was still silence. The eyes of the street, curious and silent now, were upon her. She rapped again, and at last she heard the grudging clack of footsteps on stone.

A woman dressed entirely in black opened the door a crack and peered out with an ageless, wrinkled face.

Jane's Spanish was passable.

'The English girl, next door,' she blurted. 'Señorita Osorio. Do you know –'

'*No entiendo*,' spat the wrinkled woman. '*No hay señorita.*'

She tried to shut the door, but Jane had wedged a discreet toecap, and waved Cassie's letter.

'See? She gave this address.'

'There is no English girl. Go away, go away.'

Jane found her temper rising. She didn't like the scorching dry heat, the street's contemptuous eyes, the woman's hostility.

'I have come all the way from England to see her, please tell me where she has gone. She *was* here, see the address.'

'Go away,' hissed the old woman, trying vainly to shut her door.

'I will go away. I want to go away. Just as soon as you tell me where I can find my friend.'

The woman rolled her eyes and made the sign of the cross.

'Maldona!' she mouthed in a croaking whisper.

'What?'

'Maldona! Go to Maldona, señorita, and go to the devil too!'

And with that, the old woman finally managed to

dislodge Jane's foot, and slam her door shut. Jane heard the sound of heavy bolts being drawn. She looked round, bewildered, for someone else to ask, but saw that the street was empty.

Jane sat at the bar sipping coffee, waiting for Harry Kuhl and watching *le tout* Marbella purposefully ambling past on its way from designer boutique to designer boutique. In this land of gold medallions, poodles, and spangled bikinis worn as formal daywear, Jane had decided to blend in with the local flora and fauna, so after showering back at her hotel, she had put on a red satin mini-skirt and a white silk blouse that she buttoned well below her breasts, leaving her navel bare; from her neck, a gold chain snaked between her breasts and emerged again below the blouse to loop round her waist. No stockings, just a white silk g-thong, to match her blouse, that just about covered her mink; red toenails in open slingback sandals. Maybe I'm a Marbella type at heart, she thought, and worried about this until Harry Kuhl showed punctually at one.

As she slid into the passenger seat of the shiniest, sil-veriest Mercedes coupé she had ever seen, Harry said, 'You are wearing red, the colour of blood, white for purity, and gold for the sun. Very Spanish.'

'Thank you for the compliment. I assume that was a compliment.'

As Jane made herself comfortable, she was aware that her skirt had ridden up, affording Kuhl a glimpse of her mons bulging under the skimpy silk panties, and aware too of his looking there, which sent a shiver down her spine.

'Right. OK,' said Kuhl vaguely, seeming to embrace everywhere and everything and accelerated smoothly in the direction of the crimson mountains that towered over Marbella.

'You are not afraid to travel into the unknown with a stranger?' he said.

'No . . . no, I'm not,' answered Jane, and to her surprise she knew it was true, although, logically, she was being foolhardy. Kuhl smiled.

'I sense from your aura that you are intrigued, but not afraid,' he said, 'and you are not afraid because you have perception.'

They passed the lazy suburbs of rich Marbella, rich with fountains and mosques and bougainvillea, and then the paved road became a narrow ribbon, and then a dirt track lined with wild orange trees, olives and palms.

'There are many Arabs in Marbella,' said Kuhl, as they passed an estate with a small mosque sullenly dominating the roadway. 'They were kicked out in 1492, and now with all their money they are coming back.' He pointed to a speck of white in the distance, nestling on a hillock under the baked mountainside.

'That is my house there, right underneath the *Sierra Bermeja*, the crimson mountain.'

They came to the top of a hill, where the track curved before descending into a dried-up river bed, thence snaking up towards the solitary eminence of Kuhl's villa. The view of the city, the sea and the sweep of the coastline into the glittering heat haze was breathtaking.

'Can we please stop for a moment?' said Jane. 'Just to look.'

At once, Kuhl slowed and braked, and they came to a halt in a swirl of dust. As he reached for the handbrake, his hand brushed Jane's thigh.

'It's lovely,' said Jane, then, realising what she sounded like, blushed. Kuhl made no move to touch her again, but unashamedly stared at her mouth.

'Stand up on the seat, and enjoy the view,' he said mildly.

She clambered to her feet and leaned on the windscreen frame, and then, as she was filling her lungs with the soft, scented air, and her eyes with the magnificent panorama of the coast, she felt Kuhl's lips press against her mons, through the thin satin of her skirt. His hands gently clasped her bottom as he pressed his face to her sex, not moving. Jane breathed in sharply but did not resist him. She felt mesmerised; she felt his strong tongue gently rubbing her sex, finding her clitoris through the dress fabric, and she sighed as her sex began to moisten.

53

'Oh,' she said, 'that is very nice.'

Kuhl slowly lifted her skirt and began to tongue her moist panties, with long, slow strokes that brushed her tingling clitoris and made her moan like the sighing of the sea breeze.

'You are bewitching me,' said Jane faintly.

'No, it is the place. It is a focal point of the energy of earth and sea, halfway between the ocean and the mountain.'

'So you knew I would want to stop here.'

'The place brought you, not I.'

'Please,' said Jane, 'take down my panties, kiss me on my naked cunt.'

'No,' said Kuhl, 'I must kiss you on your second skin.'

'You are going to fuck me, Harry? Oh, please.'

'Not yet ...'

'You are cruel. Oh, God, don't stop, I think I'm going to ... Oh, yes, yes.'

Jane trembled as the glowing warmth of her orgasm fluttered through her belly, and pressed Harry's blond head to her loins as his tongue worked at her throbbing clit, through the panties which by now were soaking wet. The perfume of the land and the fresh sea air mingled in her lungs, and as the sun bathed her in its pitiless rays, she felt as though the sun himself had loved her.

Shivering, she sank to her knees beside Harry and fumbled with the zipper of his jeans until she had released his penis, rigid beneath tight panties. She gasped in delighted amazement: the panties were royal blue silk, with a frothy lace trim: a girl's.

'How sweet,' she said, stroking his hard belly. 'You wear girlie things – it makes you seem, somehow, so much more virile. The contrast between your outward self and ... down here.'

'They are my wife's,' said Harry. 'I wear her second skin, to be near her always.'

Jane forced her fingers into the straining waistband and released his cock, which sprang up like a bound palm trunk. She stroked his balls and mons, which were both quite bare, and that too was sweet.

'Does your wife shave you?' she asked coyly.

'Of course. I am her baby.'

Jane slipped her mouth over the swollen bulb of Harry's rigid penis, then took him all the way to the back of her throat, and began to suck firmly, all the while caressing his hard balls. Her tongue flickered over his peehole; it was not long before she tasted the first drop of sperm, hot and sticky, and nice, like vanilla. She clasped his buttocks and pressed him into her as she fellated him, and very quickly he came, with a silent jerking of his penis as his powerful jet of seed washed her throat and she swallowed every warm drop.

'Oh,' said Kuhl, as though surprised. 'Right. OK.'

Jane scarcely had time to smooth her dress and hair – there was nothing to be done about her panties, short of wringing them dry – before Harry Kuhl gunned the motor again and they continued towards his villa. Jane was still basking in the afterglow of her orgasm, and wanted to give him a kiss, but did not dare: his manner had again become distant. She thought that his big penis would make a lovely candle.

'The energy, you see,' he said suddenly. 'Halfway between the rocks and the ocean. A woman's cunt is an ocean, her nympha, her clitoris, a proud rock bathed in the sea. I told you I was mystic-erotic.'

And Harry Kuhl turned to smile at her with, for the first time, a real smile.

The Mercedes crunched to a halt on red gravel before the sumptuous white villa. The air was heavy with scent and colour: blue jacaranda trees, purple bougainvillea, sunflowers, orchids. The bright green lawn hissed with sprinklers; across it sang a woman's voice.

'*Ich bin im Schwimmbad*, Harry.'

Jane looked for the source of the voice, and saw a turquoise swimming pool shimmering about fifty metres away at the edge of the garden.

'We have company, Greta,' cried Harry, in English, 'Miss Jane Ardenne, from London, who is joining us for luncheon.'

'How nice,' responded Greta, also in English. 'Bring her to the pool, angel, I am sure she will welcome a bathe. And get us some cold beers.'

Harry led Jane to the pool, walking in front of her and not looking back, as though he were a butler. The sun was in Jane's eyes as she came to the poolside, where she saw the silhouette of a woman bobbing on an inflated cushion in the middle of the water.

'Greta – Jane,' was all Harry said, before trudging off on his errand.

'Welcome, Jane,' said Greta. 'You must be dying for a bathe in all this heat. Jump in and join me while we wait for our beers. Harry can be so slow, at some things.'

'I don't have a costume,' said Jane, feeling rather silly at sounding so prim.

'Costume? Good heavens!' said Greta.

Jane squinted against the sun, and saw that her hostess was nude.

'Being naked suits me fine,' she said, smiling. Greta laughed.

'Very good. You make an English joke. I like it.'

'Joke?'

'Being naked *suits* you. You see? I am fond of humour.'

Jane stripped, except for her gold chain, and dived nude into the pool, sighing with pleasure as the cool water caressed her body. She swam towards the water-sofa, and Greta gave her hand to help her climb up beside her. Then she put her arm around Jane's shoulder and kissed her lightly on the cheek.

'Welcome,' she said.

Greta was small, firmly muscled, with a flashing white smile and bright eyes, and her body was nut brown from head to toe. Jane sat with her feet in the water, which made pretty darting patterns around her red toenails.

'You are new in Marbella,' said Greta. 'My, you have such a lovely pale skin.'

'Your tan is lovely,' said Jane. 'I'm so envious. There aren't many opportunities for nudism in London, and we don't have the weather.'

She looked admiringly at her hostess, her long auburn hair draped wet across the nipples of her breasts which were small and taut, like Cassie's. And, like Cassie, she had a lovely big bottom; Jane was not suprised to see that her pubis was shaved to a smooth velvet.

'It is I who am jealous,' said Greta. 'You have such full bosoms, and down there, your mink, why, it is longer than the hair on your head. And so thick. I have always shaved, ever since I was sixteen – it makes me feel more naked. Haven't you tried? It is exhilarating.'

'I thought about it,' said Jane, blushing. 'But I was a bit scared.'

'Scared of your naked sex? That is wrong, you must not be scared. Touch my mons, if you like, and see how nice and smooth it is, like a baby's bottom.'

'Oh, may I?'

Greta placed Jane's hand firmly on her shaven mons, just above the bare lips of her slit, and Jane marvelled at the touch. Shorn of hair, the ripe swelling of Greta's sex was thrilling in its purity. Hesitantly, Jane stroked it, and Greta grinned.

'At last,' cried Greta suddenly, 'here is Harry the lazybones with our refreshments.' Hastily, Jane removed her fingers from Greta's pubis, but Greta clicked her tongue and took hold of Jane's hand, this time placing it between her legs so that the palm was pressed right against her lips.

'It is permitted to be comfortable,' she said. '*Schnell*, Harry!'

Harry had a little raft, on which four beer cans were perched. He sent it expertly skimming, so that it arrived just at the women's feet. Eagerly they opened their beers, giggling as froth spurted over their bare breasts. Jane sighed with pleasure at the cold beer's taste.

'Harry's sperm tastes nice, doesn't it, Jane?' said Greta suddenly.

'What? I –'

'Of course you did. Harry always brings females here by that panoramic dirt-track. He thinks it is mystic-erotic. They always suck him!'

All the time, Greta's hand was gently stroking Jane's pubis, and Jane found her fingers irrestistibly drawn to her hostess's own shaven mount. Their lips met in a long, friendly kiss, and then Jane playfully put her mouth to Greta's tight little nipples, and licked them.

'You are a very nice English girl!' she laughed.

'You don't mind . . . about me and Harry?'

Greta kissed Jane's naked breasts and rubbed her nose against the stiffening nipples.

'Why no. He knows he will be whipped for it.'

'You whip your husband?'

'When he is naughty, which is most of the time. Today I think he deserves a really hard flogging, Jane, if you would like to watch.'

Jane felt a fluttering warmth in her belly, and her already moist sex became very wet. Harry whistled from the house, indicating luncheon.

'You mean, beat him on his naked buttocks?'

'Of course! What other way is there?'

'I should love to watch, Greta.'

'Good! It will add to his humiliation.' And the two naked friends, hand in hand, went to get their luncheon.

Luncheon was raw: that is, the two ladies ate naked, which seemed right to Jane, because the food was raw too. There were dishes of olives, cheeses, and smoked hams; an enormous salad of tomatoes, onions and iceberg lettuce; mound upon mound of shellfish. Harry waited on them, dressed in a frilly apron over his royal blue panties. He poured them chilled amber montilla wine and enquired if everything was all right.

'It is wonderful, Harry,' said Jane, 'But why don't you join us?'

She eyed his bared body with approval: he was slim and smooth – Greta must shave all of him, then – and attractive in a lithe, coltish way; veal escalope to Greta's sirloin steak.

'I am your servant,' said Harry.

'Be naked at least.'

58

'No, I must wear the badge of my rank.'

'Try one of these,' said Greta, handing Jane a smooth shell like a big clam. 'It is called a *concha fina*, and you eat it raw, of course.'

'It is the perfect animal,' said Greta, 'for it is pure muscle, and does not need a soul. Or rather, its soul is its muscle: pure power. That is why Harry likes taking photographs of such creatures. They are hard and nasty on the outside – think of crabs, or lobsters – and soft and helpless on the inside.'

'Like human beings,' said Harry.

'He likes photographing humans too,' confided Greta with a wink. 'In fact he is too modest to tell you that he is one of the highest-paid – how do you say, glamour photographers in Europe. He works with the nude form.'

'I am not modest at all,' said Harry. 'The fact is, I am good at taking photographs of the nude because I visualise my subjects as shellfish. A woman's cunt is above all a fishy place, her breasts as pink and curved as scallops. My job is to show the unity of all life! You remarked that I wear my wife's underthings. Why should I not? It helps me feel like a woman, and then I can take photographs of women. Would you like me to take photographs of you, Jane?'

'I'm not sure I feel like a fish,' said Jane, 'but I'm flattered, I think. I'll be glad and honoured to pose nude for you, Harry. I'll do anything within reason.'

'Why, Jane,' laughed Greta, 'nothing is within reason.'

'Well, that is very good mystic-erotic psychology,' said Jane, and it was in a merry and excited mood that she allowed herself to be led through the spacious drawing-room to Harry's studio.

'You can see what a good photographer Harry is,' said Greta proudly, showing Jane the walls decorated with nude studies. They were black-and-white photographs, mostly of women, and their ages ranged from Jane's to late middle age, the older women seeming to possess bodies as firm and supple as the younger. There were also some male nudes, musclemen taken outdoors, against a dramatic landscape of snow-capped mountains, although the bright light could only be Spanish. The bodies of the men were shaved, and their bulging muscles glistened with oil. Some of them stood proudly with fully erect penises. But the room was dominated by a study of Greta herself, which hung over the fireplace. She was nude, lying with her thighs up and her ankles around her neck; the camera focused on her open sex.

They passed into the studio, and Harry excused himself for a moment, saying he wished to change. Greta smiled at Jane.

'He is rather excited,' she whispered conspiratorially, 'because he knows I am going to punish him, before your eyes, Jane.'

5

The White Whip

The studio was large and white, cluttered with props, like a film set. There was a bed, no doubt for mystic-erotic purposes, screens, batteries of lights and cameras on bulky tripods. A closet bulged with bright clothing, and in the corner stood a rack of whips. Jane shivered in delighted apprehension, and touched one of the whips, a heavy braid of crimson leather.

'We like to make things homely,' said Greta.

'I don't think this is homely,' said Jane, stroking the whip's thick leather thongs. 'It is gorgeous, but I cannot imagine what it must be like to take a beating from such a fine, cruel thing.' Greta smiled and stroked Jane's bare bottom, and Jane blushed.

'You will see, shortly,' she murmured.

'Greta,' said Jane suddenly, 'do you know of a place called Maldona?'

Greta frowned.

'Why do you ask such a thing?' And Jane told her the story of her fruitless search for Cassie.

Greta took a while before answering.

'I must tell you, Jane, that Maldona in Spanish means "evil woman". I must also tell you that it is a legend, something used to frighten little girls. Or else it can mean our German *Schlaraffenland*, the land of dreams.' Jane was curious: why did Greta say that she 'must' tell her this?

'But does it exist, Greta? I have heard it is a castle, near hear, somewhere in the mountains, perhaps.'

Greta looked at her firmly, and spoke as though reciting a catechism, 'I must tell you Jane, that it does not exist, for if it did, it would be a place of unimaginable suffering and unimaginable beauty. A place where women would submit themselves to discipline beyond their wildest fantasies, beyond their wildest and most secret cravings; where their bare bodies would dance to whippings a thousand times more severe than anything our house has seen. But Maldona is the land of dreams, Jane, of every woman's dreams.'

Suddenly, Harry made his appearance, and both women clapped their hands uttering little coos of approval. Harry wore a white translucent nightgown of filmy silk, which covered his body entirely, and he had a red rose in his swept-back hair. On his feet were red satin slippers, toes curled in the Arab style, and, most intriguingly, he had made himself into a woman: he wore white panties under the robe, with a thick triangle of auburn hair, a false mink, covering his pubis, with white stockings strapped to a white lace garter belt.

'How sweet!' cried Jane, thrilled that the woman's garb should sensuously emphasise the lithe maleness of the body beneath. Greta picked up the crimson plaited whip from its rack, and smiled grimly.

'Well, Harry,' she said, 'I think you know what is coming to you. You have deserved punishment.' Harry nodded.

'Lift your dress, and lower your panties, for I intend to beat you on your bare arse. You may bend down and touch your toes.' He obeyed, shivering a little. Greta lifted the whip to the full extent of her reach, and cracked it across the centre of the man's naked buttocks. Harry groaned, and shuddered, but after that made no sound as Greta delivered seven sharp cuts in rapid succession.

Jane watched the ferocious punishment with awe, and excitement welled inside her as she saw the man's bare fesses tremble and clench as the cruel leather made them blush. With each stroke, Greta's naked breasts bounced prettily, so that it seemed her breasts and the trembling buttocks of her flogged husband were dancing together in a secret, loving rhythm.

When seven strokes had been delivered, Harry smiled. He knelt and kissed his wife's feet, then, panting, nodded at his cameras.

'To work, then,' said Greta, all businesslike. 'You are ready, Jane?'

'Try me,' said Jane, and began to strike what she imagined to be the poses required by Harry Kuhl's mystic-erotic genius. Harry positioned himself behind one of his many cameras, and switched lights on and off as Jane thrust and pouted at the glinting lens. Now, she understood why women bared themselves on stage or on camera: it was the exhilarating, childlike power of knowing that *her* body, *her* naked sex, were the centre of attention; that her every movement inspired awe.

'No,' said Harry suddenly, 'that is just kitsch.'

'I don't understand,' said Jane, crestfallen.

'Do not feign emotion: it is a turn-off. You should show disdain for the camera, even fear, for the eye of the lens is a phallos, an intruder, threatening you, invading your body. You are repelled and enchanted at the same time. Jane, you want the camera to enter your cunt, to *fuck* you.'

As he spoke, the camera's motor-drive had been whirring, and Jane realised that she was already obeying him, her poses becoming sullen and secretive, her nudity more tantalising for the hostility it contained. She thought of trapping the snake's eye of the lens inside her and crushing it with the muscles of her sex, and found that she was moist with excitement.

'Better,' said Harry. 'Yes, bend over, just so. The fesses parted, showing your anus – you are daring me, insulting me with your nakedness. Hold the breasts, yes, that's it, squeeze the nipples, mocking, contemptuous. Hand over your cunt, Jane, not coy, but sneering, forbidding me entrance. Now the cunt bared, but bend your leg so that you take your toes in your mouth: you are saying, this is my body, it is not for you.'

Jane took up that pose, then, without prompting, slid four fingers deep into her slit, which, very wet now, accommodated them with ease.

'Excellent!' cried Harry. 'Now we shall use some accoutrements.'

Greta handed her a silk robe, and showed her how to drape it, hiding breasts and mink; then she got a necklace and a silver chain to entwine round her own golden one; feathers, bracelets, the crimson whip which she pressed between the spread lips of her sex. The camera whirred, lights flicked on and off, and Jane felt lost in a heady dance, as though she were all alone. Her skin was glistening with sweat under the hot lights: she sneered at the winking eye of the camera, daring it to violate her. Harry told her to spit, and she did so, letting her saliva moisten her breasts. She was alone in a world of light and shadow, with Harry and Greta as her servants in the dark mystery of her revealed body.

Greta applauded when she seized the whip handle and pushed it to the hilt inside her, allowing the thong to dangle from her sex like a thin, evil penis, as her willing fingers exposed and caressed her stiff clitoris. She let Greta strap her into tight corsets of gaudy silk and pinching whalebone; net stockings and garter belts, stiletto heels with razor points, which Greta, lying flat, took inside her mouth and, to Jane's nervous amazement, just inside the lips of her cunt. Harry's penis was well hardened now, bulging under his false mink, and Jane was pleased and excited, her joyous fingers oily with her own juice as she continued to flick at her engorged clit, teasing herself, always drawing near to her plateau, then stopping before she exploded in pleasure.

When Greta handed her a garment made of soft black rubber, she put it on without hesitation. It was a skintight catsuit, all in one piece, which covered her whole body. Her head was encased in a pixie hood with holes for her eyes, nose and mouth, and steel zippers opening to reveal her breasts, mink and anus. Jane felt herself through the thin rubber.

'Oh,' she cried, 'this is like a second skin. It's made for me!'

'Zips open,' called Harry, and she obeyed. Greta brought an ebony carving, which looked African, and

ordered her to kneel on all fours, with her buttocks high
and spread. The carving was consisted of two penises of
about the same size, both very long and slender. Jane felt
a tickling at her anus and cunt-lips, then sighed as the two
penises slid smoothly inside both her passages. There was
no resistance, and Greta plunged them into Jane, right to
the hilt.

'Are you going to fuck me, Greta?' whispered Jane. 'Oh,
please.'

But Greta closed her zips smartly, so that the double
cock was locked insider her; only the silver chain on which
they were fastened protruded from the small opening between Jane's legs.

Greta gave a hard jerk on the chain, and ordered Jane to
stand, this time with harshness in her voice. Jane thrilled as
she obeyed, feeling the silky rubber caress her as she moved.

'It's fabulous,' she blurted.

'It is not fabulous, it is real,' snapped Greta. 'And now
you are going to be punished, girl, for your behaviour at
the swimming pool.'

'With you!'

'Of course with me. And your punishment will be real,
too.'

Greta took the crimson whip and lashed the air with it,
making a loud whistle followed by a vicious crack.

Jane gulped.

'Greta . . . I'm not ready for such a thrashing,' she said.

Greta laughed.

'You sweet, silly girl. The whip is not for you. It is for
my body. I am guilty of allowing my servant to spy on us
at the swimming pool, while we took our pleasure, and that
was undignified of me. You were my partner in crime,
weren't you? So your punishment is to beat me, to watch
as my body writhes in pain under your lash.'

Shivering, Jane took the whip from Greta, who tugged
on the silver chain and led Jane around the floor; with
each step the chain jangled and pulled on the black penises
which filled Jane so tightly. She was powerless to resist,
and watched Greta's naked body writhe in a dance of

submission as she came to Harry and knelt before him. Greta knotted the silver chain around her own bare waist, binding Jane to her. Then she parted Harry's robe and kissed his stiff penis through the hair of his false mink.

'I made this mink for him,' murmured Greta. 'It is hair from my own head.' Harry lifted her hands and placed them on his shoulders, and Greta splayed her legs wide on the floor, her back arched, and her body trembling, rigid in the shape of a cross.

'Now, Jane, my priestess,' she whispered, 'whip me. Seven on the back, and seven on my bottom.'

Jane lifted the whip, and cracked it hard across Greta's shoulders. Greta sighed, and her mouth worked furiously at the silken sheath of Harry's erect penis. A second cut, and a third, and the play of Greta's writhing muscles excited Jane so much that her fingers strayed to her own sex, feeling the slit quite wet now, and brushing her swollen clitoris through its thin covering of silky black rubber. Greta moaned; her back well flushed with the whip, she now received her seven cuts on the buttocks, squirming at each stroke, the taut flesh vivid in the shadow of the distant spotlights, her deep cleft a valley of soft shade.

'I am yours, Jane,' sighed Greta, and resumed her tonguing of her man's stiff cock until Harry too sighed and a wet stain spread across the white silk of his panties. Jane paused, and raised the whip for the seventh and final stroke on Greta's fesses, and now Greta's moan became a squeal, and she cried out, 'Sweet Jane, I am coming! You have made my body alive. Yes. The last cut, Oh please!'

And, soaked in sweat underneath the rubber catsuit, Jane brought the whip down in a final stroke, her hand fiercely rubbing her own sex, and as she saw Greta's buttocks jerk, she cried out in her own spasm of pleasure.

The spotlights winked out, and the three lay in the warm darkness, holding each other, a silent triad of filled desire.

'Maldona?' said Harry thoughtfully. 'I have heard of it.'

'Ach, Harry, it's *Schlaraffenland*, a legend,' said Greta crossly. 'Jane does not want to be bothered with such stuff.'

They sat on the verandah with wine and nuts and olives, watching the sea blaze in the crimson light of the dying sun; dressed for the scented evening breeze that cooled the hot land. Jane saw that there was worry in Greta's eyes, that she was almost pleading with her husband to agree with her, and wondered why she was concerned.

'Legends can be interesting,' said Harry slowly, toying with his wineglass. 'You have heard of the Knights Templar, the medieval order of chivalry that was born from the Crusades to the Holy Land?'

'They had all sorts of treasures,' said Jane.

'Yes, and because of that they were suppressed, by an edict of the Pope, in the fourteenth century. The land was taken, but where and if the treasures existed remains unknown. The Order vanished, scattered to the winds – except in Spain, where it was allowed to survive. It is said that those Knights who lived made their way here, and that the Order still exists, closed in isolated castles and fortresses, using its vast wealth to make pacts, shifting with the political winds, surviving. Maldona is said to be one of those strongholds.'

'But it is only a silly rumour,' said Greta.

'Cassie said it was a college.'

Harry shrugged.

'A fortress is a college of sorts,' he said. 'Anyway, this place, if it exists, is supposed to be up in the mountains, beyond Ronda. A bleak, dangerous area, and not for visitors.'

'Stay here with us,' said Greta.

'I don't understand why these people should wish to survive as an Order,' said Jane. 'I mean, there aren't any crusades any more.'

'Wealth and power have no purpose,' said Harry. 'They exist for themselves. The Templars created a structure of Commanderies, controlled by a Superior, under whom served Knights and Chaplains. And when a structure exists, its instinct is to perpetuate itself, even when its original reason is gone.'

Greta kissed her.

'You'll stay, won't you?' she said. 'At least tonight. Harry will run you to town to pick up your car and your things.'

'Yes,' said Jane. 'But, you know, I must find Cassie. If she is in this Maldona place, then I must . . .'

'Must rescue her?' laughed Harry. 'Heavens, this is the twentieth century. Perhaps she does not want to be rescued.'

Jane thought of crags and castles, and romantic dawns over snow-capped hills.

'Perhaps I wouldn't want to be rescued either,' she said.

'There is one other thing which I find piquant in this legend,' said Harry, 'and probably explains your friend's curiosity. It is said that of all the Templar foundations in Iberia, Maldona was a foundation of *women*.'

'Don't go,' pleaded Greta.

'I must. I'll go tomorrow. And I'll come and see you again, when I have found Cassie.'

Greta sighed.

'Well, we shall be here if you come back,' she said, looking daggers at Harry, who seemed quietly pleased with the impact of his words.

'Get in the car,' he said to Jane, 'and we'll go to Marbella.'

'What do you mean, *if* I come back?' cried Jane, joking. Harry gunned the engine, and his soft voice was scarcely audible above the roar.

'Well, if the legends are to be believed, Jane, nobody finds Maldona. Maldona finds you.'

That evening, Harry, Greta and Jane enjoyed a light supper, and afterwards they sat by a log fire with coffee and brandy, looking at the flames, for, as Greta explained, the hotter the day, the colder the night. Maldona was not mentioned, and neither were the events of the afternoon, although Jane burned with curiosity about her new friends.

'You must think us rather staid,' said Greta, sipping her brandy. 'We are homebodies, I think.'

'Staid?' cried Jane. 'After what we did today?'

'You liked wearing the rubber catsuit while you whipped me?'

'Heavenly. I can't explain.'

'Take it with you, then, on your wild duck chase. It will keep you warm in the cold mountains.'

'Thank you. But Greta – when I beat you – how is it you . . . you came, without even being touched?'

'Your whip touched me, Jane, and that caress is the most potent. Pain is merely a heightened form of pleasure, the nerve ends stimulated to breaking. When you bite into a juicy peach, do you not feel a moment's delicious pain as your saliva spurts?'

Jane took a deep breath.

'Greta . . . I want my bottom to be a juicy peach for you. I want you to bite me – to flog me, yes – on my bare bottom. Please say yes!'

'We shall see,' said Greta, and turned back to stare at the glowing embers through her brandy glass.

Restless, Jane excused herself and went outside to look at the starry sky and think of her journey into the unknown on which she would embark in the morning. She felt powerfully drawn to Harry and Greta, and yet the call of sweet Cassie was stronger. Was she up in those dark mountains? Jane shivered, and not just from the cold night air, and went back inside. For a while, she padded through the house, marvelling at the pictures and furnishings, rugs and cushions that looked brightly Arabian. There were jewelled scimitars, spears and daggers with curling handles; in one room she shuddered at a wall hung with chains, whips and leg-irons of shiny copper, which looked deceptively innocent, like the scythes and ploughshares in a country pub. And there was a blown-up photograph of Harry's: one of his muscled male nudes, penis well erect, crouched like a dog with a chain around his neck. The chain was held by a woman, naked except for a mask of feathers, who held a whip raised over his naked arse. Beside the photograph hung a whip of white leather: from a braided handle a foot long dangled four thongs a good three feet, gleaming white and encrusted with glittering sharp gems. Jane thought it utterly enchanting, full of beauty and menace. She picked it reverently from the wall and carried it back to the drawing-room.

'Wherever did you get this lovely thing?' she asked.

'A gift from an Arab friend,' said Greta. 'We visit Morocco a lot. They are generous people.'

'I've never seen a whip studded with gems.'

'They are diamonds,' said Greta.

'The whip must be worth a fortune.'

'It is, and not just for the diamonds. There are very few of its kind in existence, and it is a most valuable antique. That whip dates from the fourteenth century, the last years of Arab rule in Spain. It was made for Akbar, the Amir of Ubrique.'

'That is in the mountains beyond Ronda,' added Harry, 'in fact the same direction you will take tomorrow on your little quest.'

'Well,' continued Greta, 'whenever the Amir took a new wife to his harem, his custom was to whip her, to teach her obedience, to break her.'

'How cruel,' said Jane.

'They were cruel times. Much like our own. But Akbar was a generous man, and whipped his wives with such a diamond-studded quirt.'

'Generous? That would hurt far more than an ordinary whip.'

'Of course. But the stones were loosely set, and with a vigorous flogging they would be dislodged. After her whipping, the lady got to keep all the diamonds that had fallen from the whip's thongs, so the longer she could stand the lash, the richer she became, and the more respected for her bravery. The beatings took place in the public square, to the great merriment of the crowd, and soon developed into a kind of contest, with aspirant ladies travelling from far away to compete for the Amir's favours. It was not unusual for four or five such women to be flogged at the same time, the winner, of course, being the one who endured the most strokes. And it is said that once a wife was accepted after having collected every single diamond from the whip, which was left quite bare. The beatings were on the bare buttocks, not the back, which was held to be undignified and fit for slaves; for, of course, once accepted into the harem, a wife was mistress of slaves, and lived a life of sumptuous luxury, so much that poor Christian girls would convert to Islam just to enter the contest. That is the story, anyway, although I don't suppose you believe a word of it.'

'How romantic,' said Jane, 'how dark and thrilling and . . . Spanish.'

It was in the small hours of the morning that Jane, alone in her comfortable guest room, was awoken from a deep sleep. The moon beamed through the drapes, and she knew dawn was not near. There was a rustle of movement, a footfall, and she jerked her head up. Someone was in her room. She rubbed her eyes, and saw a dark silhouette beside her bed.

'Sh! It's only me!'

'Greta . . . You startled me.'

'Jane, would you mind if I joined you? I couldn't sleep, I felt so lonely.'

'Please join me. But lonely? I am the lonely one, missing my friend. You sleep with Harry.'

Greta slid beneath the duvet and snuggled up to Jane's warm body. She placed a wrapped package on the floor.

'Yes,' she sighed. 'Well . . .'

'Well, what?'

'Oh, nothing. Just cuddle me. I have brought you a present. I hope you like it – I know you will.'

'I'll open it in the morning.'

'Mmmm . . . This is so cosy. Do you always sleep nude?'

'Why, yes.'

'I must do the same, then.'

And Greta slipped off her nightdress, then pressed her bare body against Jane, her face nuzzling Jane's breasts and her hand stroking her belly. It was not long before Greta's fingers strayed to Jane's mink, and rested there, toying with the silky smooth hair which had recently begun to grow back. They lay silently embracing, drinking the stillness of the night.

71

'This is nice,' said Greta.

Jane stroked her bottom.

'Does your poor red skin still hurt?' she asked.

'A little. It's still warm and tingly, but that is nice too.'

'Greta?' said Jane softly. 'Why are you lonely?'

There was a silence, and then Greta murmured, 'Harry and I do not fuck.'

'Oh, I didn't know. I'm so sorry.'

Greta laughed.

'How can you be sorry for something that is not your fault? You English, always saying sorry.'

'Well, you know what I mean.'

'Yes, I know.'

'Tell me about it if you like, Greta. You want to tell me, don't you? That is why you have come to me.'

'Harry and I are from eastern Germany, what was once the German Democratic Republic, the communist dictatorship. I lectured in philosophy at the University of Rostock, and Harry was my student. We were lovers; we were political, and like so many, we were arrested and imprisoned by the Stasi, the secret police. We spent two years in the medical prison.'

'A medical prison,' said Jane. 'It sounds . . . well, did they torture you?'

'Not exactly. There were experiments. The doctors were interested in the effects of pain on the nervous system, and thus we received regular whippings: quite hard, strapped naked to a flogging frame, with all sorts of monitors and wires attached.'

'That is surely torture.'

'I say not exactly,' said Greta, 'because after a while you get used to it. You see, Jane, during the beatings they would masturbate me. With each stroke of the whip, my clitoris, my whole body, would tingle and glow with their clever, devilish rubbing, until I would come. And they did not stop, they made me come again and again, until I could not imagine orgasm without whipping. I craved to be beaten. It was the same for Harry; at least they had the decency to use female guards for his . . . stimulation.'

Greta laughed ironically.

'We married eventually, and came here to the Costa del Sol, like so many others, to escape the past. And like so many others, we are trapped by it. We do not fuck, as man and wife do. We need a scenario, like today's. We cannot live without it, Jane. Our Arab friends are most understanding, damn them!'

'What friends?'

'Oh! Forget I spoke. It was Arab friends in Hamburg who found us work here, that's all.'

They lay in silence, hands gentle on each other's body, and at last Jane said, 'Greta, I would love to make another scenario. But above all I should like to see you fuck. Couldn't you do that? If I whipped both of you, together?'

'That would give you pleasure?'

'The greatest pleasure.'

Without a word, Greta reached down and handed Jane her wrapped present. Excited, Jane opened the parcel, and cried for joy. Inside was the white whip of the Amir of Ubrique, sparkling with diamonds.

'It's lovely,' said Jane, and kissed Greta long and hard on her lips. Then, tenderly, she kissed the jewelled thongs of her whip and pressed them to Greta's mouth.

'Greta,' she whispered, 'it is not yet dawn, but I am wide awake. We have time. Greta, please whip me with my gift; whip my bare body, as the harem women were whipped so long ago.'

'The diamonds are yours to keep anyway, girl,' laughed Greta.

'Please,' begged Jane, and placed Greta's hand between her thighs.

'See how wet I am, wanting you to do it to me. And wet, too, thinking that the sight of my body dancing under your whip will make you and Harry fuck, for that would give me the greatest pleasure.'

Greta took her cheeks in her palms, and looked intently into Jane's eyes.

'Under the whip, Jane, a woman can find herself.'

'I know.'

* * *

A cellar, lit by flickering candles: the walls, ceiling and floor all mirror, the only sound the humming of air conditioning. On the mirrored walls, racks of whips and manacles, harnesses and gags and rubber suits, repeated in the glass to infinity. Jane lay on a frame in the centre of the chamber, strapped tight, her bare bottom perched high on its cushion. Her head was sheathed in a soft rubber hood that left only her nose and mouth bare, and she had insisted on that, for she wanted to be flogged in darkness, not seeing herself tremble as she was beaten, in those harsh mirrors. Her ankles and wrists were bound, and in addition, chains clamped her nipples and the lips of her sex, fastening her to the whipping frame.

'You have only to say stop,' said Harry, 'and the beating will cease.'

'I shall not say stop,' replied Jane. 'I am in your power.'

'And we are naked for you, Jane,' murmured Greta, 'for we are in your power. Whipped, you prove yourself mightier than your tormentors.'

'Begin, please,' ordered Jane.

She heard Harry lift the four-thonged whip, and the first cut fell, stroking her buttocks with liquid fire. She sighed, and clenched her bottom for the second stroke and, when it came, the fire seemed to tear her skin from her. Her bottom started to dance as the pitiless strokes followed silently, in measured time, and the only thing Jane could hear was her own hoarse panting; still she did not cry out. And as her bottom squirmed, she began to feel a fearful, exultant joy in her belly, a glowing pleasure in her utter helplessness, unseeing, feeling nothing except the lash, as though she were alone in the entire world with only her sweet pain to make her live.

She could feel her sex moistening, now, and as she danced to the whip's rhythm she rubbed her sex against the soft Morocco cushion, moaning with little gulps as her clitoris stiffened and tingled at the gentle pressure. Greta watched her, and moved to her head, to press her silken bare mons against Jane's mouth. Jane kissed her there, sighing as she sucked as Greta's oily slit, and with each

74

stroke of the lash on her naked skin, her tongue darted out to caress Greta's stiff clitoris. And now it was Greta's turn to moan. Jane lost count of the strokes on her bottom; she was alive in a blissful maelstrom of fire, feeling only the cut of the four sweet thongs on her, tasting only the salty juices of Greta's swollen cunt. As though in the distance, she heard a tinkling sound as diamonds flew across her back and thighs, and dropped to the glass floor. She squealed deep in her throat, a cry of victory over her pain, and triumph as she heard the jewels dislodged one by one by the force of Harry's beating, until at least he cried, 'The whip is bare! Jane has taken every diamond!'

And suddenly, the beating ceased, and she heard the white whip clatter to the floor. Harry's hands were on her burning buttocks, parting them; his swollen cock caressed her anus bud, and she thought he was going to penetrate her there, but then the bulb of his penis slid forward to the lips of her cunt, and with one powerful thrust his stiff cock was inside her sex, filling her with his exultant manhood. She was wet and oily for him, and his fucking made her cry out. He was stiff and perfect, bucking with a demonic energy that made her belly quake, and it was not long before she felt him shudder, and the hot seed spurt from him. All the while she fiercely tongued Greta's hard acorn, licking up the salt juices that flowed on her mouth, and as the last shudders of Harry's orgasm died away, Jane came to her own spasm and heard herself howl, with Greta's hands tightly on her rubber hood, pressing her to her wet quim, and Jane heard Greta cry out too, lost in an ecstasy of her own.

Harry's penis softened and withdrew, making Jane feel sad. But Greta tore off her rubber hood, and she blinked in the light. Greta's face was flushed and joyful.

'You must watch us, now, Jane. You are inspiration.'

She embraced her husband, covering his body with kisses and stroking his flaccid cock until it stirred and rose again, to a glorious stiffness, shining with Jane's love-juice. And then, in front of Jane's smiling face, husband and wife fucked, and Jane felt tears of happiness blur her eyes.

* * *

They breakfasted together after a few hours' sleep, and Harry and Greta giggled and blushed like new lovers. Greta held Harry's hand, and said to Jane:

'Harry fucks so beautifully.'

'Yes,' said Jane.

Later on, Jane insisted on pursuing her quest for the fabled Maldona.

'I have told you what I must,' said Greta mysteriously. 'I hope your search brings you fulfilment. Take these, our gifts.' She handed Jane a box, which she opened. It contained the black rubber catsuit, and the two ebony cocks, which had pleasured her so sweetly. She looked, and saw that they were not made of wood at all. Greta smiled.

'From the harem of our medieval friend, the Amir of Ubrique,' she said. 'Favourite wives received the gift of two cocks, cut from slaves to make them eunuchs, then stuffed and sewn together to make a device for their pleasure.' Jane stroked the smooth cocks, and the balls like walnuts, and shivered.

'So two men had to become women to serve women's pleasure,' she said, putting the gifts in her bag along with her white whip, and the golden fan-harness she had brought from London. She got into her Range Rover and started the motor.

'Well, I'll say goodbye,' said Harry. 'I have some photo people coming today, and must get ready. I suggest you go up to Ronda, and then to Grazalema. It is a godforsaken place, and if your Maldona exists, she might well be there.' Jane wondered why he referred to this apparently non-existent place as 'she', and why he grinned like a cat.

'Goodbye, my loves,' she said. 'We shall meet again.'

'Oh, yes, sweet Jane,' said Greta. 'In another place, perhaps.'

As Jane turned on to the main road at the end of Greta's driveway, she passed a large black van going in towards the villa, and that was followed at some distance by a white stretched Cadillac with shaded windows. Fascinated, she stopped just before the road curved, and watched. The doors of the Cadillac opened, and three gentlemen of Arab appearance got out, to be warmly greeted by Greta and Harry. Then, with the driver of the black van, who seemed to be a woman, they opened the doors, and eight young men and women stepped down. They were nude, except for skimpy thongs; their well-muscled bodies gleamed with oil in the bright sunlight, and Jane supposed them to be models for Harry's planned photo session. They were superb in their nudity: she hoped she could see the photographs when she visited again, hopefully in the company of Cassie. She hummed happily to herself as she accelerated down towards Marbella, patting the little velvet pouch of diamonds that her whipping had earned her, and stroking her purse of treasures: the catsuit, the preserved penises, and the white whip itself. Then she frowned, remembering something.

It had to be a trick of the light, but she could have sworn . . . No, it was silly. Why would models for a photo session be shackled and chained together?

6

Matron

Sometimes a day that starts off beautiful with hope and promise turns out a rotten, frustrating dud of a day, and by late afternoon, Jane was beginning to think it was one of those. It was all right as far as Ronda; a lovely winding road through the mountains, a town built across a stunning gorge with the oldest bullring in Spain, as promised, and no shortage of arrogant males who wanted to show her round its secret places. That was par for the course, even pleasant – how disturbing to be unpropositioned, however crudely! Directions to Maldona were not forthcoming, though. No one had heard of the place, and she got the 'you don't want to go there' treatment.

'But if you don't know where it is, how do you know I don't want to go there?' she said sarcastically. Eyes were rolled, and grins grinned, sarcasm being too subtle, a thing to wound the male Spanish ego. Grudgingly, she was told how to get to Grazalema, in the benighted province of Cadiz, although she didn't want to go there, either.

As she took the winding road through an increasingly poor and barren landscape, she was beginning to agree with them. This was the tail end of a tail-end province, living on past glories and government handouts, without the bubbling wealth of the province of Malaga and its golden egg, the Costa del Sol.

She had a sour luncheon in Grazalema, and there her enquiries about Maldona were met with positive hostility, signs of the cross, and even spitting. She set off none the less in the direction she felt was right, towards a looming range of forbidding crags, down a succession of increasing-

78

ly uncomfortable 'B' roads. It was roasting hot in the car, despite the elevation; the air-conditioning seemed faulty, but opening the windows only let in clouds of dust and gnats.

Through false turnings and dead ends, she came closer and closer to the mountain crags, which she felt, quite irrationally, must contain Maldona. They corresponded to her vision of romantic Spain, all dark and forbidding, and she imagined sombre *hidalgos* with jewelled swords and whips, lording it over harems of virgins.

Her fantasy was interrupted by a flock of goats, and she had to brake suddenly to avoid decimating them. The flock seemed endless, and she looked up at the sun which was already low in the sky, wondering if she should turn round and go back to the coast, or at least Ronda, which would be sure to equip her with male company for the evening.

At that moment the goatherd rounded the corner, a grizzled old boy talking merrily to himself with his eyes uplifted to heaven. Jane sighed, and called out to him that she wanted to find the place called Maldona. His response was startling, but not surprising. He emitted a fiendish cackle, and cried, 'Maldona, Maldona! Ha ha ha!'

At least this was not a downright negative. Jane tried asking him again, slower, and more insistent. He put his head into the car and leered all over Jane. She had not known what Spanish goatherds smelled like, and now all of a sudden she did.

'Maldona! *Mala dona! Mala para ti, señorita!*' was all he said before, mercifully, retreating. 'Maldona, bad woman, bad for you, Missy.'

Damn! Jane gunned her engine, and tried one last time. 'But where is it?'

And to her astonishment, he waved at a little track which disappeared in the direction of the massive crag. Looking closely in the heat haze, she saw that there was a little gap in the rock face: a mountain pass.

'Through the slit, through the slit, that is where bad Maldona lies,' cackled her friend. She nodded in thanks, and turned hastily up the rocky little track, towards the mountains.

It was, of course, further than she expected. She was alone, a *tourbillon* of dust on this isolated track, in the flickering shade of the scrubby trees and bushes that lined it like beseeching beggars, and she thought herself in the deserts of Mexico or Arizona. Wasn't it here that they filmed all those spaghetti westerns? The sun was going down, and she was hot and sticky. She didn't even know if the road would continue through that shimmering little gap, or if it would take her car.

The road twisted, and to her surprise there was a little lake, or rather, an arm of a larger lake, which was a thin ribbon of water that seemed to curl round the mountainside like a moat. The water was cool and clear, enlivened by fish and drifting with lily-pads and wavy reeds. It took her less than a second's thought to turn off the road and drive the fifty metres or so to the lakeside, stop the car, strip off all her clothes – the solitude now seemed blissful! – and dive nude into the cool water. By reflex, she took the bag containing her treasures, as well as her passport and money, and dumped it at the water's edge, although she realised, as she gasped in pleasure at the water's caress, that it was no safer there than in her car, beside it. It didn't matter; she lay on her back, floating under the magnificent purple sky, now darkening to velvet, with the stars and moon just hinting, and found all the cares of the frustrating day wash from her like grime. Little shoals of fishes fluttered around her naked body; she opened her legs wide, feeling deliciously naughty, and allowed them to brush tantalisingly on the lips of her open sex. She felt new confidence: that old fool had probably spoken with the wisdom of the simple-minded. Maldona was sure to be there, beyond the pass, scarcely a kilometre away.

Suddenly she became aware that she was being watched. The glint of two evil eyes peeped from behind the Range Rover, and she heard a chillingly familiar cackle; 'Maldona! *Mala para ti.*'

'God!' she cried, thrashing the water, and foolishly trying to cover her breasts and pubis. Here she was, alone in the middle of nowhere, with a crazy man! How had he got here? Probably, she realised, by loping just as fast as her car's tortured crawl along the rocky path. She had no idea what to do, and felt panic welling up where her joy had been. But the impasse was resolved, swiftly and efficiently. She heard the car start, the motor leapt into life, and with a screech of tyres, her Range Rover disappeared into the dust.

Jane waded out of the water, and stood on the bank by her bag, yelling and waving and doing all the things one knows to be futile even as one does them. Then she squatted down, shivering, and tried to think.

She could go back to the main road. But even that was not a main road. To get anywhere that she would find help, another human being, would be a trek of miles and miles, naked, through the Spanish twilight. She looked up at the little pass, clearer now as the heat haze dissipated.

Maldona was there. Maldona could not be far away. Her mind was made up. No signposts indeed! She would give Cassie a piece of her mind when she found her! Groaning with fury and frustration, and wishing she had a cigarette, she picked up her precious bag, and, nude and all alone in this cooling desert, started to trudge barefoot over the rocks towards Maldona.

It took longer, and was more uncomfortable, than she expected. Her muscles ached and her feet screamed with pain as she entered the canyon that led through the sheer bulk of the mountain. The car would have been useless anyway, it was so narrow! And somehow the loss of her car seemed strangely irrelevant. What was a car? She could always get another one. The safety of her body was more important, and her fitness for the punishments – yes, here, naked and alone, she could admit it! – that she yearned for, and that she hoped would await her in this mysterious place. Perhaps it was proper to arrive nude and humble, betokening a readiness to submit.

She shivered in the twilight, as though this narrow pass were a secret channel admitting her to some strange womb, intimidating her, yet sheathing and protecting her innocence.

At last, she stepped out of the pass. Beneath her stretched a great bowl of land, lush groves and meadows entirely contained by a rim of rocky crags. The highest of all the crags, sitting above them like a queen surrounded by her knights, was curved to form a vast plateau, and silhouetted against the white waxing moon in the middle of the smooth plateau, stood a castle, or a cathedral, its vaulting spires and turrets seeming to stretch all the way to the stars twinkling in the black velvet sky. And Jane knew she had found Maldona.

It took Jane three hours to cross the meadowland and reach the towering mountainside at whose top the castle of Maldona perched. At first it seemed there could be no way up, but at last she found a worn, narrow path that wound towards the top, and she had to make herself as nimble as a goat to climb up, clinging to precarious toeholds and wispy bushes. But eventually, breathless and giddy with fatigue, she found herself at the huge steel doors of the castle, which stood about two hundred metres from the rim of the plateau. The few windows were barred or shuttered, as though the building were the carapace of some giant crustacean. Jane looked in vain for a method of entrance, and could not even find a bell or an intercom. In the darkness, she could not even guess at the vastness of the structure; from the distance it had appeared slender, and now in the eerie moonlight it seemed squat, brooding and infinite. Wherever she was, it was evidently not the front door.

Feeling too faint to be ridiculous, a naked girl in the dark, empty moonscape, she banged on the huge steel portals, which echoed hollowly. Then she saw that within the huge door was another, smaller, door, and she banged on that.

'Is anyone there?' she cried in English, then in Spanish. 'Help!'

Just as she was about to give up hope, the small inset door creaked open. Inside was warm yellow light, the smell of flowers and coffee and home. A woman stood before her in the little doorway. She was about thirty-five, with a kindly face smiling beneath ironed shoulder-length blonde hair which was discreetly flecked with grey. Her trim body was sheathed in a black tunic, like a uniform. Without a word, the woman took Jane by her arm, and led her gently inside.

'You poor dear, you must be famished,' she said in an accent that was not far from Jane's native Northumberland. 'And naked too, why you would catch your death of cold outside on a night like this. You just sit down and have a nice cup of coffee, or would you prefer tea? I have it sent from Fortnum's, you know.'

'I . . . something terrible has happened!'

'Then you'd prefer tea?'

'No . . . you don't understand. My car . . . I don't know where to begin! It's awful!'

'It is always awful, love. That is why we are here. And as for beginning, your beginning was the moment you crossed my threshold. What is past does not exist here. We all arrive naked, in a manner of speaking. Tea, then?'

'Tea will be fine.'

'Splendid. Welcome to Maldona, girl.'

Bathed and robed, Jane sipped hot tea and felt life return to her. She sat on a sofa covered in a blue Liberty print, by a cosy log fire. The room twinkled with candles: through the undraped French window she looked out on an English garden of rose bushes, ivy, birdtables and even a goldfish pond, which could have been in a suburb of London, were it not for the gleaming moon in the velvet Spanish sky above. She was too dazed to ask questions, and concentrated on the glow of the hot tea, the minute sensations of comfort as her body adjusted to her new, friendly surroundings. The nightmare she had fled on the burning mountainside seemed an age away.

'Is your robe comfortable? It's the best I can do at short notice.'

'Yes, yes thank you. You are very kind.'

The fluffy pink robe and slippers belonged with the suburban garden.

'You'll get a proper uniform as soon as possible of course, it's just that it's a little late – almost third bell, and most students arrive early. But then we cannot second-guess fate, can we?'

'Uniform?' said Jane, faltering. 'I'm a little confused.'

'Of course you are. It takes a while to learn about Maldona, and even then you will never learn everything. I don't think anyone over all the centuries ever has. I certainly haven't, and I seem to have been here for ever.'

She laughed a pleasant girlish laugh that put Jane at her ease, despite her puzzlement.

'My proper title is Mistress Hospitaller, but that's such a mouthful, isn't it? So everybody calls me Matron.'

Jane noticed that Matron wore no watch, and that her only jewellery was a necklace of bright gold chains plaited together.

'My name is Jane Ardenne,' said Jane.

'Quite, quite,' said Matron vaguely, as if this fact were of no import.

'Actually, I came here to look for a friend of mine: Cassie Osorio. Do you know –'

Matron put a hand on her lips.

'Don't say any more, girl. You will soon get to know the Rules of Maldona, or those rules which affect you. There are so many rules – I think only the Superior knows them all! But for the moment, remember the two basics: tell the truth, and never ever ask questions.'

'The truth, of course,' said Jane. 'But no questions?'

Matron wagged her finger and smiled.

'There! A question already! But I won't whip you for it – this time! In Maldona, you neither ask nor are asked questions. If you told your story, you would embroider it unconsciously with half-truths or embellishments, and that is imperfection. The outside, and your past, do not matter. We are here because we are here, because Maldona wanted us.'

'It's just that ... well ...' Jane faltered, not sure if she should explain about her car and her resulting predicament. 'If I could get to a telephone?'

'Why, there are no telephones here. No maps, no electricity, no keys, and no music, save for the sound of the punishment drum. Music distracts the brain, you see, except when the solemn beat of the drum makes the flesh tingle in preparation for the lash.'

Suddenly, Jane felt overwhelmed by a rush of longing and understanding. Perhaps she had been brought here, somehow, mysteriously but rightly. Greta and Harry must have acted in some way as agents. Her heart raced as the kindly matron spoke so casually of whipping.

'There is much whipping of girls?' she said, trying to keep the tremor of excitement from her voice, and failing.

'Only when girls are imperfect. And we girls are very often imperfect, aren't we?'

'Naked whippings?'

'Yes.' Jane took a deep breath. This was it, and her decision was made.

'Matron, I should like to enrol as a student here. I can pay, of course.'

'My dear, you have enrolled in Maldona simply by entering. And we use no money here. There are ... other currencies. Now, you may keep your personal belongings – that bag you carry – although you will have no use for your cash. The only thing you must surrender is your timepiece, which will of course be returned to you in the unhappy, and, looking at your fine figure, unlikely event you should elect to go down from here. The bell of Maldona rings four times a day, and that is our timekeeping.'

Jane unfastened her gold watch and handed it over. Matron gave her a formal receipt, and told her the watch would be kept in store for her; her other belongings she could take and keep in her cell. Jane thought of the contents of her bag: the money and passport, thankfully; the diamonds she had won, the phallos candle, the catsuit, black dildos of the Amir's harem, white whip, and the Parfaite's harness. She felt it best, somehow, to keep her possessions secret.

'Is there a locker?' she asked, hoping her question would go unchided.

'Why, there are no locks in Maldona,' said Matron.

A bell rang in the distance, not the gloomy clang of a church bell, but a fresh, cheerful sound which made Jane's spirits rise. She felt a glow of warmth: this place was friendly, and Cassie must surely be here, must have liked it enough to stay. Already Jane was intrigued.

'That was third bell,' said Matron, 'and at this time you will take your evening meal in refectory. But not tonight, for you have not been inducted. There is the medical examination, your uniform to be issued, your haircut and identity chain – and we mustn't forget your name!'

'But I already have a name,' Jane observed.

'When you come to Maldona, you have none. You are virgin. Maldona names you, clothes you, instructs you, and feeds you. Tonight you shall dine with me, virgin.'

'Super! I'm famished!'

'That is not a lady's expression, virgin.' Jane blushed.

'Oh, I'm sorry.'

'And never say you are sorry!' cried Matron sternly. 'A girl must stand by her words and deeds. Break a rule, and you must accept your proper punishment, in fact you must request it, but you must not deny what you have done, nor apologise for it. It is assumed that even if you commit an imperfect act, you did so thinking it right in the circumstances.'

'I shall do my best not to be imperfect, Matron,' said Jane, feeling humble.

Matron wrote a message on her pad, folded the paper and sealed it in an envelope. Then she went to a tube in the corner of the room, running from ceiling to floor, that Jane had imagined to be a heating pipe. She opened a slot and a rush of air whooshed out, then she popped the letter inside and slammed the tube shut again.

'It is a *pneumatique*,' said Matron. 'My preferred method of communication.'

'I have seen them in old films,' said Jane.

'Yes, films. Well, we have no electricity here, but we do try to keep up with modern things, where appropriate.'

Matron's apartments were lit entirely by candles, in glittering chandeliers.

86

'Your prefect will give you the necessary instruction,' said Matron. 'Anything I tell you is just by way of a chin-wag.'

'Prefect? It sounds like an English boarding school.'

'Yes, I suppose it does.'

There was a knock on the door, and Matron cried, 'Come!'

Two girls entered, wheeling a trolley laden with crystal and silver. A delicious smell of hot meats filled the air.

'Ah, tuck,' said Matron. 'That was quick. You may prepare our table, virgins.'

Quietly and efficiently the two girls set the table for dinner. They did not look at Matron or Jane, but kept their heads bowed and their faces impassive. They wore black tunics like a schoolgirl's uniform, which came down to mid-calf, showing a brief glimpse of bare skin before white ankle-socks and black laced boots. Their blouses were starched white, the collars buttoned to the neck, and the dress held with cross straps on shoulders and breasts. Above their collars they wore a slender gold chain, wound round the neck, but of only one strand, unlike Matron's thick plait. Their hair was cut in a short back and sides, like a boy's.

When they had finished their task, they bowed low from the waist, and departed as silently as they had come, and Jane sat down with Matron to enjoy her feast. And it was a feast: oysters, champagne, roast duck, and creamy profiteroles for pudding, all washed down with decent champagne and a surprisingly good Rioja. Jane drank sparingly, wishing to keep her wits about her, but she ate everything with gusto. Matron sipped delicately but often.

Despite a few lines of age, and Jane calculated that Matron was just old enough to be her mother, her hostess's face and body had a bloom of youth. Matron was trim and strongly built, and the austerity of her uniform, the black pleated skirt, white blouse and stockings, and black calfskin shoes with sensible heels, enhanced the lithe body beneath. Jane could feel Matron's eyes studying her own body, which her rather silly pink robe, all flouncy and transparent, did little to hide. She felt a bit oopsy and girlish, faced with one of those hard suburban wives, bodies toughened by tennis courts, saunas, and adultery.

'We only have wine at special occasions,' said Matron shyly, 'but since you are quite the prettiest virgin I have seen in a long while, I have deemed your arrival a special occasion.'

The two women clinked glasses, and their fingers brushed.

'Well, Matron,' said Jane, 'I am honoured, but to avoid misunderstandings I must tell you that I am nineteen years old, and no virgin.'

'All girls are virgins when they enter Maldona,' said Matron sternly. 'In due course, you may progress to corporal, prefect, perhaps housemistress. It depends on the degree of perfection you achieve. Some virgins prefer to remain so all their lives, choosing to serve rather than command; finding in fact, that true power lies in not having any. But I think you, virgin, will progress quickly.'

She looked at Jane with probing eyes, and reached forward to touch her cheek.

'I think, I sense, that you might even have it in you to become a Parfaite.'

Jane stopped herself asking what a Parfaite was, and instead said, 'I should love to become a Parfaite, Matron.'

'In a way, I hope you don't,' said Matron, sighing. 'You are so pretty, and Parfaites are hard. They are a law to themselves, responsible only to the Superior. Theoretically, I and the housemistresses and Jocasta, the Surgeon Mistress, are of equal rank: but *we* must report to the Deputy Superior, and while the Parfaites have authority through Maldona, our rule extends only to our own domain.'

Matron paused, and added in a dreamy, faraway voice, 'Only Parfaites command the knights of Maldona, the males who serve them as slaves. And only Parfaites may carry a whip, the badge of their authority.'

Jane knew that she had to become a Parfaite.

Matron's eyes devoured Jane's body, all too visible under her gauzy robe, and there was no mistaking the sparkle of desire.

'You would be a fine Parfaite, virgin,' she said, 'for only Parfaites have the right to go naked when they please.'

Luckily, Jane's tiredness inspired her to yawn, concealing the thrill of excitement that narrowed her lips and caused her breast to swell.

'Yes, you have had a hard day, and it is late,' said Matron. 'Join me on the sofa, and we may contemplate the flames.'

They sat, contented and drowsy, with coffee, watching the flicker of the firelight, until Matron broke the silence.

'You have a very beautiful body, virgin. It has the potential for perfection although of course only Maldona herself is perfect.'

'Thank you, Matron,' said Jane sweetly, not quite sure if Maldona was a place, or a person, or both. 'But it is a little confusing to be called virgin – if I am to have a name, perhaps you would do me the honour of choosing one for me.'

Matron put her hand on Jane's bare arm. Her fingers stroked Jane's breasts, pausing gently to brush her nipples.

'I think you are worthy. I will decide on a name for you.'

'Thank you, Matron. You honour me greatly.'

Matron's eyes glowed.

'How kind of you to say so.'

The play of her fingers on Jane's breasts was becoming exciting, and Jane felt her nipples tense and stiffen under Matron's gentle stroking. Matron was aware of the effect her caress was having, and with a wicked smile she continued to stroke Jane's tingling breasts, as though daring her to say stop. But Jane did not resist; instead she thrust her breasts up and forward to meet Matron's touch.

'I think you are a lady,' said Matron. 'You have poise and manners, and physically, well, your body is very joyful. Your breasts are so soft, yet firm, and the nipples are quite ... original. With some muscle behind them, they will be very nearly perfect.'

'Thank you for the compliment, Matron,' said Jane, breathing deeply, 'and may I say that I could not imagine gentler fingers stroking my breasts.'

'You shall stay in my apartments tonight,' said Matron.

'Yes, please.'

'Then, tomorrow, you shall have your induction. It will all seem a little confusing at first, but we believe in throwing a virgin in at the deep end. You'll be assigned to an auberge – that is like a house in an English boarding school – then meet your housemistress, and your prefect, who will instruct you in the rules. Then there is the medical, the uniform and so on, but by second bell you will be a proper virgin of Maldona, and join the girls of your auberge for luncheon in the refectory.'

'I'm so excited,' said Jane, even though Matron's hands had ceased stroking her aroused nipples and rested one on each of Jane's bared thighs. 'It does sound awfully like an English boarding school, at least the one I was sent to.'

'We are an English foundation,' said Matron, 'and I like to think we maintain an English code. Although we have girls from every tribe, we use English as our common language. In fact, now that I think of it, there is a place in the Auberge d'Angleterre, the English House. Would you like it?'

'Yes, please,' said Jane, wishing Matron would stroke her a little more.

'I'll write a note to the housemistress, who is my friend; and copy it to the Deputy Superior. There should be no problem.'

She scribbled another note, sealed it and its copy in envelopes, and pushed them into the vacuum tube.

'There! I can see you already in the red of the Auberge d'Angleterre, much nicer, I think than the yellow of Germany or the blue of France.'

'Yet your uniform, Matron, is black.'

'Black is the fusion of every other colour that exists. Hence, black is the colour of Maldona.'

Matron put her hand on Jane's head, and stroked her hair.

'Such lovely hair,' she said. 'It is almost a pity it has to be shorn.'

'Well, it is already quite short,' said Jane.

'As the Deputy Superior says, there's short, there's real short, and there's Maldona short. Rules are rules, and they have worked for six hundred years. But you know, we could save some time for tomorrow if I were to cut your hair here and now.'

'I would like that very much.'

'Loosen your robe, then, while I fetch my things.'

7

Intimate Examination

Jane let her robe fall open to her waist, then pushed it off her shoulders, so that her upper body was bare.

'Splendid,' said Matron, brandishing scissors, and comb. 'My, you are handsome. How smooth and creamy that lovely breast skin is, shining in the firelight. I mustn't tremble and let my scissors slip.'

Jane bent her head back and stared at Matron with heavy eyes.

'I wish I had hair on my breasts and nipples, and all over my body, so that you could cut me everywhere,' she whispered.

Matron set briskly to work, snipping and scraping.

'I wish that too,' she said softly.

Jane's skin tingled as tufts of hair floated down on to her breasts and shoulders, and she found it exciting to be shorn, like a mountain beast. When Matron had finished, she held up a mirror for Jane's inspection, and Jane gasped, first in shock, and then in amusement. She had been well and truly scalped, and only a shock of hair, parted like a boy's, was left over her forehead. The back of her neck, and all around her ears, felt bristly and naked to the touch.

'It's really cute,' she said.

'Good,' said Matron, 'now sit still while I clean you up.'

Jane felt Matron's hand sweep across her shoulders and back, scooping up the cut locks, and then cupping her breasts, stroking the naked nipples until they were stiff and trembling. She brushed all the silky hairs from Jane's breasts, but continued to touch her, taking firm hold of the full naked breasts as Jane sat trembling and still, her breath heavy and with a delicious tingling in her belly. As the woman caressed her naked breasts as gently as a mother, Jane felt her sex become wet. Matron too was breathing hard, stroking Jane's breasts like favourite pets.

'So lovely,' she murmured. 'The muscles waiting to blossom and ripen.'

She scooped up Jane's cut hair and made a pile on the table.

'You have lovely soft hands, Matron,' said Jane.

Matron shut her eyes and sighed, then knelt before Jane with her back to the fire. She pressed her face to Jane's breasts, and with her fingers gently pinched the hard, swollen nipples. Jane felt her lips kissing her soft breast skin, and gave a little moan of joy. Matron moved her lips to the nipple of the right breast, sucking it firmly until the whole engorged nipple was inside her mouth. Jane moaned again as she felt the hot, wet tongue flicking urgently at her nipple, and let her robe fall from her thighs, so that her belly and sex were open to Matron's gaze. She took the woman's head and stroked the blond tresses, pressing her tightly against her naked breast.

Then, gingerly, she parted her thighs. Her mink glistened in the firelight with the moisture that had seeped from her sex; and she guided Matron's hand across her shivering belly to her mink, and then to her pink wet cunt-lips, where she could feel her acorn already stiff and throbbing. Matron's supple fingers closed on Jane's sex, massaging the clitoris with slow, loving strokes, while her fingers gently penetrated Jane's slit, sliding easily into the oily wetness. Giddy with pleasure, Jane whispered boldly, 'If I am to stay here tonight, Matron, please let me share your bed. I should love to be naked beside you – to serve you as your virgin.'

'Yes, yes!' sighed Matron, and her head abruptly left Jane's breast, to plunge between her spread thighs.

One hand clasped Jane's bare bottom, prising the buttocks apart, and while her mouth and tongue pressed against Jane's swollen cunt-lips, her fingers found Jane's anus bud and began to probe it, tickling and thrusting.

93

Jane squirmed in delight. Her clitoris throbbed at Matron's expert tonguing, and she felt the moisture flow hot in her slit, and then she gasped as Matron's finger – no, two fingers! – thrust deep into her anus.

'You're making me so wet,' said Jane, as her bottom wriggled. Matron's fingers parted the tight elastic of Jane's anus, and then a third finger joined them, plunging in to the hilt and tickling Jane so that her buttocks danced in squirming delight.

'Lick me, suck my clit, I'm going to come, Oh please make me come,' moaned Jane, through hoarse, panting gasps. Her belly fluttered and her whole body flowed like molten gold. She felt Matron's tongue fiercely flicking her clit, and her strong fingers fucking her in her tight anus. With her other hand, Matron gently stroked Jane's quivering bare fesses.

'Your croup is marked prettily by the whip,' she said. 'And not long ago.'

'Oh yes, friends in Marbella, Harry and Greta. Don't stop, please.'

'Harry and Greta,' said Matron thoughtfully as she continued her tonguing and arse-fucking. Jane's bottom writhed to the rhythm of the gorgeous pressure in her anus as she pressed Matron's silken head hard against her wet cunt.

Suddenly, Matron broke away.

'Oh,' cried Jane. But with one fierce movement, Matron scooped Jane up in her strong arms and carried her into her bedroom, as graceful as a bear with its prey. She laid Jane gently on the bed, and pulled off her pink fluffy robe, and stood for a moment, panting, with her hands on her hips, and fire in her eyes, her mouth raw and hanging open and moist with saliva. Without taking her eyes from Jane's naked body, she stripped off her uniform. Jane watched, terrified with the desire the older woman had awakened in her, as Matron's naked body was revealed. She spread her thighs wide, willing Matron to tongue her once more, and her own fingers crept down to rub her throbbing acorn.

Matron wore no undergarments save for a curious strip

of satin that tightly bound her breasts. She saw Jane's quiz-zical look, and said, 'Yes, I wear the strophium, for modesty. But now I am to be immodest.'

When the strophium was undone, two proud, firm breasts swelled gloriously, conical in shape and topped with bright red nipples like hard plums.

Her body gleamed in the candlelight: it was hard and muscled, the ridges and crevasses of her taut flesh a delicate ripple of light and shade. She carried no fat; every inch was sinewy muscle. Seeing Jane's rubbing fingers at their fierce masturbation, Matron spread her own cunt-lips and began to twitch at her own glistening stiff acorn, and Jane gasped, for her clit was bigger by far than any acorn. Her mons was entirely shaved, and gleamed as smooth and shiny as an apple.

'Come to me,' begged Jane.

'How I would love to lace that croup of yours,' said Matron. 'To beat those sweet orbs till they were flaming red, till they begged for mercy.'

'Do it, then, Oh please do it to me,' cried Jane. Her body shook with hot pleasure at the thought of lying helpless under this woman's powerful lash. 'Lace me as hard as you can!'

Matron knelt beside Jane, and kissed her mouth, placing her palm on the back of Jane's hand to guide her in her masturbation.

'I may not,' she said ruefully. 'Only the Parfaites may keep a whip. A beating is an official matter, and must be logged and witnessed, the whip signed for: in short, everything must be authorised. I may not lace you for my own pleasure, but . . . Oh, I am so embarrassed.'

'Please tell me what is to be done,' insisted Jane.

'At my rank, which is that of adept, it is not often that I have occasion to break the rules. So it is a long time since I have felt my bottom smart under the whip. How I long to be laced . . . for you to lace me, sweet virgin! But I have no whip . . .'

Jane sat up and took Matron by the shoulders.

'I have a whip, Matron. I am not yet inducted, remember, and I have my personal things with me in my bag.'

She delicately removed her hand from her sex, allowing Matron's bare fingers to rub her clit, and transferred it to Matron's own wet cunt. The two women sat in silence, masturbating each other and kissing mouths and breasts, until Matron whispered, 'You will whip me?'

Jane smiled.

'I must have something in return.'

'I do not dare whip you, girl: you are already marked, and more would be noticed by Surgeon Jocasta. If it were known that I had disciplined you without authorisation . . .'

'Spank me, then. A hard spanking on my naked arse will leave no trace in the morning. Spank my bare bottom, please, Matron, and make her all hot and pink.'

Jane folded her body across Matron's thighs, her head buried in the coverlet.

'Yes . . . I suppose . . .'

'Hurry!' cried Jane. 'I am so hot and wet for a spanking, I can't bear it!' Jane groaned with a great sigh of relief and contentment from deep in her breast as she felt Matron's hard palm descend with a vicious crack on her bare arse, and she thrilled at the thought that those very fingers were still warm from the depths of her anus. Matron had her other hand deep in Jane's cunt, making it overflow with wetness as she mercilessly pinched her quivering clit. Again and again Matron's hand came down on her squirming globes until they seemed to be on fire, and Jane knew she could no longer hold back, did not want to hold back, and with a howl of ecstasy, released herself into the hot joy of orgasm. The spanking stopped, and Jane pulled Matron to her, showering her lips and breasts with kisses.

'Wait,' she whispered, and ran nimbly to her bag, where she withdrew the white whip of the Amir Akbar. She returned and dangled it proudly in front of Matron's astonished eyes.

'Where . . . how did you get that?' she stammered.

Jane wagged a finger.

'No questions,' she chided playfully.

Matron clutched Jane's wrist, and fervently kissed the handle of the white whip.

'The sacred whip,' she murmured. 'I am not worthy. Wait!'

She sprang to her feet and rummaged in her closet, then returned with an arrangement of straps and buckles, also of white leather.

'You will not tell a soul,' she said faintly. 'It shall be our secret.'

'I promise.'

'This is special. Like all beautiful things, that whip carries danger. You must keep it hidden. And I must be harnessed to receive its kiss, for then I am a tethered beast, absolved from any wrongdoing.'

Matron lay spreadeagled on the bed, with her face to her pillow. Jane strapped her wrists and ankles to the bedposts, then looped the snaky white thong all around her body, binding her neck first, then passing the harness across her breasts, where it was divided in two by a buckle. The nipples were left bare, but each thong now passed across her belly and her shaven mons and bunched against her cunt-lips, forcing her gleaming clitoris to poke out high and stiff from the pink folds. The thongs then ran right across the cleft of her buttocks, cutting deep into her anus bud, and wound around her waist to rejoin the buckle at her breast. In the middle of the thongs were a series of tight clips, which Jane fastened to the woman's taut nipples and to her swollen cunt-lips, pulling the thongs tight and at last fastening each end to the bedposts beside Matron's tethered wrists. Matron could not move. She was helpless.

'But you must gag me,' she whispered, 'for it must be perfect.' She nodded at a further device: a metal clamp, like a scold's bridle, which Jane fastened around her, depressing her tongue with the metal bit. And then Jane lifted the four white thongs of her whip, and flogged the naked flesh before her as tenderly and as harshly as a musician stroking the strings of a violin. She laced the buttocks until they were fiery scarlet and squirmed uncontrollably, then moved to the shoulders, laying a pretty criss-cross on the clenched muscles of the back. Jane thrilled with power as the shuddering body before her jangled to the music of her whip, and at last, when she judged the moment right, she delivered a cool, savage stroke right in the cleft of the buttocks, so that the four white thongs snaked against Matron's brightly exposed anus bud. And at that moment, Matron's moaning became a scream, and she thrashed in the spasm of her own climax. Jane took off her gag, and covered Matron's lips with kisses, then licked away the tears which moistened her cheeks. Matron's smile was radiant.

'Oh, oh,' she moaned. 'Yes. Such a beautiful lacing. Sweet, sweet Jana. Jana, my gorgeous demon, how you have punished me, how you have made my flesh live.'

Jane slowly unwound Matron's bonds, releasing her.

'Well, good,' she panted, stroking Matron's hair, 'but my name is, I mean was, Jane, not Jana.'

Matron sat up and looked at her very earnestly.

'I name you Jana,' she said. 'No one has borne that sacred name for ... well, no matter. You *are* Jana.'

'I thank you, Matron,' said Jane, and bowed.

'There is one other thing I must tell you. It is not a rule as such, but a guiding principle. You are of Maldona of your own free will.'

Jane thought this locution interesting: not 'in Maldona' or 'at Maldona' but '*of* Maldona.'

'I understand.'

'What this means is that you may leave Maldona at any time. At any time at all, and for whatever private reason, you may cry "I go down" and you are free to leave. In the middle of a punishment, Jana, if you cannot bear it, cry "I go down" and the punishment stops at once. But when a girl leaves Maldona in this way, she never comes back.'

'Oh, Matron,' said Jane – said "Jana", I shall never want to leave Maldona.'

It was still dark when the first bell of Maldona rang. Jana yawned and reached groggily for her coffee-maker and cigarettes, taking seconds to realise that none was there.

She had dreamt of Cassie: Cassie's body lay on her, and shivered to an unseen lash. But they both were sheathed in harnesses of thick white leather, their mouths gagged, so that they could neither touch nor kiss each other's flesh. Then they were falling slowly through a great black chimney, floating down to a fierce white light, and assailed by harsh whipstrokes that lashed them from the walls of the chimney. They clung desperately to each other to shelter from the strokes, but there was no escape except the white light which seemed an infinity away.

Jana rubbed her eyes, and suddenly the bedcover was pulled smartly away from her.

'Rise and shine, Jana,' said Matron, 'you have a busy day ahead.'

She took Jana by the hand and led her to the bathroom, where she watched her squat on the commode. When Matron was satisfied with Jana's evacuation, she took her to a small gymnasium, and led her in a punishing series of exercises, including a set of fifty press-ups, of which Jana could scarcely manage half.

'You're out of condition,' said Matron merrily. 'But your first few weeks of training should put that right. The mind cannot study unless the body is fit.'

At the end of the session, Jana's body was lathered in sweat, her heart raced and her muscles were sore. Nevertheless she felt a glow in herself, a pride in the ache of her dormant muscles, and felt elated that her body had stood its punishment. And, to her astonishment, she did not desire a cigarette. After the exercises, it was time for an ice-cold needle shower, which she took with Matron. She marvelled at the smooth musculature of the body beside her, and at the gleaming swell of the shaven mons. They did not touch, now: their bathing was chaste.

'I should so love to have a completely bare sex, like yours, Matron,' she said, regretting that she had not asked Greta to shave her when she had the chance.

'You must wait until you reach the rank of adept,' laughed Matron. 'Those below, even prefects, are not permitted to shave their bodies. It is the rule.'

'Then I shall work hard to become an adept,' said Jana fiercely, 'or . . . or a Parfaite.'

'Yes,' said Matron with a wistful, tender smile, 'I expect you will. But now I think we have earned some breakfast.'

Jana was given a white starched coat, like a doctor's, with a loose belt but no buttons; no panties or stockings, and for her feet a pair of white canvas tennis shoes. Matron, meanwhile, selected a clean white blouse, rather billowing, white stockings and suspender belt – no panties – over which she slipped her black uniform skirt.

'You'll get your proper uniform later,' she said. 'First there is the medical, hence the loose coat, and then your prefect will take you to the ordnance room to get your kit. After you are dressed, your prefect will formally introduce you to your housemistress at the Auberge d'Angleterre, and you will be inducted into your house, and into Maldona. You will have quite an appetite for your first luncheon in refectory.'

The table had been cleared by unseen hands while they slept. They sat down, and after less than a minute there was a knock at the door. The same two serving virgins entered, this time with coffee, fruit and hot rolls with – Jana was pleased to see – plenty of butter and jam. Jana smiled, but Matron said curtly, 'You are a minute late.'

The virgins bowed their heads, and said together, 'We are late, Matron. We are imperfect, and deserve punishment.'

'Nonsense,' cried Matron with a grin, 'I am not going to whip you for such a small thing. Be good in future.'

The girls bowed, and retreated.

'You virgins have to be kept on your toes,' said Matron, 'or you'll be on your toes to have your bottoms tanned.' She laughed at her own joke, and Jana smiled politely.

Another knock, this one curt and imperious, rattled the door, which opened to admit a tall, proud girl of Jana's own age, dressed as a virgin except that her blouse was red. She wore pendulous earrings of red stone set in gold, and she carried a short white cane. Her skin was jet black, her hair short but piled on top in a mound of curls. Her haughty eyes gazed at Jana with disdain, her silken lashes unblinking. Around her neck she wore a wreath of entwined gold chains, like Matron's, and in her whipcord arms she held a sheaf of papers.

Matron stood, as did Jana, and the black girl curtseyed to Matron, who gave the briefest of nods in return.

'Prefect Kobo,' said Matron formally, 'here is the new virgin, named Jana, who is to be inducted into the Auberge d'Angleterre. You may take her.'

'Jana,' said Kobo thoughtfully, in a pleasing contralto voice. 'Well, come, Jana.'

Jana followed the prefect, and on leaving the room, turned and bowed low to Matron, not raising her head or looking at her lover of the night before. She walked behind her prefect with a swell of her breast, for she was proud to be a virgin.

Clutching her bag of belongings, she walked respectfully behind Kobo along an arcade which formed one side of a large quadrangle, in the midst of which the dawn light revealed Matron's English garden that she had seen under the night's moon. The place reminded her of a cloistered retreat, or an English monastery. The buildings enclosing the courtyard rose high above, alive with spires and turrets and intriguing carvings of whorls and zigzags which looked Arabic.

'This is the hospital,' said Kobo, 'which is Matron's domain, as are the armoury and the stores. The surgery, however, is the realm of Surgeon Jocasta.'

Jana admired the long legs and graceful, sinuous carriage of her prefect, who had the slender beauty of the Nilotic African. Their footsteps echoed through the silent arcade, and Jana blurted in a chatty tone, 'I do love your earrings, Kobo.'

To her surprise and alarm, Kobo whirled round with flashing eyes, lifted her arm, and struck Jana once on her buttocks with the cane, not severely, but hard enough to sting.

'Be quiet, virgin,' she hissed. 'You speak when I tell you.'

Her voice had a musical African lilt, which her harsh words betrayed.

101

Jana bit her lip, and bowed her head, ashamed.

'If you were not a new virgin, you would take a Lady's Beating for your insolence. I am not one of those prefects who believe in treating virgins gently. They must be broken, as I was.'

They walked on in silence, and came to a teak door, without any lock, whose handle Kobo turned.

'The surgery,' said Kobo, and they entered. As they went through the doorway she turned and graced Jana with the ghost of a smile.

'The earrings were a present from the Superior herself,' said Kobo proudly.

The surgery was white and spotless, and smelled like clinics everywhere, although Jana wondered how you ran a clinic without electricity. She saw pipes and gas burners, and supposed that, after all, people must have managed well enough in Queen Victoria's day. A girl in a white nurse's uniform with a red sash over her tunic approached them, smiling.

'I bring you Virgin Jana,' said Kobo, 'of the Auberge d'Angleterre.'

'The Surgeon Mistress is ready,' said the girl, curtseying to Kobo. 'Please follow me, Jana.'

'I have other business, and shall return in twenty minutes,' said Kobo.

'Forty would be better, Prefect Kobo,' replied the nurse.

'Ragusa, you forget that you are a virgin of the Auberge d'Angleterre, and I am prefect. I say twenty minutes.'

'I am not in your sept, Kobo,' said Nurse Ragusa coolly. 'Cleadne is my prefect.'

'Cleadne and I see eye to eye in matters of discipline, especially where insolence is concerned.'

'Here in the Hospital, Kobo, I am an almoner, and your authority does not run. Come back in twenty minutes if you please, and cool your heels.'

Kobo spun round and left without another word. Her face was a mask of suppressed rage. Nurse Ragusa, a pretty girl with auburn hair cut the same as Jana's, was flushed and angry.

'Some of these prefects think they own the place, she said as she led Jana into the surgery. 'I used to dream of being a prefect, but I'm honestly glad to have been posted to the almoners. It goes to their heads – and, really, most of them are frustrated that they haven't made Parfaite. That Kobo behaves as though she is a Parfaite already. She trims her mink until it's as bare as the rules let her get away with, and have you seen her cane? It is supposed to be only symbolic, but she carries the maximum length allowed.'

'And uses it,' said Jana ruefully.

'Oh, yes, you'll find that out. Anyway I don't think it's right to bend the rules. You should either have a full mink, for example, or be completely bare. like the Parfaites. Actually I think a full mink is rather nice. Well, just slip off your robe, Jana, and lie down on the couch. The Surgeon Mistress will be here in a jiffy.'

Jana lay down on a surgical bed which had leg-rests angled so that her thighs were parted for examination, like a pregnant woman's. Ragusa chattered on as she busied herself with bottles and shiny steel instruments. Her voice was bright and sharp, like the knives she handled; Jana guessed it to be Scottish, perhaps the hard, knowing accent of Glasgow.

'I mean, Kobo knows as well as I do that she has no authority outside the auberge, except in matters pertaining to the auberge. The Surgeon Mistress commands me here, just as the Mistress Manciple commands the refectory, and the Mistress of Arts the gymnasium. Kobo would be well annoyed if a Parfaite came into the auberge and started ordering *her* around! I'd fight her if I thought I had a chance of winning, just to get her off my back. But she is so hard and strong.'

'You look pretty strong yourself,' said Jana, observing the nurse's broad back and well-muscled arms.

'Oh, well,' shrugged Ragusa. 'The important thing, Jana, is to remember the rules. They contain a system of checks and balances which has been finely tuned over the centuries, so that the rules are, well, perfect. Here in Maldona, we *live* by our rules.'

103

As Ragusa prattled, the door opened and a woman of Matron's age entered, wearing a white doctor's coat, with a swathe of gold chains like Matron's wrapped around her neck. Her hair was ash blonde and tied up in a very doctorly bun, and on her nose perched a pair of gold-rimmed glasses.

'So you are Jana,' she said with a brisk smile. 'Welcome to Maldona. I am Surgeon Mistress Jocasta, and I'll just give you the once over. Don't bother to bow.' Her accent was softly German, like Greta's.

Since bowing was obviously impossible, Jana inclined her head on to her breast in a gesture of obeisance, which seemed to please Jocasta. The nurse laughed dutifully at the little joke, with the obedient smile of one well used to it.

'You look healthy enough,' said Jocasta. 'It shouldn't take long to get those muscles ripened: some work to be done on the breasts, I think.'

'Yes, Surgeon Mistress,' said Jana.

Jocasta proceeded to examine her teeth, eyes and ears. She shone lights, made her say 'aah', tapped her bones, waggled her knees, poked and prodded like any doctor anywhere. As she bent over her, Jana saw her robe fall slightly open, and was treated to a glimpse of a very full bosom tightly swathed in a white strophium, which seemed to be a primitive, perhaps medieval, form of bra. Jocasta's body smelled musky, and with a strong odour of sweat, as though she had just been exercising. At least I'll get fit here, Jana thought.

The Surgeon Mistress paid particular attention to Jana's breasts, squeezing them and tweaking her nipples unusually hard, and Jana found to her embarrassment that this treatment caused the nipples to stiffen and swell quite noticeably. Jocasta smiled.

'Not feeling cold, are we?'

'No, Surgeon Mistress.'

'Hmmm . . .'

Every inch of Jana's naked body was pummelled and prodded, while Nurse Ragusa took notes in response to her

104

mistress's rapid instructions. At last came the moment which Jana had been nervously anticipating. Jocasta donned a pair of thin rubber gloves and flexed her fingers like a boxer.

'You're in good shape, for a new virgin. Lots of potential in those breasts. But now for a look at the waterworks, eh?'

Jocasta positioned herself between Jana's open thighs, took hold of the lips of her sex between the thumb and forefinger of each hand, and gently parted them. She fingered the moist pink flesh of Jana's slit, which, to Jana's great embarrassment, was growing quite wet at the strange excitement of being impersonally examined, like a slave or beast at auction. Then she shuddered and arched her back as Jocasta's fingers pressed her clitoris, and could not help giving a little moan as the doctor took her acorn between her fingers and rubbed it. Jocasta fired instructions at her scribe, and Jana thought she heard the phrase 'nympha development a priority, potential Parfaite' which she did not quite understand. The Surgeon Mistress tweaked and stroked her clit, or her nympha as she supposed she must learn to call it, until she was quite stiff and tingly, all the way from her hard nipples to her wet slit. She felt all melting and warm, and could not help sighing; it seemed so lovely to be a helpless piece of meat on a slab, being fussed over and examined so that her examiner really seemed to be her servant, waiting on her inert body. She was aware of a measuring device applied to her nympha, clamping her, and gratified murmurs of 'Hmmm, yes, excellent,' from Jocasta.

Then, without warning, Jocasta's hand plunged into her wet sex and probed the very neck of her womb.

'Oh!' cried Jana in surprise.

'There, now,' said Jocasta with a smile. 'Remember I am a doctor. Most virgins have not experienced a lady's fingers in their gashes before.'

Jana blushed, and Jocasta smiled at her with narrowed eyes.

'Or perhaps you have,' she said.

She probed Jana's slit until Jana could not conceal her excitement, and her generous flow of oily juice.

'I must say, you have a well-formed lady's place,' said Jocasta. 'Quite tight and elastic. You have a lovely mink, too. I suppose you're dying to shave it, most virgins are. But I think if you have the potential to grow a nice full forest, and it looks as if you do, you should enjoy it. How envious we woman can be, always wanting to change our bodies!'

'I suppose we feel there is something brutish about it, Surgeon Mistress,' said Jana.

'We are all brutes, Jana.'

Abruptly Jocasta removed her hand from Jana's sex, but allowed her fingers to remain on her swollen nympha, continuing to tickle it gently as she applied the fingers of her other hand to Jana's anus bud.

'Most interesting,' she murmured. 'Measure the nipples again, Ragusa. They are rather splendid and stiff, with a most intriguing elevation.'

Suddenly she had two fingers inside Jana's anus, pushing hard right the way inside until Jana felt her knuckles pressing to the cleft of her bottom. The sweet tickling pressure in her bumhole, with the tingling in her hard nympha, made Jana's pelvis start to writhe against the surgeon's probing fingers. Her face was hot, her breath hoarse, and the thought crossed her mind that if this stimulation of her lady's places continued she would be unable to avoid the embarrassment of shivering in orgasm.

Jocasta stared at her with rapier eyes.

'Yes, most interesting, almost a perfect specimen,' she whispered. 'Now, Ragusa, the lavage, please.'

The nurse retreated to the corner of the surgery, where glass jars bubbled over gas burners. As she sorted her equipment, Jocasta kept up her tender kneading of Jana's nympha, at the same time sliding her fingers deliciously in and out of her anus. Jana's buttocks clenched and relaxed, squeezing the supple fingers inside her, and her hips thrust her stiff clit towards the hand that, maddeningly, brought her to the brink of climax, then paused to let Jana's trem-

106

bling subside, before bringing her back to the very edge of her plateau.

Ragusa returned with two large syringes of clear plastic, with a squeeze bulb at their base. The syringes were filled with a green liquid that misted the inside of the container with steam. Now Jocasta removed her fingers from Jana's anus in one rapid movement, sliding out with a nice tickling plop, and Ragusa positioned the nozzle of the first syringe.

'Excuse me,' said Ragusa with a grin, and pressed her fingers to Jana's slit, moistening them with the love-juice which coated her cunt-lips, then applied the oily liquid to her syringe as a lubricant. She pushed the syringe, bigger than an erect penis, all the way inside Jana's bumhole.

'Oh,' cried Jana, not sure whether she felt pain or delight. Jocasta's hand was still on her nympha, and with her other, she caressed Jana's nipples, which seemed stiff to bursting. She made way for the nurse, who positioned the second syringe, and Jana felt it thrust right to the hilt into her squirming slit.

'Don't worry, I'm just going to give you a good clean,' said Jocasta with panting breath. 'It's pure warm, olive oil, extra fine. Ragusa, are you monitoring breathing and heartbeat?'

'Aye, Mistress.'

'Then, both barrels, please.'

Ragusa squeezed hard on the rubber reservoirs, and Jana bucked as she felt a surge of the hot oil fill her anus and cunt, until she thought she would burst. She groaned, and looked at the syringes, to see that they were scarcely depleted. Ragusa squeezed again, and again, and with each spurt of liquid, Jana felt she could take no more, yet still her body accepted the lavage, and she found herself gasping and squirming in pleasure at the pitiless filling of her cunt and bumhole. And all the time, her nipples and clit quivered at Jocasta's sweet rubbing.

'When Ragusa removes the syringes,' said Jocasta crisply, 'you must hold the oil inside you until I give the order to evacuate.'

'I shall obey, Mistress,' gasped Jana.

Suddenly, Ragusa pulled the syringes out of her two tightly-clenched chambers. Her belly and tripes, filled with the hot oil, seemed on fire, but grimly she clenched her sphincter muscle, willing the flood to hold back for a minute, two minutes, three . . .

'Mistress, I can't hold it!' she cried at last.

'You must! Or do you want to earn your first beating? Ragusa, take over the examination of the nympha, while I apply myself to the teats.'

To Jana's astonishment, Jocasta proceeded to drop her doctor's robe, revealing herself to be quite naked, apart from the constricting strophium, which she rapidly unwound to free a pair of breasts that popped joyfully out of their confinement, and, thanks to the taut muscle Jana could see behind the soft breast skin, were almost as full as Jana's own. Jocasta bowed and fastened her teeth and tongue on Jana's engorged nipples, while the nurse rhythmically stroked her stiff nympha. Jocasta took Jana's hand and placed it on her own trembling breast, and Jana eagerly caressed the swollen nipples as the Surgeon's mouth sucked at her own teats. And then her hand slid down across Jocasta's firm belly, gliding over the superb naked mons, to Jocasta's parted thighs, and found her cunt, the lips already engorged and soaking wet. Jana gasped as she clutched Jocasta's clit, impossibly big and stiff, and rubbed it fiercely until she could hear Jocasta's hoarse pants and knew that she was bringing her to orgasm. She felt her own belly quake with her approaching spasm, and knew that when it came she could not hold the hot oil inside her any more, and just as she was about to convulse in her spasm, Jocasta cried, 'Now, Jana, release the lavage!'

With a groan, Jana relaxed her sphincter completely, and felt the oil spurt from her. Jana saw that the nurse had her hand between her legs and was masturbating quite fiercely. There seemed no end to the hot tickling flow from her anus and cunt; she finally shook with a sweet, honeyed orgasm, her loins bucking and writhing on the bed.

As she came, she mastubated the trembling Jocasta with

frenzied fingers, while Ragusa pleasured herself no less fervently with her own hand, and as Jana's spasm calmed, she heard the two women convulse in their own climax, Jocasta with a great whinnying sigh, and Ragusa with little moaning yelps like a puppy's. The flow of hot oil dwindled to a trickle, as though little mice were scampering on Jana's thighs, and finally stopped. Ragusa then bent down to give Jana a firm kiss of thanks on both her sex and her anus bud. Jocasta, panting, snapped her fingers, and Ragusa obediently wound the strophium once more round her quivering breasts, and slipped on her doctor's robe. Jana sank back, happy and exhausted, hoping that Maldona was as keen on frequent medical examinations as she was on obedience to the rules.

'Well, Jana, I am pleased to say that you are perfectly healthy,' said Surgeon Mistress Jocasta, wiping her misted glasses on the hem of her tunic. 'I think I have accomplished some very useful research for Maldona. Now I expect your prefect will be waiting to escort you.'

Jana bowed low, and left the surgery, to find that Kobo was indeed waiting, livid with rage. Jana lowered her head to her prefect, while Ragusa winked and blew a cheeky kiss. Kobo flung open the door and stormed out, obliging Jana to trot, her bag bumping awkwardly against her.

'Forty minutes!' ranted Kobo. 'I have been kept waiting an hour and a half!'

Jana suppressed a giggle, and, prudently, kept silence.

8

Virgin's Beating

Kobo led Jana rapidly through arcades and corridors, thronged with girls in virgins' uniforms who eyed Jana curiously. Kobo made no attempt to explain where they were, and Jana soon felt lost and overwhelmed by the immensity of the labyrinth. Many of the virgins bowed their heads to Kobo at her passage, presumably since they were of the Auberge d'Angleterre. At length they emerged into a spacious herb garden, scented with flowers and washed with fountains. In the distance, beyond the spires of Maldona, Jana could see a range of shimmering snow-capped mountains. But her joy at the seemly garden was broken by the sight of the line of girls working with spade and hoe. They were naked, save for a strange garment at their waist, like panties, only made apparently of steel, and their mouths were clamped by metal gags. A loose chain bound them together at their waists. Only one of the girls was clothed, and she carried the heaviest spade, as well as a brimming sack of rocks strapped to her back. She wore, to Jana's surprise, a rubber catsuit like the one she had in her bag, and in the hot sun, the sweat poured from her eyes and nose.

This was evidently a punishment gang, and its overseer wore a virgin's uniform with a red rosette on her breast, and her hair was not shorn, but collar-length, as Jana's had been. She carried a short cane like Kobo's and, as Kobo passed, she bowed her head. Jana saw that, as she did so, she squinted at Jana with keen, malevolent interest. They reached the arcade at the far end of the garden, and Kobo said, 'That is Miriam, the corporal in charge of your corridor. Corporals deal with day-to-day matters of decorum and discipline. And now I wish to visit the fountain. You will wait here.'

They arrived at a doorway whence wafted the smell of disinfectant and the gurgling of pipes, and Jana understood that a fountain was, in Maldona's quaint terminology, the lavatory.

'Oh,' she blurted, 'I need to go . . . I mean, I should like to go to the fountain as well, please.'

In fact, Jana realised, she was absolutely bursting.

'No. This fountain is for prefects only. You must wait and control yourself.'

Then, seeing the anguish on Jana's face, she relented.

'Very well,' she snapped, 'seeing as it is your first day, and you are not yet inducted. Come in.'

The fountain contained six Turkish commodes, holes in the ground with porcelain frames and footpads, all arranged in a circle, so that the users were in full view of each other. A virgin dressed in overalls acted as attendant, with buckets, cloths, tissues and scent. From her post by a row of washbasins, she bowed her head to Kobo who lifted her skirt and permitted the attendant to remove her panties, which Jana saw were a rather striking confection of black lace and silver sequins. Kobo proceeded to squat on one of the commodes, and Jana lifted her robe and did the same, not having any panties to remove. She saw that Kobo's mons was indeed shaved very close, a shiny black hillock dotted with spare little curls, and she felt a pang of envy at the rippling swell of the prefect's powerful thigh muscles clenched against bulging calves. She sighed a relief as her sphincter relaxed and, after a moment, Kobo permitted herself to sigh also.

At that moment, another person entered the fountain and, to Jana's surprise, it was a male: a tall boy with an arrogant curl to his lips and a mane of lustrous black hair that cascaded over a rich embroidered tunic. His arms and legs were bare, and covered in slabs of hard muscle which made Jana curious to see the powerful chest that swelled underneath his tunic. Jana felt suddenly happy to see a

111

man in this place. Ignoring the full bow of the attendant, he took the commode beside Jana, facing Kobo, and did not squat, but with jaunty insolence raised the skirts of his tunic, giving Jana a tantalising view of his naked bottom, which was as pert as two downy little peaches. He looked up at the ceiling as he noisily made water, as though the girls were not even there; Kobo lowered her head to avoid looking at the boy's penis, only inches from her face, and when his business was over, he smoothed down his skirts and strutted out without a word or acknowledgement.

Kobo glowered.

'What took you so long in surgery, virgin?' she demanded harshly. 'Have you a problem?'

'It seems not, Miss. The Mistress Surgeon pronounced me healthy.'

'So you are fit for rigorous discipline.'

'I suppose so, Miss,' said Jana uneasily.

'Jocasta is always intriguing,' muttered Kobo balefully. 'Are you up to something with her?'

'No, Miss, I assure you! How can I intrigue when it is only my first day?'

'Hm. You virgins are deceitful.'

Jana sighed again as her bowel finally emptied.

'Prefect Kobo, it is the greatest honour to be in your charge, and I promise I shall not be deceitful.'

'Hm,' grunted Kobo again. She got up, wiped herself with the scented tissue handed over by the attendant, then washed.

'Perhaps you will do, Virgin Jana,' she said. 'Tell me, do you find me beautiful?'

'Why, yes, Miss,' said Jana, unable to think of any other answer to this unexpected question.

'It is not enough, though, to be beautiful. Only perfection is enough.'

Jana hurried to complete her toilette, and followed Kobo outside.

'And tell me, Jana, did you find *him* beautiful? The knight who insolently came into our fountain?'

'Well . . . in a way, Miss. But it surprised me to see a male in a ladies' fountain.'

'Ha!' snorted Kobo. 'Knights, like Parfaites, whose slaves they are, may go anywhere they please. That Jason – he is so arrogant, just because he belongs to Leandra. He followed us deliberately, to humiliate me. Men think they are already perfect, because of that fat cock they carry between their legs, and the balls below which contain so much vital heat. But we women understand that perfection is not in balls, that only discipline, training, and submission to the rules can make us perfect.'

'I think I understand, Miss.'

'You will understand when I have finished with you,' said Kobo, opening another door, and they entered the armoury.

The armoury was a long, low chamber, with a counter on one side running all of its length, behind which shelves were stacked with clothing, tools and machinery, and opposite a row of doorways leading to offices. Virgins scurried with boxes and bags, or waving chits, and the atmosphere was the controlled chaos of a restaurant kitchen. Kobo spoke briefly to the virgin behind the counter, who wore a blue rosette, meaning she was a corporal of the Auberge de France.

'Prefect Kobo, of Auberge d'Angleterre, with new virgin to receive kit. The Mistress Armourer is expecting us.'

'Please wait a moment, Prefect Kobo,' said the French girl, without deference. She lifted a flap in the counter and crossed to one of the office doorways, leaving Kobo to stare at the ceiling, evidently taking every second that delayed her life as a personal affront. Jana stood meekly, beginning to understand her position as the lowest of the low.

'Good morning, Mistress Armourer,' said Kobo, inclining her head at the thin brown woman whose thick shock of grey hair was made to seem curiously youthful by the leathery sinews of her strong bare arms. She nodded curtly, and they were taken into an office, where the Mistress Armourer told Jana to strip. Jana looked around her as she slipped from her robe, and saw a room piled high with papers and ledgers, all higgledy-piggledy, like a scene from

Dickens. Kobo and the armourer did not bother to look at her, and Jana was secretly pleased at being no more than an object, a body to be dressed and equipped. She was made to stand naked against the wall, while the armourer took all her measurements, including the most intimate, and wrote it all down on a chit, which she gave to the counter attendant who scrutinised it and, without looking up, departed to fetch what was ordered, mumbling sizes and colours and quantities to herself like a dutiful shoe-store assistant.

Assuming she was finished, Jana reached for her robe, but Kobo shook her head. The armourer opened a curtain on the far wall of the office, to reveal a five-by-four camera mounted on a tripod. She flicked on a battery of spotlights, and Jana imagined herself back at the villa of dear Greta and Harry.

'Your photographic record goes into the files of the Mistress of Art,' explained Kobo. 'It is renewed every three months, to keep a record of your prowess and development.'

Gruffly the armourer barked out the poses she wished Jana to adopt, and Jana obeyed enthusiastically, for they were as intimate and detailed as the taking of her measurements, and the session seemed remarkably like the mystic-erotic procedure of Harry's, including, to Jana's pleased surprise, several close-up shots of her exposed lady's places. When it was over, Jana was permitted to replace her robe, and after bowing low to the Mistress Armourer – Kobo merely nodding – they returned to the counter.

A kitbag like a sailor's, fastened with a red buckle, awaited her. JANA D'ANGLETERRE was stencilled on it, which made her feel tremendously grand, and she signed for it with that name, trying to seem casual, but really tingling with pride. She shouldered the kitbag and puffed, because it seemed to weigh a ton, and with the bag over her shoulder, and her personal bag in her hand, she followed Kobo back into the sunlight. They left by the door at the other end of the long room, and as they passed the last section of the counter, Jana saw that the contents of the shelves were row upon row of snaky, beautiful things that gleamed in the sun's shafts: every imaginable variety of cane and whip, ranged and tagged in loving profusion.

They proceeded through the labyrinth that was Maldona, past halls, gardens, down endless corridors and arcades sweet with birdsong. Jana had earlier imagined that Maldona would be a cold, austere place, laid out with rigid geometry, but now it seemed more like a maze that had grown willy-nilly like the petals of a huge wild flower. She sweated under the weight of her belongings.

'I think I should need a map to find my way round this place, Miss,' she panted.

They halted before a great oak door emblazoned with St George and his speared dragon. Above them loomed the crenellated towers of the Auberge d'Angleterre, and Jana noticed that the spear-wielding St George was depicted in a rather novel way, with flowing shoulder-length tresses and a slim figure in a long robe that looked like an evening gown. His features were clearly androgynous, while the half-human dragon showed, under his scales and claws and wings, a physique that was brutally male. As Kobo pushed the door open, she said, 'There are no maps in Maldona, Virgin Jana. Do you need a map of your own soul?'

Jane entered her new home, the Auberge d'Angleterre.

The entrant to the Auberge d'Angleterre found herself in a magnificent hallway, the floor marble and the walls panelled with English oak on which hung martial tapestries, depicting Boudicca, Joan of Arc, Greek Amazons; paintings on similar womanly themes, including numerous depictions of bare-breasted Britannia ruling the waves, and her equally naked French counterpart, Marianne, leading the citizenry to the barricades. Around the pictures hung pikes, swords, guns, and whips that Jana hoped were intended for animals rather than human backs. Ahead, a dazzling marble staircase led to the mezzanine, from which radiated a dozen corridors. Light streamed through mullioned windows, glinting on the crystal chandeliers laden with candles, and creating a chiaroscuro that made the auberge's vestibule the entrance to a magic world.

A tall girl had just descended the staircase and was striding towards them, her snow-blonde hair swaying waist-length over a robe in silk brocade pieced together in a rainbow swirl of colours, and lined with white fur. Her tanned face bore an expression of imperial hauteur which perfectly matched her striking costume; below her robe, the calves, firm with rippling muscles, disappeared into white leather boots, also trimmed with fur. Around her neck she wore a thong of gold chains, not pleated like Matron's, but forming a shimmering band at least two inches wide. In her right hand, she carried a four-foot whip with a wicked snake's tongue at its tip.

Jana thought her the most beautiful creature she had ever seen.

As the girl approached the door, Jana instinctively stepped back to let her pass, but Kobo grabbed her wrist and pulled her through the doorway, obliging the tall girl to step aside. No greeting was exchanged, and the girl's expression was stony as she finally stepped out. Kobo looked at Jana with the hint of a smile.

'Ha!' she cried. 'That was the Parfaite Leandra, the mistress of that knight Jason, who was so insolent to me in the fountain. You see? I passed her *inside* our auberge, and thus was not obliged to show obeisance. If I had met her outside, I should have had to bow.'

Kobo led Jana up the stairs, and into a sumptuous corridor that led from the mezzanine. This led to a slightly less sumptuous corridor, which, after many twists and turns, gave way to one that was drab and bleak, with a floor of unpolished rough boards and tiny slits without glass that barely admitted enough light to see by in the dusty gloom. Jana's hot sweat turned cold on her skin. Along the corridor were wooden doors with small apertures at eye level. There was no one around, but there was a lingering smell of bodies, rough soap, drains and sweat, which Jana remembered only too well from her boarding school. Kobo stopped at the second last door, and opened it.

'This is to be your home, virgin,' she said. 'Cell number seven. The fountain is next door, and your corporal, Miriam, lives in cell number one.'

Jana found herself in a cubicle of minute dimensions, with bare white walls, and furnished with closet, chair, desk, and candlestick. The bed, anchored to the wall, was of bare boards, with a cushion and a coarse rug on it. Jana fought back a sigh of dismay.

'Now you will sort your kit, and I will instruct you on its proper presentation for morning inspection,' said Kobo. Jana obeyed, removing all the items from her kitbag and placing them on the bed. She left her own personal bag on a shelf inside the closet which Kobo had indicated was the permitted place.

Opening a bag of presents is always exciting, even if it contains only a uniform of obedience. Jana had three brand new virgin's strapped skirts, seven pairs of black calf-socks, three pairs of black lace-up shoes and one pair of best shoes, which were leather boots that came to the knee; two denim work tunics, and two pairs of gorgeous red satin panties, which Jana held up with a coo of delight.

'Those are for special days only,' said Kobo severely. 'Virgins wear no panties, neither do they wear the strophium on their breasts. You are accustomed to wearing a . . . a brassière, I suppose.'

She pronounced the word with some distaste.

'Why, yes,' said Jana.

'Here, you must leave your breasts free. That way, you will be encouraged to build the muscle that will hold them firm and proud. Like mine.'

And Kobo swelled her bosom so that Jana could see how serene and pert her breasts stood, pressed against the thin cloth of her blouse with her nipples jutting like chocolates.

There was indeed a full kit, with toilet things, paper, pens, and folders, laundry bags, brushes and pans. There was even a small vial of perfume.

'That, too, is for special days,' said Kobo. 'It must be kept shut away with your panties.'

When Jana had folded and arranged her things according to Kobo's instructions, the prefect told her that her kit would be inspected every morning one hour after first bell.

That hour would be spent at exercises and toilette. After inspection, and the awarding of punishments for any imperfection in the display of kit, the duty virgin would collect the previous day's soiled garments and then the corridor would form a line behind Miriam, their corporal, and march to the refectory for breakfast.

'The corporals are in charge of everyday discipline,' said Kobo. 'Uncleanliness, insolence, or improper display of kit may be punished at the corporal's discretion, whether with a Lady's Beating, or labour in the garden. Any disputes may be brought to me, but my rule is that you must accept your punishment first, and appeal it afterwards if you wish. If I grant your appeal, then you are entitled to inflict double the punishment on your superior, for her imperfection. But be warned that frivolous complaints will result in your own punishment being doubled. I am busy, and do not take kindly to disputes, for I have seven corridors in my sept, and make sure I inspect every virgin myself, regularly. You must keep your cell spotlessly clean, of course, and these –' she reached into the top of Jana's closet, and took out two appliances of shiny steel '– must be polished every day. They are your gag and your restrainer, in the event that such discipline is prescribed either by me or your corporal.'

Jana swallowed nervously, for these appliances had been borne by the naked bodies of the girls at labour in the herb garden.

'The restrainer,' continued Kobo, 'is a protective device against bodily indiscipline, and is worn by all new virgins at night for their first two weeks in the auberge. It is also worn for formal interviews with your housemistress, as a reminder of humility, and over it your panties. As you are shortly to be presented to your housemistress for induction, both items will be worn.'

Both restrainer and gag had 'Jana d'Angleterre' engraved on their shiny steel. The gag looked fearsome enough, but the restrainer was a waistband and a flap to cover the buttocks and pubis, and from this flap protruded a shaft of solid steel, the size of a man's cock, directly opposite the anus.

'And now,' said Kobo, 'put your soiled robe into your laundry bag, and go to the fountain to bathe, before dressing to meet our housemistress. Don't forget, you will wear your restrainer, and panties too, and may apply a dab of perfume between your breasts and behind your ears.'

Jana stripped, and padded to the fountain, carrying her washbag. It was a far cry from the luxurious prefects' fountain: a small chamber with four metal commodes, a single washbasin, and a row of four shower-taps. Jana thought it advisable to squat again, and used one of the commodes, listening to her liquid tinkling eerily away into the bowels of Maldona. Then she opened a freezing shower, and scrubbed herself with the gritty soap-cake until she glowed pink. To her surprise, she was enjoying herself. The spartan regime which she was to endure was invigorating, even ennobling, and the contrast between her modest kit, her drab, uncomfortable quarters, and the radiance of one such as Leandra inspired no envy, but rather the pride of a foot-soldier in the hardships she must bear.

So it was with a merry grin that she skipped back to her cell and crouched down to spread her buttocks wide, and allow Kobo to show her the correct fitting of her restrainer. She flinched involuntarily as the cold steel tickled her anus bud, then pushed all the way into her shaft, but even Kobo was surprised at the ease with which Jana's soft anus welcomed her new tenant. Kobo snapped the clasp shut. There was no lock, although Jana had expected one, as on a medieval chastity belt.

'I suppose that I am on my honour to wear the restrainer at the appointed times,' she said, 'since it is unlocked. I mean, not to be sneaky and take it off.'

'Sneaky?' said Kobo, looking puzzled. 'I do not understand. Why would you wish to remove your restrainer, knowing that you are obliged to wear it? As for honour system, what other system is there? There are no locks in Maldona, because such things imply imperfection.'

Jana dressed in her brand new uniform, with the super panties pulled tight over her steel girdle, and put dabs of perfume, a lovely musky scent, on ears and breasts, and felt

119

as excited as a new girl at school, soppy with enthusiasm. She was proud to be permitted to walk at Kobo's side as her prefect sketched for her the organisation of Maldona: the division into three auberges, France, England and Germany, each of which was subdivided into three septs of seven corridors. A sept was controlled by a prefect, under whom served seven corporals – one for each corridor of seven virgins – of which the corporal was the first. Above them all was the housemistress, one of the class of adepts, like Matron, the Surgeon Mistress, and the Mistress of Art. Above the housemistresses ruled the Deputy Superior, above her the Superior, and above her – Kobo spoke the name in awed tones – Maldona herself. Jana still could not get used to the way in which the place Maldona and the person Maldona – for she assumed it *was* a person – were referred to interchangeably.

Aside from the social structure of the auberges existed the structure of function, the domains of Matron and the other adepts who supervised the physical needs and activities of Maldona, from refectory, surgery, gymnasium and library, to the range of services, arts and crafts which, Jana was intrigued to learn, included an important fabrication of candles. She reflected that in a place without electricity candle-makers must obviously be at a premium. It was nevertheless very easy for a girl who had attended an English boarding school to grasp the basic division between the 'school' activities like classwork, sports and recreations, where girls from every auberge mingled freely, and the auberge system in which a girl had her social being. And outside these, governed by their own laws, were the Parfaites, responsible only to the Superior and to Maldona herself. The Corps of Knights were the slaves of the Parfaites, and answered only to them; they had no legal existence of their own, but in any situation their physical presence and their actions were deemed to be those of their Parfaites themselves. So when the fountain attendant had bowed to Leandra's Jason earlier in the morning, she was in fact bowing, not to the mere male, but to Leandra his owner, manifesting herself through him.

Jana pricked her ears up when Kobo touched the subject of promotion, how a virgin could rise to become a corporal, a prefect, or even a Parfaite. It seemed that a girl was judged on her prowess, and names suitable for promotion 'emerged' after lengthy and mysterious soundings amongst the adepts. Prowess meant skill at wrestling, and the measure of prowess was the number of neckchains in a girl's torc. For wrestling was the way in which disputes were decided, or else dominion and obeisance were established. Any girl might challenge another; the girl who could fight her opponent to a submission gained her identity necklace for herself. Furthermore, there was a fast track to promotion, for a challenge could be presented not just for the neckchain, but for the rank itself. A virgin who was foolhardy enough to challenge her prefect might take her position as well as her necklace, thus reversing their roles: foolhardy, because an unsuccessful challenger had to accept as savage a punishment as the victor cared to inflict.

Kobo seemed rather nervous as she described this system, and Jana smiled, keeping silent. As far as becoming a Parfaite was concerned, the same fast track was available, but the punishments available to Parfaites who were unsuccessfully challenged were so awesome, and known only to the Parfaites themselves, who shared their own special rule book with the Superior and Maldona herself, that few dared try their luck.

Leandra had been one of those few.

Finally, Jana learned that one of the Parfaites' jobs, insofar as they had jobs, was to oversee and nurture the development of selected virgins. Kobo had her own Parfaite, and she expressed a polite if insincere hope that Jana would be lucky enough to be chosen.

They came to the housemistress's apartments and, before knocking, Kobo turned to Jana and said, 'Is your restrainer comfortable?'

'It hurts a little.'

'Good. Yet I think your bottom hole is no stranger to such an implement.'

'Not exactly a restrainer,' said Jana coolly.

'What then? A man's penis?'

'Perhaps.'

'Tell the truth!' thundered Kobo. 'Or I will whip you!'

'Many men's penises,' cried Jana defiantly. Kobo grinned.

'That is one of the forbidden things. Maldona is chaste. It is the rule . . .'

'Welcome to the Auberge d'Angleterre, Virgin Jana,' said the petite woman who opened the door, gracing Jana with a sparkling smile. Jana and Kobo entered, and fell to their knees.

'I am your housemistress, Hera. You may both rise.'

Jana and Kobo rose from their position of obeisance.

'Thank you, Mistress,' said Jana.

Kobo hung her cane from her belt, and stood beside Hera's desk, leaving Jana to stand before it with her hands behind her back. The housemistress's study was cosy and dark, even spinsterish, with many books and china ornaments, a globe, office paraphernalia, and in the corner, very prominently, a rack of switches, canes and whips. The air was fragrant and scholarly, and Jana thought of the den of an English headmistress.

But Hera was not English: her accent was decidedly French. She was a small, strong woman of early middle age, shiny black hair tied in a bun, and her trim body enclosed in a dress of crimson satin that covered her from neck to ankle, curiously Victorian, except for the thick torc of gold chains which perched on her lace collar.

'Prefect Kobo has explained the rules to you?' she asked.

'Yes, Mistress.'

Jana smiled dutifully, and Hera got up from her chair to examine her.

'Yes,' she said, 'you are finely built. Your medical report is first class, and you are fit for discipline at every degree. I see your eye on my rack of instruments, though, and I dare say you do not wish to feel their kiss on your naked croup too often.'

'I shall be proud to endure whatever Maldona decrees, Mistress,' said Jana.

The housemistress consulted Jana's file.

'You have probably bought with you a few articles of personal adornment?'

'Well, Mistress, I normally – I mean, in my previous life, I used to wear a gold body-chain.'

'How fetching. I am sure Kobo will give you permission to wear it on special days.'

Kobo nodded, grudgingly.

'Normally the only adornment should be your identity necklace, which you must not remove, but here at Angleterre we are quite tolerant about small loopholes in the rules, unlike the puritanical Germans. And as for the French . . . She rolled her eyes. 'Oo là là!'

She laughed prettily, flashing white teeth against the pink lips which contrasted with her olive skin. Like Cassie's, Jana thought, and felt a pang of longing.

'However,' continued Hera, 'I am quite strict as to our dress code. Nudity must not be casual, and the enjoyment of its delicious freedom is restricted to training, bathing, bed, and punishment. Now, of course, punishment plays an important part in the teaching of discipline, and our most common form of punishment is corporal chastisement, using the whip or cane. Do you know why?'

Jana took a deep breath, and said, 'Mistress, the kiss of the whip on our naked flesh humiliates the body, and stings the soul into understanding.'

'How prettily put,' said Hera with a surprised smile. 'Yes, I think you will go far.'

Kobo looked jealous.

'To put it in the nutshell,' she continued, 'a good lacing is the best lesson in philosophy, and it is a lesson which you will wish to taste sparingly, but one which you will wish to taste.'

'Mistress,' said Jana, 'I crave instruction.'

Hera nodded in approval.

'You should be aware of the various degrees of punishment, and Prefect Kobo will no doubt tell you more, or indeed –' her eyes sparkled mischievously '– show you by example. First of all, beatings are given on the naked buttocks. Does this cause you unease, Jana?'

'No, Mistress. It is the correct way.'

'A Lady's Beating is taken in private, except when an imperfection has been committed outside the auberge, in which case the prefect may use her own cane to punish you there and then, with your naked fesses exposed to the gaze of others. For a Lady's Beating, therefore, the offender must lift her skirt and hold it well clear of her bare fesses until the beating has been satisfactorily completed. A Grand Beating is more serious. This takes place indoors, in front of at least six other virgins, and the offender must strip completely naked, to take the cane, whip or tawse on her buttocks, or shoulders, or both. A Noble Beating is harsher and less frequent, and is *en auberge*, that is, witnessed by the entire assembly of the auberge. The offender now is naked, gagged, and bound to a flogging-horse in full view of her peers.'

Hera paused, her eyes bright, and her face flushed with excitement.

'What is your reaction, Jana?'

'I have none, Mistress. I listen and accept.'

In truth, Jana felt her sex becoming quite moist with desire as the housemistress so casually recited these thrilling ordeals which no doubt awaited her.

Hera licked her lips and continued, 'The Noble Beating is given with the birch, or the *flagrum*, the many thonged scourge, on the back, buttocks and thighs. I myself am required to deliver the first stroke or strokes, and thereafter each prefect takes a stroke in turn. The Noble Beating, too, is witnessed by the auberge, but the offender is chained as well as strapped to the flogging-horse.'

She took a deep breath, and swallowed hard.

'A Lady's Beating is normally of seven strokes, when delivered by a corporal, or, with the prefect's permission, a maximum of fourteen. A prefect may administer a Lady's Beating of fourteen, or, with *my* permission, a maximum of twenty-one. It is the same for a Grand Beating, but this may only be administered by a prefect. For a Noble Beating ... there is no maximum. I decide each case on its merits. All these, of course, are punishments within the auberge. Should you infringe the rules outside the auberge, you may incur a Parfaite's punishment, and should a Parfaite have cause to discipline you, I am afraid the place, nature and severity of the punishment are entirely up to her. Some Parfaites are more in love with the whip than others. You have already seen a Parfaite?'

'I have seen Leandra, Mistress.'

'Ah yes, Leandra . . . she happens to be one of those.'

'Mistress,' interrupted Kobo, 'there is the *Perfect* Beating.'

'Well,' said Hera rather crossly, 'since its form and severity are contained only in the higher rules, to which none but Maldona herself has access, I think we will leave that a mystery. And now it is time to induct Jana into the Auberge d'Angleterre, and present her with her necklace.'

Jana smiled eagerly.

'But before that, Jana, there is a small ceremony which you must undergo. Call it an initiation rite, a sign that you accept to be broken to our ways. It is called a Virgin's Beating, and it will only happen to you once. Do you accept?'

'Gladly, Mistress,' cried Jana, her slit very wet now, and her bottom tingling with anticipation.

'Remember that you may cry out at any moment for the beating to stop, and to be released from Maldona.'

'I beg you to chastise me, Mistress,' pleaded Jana.

'Very well. Denude yourself, virgin.'

Trembling, Jana undressed under the hooded eyes of Kobo and the housemistress, and noticed Hera's nostrils flare, with a deep breath, as she slipped her blouse off to expose the ripe fullness of her naked breasts and the wide nipples that were already stiff and swollen with her excitement. Now she stood naked but for her steel restrainer.

'Unfasten the clasp of the restrainer,' ordered Hera, 'and let the panels hang loose.'

Jana obeyed, thus exposing her mink and bare buttocks.

'Such a lovely looking mink,' murmured Hera dreamily, as she took Jana's hands and placed them on two grips fixed to the wall, then positioned her feet on two painted marks, wide apart on the floor. At a nod from Hera, the prefect fetched three instruments from the rack, and held them in Jana's view.

'You have the choice of implements,' said Hera softly. 'There is the cane, quite fearful, half an inch thick and four feet long. Or the leather tawse, with three tongues; or my personal favourite, *betula pubescens*, the English hairy birch, unfortunately the most painful of all.'

Jana gulped as she saw the bunch of hard, whippy twigs, bound by wire.

'I shall take the birch, Mistress,' she whispered.

'A Virgin's Beating is only seven strokes,' said Hera softly, 'but with the birch, it can seem like more.'

She swished the birch in the air, and it made a dry crackling sound.

'The *betula pubescens* is very stimulating indeed. But, Jana, the true beauty of a whipping is not pain, but the submission to pain, the giving up of the self. Hence, the whips of Maldona never draw blood, for that would not be beautiful.'

Hera took her time inspecting Jana's body, and the suspense of this anticipation made Jana quite wet with excitement.

'You have been whipped before, I suppose?'

'Yes, Mistress.'

'On the bare bottom?'

Jana nodded.

'Never on the naked breasts?'

'Why, no!' gasped Jana.

'Or on the belly? Between the thighs, on the naked lips of your fount, your sex?' continued Hera implacably.

'Oh, no, Mistress, not there!' cried Jana, numb with fear.

'Well . . . it is only seven strokes, and remember, virgin, you can stop the punishment at any time.'

'Please, Mistress,' blurted Jana, choking back a sob, 'I shall take your beating, I swear.'

She felt Hera's hand stroking her shivering bottom.

'Such firm, ripe young fesses,' murmured the older woman. 'How frightening, yet how beautiful, to stripe them.'

Hera positioned herself behind Jana, and her dress rustled as she lifted the birch. Jana's buttocks clenched in anticipation of the first cut, and the birch swished alarmingly, to descend on Jana's bare skin not as a stinging lash, but as a caress which stroked her like a feather. Jana moaned at the tickle of the birch rods, knowing that Hera was playing with her, willing her to begin the beating proper.

'Please, Mistress, whip me,' she sighed.

But again the birch rods descended, this time to stroke the cleft of her buttocks and tickle the backs of her thighs. It was almost unbearable, and Jana could feel the gushing wetness in her cunt as her body thrilled to the birch's caress. The birch reached through her cleft and found her anus bud, pierced by its hard steel dildo, and stroked the stretched skin of Jana's anus.

'Oh,' moaned Jana, 'beat me, beat me.'

The tips of the birch found her gash, then the nympha, the stiff clitoris, which was hard and tingling, and Jana groaned again as a spasm of pleasure shot through her body. Hera was relentless in her caress. The birch twigs went to her mink, soaked with sweat, and, in its underpart, with Jana's oily love-juice; then across her belly, up to the nipples, which she stroked long and vigorously until they stood like little cathedrals, sending electricity down Jana's spine and into her trembling nympha. She felt her cunt flow uncontrollably, and knew that, incredibly, she was on the verge of coming. She squeezed on the dildo that so sweetly filled her anus, and wished she was free to take her nipples into her mouth, to tongue them and chew on their hard tender points. The birch would not stop, and Jana thought her cunt, her whole body, had melted into a hot pool. She did not want this strange beating ever to end, and moaned as the birch stroked her spine, all the way down to its sensitive base, where it lingered, tickling her at the top of her crack, and the waves of pleasure this sent washing over Jana's body made her finally break, and with a cry of pain and joy she exploded in a trembling climax. And as her body jerked in her spasm, she felt Hera's lips on hers, as the housemistress fastened a golden chain round her neck.

'Congratulations, Jana,' said Hera, 'you are now a virgin of the Auberge d'Angleterre.'

9

Erato

The refectory was as big and gloomy as a cathedral, and the girls of Maldona took luncheon in an atmosphere of hushed reverence. Talking was conducted in whispers, and the loudest sound was the clinking of spoons on plates, or the rustling of skirts. On a dais at the head of refectory stood the high table, where sat the adepts. Below it stretched tables seating fifty girls each, three for each of the auberges and one table for each sept of the auberge, with its prefect at table's head. Jana was seated at the very end of the third table of Angleterre.

She met the curious stares without blinking; those that were friendly received a response in kind. She was full of hungry vitality after the tumultuous events of the morning. Her restraining phallus was stored away in her cell, awaiting its reinsertion in her anus at nightfall, and she rather missed its friendly stiffness. She wondered how many of her fellow-virgins secretly relished the wearing of the phallus, or even adapted it so that it would fit into their lady's place.

Jana saw Ragusa the nurse seated at the next table, the prefect Cleadne's, and was pleased to receive a friendly smile. She returned the smile and waved, but this drew a frown of rebuke from her own corporal, Miriam, who ominously tapped the hilt of her cane, and Jana quickly lowered her head.

The girl sitting next to Jana, to her surprise, was wearing her steel gag, which seemed odd, unless part of her punishment was to go without food. But halfway through the soup course, Miriam seemed to relent, and nodded that she could free her mouth. She gratefully took off her gag and rolled her tongue across her teeth and lips, stretching it after its long confinement, then attacked the plate of cooled soup before her.

'Mmm,' she said, 'gazpacho. That's good, it should be cold anyway. These English cooks!'

'What is it?' said Jana. 'It tastes of cucumber.'

'That's right,' said the girl, slurping noisily. 'Cucumber, tomatoes, olive oil, onions and garlic. You could fuel an army on this stuff. Every meal, they like to put in just one little Spanish dish, as a sop to the land we occupy. But girls are so conservative, aren't they?'

Sure enough, the rest of the meal was as familiar and reassuring as a wet day in Golder's Green: strips of roast beef shining with every colour of the rainbow, mash, peas and gravy, followed by roly-poly pudding with custard, and studded with raisins as hard as bullets. Jana grunted as her teeth cracked on one of the pellets.

'What are these raisins, fossilised?' she said.

'You must clean your plate,' said her companion. 'It's the rule. Otherwise, a whacking.'

Hungry, Jana was glad to eat everything, washing it down with gulps of water which was the only refreshment available. There was not much talk at the table, the girls wolfing their food as though afraid it would be taken away at any moment, and through the noises of munching rang the voice of Miriam the corporal, 'Harriet! back straight, please! Naomi, don't dribble, it is not ladylike! Sylvie, eat quietly, you are not a pig!'

It was difficult to combine greed with decorum and, as the meal progressed, Miriam's tone grew harsher, and she barked from grease-smeared lips, 'Right, Sylvie, you've been warned. One!' Sylvie made a rueful face. 'Naomi! I'm tired of you. Two!' Harriet, you won't learn. Three! Carla, three for you as well.'

The girl Carla rolled her eyes, as if to say that this was one of Miriam's off-days, although Jana suspected that every day for Miriam was an off-day. Her face would have been handsome were it not for the cruelty in her lips and eyes.

Only Jana and her neighbour had not yet been singled out by Miriam's wrath, and Jana turned to the girl with a shy grin of complicity, in doing so she knocked over the water glass by accident, and spilt water on to her skirt.

'So,' barked Miriam, 'we have a new slut, have we? Jana, I believe. Well, slut Jana, you have earned four!'

There were murmurs of astonishment and approval from the other virgins.

The end of the meal was indicated, and the virgins formed lines to troop back through the maze of corridors to their own cells, where the early part of the afternoon was a quiet time, and they were free to rest, or to take recreation. Jana felt curious to explore, but first, there was the matter of Miriam and her rota of numbers. Jana had a keen idea what those numbers referred to, and she was not long in finding out. Her neighbour had replaced her gag before leaving the refectory, and it turned out she occupied the cell next to Jana's. She winked as she went inside, and as Jana opened her own door, she was recalled by Miriam's harsh cry, 'Where do you think you're going, slut? You're getting four, remember? Outside and hitch your skirt up, with your bum cheeks well spread, slut!'

Jana saw that the other girls were standing in their doorways, pleated skirts raised to reveal a pretty row of bare bottoms, framed by their suspenders and stocking tops. All except one, the girl Sylvie, who revealed herself to be wearing a striking pair of turquoise panties.

'Well, Sylvie,' sneered Miriam with heavy sarcasm, 'I don't believe it is a special day, is it?'

'No, Miss,' quavered Sylvie.

'So we are not supposed to be wearing panties, are we? And certainly not turquoise ones. You are supposed to be bare bum like a proper virgin.'

'Yes, Miss.'

'Just for that, you'll get two extra!'

There was a subdued titter from the rest of the corridor.

'So you think it's funny, do you? Just for that, *everybody* will take two extra.'

The titter gave way to a groan, as Sylvie glumly rolled

down her panties and presented her bottom naked like the rest. Jana shivered, for now she was to receive six strokes of Miriam's cane on her own bare fesses. She began to understand Miriam's game: a beating of less than seven was not official, and could be delivered informally and casually at the corporal's whim.

'We'll start with the new slut,' said Miriam, and obediently Jana lifted her skirt, pleased at the draught of cool air across her croup, and pleased at the gasps of admiration as she spread her thighs and thrust her bottom boldly up to invite the cane's kiss. She felt a tickling in her belly and sex, and realised that she had indeed spilled her water on purpose, for she wanted to be caned like the others, and was proud, too, that she was to take more than any of them. *Why*, she thought, why do I want this? Cassie will explain it to me. Oh, Cassie, I must find you.

'Daydreaming, slut?' hissed Miriam, and an instant later her cane laced Jana's bottom. A delicious thrill of pain leapt through her body, and she squirmed, relishing the humiliation of her smarting bare skin. Miriam chuckled and laced her again, then again, the cuts coming with cruel rapidity, and soon, too soon, it was over, and Jana felt a lovely fiery glow suffuse her naked rump as her cheeks trembled and jerked. Coolly, she smoothed down her skirt, and bowed to Miriam, who was quite taken aback.

'Well, slut,' she muttered, 'you can certainly take it, I'll say that for you. Dismissed!'

Jana retreated to her cell, and lay down on the hard bed. Outside she heard the crack of the cane on the bottom of her fellow virgins, and their yelps of anguish. She smiled at the knowledge that she had taken her beating in silence. Her bottom smarted, irritating her, and she sighed, lifting her skirt once more to let her fingers stroke her mink, then stray to the lips of her sex, and find the swollen nympha within, the hard clit that begged to be touched and caressed. She found her cunt gushing wet, as she knew it would be: her beating, and the cries of the other beaten girls, excited her. As she heard the corporal's cane gleefully descend, she closed her eyes and imagined those squirming white fesses naked and blushing from the cane, and spread her thighs wide. With shivering fingers she smeared her love-oil all over her belly and breasts, rubbing it into her stiff nipples, then brought her fingers to her mouth, where she sucked and swallowed her own salty fluid, all the time rubbing her stiff nympha, until as the last stroke of the cane descended outside, she writhed in a lovely swooning orgasm, her spasms making her shudder all the more intensely for the silence she was obliged to keep.

Bright sunlight slanted through the window, lighting the glistening hairs of her mink, and Jana lay motionless, her thighs spread, dozing and dreaming of Kobo and Miriam strapped together and whipped naked by Jana, with the white whip. The knight Jason drifted into her daydream. He had been watching the flogging of the two girls, and his prick was bulging under his tunic, so she stripped him and made him bend over, making the girls laugh as she laced his juicy bare buttocks as hard as she could.

She awoke with a start as the door to her cell slid open.

'Oh!' cried Jana, flustered, and smoothed her skirt hurriedly down over her thighs.

Her visitor was the girl in the punishment gag, which she removed as soon as she had closed the door behind her.

'That's better,' she said. 'Mind if I sit down? I'm Erato, by the way. Don't mind me, carry on with what you were doing, everybody in the corridor will be at it by now. A caning always does that, funnily enough.'

'Well, I've done it already,' said Jana, blushing.

'Pity, I was hoping I might help,' said Erato jauntily.

'Is it permitted for us to be in each other's cells?'

'Of course not, but rules are made to be broken. Look at Sylvie, and her wearing her panties *in flagrante*.'

'Why must you be gagged, Erato?' asked Jana, assuming that questions were permitted amongst friends and equals.

'Oh, I cheeked Kobo,' said Erato airily. 'I'm always doing it. She hates me. Then I get the gag, and a beating, and have to wear the catsuit and the phallus as I work in the garden. I don't mind the phallus up my bum, in fact it's rather sweet, but that catsuit makes me sweat like a corporal.'

'I think Kobo is rather cruel,' said Jana gloomily.

'To me she is, and with good reason. I used to be prefect in her place, you see, when she was only a corporal, and one day I caught her shaving her mink, the vain cow. I ordered her a beating, and then she was insolent, so I got it bumped up to a Grand Beating. How I enjoyed making that naked bum squirm – fourteen juicy cuts in front of my whole sept. But then, the scheming, self-righteous bitch appealed against the sentence, and wheedled her way in front of the Council of Adepts, and they inspected her wretched mink, all scientific, and found that it was according to the rules, just a millimetre longer than the allowed limit. So my forfeit was to take a double punishment from her.'

'Twenty-eight!'

'With a long cane. I was ready, but Kobo challenged me for my prefectship instead, and since the challenge was thrown in front of Hera, I could not refuse, though I should far rather have taken the flogging. I knew the bitch would beat me, and she did. So here I am, broken to virgin.'

'How awful.'

Erato shrugged.

'All in the game. Kobo knows I'll challenge her when my strength is ripe, and that's why she's trying to wear me down. But still, I don't envy Kobo. The poor cow wants so desperately to be a Parfaite, and she makes it so obvious, that she will never get promotion. She'll have to fight for it and, strong as she is, she'll have trouble beating any of the Parfaites.'

'I should love to be a Parfaite,' said Jana softly.

'Well, well,' said Erato, scrutinising her intently, 'you know, you might just make it. You have a look – it's hard to explain. A lot depends on whether you get taken on by a Parfaite, as her student.'

'I'd choose Leandra,' Jana suddenly blurted out.

Erato laughed.

'You don't choose a Parfaite. She chooses you, *if* you're lucky. I say, can I have a look at your bottom? You took quite a whacking, and without a murmur.'

'Gladly,' said Jana. She got up and raised her skirt.

'Gosh, how pretty,' said Erato. 'All pink and glowing, like a rose.'

'Touch if you like,' said Jana.

'Thanks every so much,'

Jana felt Erato's cool palms stroking her, and smiled.

'Such a firm croup, and so big! I'd love to give her a little kiss.'

'Be my guest.'

Now she felt Erato's moist lips caress her bare skin, and shivered.

'Mmm,' murmured Erato. 'I'm getting all wet . . . you know where.'

'Would you like me to do something about it?' whispered Jana.

'Yes, please.'

Erato snapped open her steel restrainer, revealing a thick mink and a nympha, already stiff, peeping from the curls.

Jana put her fingers on it and began to rub gently.

'It's awfully big,' she said, admiringly.

'Ooh! That's lovely,' gasped Erato. Shall I . . .?'

'Later – I've just diddled myself, you see, and I'm quite sated.'

'I'll look forward to that. Oh! How gorgeous! What sly fingers you have.'

'You are lovely and wet,' said Jana, enjoying the sight of the girl writhing at the touch of her fingertips, which were slippery with love-oil. Erato lovingly stroked her inflamed bottom, faster and faster as she approached climax.

'Are you sure . . .?' she said with raised eyebrows.

Jana laughed, for she was becoming wet again.

'All right, then,' she said, and thrilled as Erato's hand pressed her sex, and began to massage her own nympha into a tingling stiffness.

'You are big, Jana,' said Erato. 'Your nympha is really well-developed for a new virgin, why, it's as big as many of the Parfaites'.'

'Does my raw, flogged bottom really turn you on?' asked Jana.

'Oh, yes. And what a lovely fount you have – I mean, your cunt. So soft and wet and sort of squeezy.'

'I haven't heard the word fount before. It seems that Maldona is fond of her own terms for, well, intimate things. Like fountain for toilet.'

'There are a lot of words from Greek, or French, or Latin, left from the old days. English can be so limiting, can't it? I mean, *buttocks* – what a coarse word, when you have fesses, or croup, or gloutos. "Fount" is from the French "fente" – a slit, or there is the lovely Greek "trema", which suggests trembling. Mink, bush and forest, those are all nice words, but sometimes we use the Greek "trix" or "kytai", which gives us the little joke, to describe masturbating: "teaching tricks to Katie". Well, it's slightly funny.'

'What you are doing isn't funny,' gasped Jana, 'it is gorgeous.'

'Are you going to . . .?'

'Very soon.'

'Oh! Yes! Me too . . . Me . . . Oh, Jana, Jana!'

The two girls embraced as their soaking fingers brought each other's bellies to their fluttering, sweet spasms.

'Tired?' said Erato.

'Not really. I'm only glowing and drowsy. I feel I've made a friend.'

'Me too. I'm glad we diddled each other. Myself, I always masturbate after a lacing, and I bet most of the others do too. You feel so hot! I wish we had a cane, and you could give me a lacing like the one you took. That is the funny thing about Maldona: we crave what we dread.'

Jana decided against telling her new friend about her white whip, so early in their acquaintance. She wanted to find out more about the secret of its provenance, why Matron had been awestruck by the simple flogging tool.

But she did tell Erato about her search for Cassie.

'There *was* a girl like that, very striking, in the Auberge de France, I think. But only for a short time. The boy-friend she mentioned would have been a knight, for they are used by the Parfaites as messengers to the outside.

There was some rumour that she was sent for a Noble Beating, for asking questions, very dangerous questions, concerning the higher rules, which only Maldona herself may know. Wait – it may have been a *Perfect* Beating –' Erato gave a little shudder. '– on Maldona's orders. But she cried "I go down", and went away. But that is only hearsay, like most things here.'

'How do I get to see Maldona herself?' asked Jana.

'You don't! Unless you are the Superior, or a Parfaite.'

'Then I must become a Parfaite as soon as possible.'

'Why not try for Superior while you are about it?' replied Erato sarcastically.

'I could.'

'I do believe you mean it. Listen, come with me to swim, I think you need to cool down. And afterwards we could have a sauna, perhaps a wrestle in the gymnasium.'

'I'd love to,' said Jana, and gathered her wash-things.

'Good. At bath, you see, I may go ungagged,' said Erato, 'although I have to walk through Maldona with the cursed thing till we get there.'

They set off through the labyrinth, which, with Erato's expert guidance, no longer seemed so confusing, and soon came to the bath complex, announced by the smell of scalded flesh and the giggles of swimmers by the open-air pool. They left their clothing in the apodyterium, which Jana thought a rather fancy word for changing-room, and took their places on the grass beside the blue water. They baked in the sun until they were sweating freely, then dived into the icy water and swam energetically for twenty minutes. Jana looked up at the fairy-tale turrets towering above them, and the snowcapped mountains beyond, and thought herself in paradise; even the smarting of her bottom seemed like an old friend.

'Where exactly does Maldona live?' said Jana as they splashed.

'Up there, at the very top ... I *think*. But don't point, or even look.'

'Well, how is Maldona chosen? By challenge? Surely not by promotion, since there is no one to promote her.'

'Maldona is not chosen. Maldona is eternal,' said Erato very seriously.

Jana's flippant comparison with the Dalai Lama of Tibet, who is endlessly reincarnated, was fortunately interrupted by the tall, nude figure which Jana recognised as Leandra, accompanied by her knight Jason. She stood for a moment, haughtily surveying the bathers, with the sun illuminating the valleys and hills of her musculature. Her body was hard, sculpted rock, and below the shining hillock of her shaven mons hung a clitoris that glistened so fat and pink that Jana yearned to rush to her and take it in her mouth, right to the back of her throat, and caress it and suck it until that proud body melted with joy.

'Out,' ordered Erato, and along with every other virgin, they left the swimming pool.

'She is so beautiful,' whispered Jana, as Leandra dived into the empty pool and swam a length with the grace of a salmon, entirely underwater. 'I want her for my Parfaite.'

'You make me jealous,' said Erato, as they towelled each other, 'but I have an idea, if you are so desperate to be taken by Leandra. You'll be shown to the assembly of Parfaites, to see if you will be one of the lucky few virgins who are adopted. My own Parfaite is Circe, and I'd put in a word for you, but she is a bit too . . . nice for you. Leandra, now, is very strict. She can take any punishment, and will only countenance a virgin who can equal her. I'll borrow a cane, never mind where, and give you the hardest lacing you can take, so that she will see your marks and kisses and hopefully be impressed. It's against the rules, of course, but since you are new, you can pretend you took the beating before you got here, which should impress her even more.'

'That's awfully kind of you,' said Jana. 'I agree, then.'

'Not kind,' said Erato, taking Jana's hand, 'for I'll enjoy it no end. Now let's wrestle, and then we can relax in the sauna.'

Jana lay pinioned for the umpteenth time between Erato's powerful thighs, the coarse fiber of the wrestling mat scratching her back. Both girls were panting, slippery with sweat.

'You're good, Jana, but you're not as good as me,' said Erato. 'Now submit!'

'No.'

Erato slapped her breasts, quite hard.

'How beautifully your teats quiver! Now submit, or I'll slap them till they glow.'

'Never.'

'You asked for it!'

The crack of her palm on Jana's breasts reddened the firm quivering flesh, but Jana remained silent.

'Damn, you are enjoying it!' cried Erato in mock anger.

'Yes, I am, rather. See how stiff you've made my nips. But about Maldona – how can a woman's body be eternal?'

'She appears in the woman's form she deems suitable, when the time is perfect. Now submit!'

'And she is recognised?'

'Yes, she is recognised. Submit, Jana, or I'll squeeze you to death.'

'I'd love you to squeeze me to death. You know, Erato, I want to be a Parfaite . . .'

'So you said. Submit!'

'. . . perhaps even the Superior herself. But most of all . . .'

'Submit!'

'Certainly not. You'll have to hurt me much harder than that.'

'Oh, I don't want to hurt you. Just submit, please?'

'But if I can't get to be Superior, or not even a Parfaite, perhaps I could just be content to be Maldona.'

'What?' cried Erato.

She was momentarily off guard. Jana delivered a savage kick that twisted her and threw her neatly off. But she did not leap up to pinion her felled opponent. Instead, she spread her arms and legs, and lay immobile and smiling on her back. She looked at Erato and shrugged.

'I submit, Erato,' Jana said.

10

The Secret Book

In the days that followed, Jana quickly adapted to the rhythms of Maldona, at once brutally strict and casually indolent. She supposed it to be like the army, where the enforcement of ferocious rules went hand in hand with a system of nods and winks and highly refined shirking. And she came to understand that Maldona depended on her rules, for the rules *were* Maldona, an infinite network of petty or incomprehensible regulations whose only purpose was to offer opportunities for being broken. The rules existed because without them there would be no rules.

Outside the strict discipline of classroom or gymnasium, the girls were free to wander and play, always deliciously aware that they walked a minefield, where the slightest infraction of rules unguessed at invited the lash; the wrong curtsey or bow, even an imperfect facial expression, could lead to a vigorous lacing of the bare croup.

The day began with gruelling exercises, when the virgins, auberge by auberge, would trot to the cold gymnasium, and perform punishing sets until their bodies glowed, then return to their corridors to a freezing shower, hosed down by grinning corporals. Jana enjoyed herself. The gymnasium introduced her to light muscle-building equipment, instead of mere body exercises of the aerobic type. She worked with springs, isometric machines and the light weights permitted to virgins, finding that she mastered them easily. As her strength grew, and her muscles began to swell most pleasingly, she hoped that she would soon be able to apply to join the Corps of Body Sculptors, and work out with the heavy weights that built muscle rather than merely toughened it. Her wrestling improved, and she wondered when she would dare to throw her first challenge, and gain another gold chain for her neck.

Miriam the corporal seemed an obvious candidate for a challenge. She was really a beast – perhaps I will become a beast if I take her corporal's post from her, Jana worried. Miriam delighted in tormenting her virgins, whether by awarding arbitrary canings after mealtimes, or by lashing their bodies in the fountain with a severe jet of water from her hosepipe, usually aimed between their legs, and, moreover, usually aimed between Jana's legs. She had taken a jealous dislike to Jana, which increased as Jana's muscles and strength grew. Jana knew that if she challenged Miriam and lost, she would suffer, and her beatings would be more frequent and brutal; then she reflected that that was hardly possible. Few meals passed without a postprandial caning, and few inspections did not reveal the hapless Sylvie to be illicitly wearing panties, or perfume, or some other infraction, which of course earned extra strokes for the entire corridor. Jana reckoned that Sylvie must be a little stupid to continue her offences thus.

The day proceeded with classwork, lectures in 'philosophy', mostly given by Parfaites, with the staff of armoury, surgery, or gymnasium covering more specialised knowledge. The Parfaites were a strange, arrogant bunch, Jana found. They lectured nude, cool and relaxed in front of their perspiring audience, and 'philosophy' seemed to mean any subject that came into their impossibly elegant heads. The absorption of all this knowledge was intended to help propel the girls towards the elusive perfection. Nothing, except physical training, was actually compulsory, yet it was bad form to be seen slacking or idle. All activities must lead to improvement, whether sunning by the pool (for physical beauty) or browsing in the library (for mental beauty) or, for 'social awareness', attending the innumerable councils and tribunals which argued over minute points of discipline and settled the passionate disputes which erupted frequently between girls of every rank, and of course gleefully witnessing the punishments and forfeits which were handed down.

Jana liked watching the punishments, and together with Erato she would go to watch Grand Beatings, which were at first terrifying, but became a savage pleasure as Jana allowed herself to be charged with the electric excitement of the crowd, sighing at each vicious stroke of tawse or whip on trussed naked flesh. Jana liked the tawse, for it made more noise.

'Shouldn't be long before you get called before the Parfaites,' said Erato one day. 'I hear that you are showing good prowess. Don't forget my little offer of help.'

'I won't,' replied Jana 'But, honestly, I'm caned every day by that beast Miriam as it is.'

'Miriam is small fry,' sneered Erato. 'I'll make you wriggle like an eel, Jana. And you can pretend it was Miriam's cane that did it.'

'Mmmm,' said Jana, and squeezed Erato's hand.

Wrestling was also exciting to watch, and Jana found she always became wet in her sex at the sight of two naked girls, slippery with oil, fighting with no holds barred. This was a common way of settling disputes, but when the dispute also involved an alleged breach of the rules, the two contenders were put to the trial of the lash, and Jana enjoyed watching that most of all. The two girls were strapped naked together, and tied hand and foot, their wrists suspended from the ceiling so that they must stand on tiptoe. With a prefect behind each girl, they were simultaneously flogged, until one girl admitted her wrong and begged for an end to the ordeal, even as she knew she was incurring a further flogging the next day. It was curious that the two whipped girls would usually embrace fervently after they were cut down, with love grown from a shared ordeal. And, after witnessing these spectacles, it seemed the most natural thing in the world for Jana to take Erato to her cell, where they would lift their skirts and masturbate each other cheerfully.

It was not easy to make friends, so Jana was especially glad to have met Erato. Friendship was based on power and interest, and Jana, as a new virgin with a solitary necklace, had little to offer. But she was not quite the lowest of the low. That title was reserved for the 'whipping girls', those who had lost their identity necklace in a foolish wager or challenge, and were obliged to sell their bodies in return for a new one. This meant that they agreed to take all the beatings their 'protector' might incur, on her behalf, and the system was legally recognised in the rules. They were a strange breed, mostly gloomy, for their croups bore the marks not of fortitude and dignity, but of folly and humiliation. Yet some of the whipping girls seemed to thrive, making a career out of their abject status. Harriet, on Jana's corridor, was one of those. She was slightly older than the rest, tough and with a tanned, leathery skin that seemed impervious to the hardest lacing. She was always smiling, and rare was the day that she did not endure two or even three severe punishments. Her body was wiry and mannish, with the narrow taut muscles of a runner, and her tight croup bore the marks of years of chastisement. One day, Jana asked her why she put up with her lot.

'I'm just a fool,' she said gaily. 'Always gambling, always losing. I love to fight, and I always get beaten. Look at my muscles, I can never put on weight no matter how hard I try.'

'They are nice muscles,' said Jana, feeling her arm. 'Very strong.'

'But too small. I haven't the weight, you see. And so it goes, my bottom pays for my scatterbrained notions.'

But later, Erato said gruffly, 'Don't you believe her act. Harriet is a whore. She sells herself for sex, to the high-ups, adepts who don't want the shame of enduring a punishment, or having their offence known. There is more goes on here than meets the eye, Jana.'

In this as in much else, Maldona was a strange blend of the stern and the tolerant. In theory, a virgin might not go without a necklace; but where she had obtained it was not questioned, and there was a thriving trade in neckchains, stolen, pawned, or abandoned by girls who had gone down. And for lesser transactions, there was a market in signs of erotic prowess. Love-bites were esteemed as jewels, whether on the neck, the breasts, or the very fount-lips, and these visible caresses were begged, stolen and fought for as fiercely as for any treasure. Such was the 'other currency' of Maldona.

There seemed to be little religion in Maldona, and Jana realised this was because Maldona was a religion in herself. The paintings clustered on the walls were catholic in their inspiring depictions of great personages: the Buddha rubbed shoulders with Hermes Trismegistus, King Arthur with Nostradamus, alongside a pantheon of goddesses from every religion. Saints appeared in scenes of torment: the martyrdom of St Anthony, the scourging of St Sebastian, St Catherine broken on the wheel, or the severed breasts of St Agatha. Maldona was pagan in her voracity for images of ordeal.

It was expected that, in this quasi-secular institution, a girl with skills should make herself useful. Accordingly, Jana went to the Mistress Armourer and offered herself as candlemaker. Her proposal was accepted with enthusiasm, for the candleworks was short of artisans. She was familiar with the hot and arduous work, and was thus made welcome in the tribe of a dozen candlemakers, who worked at all hours in a roasting cavern deep under Maldona, to satisfy the insatiable demand for their humble products. Because of the importance of their work in keeping the vast, dark labyrinth alight, candlemakers enjoyed certain privileges and freedoms: to work late, and thus skip classes or training sessions, and to wander the corridors of Maldona when other virgins were required to be in their cells sleeping.

They were also permitted to work naked except for a protective apron, because of the heat, though Jana scorned the protective apron, not flinching even when a drop of molten wax splashed her bare body. They made standard white candles, but in addition, each virgin had her clients for 'specialities', artful, coloured creations for individual prefects or adepts, made with jealously guarded recipes of tints and dyes. It was easy to get such supplies from the armoury, and a chit could be had to secure almost anything that could be imagined useful for candlemaking. The atmosphere was occasionally fraught with tension, and

144

scuffles broke out over some petty jealousy or suspicion, so that a corporal seconded to the armoury was generally present, cane in hand, to quell such unseemliness. Jana remained aloof, content to make the plain white candles, while all the time eyeing the artistries of her colleagues, to see if she could spot a marketing window, as Henry Gordon Playste would say ...

She became nocturnal, by night toiling in the hot cavern in smoky darkness, and by day glorying in the rays of the sun as she basked by the swimming pool. She gave up going to the lectures in philosophy, finding herself philosopher enough. She trained and wrestled hard; her muscles grew and her skin became golden, exciting the jealousy of Kobo and Miriam, and the admiration of her fellow-virgins. And, as her body firmed, she found to her delight that her nympha had indeed grown, jutting now from the lips of her fount like a blood-red ruby.

The time came when she was no longer obliged to wear her phallus at night, but she found she had grown used to the hard steel comforting her anus, and wore it anyway. She whispered this, giggling, to Erato, and was overheard by Harriet the whipping girl, who announced loudly, 'Oh, *I* wear my restrainer all the time, you know.'

The candleshop suited her. She loved the hard work, the sweat and dirt and stink of ashes and wax, the humility of toiling naked like a slave, with the overseer's cane always gleaming. And she saw that there was indeed a marketing window, for the special creations of her well-meaning colleagues were pretty but bland, frothy things of flowers and mushrooms which were decorative and nothing else. Jana began to make trips to the stores to obtain her own store of ingredients.

And as she became enmeshed in the life of Maldona, the reason for her presence began to seem distant, not forgotten, but like a light at the end of a tunnel which would be reached in due course, without urgency. Her prowess at wrestling improved so much that she was able to beat Erato with ease, and she adored the feeling of raw power as she pinned her naked opponent helpless to the mat.

'It's time you threw out a challenge, Jana,' said Erato one day. 'The Parfaites will be seeing you any day now, I'm sure, and it'll look good if you have a couple of neckchains to your credit. Why not take Miriam? That was a sneaky thing she did to you.'

Miriam had goaded Jana so much at luncheon that she had answered her insolently. Rebuked for her table manners, she had cried, 'This slop doesn't deserve table manners!'

For that she had earned a Lady's Beating; Hera sent for her, and together they chose the instrument most suitable for her punishment. Her offence was an insult to her corporal, but to the refectory of Maldona too. Jana herself chose the birch, the *betula pubescens*, and carried it to the smirking Miriam, who made her kiss the rod, and bend down with her skirt pulled high to receive a full, slow seven on the spread naked buttocks. It was the juiciest lacing she had yet received, and when it was over, her eyes brimmed with tears and she rushed to her cell to lie on her belly with her stinging bottom in the cool air. After a while the smarting turned to a glow, and she felt proud that she had taken the punishment without a sound, and purged herself of her stupid offence. And with this knowledge, joyously and fiercely, she masturbated to a delicious orgasm.

Jana frowned.

'Not Miriam,' she said.

'Harriet, then. Or even poor little Sylvie.'

'You don't understand. Miriam is beneath my dignity. It's Kobo I want.'

'Kobo!'

'Or more than Kobo.'

That night she was restless. Her bottom still smarted from her Lady's Beating, and she was glad, for she knew she had deserved it, Miriam's spite notwithstanding. The half moon gleamed through the window, and knowing that she could not sleep, she dressed and crept out of her cell, hurrying down to the candleworks. She found herself alone there, and flung herself furiously into her work until it was long after fourth bell, and first bell could not be far away.

146

Sweat poured from her as she fashioned her own private creations, glad to be alone and away from prying, jealous eyes, for these creations were like none Maldona and seen before. At last, satisfied that the radiant flesh-coloured wax – and the colours were a pretty rainbow of flesh, like the flesh Jana herself had known – had turned out correctly, she stowed her products in her personal cabinet, and started on her way through the winding underground corridors, back to her cell.

Suddenly fatigue hit her, and she felt dizzy, and then after stumbling through unfamiliar corridors, it dawned on her that she had lost her way. She cursed, and tried to retrace her steps to familiar territory, but the further she went into the maze, the more confused she became. At last she found her path blocked: she was in a cul-de-sac, lit by one solitary candle at its mouth, and the rest totally dark. She was about to turn back when an eddy of hot air made the candle flame dance, and its flicker was suddenly reflected at the closed end of the cul-de-sac, as though from a mirror. Curious, she followed the passage to its end, and came to a huge steel door, flush with the cavern wall, and so tightly fitted that not a glimmer of light passed underneath, if light there was on the other side.

She touched it, tried to push it open, but it would not move. Then, in the stillness, she felt a faint vibration through the slab of steel. She put her ear to it, and heard a noise, a low, insistent humming, like an engine or genertor. Then the noise deepened to become a throb, which she had heard before as she neared the cul-de-sac, dismissing it as the sound of the mountain cooling and creaking in the night. Now it sounded like the motor of a truck, growing fainter as it moved away.

And looking down at the door, she saw a lock. In Maldona, where there were no locks.

Jana hurried away with dark fear clutching her. She managed to grope her way back to a familiar corridor, when suddenly she heard footsteps. As the newcomer approached, she hid in a side passage, even though a candle-maker was permitted to be about at this hour. She held her breath as Surgeon Mistress Jocasta passed by on her way to the secret door.

Back in her cell at last, Jana slept for the few remaining hours before first bell. But she awoke feeling unexpectedly refreshed and eager. Now she had a mystery of her own to solve. She knew a secret!

The next morning, the Deputy Superior announced at breakfast that the whipping girl Harriet, of the Auberge d'Angleterre, was to receive a Noble Beating in front of all Maldona. Following custom, no reason was given, and the hall was immediately abuzz with excited rumours. Whose punishment was Harriet taking? An adept, perhaps a Parfaite ... Naomi was cheeky enough to suggest it was the Superior herself. Miriam snapped at her to hold her tongue, but even Miriam was made nervous by the impending ordeal, and let the blasphemy go unpunished. Harriet was to receive twenty-one strokes of the birch on her naked buttocks.

Sylvie looked tearful, and put her hand on Harriet's, and said in a soppy, melodramatic voice, 'Oh, Harriet, I'm sorry if I've ever said anything rotten to you, truly I am. Our hearts are with you.'

Harriet laughed.

'I'll bet you're glad your bottoms aren't with me. Tra la la, a Noble Beating! I've taken worse! You won't hear me squeal, tra la! And I'll look pretty for a day.'

It was the custom that the victim of a Noble Beating had a day's notice of her punishment. This was not designed as a subtle torment – twenty-four hours' wretched brooding – but rather as an occasion of joy. For the girl who was to be flogged wore a robe of silken rose petals for that day; it was always known when a Noble Beating was in the air, for the rose bushes would be denuded and the seamstress virgins set to work. The victim would glide through Maldona, free to go, do or say whatever she wanted, and be greeted with love and awe.

Jana watched Harriet the next day, sumptuous in her fragile robe of delicately gummed rose petals, a paintbox of pinks, reds, and yellows. A posse of excited virgins attached themselves to her, following her through Maldona, and sometimes bending to kiss her bare feet. Harriet's face wore a faraway expression as she accepted tributes and prayers with the grace of a goddess.

The punishment was a sombre occasion, save for Harriet's dreamy smile. She entered the hall wearing her robe of petals, but carrying her virgin's uniform which she would soon wear again. The Parfaites stripped her of her robe, and she was stretched nude across a wooden flogging frame. Chains were fastened tightly to her legs and arms, and her wrists, ankles and waist were strapped to her punishment frame with cruel leather thongs. Finally, she was gagged with a steel harness.

When this was complete, the Parfaites tore her robe of petals, and with sweeping gestures, scattered the petals over her naked body. And then the flogging began. The Parfaite Leandra stepped forward, for it was she whom Harriet had allegedly offended, accompanied by Hera, who as Harriet's housemistress had the honour or obligation to deliver the first stroke. Hera was dressed in her finest robe, while Leandra was nude, save for a mask of bright feathers which covered her face and head all except for her eyes, giving her the aspect of a savage bird of prey. Jana had seen such a mask before, in the photograph on Greta's wall, in which a naked masked woman wielded her whip over a naked male on a dog-leash.

Hera carried her beloved birch, and at a nod from the Superior, raised it high and cracked it loudly across Harriet's buttocks. There was a gasp and a ripple of excitement amongst the audience, but Harriet herself made no sound. Hera then ceremonially handed the birch to the naked Parfaite, who continued the whipping with graceful strength, her taut muscles rippling beautifully at each stroke, until Harriet had received twenty-one merciless lashes. And still she did not even whimper. She was cut down, knelt, and kissed the whip that had flogged her, then the bare feet of her dominatrix, and bowed to the adepts.

She then turned and bowed to the assembly, and when

she picked up her uniform and walked naked and erect from the hall, the girls burst into spontaneous applause.

'That was awful,' said Jana to Erato. They were in Erato's cell, and both girls had their skirts up.

'Awesome, perhaps, not awful,' said Erato, fiercely rubbing Jana's nympha. 'The birch holds no terrors for me, nor does it for that whore Harriet.'

'Don't, Erato,' said Jana, 'I'm not in the mood. I've a lot on my mind.'

It was not so much the punishment that troubled her as the bird-plumage Leandra had worn, and the memory of Jocasta's visit to the secret door.

Erato took her hand away.

'Don't you want to do me, then?' she said hopefully.

'Of course I will, you chump.'

Jana busied her fingers on Erato's stiff clit, and received sighs of pleasure in return.

'That better?'

'Yes, oh yummy,' moaned Erato.

'What did you mean about the birch?'

'Oh, it comes of being Finnish. We birch each other in the sauna, and it's supposed to be medicinal, but sometimes it can be quite fierce. And fun. Oh, yes, that's nice. I won't be long. I'm so wet.'

'You are indeed. I didn't know you were Finnish. You sound as English as me.'

'English boarding school. But anyway, up in Northumberland, you people are half Finnish. Look at yourself, the same broad face and high cheekbones as me. We colonised you, and became the picts.'

'Oh, stuff.'

'It's true. We're all descended from Genghis Khan. That is why we are so hard.'

Jana laughed.

'And love the birch?'

'And love . . . the . . . birch . . . Oh, yes, yes. Thank you, thank you Jana, thank you! Are you sure you don't want me to . . .?'

'No, thank you. I've got a lot to think about just now.'

'Thinking, eh? Dangerous sport.'

'Well, I'm going to the library now. I want to look up some things.'

'The assistant won't be there.'

'Why not?'

'Don't you know? It's Harriet, she is the Mistress Librarian's slave. Another one of her forfeits.'

'I'll find what I need on my own.'

'No you won't. It's all arranged according to Harriet's system, which is no system at all. And if she's not there . . .'

But Harriet was there.

'Hello, Jana,' she chirped brightly, as Jana entered the musty library, breathing the sweet scents of leather and old wood.

'Harriet, I didn't expect to see you here.'

'Why ever not? It is my job. No rest for the wicked, you know.'

'But that terrible flogging . . .'

'What? Oh, my little lacing this morning. What a lark! That Leandra can't whip for toffee. Still, breaks the monotony, don't it? Are you looking for anything special?'

'No,' replied Jana carefully, 'I'm just browsing.'

'It's all jumbled up, and only I know where everything is,' said Harriet proudly. 'Anyway, half of it's in Latin, and the other half in Greek. Pretty pictures, though. But you might find something to interest you over here.'

She showed Jana into a dark alcove where most of the books were in English.

'Thank you very much,' said Jana, but Harriet showed no sign of going away. She stood leaning against the ceiling-high bookcase, with an impish grin on her face, stroking her hair and holding her hand on her pubis.

'See anything interesting?' she said.

At that moment, a title caught her eye. Gold embossed on an old leather spine, it read: *Witches of Northumberland*.

'Well, well,' said Jana, reaching for the book and withdrawing it from the shelf. 'May I borrow it?'

'Of course. I don't see the point in books myself, they're so boring. All those words!'

151

'It's about my home county, in England.'

'Home? Your home is Maldona, the outside doesn't count.'

'I'm sentimental, I suppose, and curious.'

'Well then,' said Harriet slyly, 'aren't you curious to see my croup? All the other girls wanted to.'

'And did you let them see?'

'Of course.'

'I suppose I'd better have a look too.'

In fact, Jana was quite bursting with curiosity, and had been wondering how best to raise the subject.

'Come with me.'

Jana left the book by the door of the library, and followed Harriet who skipped merrily down the aisles to the little office at the very back of the chamber. Once there, she lost no time in stripping off her uniform, and stood naked in front of Jana, save for her shoes, stockings and suspender belt.

'Surely you are not permitted to be naked here,' said Jana.

'Poo! What are they going to do, whip me?' cried Harriet with a peal of tinkling laughter. 'I am just a whipping girl and I can do anything I want.'

Jana scrutinised the girl's body. It was well-muscled, tough rather than voluptuous, and skinny like a boy's, which went well with her pixie's face. The breasts were hard, and looked like a boy's breasts, with small nipples. Her mink was sparse and skimpy, but that served to emphasise the huge growth of her fount-lips, which were the biggest Jana had seen. They hung like tender pink meats, all wrinkled and shiny, and left no doubt that Harriet was all girl. Jana found herself attracted to this whore, as Erato had bitchily described her. She was a tough little hoyden, hard as nails, and radiating a sexual aura of dangerous innocence. The French would have called her *joli-laide*, meaning, literally, 'pretty and ugly', or in English, perhaps, 'tomboyish'.

'You like me?' said Harriet with a pout.

'Why, yes,' said Jana. Harriet stood in a shaft of sunlight

streaming from the skylight, and were it not for her under-things, would have seemed a Greek statue of some naiad or forest nymph. 'Yes, I do. Aren't you going to turn round and show me your bottom?'

'Come closer.'

Jana approached, and stood inches from the naked girl. Her nostrils filled with a rich, animal scent, the odour of horses and foxes. Harriet turned round, and Jana gazed at the crimson striations Leandra had painted with her birch-rods. She reached out and touched Harriet's tight little bottom, deeply reddened with the strokes of her lacing. Delicately, she ran her fingers across it, in awe at Harriet's endurance.

'Does that hurt?' she asked quickly.

'No,' laughed Harriet. 'But it's nice.'

Jana stroked Harriet all down her back and across her fesses, then on to the backs of her thighs, feeling the excitement swell in her own sex as she touched the smooth leathery skin of the flogged girl.

'Don't you want to diddle me?' said Harriet suddenly.

'What? I mean – here in the library?' stammered Jana in surprise. 'It's not very romantic.'

'Who said diddling was romantic? It's fun, that's what it is. Anyway if I went to your cell, that bitch Erato would know. She thinks I'm a whore.'

'Are you?'

'Of course.'

Jana smiled; in truth, she felt her sex moistening rapidly.

'All right, I'll diddle you, Harriet.'

'Oh, I'm so glad! Everybody else has. But it's you I really, scrumptiously fancy, Jana. Ever since I saw your sweet bum take the first lacing from that pig Miriam. It's the sweetest bum in the whole world!'

'You sound like a whore. But you must do me in return.'

Harriet pirouetted round to face Jana, and her hand at once delved under her skirt. She clamped her fingers on Jana's nympha and began a fierce rubbing.

'Nice and wet,' she panted.

'Mmmm,' moaned Jana. 'You're very fast.'

Her own hand crept between Harriet's parted sex-lips, which were swollen and red and glistening with Harriet's gushing love-juice. Jana inched her fingers forward in search of Harriet's clitoris, which she imagined should be as stiff as her own, but suddenly felt lost inside those huge cunt-lips which enfolded her like a sea anemone.

'Just a minute,' said Jana.

'No,' said Harriet, guiding her hand inside her slit. 'Further up. I haven't got a nympha. You must go up . . . here, by the bone, a little over there . . . Ah! Ah! Ah! Ah! . . .'

Harriet's orgasm was as sudden as it was unexpected, and thrilled Jana so that her own belly shook in a warm, melting spasm a few seconds later, flooding her body with delicious relief from the doubts and tensions which had been gnawing at her mind since her trip to the secret door.

'I needed that,' she gasped. 'It was lovely. You're very good, Harriet.'

'Whores get to know things. I suppose you're wondering why I haven't a nympha.'

'I didn't like to ask. It's just that most of us in Maldona seem to be rather ripe in that area.'

'Well, it was cut off.'

'My God!'

'Clitoridectomy, it's called, or female circumcision.'

'That's barbaric!'

'I was living with barbarians, or rather, they kidnapped me from my father's house in El Aiun when I was eight or nine years old. They were a tribe of desert Tuareg – El Aiun in those days was the capital of the Spanish Sahara, which is now part of Morocco, and my father was an American Baptist missionary. A very unsuccessful one, I must say. The Tuareg kept me and made me their whore, and when my breasts grew and my mink sprouted, they circumcised me, so that I would not feel pleasure. It is the custom throughout West Africa, including the Maghreb. Well, eventually I was rescued by a platoon of the Spanish Foreign Legion, out hunting rebels, and they made me their whore, too. Jana, have you ever been fucked by twenty strong men, in your cunt and your bumhole, day after day for two months?'

'No.'

'I have. And do you know –' she put her lips on Jana's, in a kiss. '– I loved it. I had such power over those men. I was made to be a whore, to be fucked and open my legs to everybody, for I found that the rougher my treatment, the nicer they were to me afterwards. I wouldn't recommend it to everyone, but then not everyone is born a whore. And by that time, I didn't mind not having a nympha, because I had discovered the spot. The Grafenberg spot, or the G spot.'

'That is an amazing story,' said Jana weakly. 'But how did you get to Maldona?'

'I heard of it. You see, the communication lines here run down to Africa, not to the north. This isn't really Europe, it *is* Africa. I think of Maldona as the furthest outpost of the Sahara. The rest of Spain is a foreign country, and beyond the Pyrenees is another world. In the desert, I found that I was a whore, that I loved to be whipped and fucked like a beast, and that is why I came to Maldona. Didn't you?'

'My God,' said Jana.

'Well?'

'Yes, damn you. Yes, yes, yes.'

Harriet exploded with laugher.

'Don't forget to take your book,' she said. 'I know you'll find it interesting.'

Jana walked unsteadily to the library door, and picked up her book. She looked back, and saw Harriet, still a naked statue in the bright pool of sunlight, and all around her shadow.

'Just one thing,' cried Harriet. 'Never believe anything a whore tells you!'

Jana lay on her bed, daydreaming in the hour that remained before luncheon. She thought of the brilliant clarity of the desert, of lying helpless with her legs apart, to be fucked and fucked again in each of her holes by brutal, sweating men with olive skins. She sighed, and lifted her book. It fell open in the middle, where a folded paper, a bookmark, had lodged in it, and she was about to open the piece of paper to see whose it was, when a passage caught her eye and she sat up, wide awake. Her hands trembled as she read:

... one of the victims of popular rage was a widow named Jana Ardenne, the mother of seven children though not yet thirty years of age. She was alleged of calling herself by the witch's name Jana. In 1348 she was accused of conspiring with the Moorish Sultans of Andalusia to introduce the plague known as the Black Death into the County of Northumberland. Further, she was accused of adherence to an heretical sect of Maldon in Essex, founded by the forbidden Order of the Knights Templar for the enslavement of women, who became besotted enough to submit themselves to the most lustful cruelties and fearsome chastisements of their bare bodies with full willingness and consent.

The Ardenne woman was said to possess, in the form of a wax candle, the likeness of a membrum virile, either of the Caliph of Cordoba, or the Amir of Ubrique, and this manhood had two members, dark in hue, in token of the virility of the Moorish races. With this obscene device, she forced the virgins of the county to submit to the foulest violation of their chastity, and in addition, she introduced them to the barbarous indecency of uranism, or unnatural embraces of women, which they would commit in each other's view at their blasphemous ceremonies.

The deluded women would dance naked save for masks of bird feathers, whipping each other to a lustful frenzy with a four-thonged whip of white leather, in imitation of the German sect of Flagellants, and they held that the soul was a feathered bird, which would be released from its corporeal prison by the torment of the lash. As the flagellants danced, said Ardenne would flog the naked croups of new virgins, who were crouched like dogs, with the evil member lodged in *cunno et in ano*, and would caress them at the base of their spine with a feather, in the cleft of their posteriors, since they held this place to be the seat of the soul and all pleasure.

Refusing to abjure her sinfulness, said Jana Ardenne was sentenced to be put to death by whipping with a switch of rose branches, since she and her sinful acolytes would dance naked around the rose bush. She was strapped naked to the flogging post at the village green in Alnswick, with her obscene Moorish instrument fastened in her intimate places, to mock her lustfulness. Her male servant Aelfric, said to be her familiar in debauchery, was also the object of righteous popular wrath, but he fled, some thought to the Moorish lands of southern Spain, so she endured her punishment alone.

After she had taken so many strokes that the rose branches were denuded of thorns, she is said to have cried out that she was free, and the spirit appeared to leave her. Some of the village folk swore that at the moment of her expiring, two golden birds were seen to fly from her most intimate lady's place, toward the heavens.

Jana shuddered as she read. Alnswick, she thought, the place where I was born! She steeled herself and read further:

Little is known of the fate of Ardenne's children, except that, curiously, the manor of Alnswick was in a later century purchased by a wealthy merchant named Elias Ardenne, who had made his fortune in the manufacture of candles and metal hardwares. This was in the year 1767 or 1768. In addition to continuing his prosperous household trade, it seems that Mr Ardenne expanded his metallurgic trade to include the manufacture of chains, shackles, whips, and other awful instruments of correction for the slave trade between Africa and the Antillean islands, which throve at that time, and from supplying the vile traders of human merchandise it was an easy step to become such a trader himself, owning both the ships which carried the wretched cargo to their enslavement and also the prisons on the west coast of Africa in which they were confined prior to embarkation, and the restraining devices which served to confine them. Thus, by the time he purchased Alnswick, Elias Ardenne had made Newcastle upon Tyne a slave port, lesser known and smaller than Liverpool or Bristol, but just as vigorous in its pursuit of ill-gotten profit, and had himself become the richest man in the County of Northumberland.

Jana snapped the book shut. My God, she thought numbly, Elias Ardenne was the name of my ancestor, my great-something grandfather. She lay down and wiped her brow of sweat, her heart racing. Had Harriet known what I would find here? Why else did she point me to that bookshelf? And to what purpose?

Her hand fell on the folded bookmark which had fallen from the book at that fateful page, and she picked it up. There was handwriting on the outside: TO JANE ARDENNE, KNOWN AS JANA. And the handwriting was unmistakable. It was Cassie's.

Sweet Jane, or Jana, for I'm sure that's what they've called you, I knew you'd come to Maldona, and I knew you'd find this book – this very page.

At first, Maldona seems strange, until you realise that Maldona is the real world, or rather, a distillation of it, clear and pure, with all pretence and façade stripped away from its crystal heart of naked power and naked submission – nothing else. They're coming for me now, for I've been sentenced to a Perfect Beating, and you're not supposed to survive that. I've found out too much – silly old inquisitive me! One thing is that if you cry 'I go down' it doesn't work. The whipping stops – but you don't leave Maldona.

They take you somewhere, somewhere awful, underneath ... I'm not sure. The terrible thing is, I know
I belong here, whatever they do to me, for Maldona
is life, and you belong here too, Jana: you must
achieve perfection the hard way. The easy way to
perfection lies behind the locked door. Beware of
Leand ...

And there it ended. Cassie had stopped writing because
she heard their steps clattering through the library, coming
for her, and she had hidden her letter in a place where
Jana, one day or another, would be sure to look.

Suddenly Jana's trembling turned to an icy feeling of
perfect control. Her fear of what had passed centuries ago,
and of what was to happen to her, now, was still within
her, but it had dwindled to a little point of light far away,
as though she were observing it through a glass.

If Cassie had survived her Perfect Beating, or if she had
cried 'I go down', either way, she must still be in Maldona.
Had she survived the beating and gone to achieve perfection; was enduring a Perfect Beating *part of* that achieve-
ment? Cassie's name was no longer Cassie, of course, but
now more than ever, Jana wanted to find her.

11

Leandra

Jana was summoned to appear before the assembly of Parfaites, and Erato, as promised, gave her a lacing of such artistry that the blossoms on her whipped croup resembled the flower of a beating endured long before. They met, as arranged, in the sauna after Jana's parade.

'At last,' said Erato, pink and perspiring in the scented heat. 'Well, how did it go? Did my ruse work?'

'It worked.'

'Whoopee! So you got Leandra.'

'Yes,' said Jana softly, 'I got, as you put it, Leandra.'

'What happened? Tell me everything.'

'Erato, I don't think that is fitting.'

'I knew it,' sighed Erato. 'You are going to grow away from me, sweet Jana. Already you feel yourself superior.'

'No, Erato. You will always be my friend. It is just that it's a private thing. You understand.'

'Unfortunately, I do. Oh well, that's the game. I hope your lovely back isn't a private thing, because I intend to scrub it with my loofah.'

Jana smiled, and stroked Erato's thigh.

'No, it's not a private thing, not to you, silly. So scrub me.'

And as she felt the pleasant massage of her back, and the dry, fierce heat of the sauna opened her pores and made the sweat flow, Jana found herself daydreaming about the strange new world she had just entered . . .

Jana was nervous as she knocked on the door of the Parfaites' hall, and the haughtiness of the virgin, wearing the yellow rosette of Allemagne, who admitted her, did not ease her nervousness. She was taken to an apodyterium, where she was ordered to take off her uniform, and was then led naked and barefoot into a wood-panelled chamber, where all twenty-one of the Corps of Parfaites sat at a crescent table with their whips coiled before them. Some looked at her with interest, others with (perhaps feigned) indifference. Kobo had felt obliged to give her instruction: that ambitious Parfaites were eager to acquire new, promising slaves, while the seniors were more loath to fuel the intrigues of the harem they already possessed, but would sometimes make a play for a new virgin simply to stop a rival taking her. All the Parfaites were naked, save for their finery of golden chains, and their bird-masks of gaudy plumage, and suddenly Jana started, for she knew the answer to the question that had nagged her. Harriet's body was strangely familiar under her caress in the library. She knew she had seen that lithe young colt before, and now, seeing the Parfaites arrayed like eagles, it came to her. Harriet had been the masked, naked domina holding the man on her leash, in Harry's photograph!

'Well, virgin? Answer,' rapped the convener.

'I . . . didn't hear?' stammered Jana.

'Who dares disturb the serenity of the Parfaites?' thundered the convener.

'Oh . . . a virgin, seeking discipline.'

'Whence come you, virgin?'

'From the Auberge d'Angleterre.'

'Do you long to obey a Parfaite maiden? To bend your will to hers, to bare your body to her chastisement, to serve her body and soul?'

'I do.'

'Show your face, virgin.'

Jana lifted her bowed head, and gazed straight in front, thrusting her breasts proudly forward and standing at ramrod attention. In the corner of her eye she saw Leandra at the far end of the table; despite her mask, her body's proud magnificence was unmistakable. Leandra gazed out the window with lips pursed and fingers drumming, studiously not noticing Jana. The Parfaites scrutinised her for what seemed an age, and she prayed that Leandra would look. They began to scribble notes which were picked up by the German girl who passed them to the convener. They were questions, which the convener solemnly read out, and were much as Kobo had led her to expect, portentous but banal queries abut the rules and ethos of Maldona which required a safe but speedy response. Her confidence grew as she fielded the questions with ease and even eloquence, but Leandra's proud face remained a mask of indifference.

Suddenly, she saw Leandra scribble a note, which was passed to the convener, who read it, and ordered, 'Turn around, virgin, and show your hindquarters.'

Jana thankfully swivelled so that her back was presented to the company.

There was a rustle of interested voices:

'. . . no stranger to discipline . . .'

'. . . quite a flogging . . .'

'. . . tough . . .'

'. . . marks from outside . . .'

When she was ordered to turn and face the company again, she saw that fifteen of the Parfaites had uncoiled their whips and let them dangle off the table in front of Jana. And one of them was Leandra!

'Fifteen Parfaite maidens are willing to put you to the test, virgin,' said the convener. 'You will wait in the apodyterium while we deliberate.'

Suddenly a low, thrilling contralto voice murmured, 'Wait.' Leandra wrote something, and did not give the note to the messenger, but passed it one by one all down the line of Parfaites, leaving out the convener. Each of them studied it with varying degrees of disquiet while Leandra's big cool eyes rested with smiling indifference on Jana's trembling body. When the note had been read by all, the Parfaites exchanged nervous looks, and, one by one, every whip was withdrawn and coiled again, except for Leandra's. The convener spoke again, and finally.

'The virgin Jana will be tested by the Parfaite maiden Leandra alone,' she said drily. Leandra stood, and swept out of the room, glancing at no one else, least of all the virgin Jana.

Leandra's apartments lay at the very top of the vast, rambling edifice of the Auberge des Parfaites, as the Parfaites' hall was named. Jana was admitted by the knight Jason, gorgeously attired, and just as arrogant as when he had disturbed Kobo and Jana in the fountain. Jana found herself in an apartment furnished with cool simplicity, contemporary in style apart from the many candlesticks, with big French windows, opening on to a balcony enclosed by a turreted wall. Beyond the balcony stretched a panorama of mountains and plains, shimmering purple in the heat haze. Jason led Jana wordlessly to the French windows, then withdrew, pouting.

Nude, on a reclining chair, sat Leandra, her body glistening in the bright sun, and her gold chains a cascade of glittering light. Beside her on the table was a tall cool drink, and her lips dribbled smoke from a fragrant cigarette. She was occupied in dabbing varnish on her long toenails. Jana realised with surprise that she had not even thought of a cigarette for ages. But she could have used one now, for the sight of Leandra's nude body close up was electrifying.

Jana had never seen a female bodybuilder before, except in photographs, where the forced poses to emphasise pumped muscle and striations made the women look unnatural. But now, looking at Leandra, she wondered how a woman could be thought beautiful without that sleek, swelling strength. Every muscle was a sculpture, from proud, firm breasts to flat belly and deliciously tensed thighs, and at each breath her whole body rippled sensuously, the muscles playing one on the other to make Leandra a symphony of power and beauty. Jana fell to her knees.

Leandra looked up, expressionless, then resumed her nail-painting, playfully flexing her lovely biceps or blowing blue smoke, as though to furnish the sky with clouds. Jana perspired in her uniform. She longed to be naked with Leandra, to touch her and kiss her bare body.

'You are said to be a good wrestler,' said Leandra, her voice soft as a flute.

'I believe I have mastered the techniques of *pankration*, Mistress.'

'Hmmm. That is not dishonourable. So you can kick and gouge. Would you like to fight me?'

'Yes, Mistress.'

Leandra's laugh was scornful music.

'But you would be beaten. I would hurt you.'

'That is why, Mistress.'

Now, Leandra looked at Jana, with an amused curl to her lips.

'Do you wish to receive my guidance?'

'Yes, Mistress.'

'You must be my slave in all things. Your duties shall be whatever I choose, and your obedience must be absolute.'

'In that way I shall approach perfection, Mistress.'

'I have seen that your body is no stranger to punishment.'

'My body is nothing, Mistress. It lives to submit to you.'

'Prettily put. You have a fine body, no stranger to the lash, and a fine tongue in you too. But can you hold your tongue when your naked croup feels the kiss of the whip?'

'Yes, Mistress,' said Jana fiercely.

'We shall see,' drawled Leandra. 'In the meantime, let us put your slave's tongue to happier uses.'

She rang a little bell, and Jason appeared smartly.

'The palette of rouge,' Leandra ordered, and Jason fetched a tray bearing pots of paint in different shades of red. He waited expectantly, but Leandra dismissed him.

'I do not need you, Jason,' she said. 'The virgin can dress me.'

Jason scowled and flushed, he bowed stiffly, before retreating.

Leandra pointed to one of the pots of rouge, a fiery scarlet. 'Adorn me, virgin,' she said. 'Here –' she indicated the brown cupolas of her nipples '– and here.' She touched the dark petals of her sex.

'There is no brush, Mistress.'

'You have a tongue, girl!'

Jana bent down and dipped her tongue in the paintpot,

finding a taste of bitter fruit. She squatted and positioned her head by Leandra's breasts, then touched the right nipple with her tongue. It was as big as her own, and rose as high as a thumb, with a wide areola that was covered in little brown pinheads that felt sandy on Jana's tongue as she licked. Leandra tasted sweet, like flowers. Jana felt her excitement and pleasure growing under Jana's tonguing, with the smeared red paint. She returned to the pot for generous replenishments until both Leandra's stiff nipples gleamed a gaudy scarlet, like her toenails.

'Now,' said Leandra, 'my lady's place. The lips first, and then perhaps a butterfly or a little flower on my mount, and then of course my little nympha must be well rouged.'

Heady with the lush scent of her mistress's body, Jana bent to her task, damp with sweat under her uniform, and her sex wet with excitement. Tenderly, Jana licked the ripe cunt-lips, which swelled visibly at her tonguing. By mistake, her tongue slipped inside Leandra's moist slit, and she tasted delicious salty love-juice for a moment. Leandra's hips gave a little jerk.

'You must adorn me thoroughly,' she said. 'Not one part of my fount must go without rouge.'

Jana licked firmly, applying the paint in lavish smears, and now her tongue could not help but penetrate Leandra's quivering cunt, because the juice gushed from her slit and made the inside of her thighs and fesses glisten.

'I hear you are fond of the library,' said Leandra suddenly.

'Why, yes, Mistress. One can learn such a lot from libraries.'

'Well, keep me informed of anything interesting. It is your duty.'

Was that a veiled threat? Jana did not care as her tongue flickered over the swollen lips of Leandra's cunt, causing her whole pelvis to writhe sinuously. Emboldened, Jana lowered her mouth, and with her nose pressed into Leandra's oily gash, her tongue found the anus bud and tickled her there.

'How thoughtful,' panted Leandra, 'yes, she would like some rouge too.'

Jana applied her tongue to the little wrinkled hillock, and slipped the tip inside, which made Leandra gasp.

'That's nice. Go on,' said Leandra, and stroked Jana's hair. Jana tongued Leandra's anus and penetrated the hole to a depth of an inch, smiling as Leandra squeezed her with her powerful sphincter.

'I think my nympha is ready,' said Leandra, unsteadily lighting another cigarette. 'Give her a little rouge.'

As Jana put her mouth to Leandra's semi-stiff clit, the older girl lifted her thighs and locked them around Jana's head, pressing her face against her wet cunt. The nympha stiffened abruptly and Jana felt it push all the way into her mouth, filling her with its tingling wet hardness. She gasped, and sucked the quivering stiff muscle like a lovely moist sweetmeat.

'Mmmm,' said Leandra thoughtfully. 'Go on.'

Jana needed no encouragement. Her own cunt felt as though it were melting into a pool of warm liquid as she sucked the Parfaite's distended clitoris. She felt Leandra's belly tremble, and the steel thighs around Jana's neck began to shake as Leandra's fount became a river of love-oil gushing over Jana's vigorously working lips.

'Aah,' said Leandra softly, 'Aaaah.'

Her thighs shuddered and relaxed, releasing Jana from their grasp.

At that moment Jason reappeared.

'Mistress –'

He stopped and his eyes traversed the scene: Leandra's flushed face wet thighs and quivering belly, and Jana, kneeling, her mouth smeared with rouge and dripping with the Parfaite's glistening love-oil.

'What is it now, slave?' drawled Leandra, making no attempt to hide her stiff clitoris and wet cunt from the eyes of the male.

'The package from Casablanca –'

'You disturb me for that?'

'Mistress, I thought it was –'

'I think, Jason, and you obey. But since you are here, observe how prettily the virgin has adorned me.'

166

Jason's eyes glowed with jealousy.

'In certain matters, a girl makes the best slave. Agreed, Jason?'

'Yes, Mistress,' he replied sullenly.

Leandra blew smoke at him.

'But then, in certain matters, not. You may denude yourself, slave.'

'Before the girl?'

'Of course before the girl.'

Slowly, Jason removed his tunic, and stood naked except for a silvery g-string, revealing a musculature as massive and supple as Leandra's own. His body was smooth and hairless, and gleamed proudly in the sunlight, making Jana feel out of place in her stuffy uniform.

'I said denude yourself, or do you need a thrashing to cleanse your ears?'

Jason hooked his thumbs inside the waist of his g-string and pulled the garment away from his body, to reveal a pubis that was shaved like his Parfaite's, and a huge, hairless penis that hung limp and menacing between the mountains of his thigh muscles. Jana gasped in astonishment, for she had never seen a man's cock like it. It glistened like a huge red nympha, for the bare crimson membrane of the bulb did not give way to the soft skin protecting the shaft of the penis. Rather, the flesh was skinned, raw and bare all the way down to the balls.

Leandra saw Jana's eyes on Jason's skinned cock, and laughed.

'My slaves,' she said, 'are circumcised, not in the European way, but according to the African rite. Not just the foreskin, but the whole skin of the penis is removed. The effect is to reduce the sensitivity of the nerve ends, and enable the male to pleasure his mistress for ages and ages before he must spurt his seed. Always assuming the male is in a state of excitement, which, regrettably, does not seem to be the case here. I think a demonstration would be instructive, so please see to the matter, Jana.'

Leandra stretched herself and yawned, lazily observing Jana as she approached the naked male. Kneeling, Jana took the tip of the magnificent cock between her lips, trying to feign a cool indifference. She tongued his peehole until she felt the shaft tremble and stiffen, and then with a swift gulping motion, took the cock all the way to her throat and with rapid darting movements began to suck it vigorously.

'Prettily done,' cried Leandra.

It was hard and smooth, like icing on a cake, and she wanted to bite into it and swallow the sweet morsels. But as the cock rose to full, throbbing stiffness, she had to widen her mouth to accommodate it, and clutch Jason's bare buttocks to steady herself. Jason's engorged penis stuck out from his thighs like a lance, and she longed to feel its sultry man-meat enter her wet cunt and pleasure her with a hard fucking, to bounce her body against him like a doll as he fucked her for ages and ages . . .

It was not to be.

'Enough,' rapped Leandra. 'Jason is now in a manly state, and can fuck me.'

At once, Jana disengaged, and Jason leapt obediently to place his stiff cock over Leandra's open sex. He plunged inside her pink, wet slit, so that with his thrusts, the shaft of his penis rubbed against her hard fount. And as he fucked her, with fierce slaps of his thighs on hers and a rapid pumping of his clenched buttocks, it seemed as though cock and clitoris were two appendages of the same engorged limb.

Leandra did not move or tremble as she was fucked, but sipped her drink with a faint smile on her flushed face, and seemed to be watching Jana rather than her stud. Jana could not take her eyes off the frantic thrusting of the livid red cock in Leandra's swollen gash, and she was so wet in her own cunt that she thought she would burst. Suddenly, Leandra's hand snaked out and reached under Jana's skirt. Jana felt cool fingers touch her cunt-lips, and sighed with joy, then parted her thighs to let Leandra touch her nympha, which was already stiff and tingling. Leandra gently squeezed and tickled the swollen clit, until Jana moaned.

'You are very wet, girl,' said Leandra. 'And how big and stiff your *nympha* stands! Hmmm.'

Deliberately, thoughtfully, she proceeded to masturbate Jana with firm, expert strokes, until Jana knew she was near her plateau and would shortly come if the maddening pleasure continued. But as though she sensed this, Leandra withdrew her hand and said, 'It seems wrong that a poor *Parfaite* should be left out of all this excitement,' as though the thrusting cock of the male who served her belonged to some unimportant automaton. 'My little *nympha* is standing up all forlorn, and I think she would feel at home in your nice wet cunt, Jana, so you will therefore straddle me.' She pushed Jason off-handedly away, and his gleaming raw cock emerged from her slit with a loud plop. Jana obediently pressed her cunt to Leandra's, getting on top of the prone woman, and as she did so Leandra indicated Jana's buttocks to Jason.

Jana said 'Mmm!' as Jason's strong hands grasped her hips, forcing her down hard so that Leandra's swollen *nympha* penetrated her gash like a penis. Then she felt her buttocks forced apart, and the pressure of Jason's cock on her anus bud, and suddenly the shaft was inside her, sliding easily all the way into her squirming anus with its lubrication of Leandra's love fluid. Jason rammed her body up and down on Leandra's clit, matching the vigorous thrusts of Leandra's writhing pelvis, and at the same time he followed the rhythm with a fierce arse-fucking.

Her cunt gushed uncontrollably, and her pleasure at this double fucking was so intense she felt like howling, but she managed to control herself, for she had a sly plan to show off her *prowess* to her mistress.

Relentlessly, mischievously, she squeezed her practised sphincter on Jason's pumping cock, giving him a stimulation he had not expected from a mere virgin. He grunted in surprise as her elastic anus milked his throbbing penis, sucking it into her and trapping it so that her innermost fundament rubbed and squeezed his sensitive peehole.

Jana knew it would not be long before she reached her own climax, so intense were the spasms that shook her at

169

each slap of Leandra's nympha against hers, so she concentrated on the task of milking Jason's balls of every last drop of sperm. He grunted more and more harshly as though in protest; his hands, his belly and thighs, and his whole body trembled as though wracked with pain, and then the first hot drop spat from his cock into her anus, and his cock shuddered and bucked as the powerful jet spurted fiercely into her, as Jason cried out and mewled half in ecstasy and half in fury at what she had wrung from him. The flood of his hot seed in her squeezing anus tipped Jana over the giddy edge of pleasure, and she cried long and loud as she let the sweetness of orgasm wash over her. To her surprise and joy, at the end of her ululation, Leandra arched her back and let out a single, piercing yelp as her belly convulsed under Jana's sticky thighs.

They were all breathless. Jason moaned as Jana's sphincter expelled his squishy soft penis from her anus, his powers of endurance having been defeated by Jana's ruthless milking. Jana hoped he would see the humour of the situation, but suspected that, like most men, he wouldn't.

'*You* didn't last long, Jason,' mocked Leandra.

There was a loud knock on the door.

'Well, go and open it, Jason, if you have the strength,' she said. 'I have to give one of my girls a lesson in moral philosophy. What a busy life!'

Jason hurriedly dressed and went to open the door, while Jana smoothed her rumpled uniform and patted her hair. There were footsteps, and the new arrival entered, to kneel before Leandra.

'I dare say you know each other,' said Leandra nonchalantly.

It was Kobo.

'Jana is my newest acquisition, Kobo,' continued the Parfaite.

'Congratulations, virgin,' said Kobo sullenly.

'Oh, thank you, Mistress,' cried Jana, and kissed Leandra's feet.

'Before you go, Jana, show me those lovely fesses once more, those wonderful globes that can bewitch Jason into giving his sperm so very quickly.'

Jana lifted her skirt, and in full view of the others' jealous eyes, Leandra planted a full kiss on her bared bottom, and then, with her nose rubbing Jana's cleft, tongued her bum-hole for a full minute.

'Mmmm,' said Leandra, licking her lips, 'that is a good lesson in moral philosophy, isn't it, Kobo?'

'If you say so, Mistress,' replied the prefect.

'So you must wish to imbibe wisdom at the same source.'

'I . . . yes, Mistress.'

'Then kiss your virgin as I have done.'

Jana presented her fesses to Kobo, who kissed her anus bud, and then put her tongue inside it as her lips caressed Jana's cheeks. Jana thrilled, for it was a real kiss: to Kobo, obedience had to be heartfelt.

At last, Jana was dismissed, knelt before Leandra, and was escorted to the door by Jason. When they were in the apartment, and out of sight, she suddenly put her arm round his waist and kissed him full on the rosebud lips, her other hand tightly grasping his balls. He flinched, and took a step back, dislodging a piece of paper from the table, which fluttered to the floor, but he did not resist, and after a while, answered Jana's kiss with his own. Their tongues met and wrestled for a little while before, breathless, she broke away, pleased that she could feel another stirring in his cock.

'Thank you, Jason,' she said, 'it was very nice.'

'I obey Leandra's orders,' he said stiffly.

'Next time, perhaps she will order you to fuck me in my fount. I should like that.'

'Perhaps,' he said, embarrassed, and opened the door.

Jana automatically tidied up the paper that had fallen, and found that it was still in her hand when she emerged into the sunlight. She read, 'This virgin is mine. I shall fight and destroy any of my sisters who tries to take her from me.'

It was the note Leandra had passed round the assembly of Parfaites.

171

12

The Challenge

'Well, are you happy?' said Erato, as she laced Jana's back with the birch twigs. The two girls poured with sweat as they took turns at throwing more water on the stove of the sauna, gasping with pleasure as the wall of heat struck their bodies and the steam hissed like an angry dragon.

'Yes, I am,' said Jana. 'But you did not tell me Kobo was one of Leandra's slaves.'

'No point in muddying waters. Cross bridges when you come to them, and all that. Did she lace you?'

'Not yet.'

'She will.'

'I hope so.'

Erato laughed.

'Funny, really, how we come to long for it, yet are frightened too. I suppose that is the excitement: to tempt pain, to endure it, to conquer it. When I was in London, I got into what they called the "scene", groups who would meet to dress up as schoolgirls and schoolboys, masters and mistresses, and then beat each other for imagined misdeeds. Some of our scenarios were quite subtle and intricate, and the border between life and play-acting became blurred. But it was only play-acting, after all. Maldona is for real, and that is why I was drawn here. Beneath our delightful corsetry of rules, punishment means punishment.'

The door opened, and Sylvie entered, wearing only her unlawful turquoise panties, which she took off and politely folded inside her towel, before sitting at Erato's feet on the lowest, coolest bench.

'Look at Sylvie, for example,' Erato went on. 'Every day

she is caned by Miriam for wearing her panties when she shouldn't – earning us an extra thrashing into the bargain, the little slut – and yet she continues to offend. What is the conclusion?'

'Sylvie is asking for it,' said Jana. 'She wants to be punished.'

'Why shouldn't I wear what I please?' squealed Sylvie.

'Because it is against the rules. Ergo, you want to be beaten, and moreover, you want to be beaten by Miriam. For that is the only way she can show you affection.'

'No! I hate the lash! You are a beast to say such things!'

'Everybody knows about you and Miriam,' sneered Erato, quite angry now. 'She loves nice red hair and nice red marks. You won't be the last, Sylvie.'

'Liar!'

'Is that a challenge?' asked Erato, flexing her thick biceps in Sylvie's face. 'Do you want to wrestle in the rules of *pankration*? How I'd love to strangle your scrawny little neck into a submission.'

'I'm going to tell Miriam on you!' cried Sylvie.

'What's that? A sneak, a grass? Grasses need to be taught a lesson,' hissed Erato, and without warning threw herself on Sylvie, pinioning her with her powerful thighs around her breasts, and forcing her legs apart.

'Ow! Get off!' squealed Sylvie.

Erato held her legs open so that her sex was defenceless and spread wide. Jana was curious to see the tip of a gold chain protruding from the lips of her fount.

'I knew it,' said Erato. 'Reach into that little honeypot and see what you find, Jana.'

Jana put her fingers in Sylvie's fount and followed the little chain inside her squirming slit. She felt hard little ball-bearings and, to her surprise, Sylvie's fount was quite moist; she tugged on the chain, and out popped a set of four balls, not of metal, but of oily teak.

'Miriam makes her wear slave balls, to remind her during the day of all the sucking and diddling they get up to at night, and keep her fount well moistened. Isn't that right, Sylvie, you whore?'

'Give me back my things, you bitch! Let me go!'

'This is all against the rules,' said Jana sternly. 'I know your game, Sylvie. You want the slut Miriam to lace you, but a proper beating has to be formal. Too many, and tongues would wag. So you arrange it that every day you can get a casual corporal's beating – and we suffer because of your lust!'

'That's libel!' cried Sylvie. 'Stop that, Jana, you beast!'

Jana had her hand well inside Sylvie's fount, and was thrusting her fingers firmly in and out of the wet slit, while kneading her trembling little nympha.

'No it isn't, it's slander,' corrected Erato. 'And anyway it's true, isn't it?'

'No . . . no . . .' moaned Sylvie, her pelvis writhing now under the vigorous massage of Jana's fingers.

Erato poured a bucket of water on to the stove, and the heat flattened them with its scalding ferocity.

'It's too hot! gasped Sylvie.

'Not as hot as your croup will be after I've birched you,' snarled Erato.

'Pah!' said Sylvie defiantly. 'Call that a birch? It's a sauna toy.'

Erato flipped her roughly on to her belly so that her bottom was high in the air, and Jana kept up her fist-fucking of the groaning girl as Erato scooped up six bundles of the light sauna birch twigs.

'With six of them, you won't find it too playful,' she said, and as Jana held down the wriggling Sylvie, she began to lash Sylvie's squirming naked bottom with the bush of birch twigs. Jana implacably masturbated the helpless girl as the blows rained down in rapid succession on her buttocks, raising a crimson blush on the naked skin, and Sylvie's squirming became wilder, her moans louder and more piteous.

'No! No! Oh, God! Faster, harder,' squealed Sylvie as the stinging strokes of the birch cascaded on her bottom. 'Oh, I hate you! Oh, birch me, you're better than Miriam, you horrid bitch. Oh, diddle my nympha, feel how stiff she is, you're rotten, that's what you are, Jana, fuck me in my wet fount, Oh, God, I'm going to . . .'

The door opened at the moment the writhing Sylvie cried out in tormented orgasm, her sex bouncing on Jana's merciless fingers, and her bottom leaping up to meet the birch's kiss.

'*What* is going on?' cried a voice.

A dark body was dimly visible through the clouds of steam, but the voice was unmistakable. It was Kobo.

'Erato birched my fesses, while Jana diddled me, and I didn't want them to!' whined Sylvie. 'It was a cruel assault.'

'That is most unlawful,' said Kobo severely. 'But ... what are these?'

She picked up Sylvie's slave balls from the bench.

'Slave balls,' she continued in a puzzled tone, 'may only be worn on the orders of a Parfaite. Your Parfaite, Erato, does not favour such gewgaws, I know. They cannot, of course, be yours, Jana, for you have yet to merit such adornments from Leandra. So, Sylvie, they must be yours. And you have no Parfaite.'

'Erato forced them on me!' sobbed Sylvie.

'Liar!' cried Jana, furious.

'Is that true, Erato?' demanded Kobo.

'You wouldn't believe me anyway, Kobo,' sneered Erato. 'You want any excuse to lace me.'

'I did it,' cried Jana, desperate to protect her friend. 'It's my fault. I diddled her, yes, but she asked for it, and took unlawful pleasure.'

Kobo abruptly put her hand on Sylvie's fount, and rubbed the engorged lips.

'You are wet, Sylvie,' she said, 'and your nympha is stiff. Does Jana tell true?'

'No, I swear,' pleaded Sylvie.

'The slave balls are Miriam's,' Jana cried out crossly.

Erato hissed at her to be silent, but it was too late.

Kobo stared in cold fury.

'You make a serious accusation against your corporal.'

'It is true,' said Jana. 'Sylvie is unlawfully her slave. She flouts the rules by wearing her panties on ordinary days, so that Miriam has an excuse to lace her for her pleasure, in excess of what is proper.'

Kobo spied a corner of turquoise peeping from under Sylvie's towel, and removed the panties.

'Yours, Sylvie?' she accused. Sylvie nodded miserably.

'This is a complicated and disgraceful affair,' said Kobo. 'You are lucky we are all from the same auberge, so that although we are outside Angleterre, I may bring the matter before our housemistress. Otherwise the Parfaites would be involved. Tomorrow morning I shall take you before Hera. For the meantime, I am not going to let you spoil my sauna. You three can cool off under a good icy shower, until I am finished, while I sit and think of the pleasure I'll have lacing all three of your juicy bare croups lined up in a row.'

With Sylvie sobbing quietly, the three girls trooped obediently to the cold shower, and stood for over half an hour under the freezing spray before Kobo, in more relaxed mood, came to join them. Erato, Jana and Sylvie were blue with cold and their teeth chattered.

'How cosy I feel,' said Kobo, gloating. 'There is nothing like a good sauna. I think you may soap me before I release you, girls.'

Three pairs of shivering hands applied scented soap to Kobo's body, and Jana forgot her discomfort as she marvelled at the suppleness of her curved figure, and the hard rippling muscles underneath the satin skin. Casually, she let her hand slip between Kobo's legs, and felt her tense, but not resist. She rubbed the inside of Kobo's thighs with the soap cake, and as Kobo gently parted her legs, put her soapy fingers firmly on the hot skin of Kobo's mons. Kobo gave a little sigh; Erato and Sylvie were shivering with cold, and half-heartedly soaping her back and legs, so Jana let her fingers slide to the lips of Kobo's fount, and rubbed them, while her hand slipped easily inside Kobo's slit.

'How I love to watch a girl's naked bottom squirm under my lash,' murmured Kobo dreamily. 'I'll really make you jerk, Erato. You would do the same to me, I know.'

'Yes, Kobo. It is the game.'

'And I am the winner, because I am more beautiful than any,' purred Kobo.

Kobo's fount was hot and oily, and what, for Jana, had begun as a game, now became in all seriousness, an exercise in power. So, boldly, Jana pressed Kobo's stiff clitoris, and tweaked the throbbing acorn firmly.

To her surprise, Kobo's body jumped and stiffened, and the black girl's magnificent muscles became as rigid as a statue.

'Aah!' howled Kobo, a short, staccato burst that drowned the rattling noise of the shower. The merest touch of her clitoris, and she had climaxed at once!

'Well,' panted Kobo, 'that will do. You are dismissed. Oh, Jana – just one thing.'

Jana turned, and saw Kobo's eyes piercing and malicious.

'You are very good at soaping.'

'Thank you,' said Jana coolly.

'I hope you are as good at taking my lash, tomorrow.'

'I shall aim to give satisfaction, Kobo.'

'Just don't get any ideas that because Leandra's taken you, one day you might have *my* bottom squirming for *you.*'

'Stranger things have happened, Kobo.'

'Pah! Tomorrow morning at Hera's office, after breakfast. Until then you will wear your gag and your restrainer.'

'It shall be my pleasure, Kobo,' said Jana, bowing, 'which is only fair, since I have already given you yours.'

'Why don't you take off the gag, Jana? No one will know,' said Erato.

Jana shook her head, and tapped her breast.

'Oh, *you* will know, is that it? Obedience, obedience.'

Jana nodded in agreement.

'Well, if you can't speak, you can listen. We're in trouble, all these accusations and counter-accusations. And the simplest way to solve a complicated situation is to punish everybody, regardless of legal niceties. So we're in for a sound thrashing, and it won't be given with kindness.'

Jana stared glumly at the floor of her cell. So this was what you got for telling the truth!

'However, there is a way out, cutting the Gordian knot, as it were. You, Jana, are the one who accused Miriam. So you must challenge her for her rank, in front of witnesses. That way, everything to do with this case will be purged by the outcome of your contest. Do you agree? Wouldn't you like to be my corporal?'

Jana mimed, what if I lose?

'If you lose, well, you lose your necklace and we'll get the lacing we would have got anyway. And you'll have to become a whipping girl for a bit. But you won't lose.'

Jana nodded eagerly, and gave the thumbs up sign. No, she wouldn't lose.

Hera picked up the slave balls from her desk and examined them with a frown.

'A complicated case, and a serious one. Don't smirk, Miriam. If I find that these items are indeed yours, you will pay dearly.'

Miriam stopped smiling. Only Kobo's lips curled in a faint grin of satisfaction, as the five girls, heads bowed, faced their housemistress.

'You have given me your explanations, and they are all at odds,' said Hera. 'Erato does not help her case by keeping silent.'

'Mistress, Jana speaks for me,' said Erato.

'Silence, virgin, you have had your chance to make a case. Sylvie maintains the slave balls were from you, Erato, and since you admit to assaulting her, it is logical to assume that Sylvie's accusations are correct, and that these improper items were . . . inserted into Sylvie's fount as part of that assault. However, Kobo has testified that Sylvie was taking pleasure in her treatment, that her fount was wet and her body in a state of excitement, so that she was in fact conspiring in this illicit punishment, for her own improper pleasure.'

'No!' wailed Sylvie.

Hera paused and, frowning, stroked her chin.

'Sylvie, Erato, and Jana, you will each receive fourteen strokes of the birch before the whole Auberge d'Angleterre,' she said. 'You shall be tied and gagged; I shall deliver the first two strokes, and Kobo and Miriam six each. You are dismissed.'

Jana's mouth was dry from the gag she had removed minutes before, so her voice was hoarse as she cried, 'Permission to speak, Mistress.'

'Granted.'

'I shall prove my case, Mistress. I hereby issue a challenge, and if I win, all accusations against myself and my fellow-accused are nullified.'

Hera smiled.

'So you wish to challenge Miriam for her rank? A smart move, Jana. You have certainly learned well of our rules.'

'No, Mistress.'

'Do not speak in riddles, virgin.'

Jana took a deep breath.

'Mistress, I hereby challenge Prefect Kobo.'

Kobo flushed in anger and astonishment, then bit her lip.

'Why, this is unheard of,' cried Hera. 'An untested virgin to challenge a prefect, before she has become corporal!'

'It is lawful, Mistress,' said Kobo stiffly. 'It is in the rules.'

Hera went to her bookshelf and took out a volume through which she leafed, frowning.

'You are right,' she said at last. 'And I find that in such cases, the loser takes all guilt upon herself, and must purge all punishments awarded. If Kobo loses, she will be punished by removal from her rank. If you lose, Jana, you must take the whippings of Sylvie and Erato as well as your own. Do you wish this challenge to stand?'

'Mistress,' said Jana coolly, 'a challenge given before witnesses, and where the offence has been committed outside the auberge, is a matter for all Maldona, and cannot be withdrawn.'

'She is right, Mistress,' said Kobo gruffly. 'Furthermore, the contest must be open to the witness of all Maldona.'

'Oh dear,' said Hera, 'I was hoping to keep it within the auberge, but I see that you are right. Very well, there is a

Special Day a week from tomorrow, so I shall see the Deputy Superior and arrange for your contest to be included in the programme. Are there any other questions, or may we consider the matter settled, as I fervently hope?'

'Just one thing, Mistress,' said Jana, looking coolly at the flustered face of Kobo.

'Yes?'

'May I have permission to remove my restrainer? I am just bursting to go to the fountain.'

By the rules, Jana was removed from Kobo's jurisdiction and placed under that of her newly-won Parfaite, Leandra. For the week before her contest, she was the property of Maldona, not of her auberge. The fact that Kobo was also Leandra's slave caused much merriment, at least to Leandra. The corridors trembled with gossip and the feverish laying of bets. The odds against Jana were very great, and only Erato had the courage to bet heavily on her friend, wagering all her accumulated necklaces save her last.

The Special Day was a day of fighting, and the Deputy Superior agreed that Jana and Kobo should be admitted. Personal contests, challenges and forfeits were all settled in the great ring, a miniature version of the bullring at Ronda, and unshaded from the merciless sun. The focal point of the day was the gruelling contest for the Grail of Maldona, fought among the three auberges. Three virgins from each auberge had to wrestle with all of their opponents, making six fights to each girl, and a total of twenty-seven matches in all, spaced throughout the day. The current holders of the Grail were the Auberge d'Allemagne, who, it seemed, were accustomed to winning. Jana noticed that the team of Angleterre included Harriet, and Ragusa from the surgery.

In the intervals of fighting, there were to be five Noble Beatings, one administered by the Deputy Superior herself, whose prowess with the whip was spoken of with awe. Jana looked forward eagerly to the day, not least because she would at last see Maldona herself, as she presented the

Grail to the team from the winning auberge. There was her own contest, of course, which she intended to win, and the high point of the occasion was the contest between Leandra and Erato's Parfaite, Circe.

The cause of the fight might not be known. Nevertheless it was rumoured that Leandra had delivered some deadly insult to Circe, her rival, provoking her unavoidably to a challenge. The loser in such a contest took a whipping from her conqueror, in full view of Maldona's assembly, and of course Maldona herself. After she had been whipped, the loser was then required to kiss the victor's feet and swear obeisance, handing over her whip and mask of plumage. It seemed that a Parfaite thus defeated generally took her whipping, but cried 'I go down!' rather than endure crueller humiliation. However, Jana had no doubt at all that Leandra would be the victor, and that Erato would join Jana as her slave.

Kobo treated her very civilly in the days of preparation, and watched her strenuous training with weights and springs, smiling wryly, almost in pity. Jana knew this was a tactic designed to wear down her resolve, but could not help wondering in moments of tiredness whether her confidence was unfounded.

'Don't worry,' she told Erato. 'I know how I shall beat Kobo. She has an Achilles Heel, only it isn't her heel, if you follow me.'

13

Jason's Wager

Jana took to visiting the library often, drawn either by her love of books, or her amusement at the girl Harriet and her fondness for 'diddling', as she quaintly put it. She did her best to give the whipping girl her simple pleasure, and did not mention the book to which Harriet had directed her, hoping that, if it had indeed been a strange, deliberate scheme, Harriet would reveal something more in good time. And reveal she did.

One day, Jana found herself browsing in a stack of books that were bound collections of handwritten documents, all in what seemed to be Greek. They were a jumble of notes, essays, letters, and columns of figures, like ledgers. Jana had struggled through a couple of years' Greek at her boarding school, and remembered little more than the alphabet, but she knew also that the rudiments were still there, and would come back easily enough if pressed into service, since a language is never truly forgotten. Yet she could not make head or tail of these books. Harriet interrupted her with a pat on the bottom.

'You don't want to be looking there,' she whispered. 'Come to my office for a diddle.'

Jana allowed herself to be tugged away by the lustful little virgin, and it was only when they were in full embrace that she murmured something about her puzzlement at these unusual books.

'You don't want to bother your pretty head about that,' said Harriet, stroking Jana so beautifully that indeed she did not want to bother about anything else for a while. 'Those books shouldn't really be on display at all, actually.

They are only for the Superior's eyes, but of course there is always the problem of storage space.'

'But what are they?' asked Jana, panting as she embraced her friend. 'They seem to be Greek, but it's no Greek that I recognise.'

'I wouldn't know,' said Harriet. 'I'm just an ignorant whipping girl, and they didn't teach me Greek in the slave camp in Africa, they were too busy with other things ... like *this*.'

'Ooh! Yes ... but another thing, Harriet,' continued Jana, her curiosity as usual getting the better of her, 'why is it that the Superior is never seen? Not in the refectory, never in the gymnasium, not at all, in fact.'

'Why, Maldona herself is never seen.'

'That I understand, but surely the Superior ...'

'You see the Deputy Superior, don't you?'

'It is not the same. Have you ever seen the Superior?'

'Well, no.'

'Not even on Special Days?'

'Now you come to mention it, not there either. It is a puzzle, isn't it?' said Harriet gaily. 'In fact there was one school of thought, in the sixteenth century – I shouldn't really be telling you this, Jana, but you bewitch me so – ooh, don't *stop*! – and they thought that Maldona and the Superior were one and the same person! But you know what girls are like, always curious, always gossiping, and gossiping can be dangerous, can't it? Whatever is, is, that's what I say, and that's what Maldona says too.'

Jana was surprised at this burst of eloquence from the normally merry Harriet, and said so.

'Well, it doesn't do to think too much, though I admit I'm as curious as anybody,' said Harriet.

They paused for a while, intent on completing their loving embraces, and when both girls were flushed and wreathed in smiles, Harriet said, 'I say, it would be a lark to find out what's in those books, wouldn't it?'

'I suppose so. But we are warned against curiosity.'

'Oh, pooh! You know Greek, you can find out what is

in them. I bet there are some spicy stories that we virgins aren't supposed to know.'

'My Greek isn't that good.'

'It has to be better than mine. Don't be modest. Come . . .'

Harriet led Jana back to the stack of indecipherable books, and selected one at random.

'Here! Take this, it's a short one, and there aren't any of those silly numbers. I bet it's stories. Go back to your cell and see what you can make of it, and tell me tomorrow. Please, please, pretty please?'

'OK, Harriet,' said Jana, smiling at the girl's childish enthusiasm. 'But don't expect miracles.'

'Mmm!' said Harriet, giving her a hearty kiss on the lips. 'Till tomorrow, then.'

'Till tomorrow, Harriet.'

But tomorrow turned out differently than planned.

In her cell, Jana tossed and turned, trying to make sense of the small handwritten volume which Harriet had given her. The writing was very old, the paper yellow and cracked, and the book smelled of the centuries. The script was definitely Greek, the language no known language at all. As she was about to give up her seemingly fruitless effort, a phrase caught her eye. It consisted of two words which seemed to be repeated over the course of a chapter.

Something nagged at Jana, something familiar, and then she clapped her forehead as she realised the simplicity of it. Transposed into English script, the phrase read: JANE ARDENNE.

Nervously, afraid of what she would find, she began to read again. It was terrifyingly simple. The book was written in English, a strange, crabbed medieval English, but recognisably English just the same. But in a clumsy attempt at camouflage, the Greek, not the Roman, alphabet had been used. Αλβιων meant Albion, or England; Αλημανιη was Alemania, Germany; Φρανσ was France, and so on. Enthralled yet fearful, Jana began to read: 'ατ θη φωνδητιων οφ Μαλδωνη βη Ζηνη Αρδεννη.' 'At the foundation of Maldona by Jane Ardenne . . .'

184

Jana read until it was late, and knew that she could tell no one what she had learned, or that she had learned it, for if more than one person knew the secret, the very edifice of Maldona would crumble. She closed the book with the nagging doubt that she was surely *not* the only person privy to the secret. Twice Harriet had directed her to a book of importance, as though by chance. Jana now was certain that it had been no chance. Was she being initiated into a mysterious sisterhood of adepts within Maldona? Or being set up as a scapegoat in whatever murky events were fated to take place?

Her fearful reverie was interrupted by Erato, who burst into her cell, in cheerful mood.

'What are you hiding yourself for, Jana?' she cried. 'I haven't seen you for ages!'

'You saw me at lunchtime, Erato,' said Jana in mild irritation, covering up her book. This weak concealment naturally drew attention to it.

'What's that?' said Erato, grabbing it.

'It's a book,' snapped Jana, trying and failing to snatch it back.

'What a funny book!'

'It's in Greek, you wouldn't understand it.'

'No it isn't, it's in Russian! I know Russian, and that is the Cyrillic alphabet.'

'All right, it's in Russian,' yawned Jana. 'It's the same alphabet.'

'Then it's no use to you, clever clogs,' said Erato. 'My dad was in the Russian Army, and I know Russian, so I'll have a bash at it.'

'No!'

'Fight you for it!'

'Stop showing off,' said Jana, suddenly sick and weary. What did it matter if Erato learned what she had learned? It might even be a good thing, since Erato was her friend, and could be trusted. But she wouldn't work out what the book meant, anyway.

'All right, take it,' said Jana, 'but leave me to get some rest.'

She had not realised how late it was, well after fourth bell, and fell at once into a troubled sleep. But she awoke after scarcely a few mintues.

'What's the meaning of this commotion?' shrilled Kobo's voice. 'I am doing my rounds, I expect to hear nothing but the sounds of sleep. You and Jana . . .'

'Now *you're* making a commotion, Kobo,' retorted Erato cheekily.

'Insolence! You've earned a whipping!'

'Pah! You can find any excuse to lace me, Kobo. But when Jana fights you and strips you of your rank, why you'll have your cruelty returned with interest.'

'Well . . . this time . . .' muttered Kobo, backing off. But then her voice shrilled again, 'What is this?'

'I . . . I got it from the library.'

'Liar! These books are forbidden to all but the Superior. That Jana, I smell her wicked hand in this. She stole it!'

'No!'

'You mean you stole it yourself?'

'Yes, just me! I mean, I didn't steal it,' blurted out Erato, confused.

'To have this book is to have stolen it,' thundered Kobo. 'Get dressed, Virgin Erato.' Her voice was calm and steely now. 'And accompany me to the office of the Deputy Superior, for you have committed the gravest offence against Maldona herself.'

'Don't be silly.'

There was a crack of Kobo's whip.

'There is nothing silly, Erato, about a Noble Beating, for that is what you have earned.'

Jana leapt from her bed and burst into her 's cell.

'Kobo! You are right! It was my doing, and I am the one who must be punished.'

Kobo leered.

'Oh, no, little virgin. You will be punished in the arena when I thrash you for your insolence in challenging me. Meanwhile, here I have my guilty one.'

'It was I!' cried Jana. 'Leave Erato alone!'

'Such commendable loyalty,' sneered Kobo.

'Don't be foolish, Jana,' said Erato. 'I'll take what's coming to me. It's nothing! Go back to bed.'

'A Noble Beating is nothing?'

'Almost nothing,' said Erato bravely, and Jana could only retreat, to listen sadly as her friend's footsteps echoed forlornly in the cold corridor.

Erato paraded like a queen in Maldona, sumptuous in her robe of rose petals. Her manner was cool and distant, with none of the serene bravura of Harriet the whipping girl. And her beating took place the next day at noon, in the blistering heat of the arena, due to the gravity of her offence of possessing a forbidden book. The beating was terrible to behold.

All Maldona was assembled to watch, the virgins sweating in their best uniforms, the Parfaites resplendent in their finest plumage, and their nude bodies oiled to gleaming with scented unguents. The Deputy Superior addressed the throng, to explain that Erato was guilty of an offence so heinous it could not be named, save that it was an assault on the sanctity of the Superior, even of Maldona herself.

But the Superior was absent; Jana wanted to know why this victim of assault was not there to exact her own vengeance. Maldona, too, was missing, until Jana looked to the topmost tower and saw a flash of binoculars from her apartments: she would witness the cruel punishment. And it was crueller than anything Jana had imagined.

The Deputy Superior was nude, to allow her complete freedom of movement. As the Parfaites tore Erato's robe of petals, strapped her to the whipping frame and gagged her tight, the Deputy Superior donned a black mask of skin-tight rubber, like an executioner. The petals were showered on Erato's stretched nude body, and her sentence read out. She was to receive twenty-five strokes from the six-thonged flagrum, a quirt so vicious that it was handed with reverence to the Deputy Superior like some dangerous beast freed from its cage.

The Deputy Superior lifted her flogging arm, and Jana shivered at the sensuous ripple of her powerful muscles, so inviting to love yet so awesome in cruelty. The quirt cracked on Erato's naked shoulders, and the force of the stroke rocked the entire whipping frame and its occupant. She groaned pitifully, but as the strokes followed, she did not make any further sound. The jerking of her body, straining with futile shudders against her bonds, spoke sufficiently.

The silence in the arena was total, broken only by the sound of the lash on Erato's bare flesh. The Deputy Superior was expert; she worked from the shoulders across Erato's broad back, and finally attacked her thighs and buttocks, making the superb fesses quiver like jellies as the whip kissed them. It was strange, and horribly thrilling, to see her friend stripped of her dignity, her personality, and to exist merely as a naked animal consumed by pain's caress. Jana's brow poured with sweat; the beating seemed to last for ever, but it must have been about the fifteenth stroke, when Erato suddenly let out an explosive wail, that rose in a crescendo to a scream of despair. '*I go down!*' shrieked Erato as her whipped body writhed in its bonds. 'For pity's sake, *I go down.*'

At once, the Deputy Superior dropped her whip and summoned her assistants to unfasten Erato's bonds. At the same time, she gestured to Jocasta, who, accompanied by Matron, rushed forward at the head of a party of stretcher-bearers, of which, Jana noted, Ragusa was one. Carefully and speedily, they loaded Erato on to the stretcher, giving her smelling salts, and bathing her face and body with cooling unguents, and hustled her away.

'Where are they taking her?' said Jana to Miriam, who was beside her, licking her lips but disappointed at the termination of the spectacle.

'To the surgery, of course,' said the corporal. 'They'll patch her up, the pathetic weakling, then let her go ... outside. And she'll never get back into Maldona! Good riddance, I say.'

Jana was in sombre mood as she went to the refectory, and sat down for luncheon with the place beside her unoccupied. Her own ordeals to come seemed to have faded into insignificance, and she felt guilty at having been the author of her friend's misfortune. Still, she thought, maybe she is happier outside. Maybe *I* should be happier outside . . .

Leandra, of course, quizzed her at the first opportunity about her friend's crime, but Jana pleaded complete ignorance, knowing, and not caring, that Leandra would not believe her. After luncheon she went down to the surgery to visit Erato, and beg for her forgiveness, and wish her well, and tell her to keep in touch, and give her a last embrace.

But there was nobody to embrace, nobody to grant forgiveness. Erato was not in the surgery. The surgery was completely empty.

Jana sweated heavily in the blistering heat as she climbed up to Leandra's apartment; she longed to be free of her heavy uniform and sport nude in the bathing pool. But Leandra's summons was to be obeyed, properly dressed. The door was opened by Jason, perspiring also even in his light brocade tunic with its short skirt, the sulky beauty of his face glistening with droplets of sweat. The interior of southern Spain is called 'the frying pan' in summer, and Maldona was well at the centre of that frying pan.

'You are too early,' said Jason with a sneer. 'Mistress Leandra is at training and will not return for half an hour at least.'

'I'll wait, then,' said Jana, pushing past him.

'No! What? I mean . . . Well, you must wait on the balcony,' stammered the nonplussed Jason, his words sounding feeble, since Jana was already there. Cheekily, she settled herself in a sun lounger and stretched out to admire the vista of the purple and gold mountains shimmering in the heat under a cloudless sky of perfect azure. Jason stared at her, and she stared back, wondering where he came from. With those sultry good looks, he must be Mediterranean – Italian, perhaps, or Greek. In a way he reminded her of Cassie.

Jason continued his unblinking stare, and she noticed that he was actually staring at her feet, unlike most men, who stared at her breasts. Lazily, she stretched out her legs and rested her feet on a stool.

'That's better,' she sighed, stretching to show off her bosom. 'How hot it is!'

'It is not permitted to rest your legs thus,' said Jason. 'It is not ladylike.'

'Oh, pooh,' said Jana. 'Go and fetch me some lemonade, slave.'

'I . . . I am not your slave,' muttered Jason.

'Well, go and fetch me some lemonade, not-my-slave,' and, glowering, he obeyed.

She heard Jason clattering in the kitchen, and when he returned with a tray, pitcher and glasses, she had her thighs spread and her skirt hitched up, so that the tip of her mink was just visible, and the lips of her fount peeped coyly from their glistening forest. Jason saw her nudity, but his eyes were still riveted on her booted feet. She yawned, and scratched her naked mons, making no attempt at modesty, as though the presence of a mere male slave did not matter. She saw that as he stared at her feet, he had gone slightly pale, and the arrogant curl had vanished from his lips, to be replaced by a pout of puppyish longing.

'*So* hot!' she said, 'I think I must take my boots and stockings off.'

'It . . . it is unseemly,' said Jason, swallowing.

'Why, Leandra won't mind. *You* don't mind, do you, Jason?'

'I am a slave,' he mumbled uncertainly.

'Then, slave, help me off with my boots and stockings.'

Jana raised her skirt, exposing the full nakedness of her mink and sex-lips, and unfastened the tops of her stockings from her garter belt. She sighed as she felt the sun's hot rays bathe her naked thighs and fount.

Jason watched her unlace her boots, and gulped. When her left boot was unlaced, she pulled the flaps back as far as they would go, stretching the laces tightly over the exposed tongue.

'Oh,' said Jason faintly, and spilled lemonade from the jug as his fingers trembled.

190

'You naughty slave,' said Jana. 'I shall have to tell Leandra of this imperfection.'

'No . . . please,' whimpered Jason.

'What? Afraid she'll lace your bare bottom? Well, help me off with these things and perhaps I shall be nice to you.'

Jason needed no persuasion. He fell to his knees and with trembling fingers freed Jana of her boots, hugging them to his body and sliding them across his manhood with a little gasp of pleasure before placing them reverently on the deck. Jana saw to her satisfaction that under his frilly little skirt, his cock was stiffening. Coquettishly, she wiggled her toes.

'Isn't it a pity my boots are too small for you, Jason? I bet you'd like to wear them.'

'I . . . yes, Miss.'

'You can kiss them, if you like.'

Jana put her fingers on her quim, quite casually, and spread her lips so that Jason could see the glistening pink flesh of her slit. His gaze riveted to her open sex, he placed one of her boots inside his skirt and rubbed himself, while he raised the other to his lips and licked the leather toe, his nostrils flared as he sniffed hungrily at her aroma.

'They must be awfully smelly,' said Jana brightly. 'Look how wet my stockings are. I've been sweating like a pig!'

'Oh, Oh,' moaned Jason, as he rubbed her boot against his hard cock.

'Put the boots down and help me off with my stockings,' she ordered. 'I've unfastened the straps, so you can roll them down, but no touching my bare skin, mind.'

Jana watched him, trembling, roll down her stockings, as she let her fingers wander idly over her stiffening clit. She felt quite wet between her legs as the tingling started in her belly and the love secretion seeped from her gash. When Jason had taken off the stockings, she wiggled her bare toes, and exclaimed, 'Pooh, how they stink!'

Jason pressed the wet stockings to his nose and lips, with a sigh of ecstasy, and crammed the silken fabric into his mouth.

'Do you hope to wring them dry?' asked Jana. 'Well, my toes are all wet and itchy, so suck them, slave.'

Jason's eyes rolled as he took her toes into his mouth, which opened wide to take both of her feet at once, like a ravenous shark. His tongue flicked frantically against her slippery toes, making her squeal with laughter at the tickling, as she continued to rub her engorged nympha with slow, giddying strokes. Beneath his skirt, his cock was a stiff pole; abruptly, she reached down and lifted the skirt, revealing the crimson shaft, magnificent in its raw, menacing nudity.

Jason's tongue darted like a lizard over her wriggling feet. She could feel her nipples stiff and erect against the damp fabric of her blouse, and her throbbing clit sent tingles of pleasure along her spine, making her whole body electric with desire.

'Your cock is lovely, Jason,' she said softly. 'So tender and naked, yet so hard, naked for love like my own nympha. How well Leandra's knife has prepared your manhood, stripping it so harshly for a woman's pleasure.'

'Leandra ordered,' said Jason, his voice a mumble. 'Jocasta cut me.'

'The Surgeon Mistress, of course. So, in her surgery, Jocasta has removed the skin of your penis, and turned you into a wonderful machine who can fuck for hours without spurting. She is clever. But I am cleverer, for when you fucked me in the bum-hole, I made you spurt in seconds!'

'It was not in the surgery,' said Jason. 'For such operations, one must go to the finishing school. Anyway, I only spurted because you cheated.'

'Ha! To squeeze a man's cock with the bum muscles is not cheating, it is an act of love. But what is this finishing school?'

'Mm, mm,' said Jason, shaking his head. His eyes were fixed on Jana's open cunt as he sucked and licked her slippery toes, and she increased the speed and force of her caresses to her nympha, until she knew it was standing shiny and wet before his pleading eyes. She opened and closed the lips of her cunt, rubbing her fingers along their swollen ridges, and plunging them teasingly in and out of her slit.

'Don't you want to fuck me in my lovely wet gash?' she murmured shyly. 'I'll make you spurt twice as quickly as you did in my bum-hole.'

Jason released her feet and looked up, his mouth shining with his saliva and Jana's sweat. His lips creased in a sneer.

'In a woman's fount, I can last for hours, little virgin. Even with the Mistress Leandra, who knows every art.'

'That would please me, proud chevalier,' said Jana, her eyelids heavy, and her sex drenched in desire, 'but it would please me still more to see you humbled.'

Jason stood up and unfastened his tunic, then dropped it to the deck. He stood naked and haughty before her, his cock magnificent as it rode up over his muscled belly, almost touching the dimple of his belly-button.

'It is you who shall be humbled, virgin. I shall fuck you until you squirm on my rod, begging for mercy. I shall fuck you until you want nothing in the world except my cock in your quivering fount, for ever.'

'You may try, Jason, but only if you accept a wager.'

'What have you to wager with, girl? Cunts are mine for the asking.'

'Really, my vainglorious slave?'

Suddenly Jana closed her thighs, and folded her feet underneath her bottom. She sat kneeling thus, and saw the dismay on Jason's face, and a slight wilting of his penis.

'Oh,' he moaned. 'Do not hide those pretty feet.'

'A wager, then. You may love my feet, or pay your forfeit.'

'Yes, damn you! I accept! But what forfeit?'

Jana showed her feet again, and Jason gasped in relief.

'You must tell me everything about the finishing school.' Jason paled.

'No! It is forbidden!' he cried.

'You agreed. Are you a man of honour?'

'*Sin verguenza!* You shameless slut!'

'Or shall I put my boots and stockings back on, and never let you see or touch them again?'

'Very well, I agree, on my knight's honour. But a wager is pointless. I am sure to win. Spread the lips of your fount, my dove, and I shall fuck you until you faint from coming, without moistening your womb with a single drop of sperm.'

'My fount?' cried Jana. 'Who said you could fuck me in my fount? I wagered I could make you spurt in a minute, and that is all.'

'You have tricked me!'

'Indeed I have, but a wager is a wager. You will please honour your agreement, and kneel for your lady's pleasure, proud chevalier.'

Puzzled, his face stony with rage, Jason did as he was told. Jana uncurled her legs, and stretched out her left foot so that her toes pressed hard on his tight balls, and Jason moaned, half in desire and half in rueful anticipation.

'Part the cheeks of your croup.'

He spread his buttocks, and Jana's big toe found his quivering anus bud. She pushed into it, and tickled his tight passage with rapid strokes.

'Oh, sweet lady,' he sighed in anguish.

'Watch me pleasure myself, knight,' she commanded, and recommenced her vigorous masturbation. At the same time she raised her right leg and grasped the swollen bulb of his cock with her supple toes. She began to caress both bulb and shaft, squeezing hard and rubbing him with firm strokes, pausing sometimes to tickle his peehole with the nail of her big toe. Lovingly, she caressed her own stiff clit, filled with joy at the impressive size to which Maldona had grown her, at her own *prowess*. Every time she touched Jason's peehole, he shuddered and whimpered, for Jana was in control, and knew that she could melt any man alive, especially with the relentless thrusting pressure of her toe in his squirming anus.

At every stroke of her cock-rubbing, she squeezed his balls hard down on to her left foot. He writhed, stroking her foot with his balls, and clenched his handsome fesses, trying to squeeze her toe deeper into his anus.

A white droplet appeared at the slit of his peehole, and Jana paused.

'Why, only half a minute, Jason, and you are about to

spurt! Admit it – I see your spunk already, and your balls are tight and trembling to be milked.'

'Oh, yes, you have won, sweet Jana. Please don't stop caressing me with those lovely feet, dearer than any fount. Make me spurt all over your pretty toes, please, Oh Mistress, please . . .'

'First, your forfeit,' said Jana coldly. 'What, and where, is the finishing school?'

'Beyond the secret locked door, deep beneath Maldona, in the mountain. Leandra took me blindfold, and I was asleep for my alteration. I remember men's voices, guttural, a language I did not understand; the noises of motors and the whirring and clicking of cameras, but also girls' voices, the happy singing of virgins and the wafting aroma of their scented bodies, and sometimes their shrieks of orgasm. And I heard the lashing of whips, sometimes in punishment, which made the girls sing out joyfully, sometimes as a driver would herd his flock, with the scampering of bare feet and the laughter of girls together. It was all confused: when I awoke, my penis was as naked as a girl's nympha, and I felt great pain, and thought I should rather take a Perfect Beating than have it again. But now I am glad, for I am pretty, and Leandra loves me.'

'So Leandra took you there? She has the key. Where does she keep it?'

'I don't know . . . perhaps with her jewellery.'

'I wish to borrow it,' said Jana, caressing the full shaft of his cock between the soft soles of her feet, rubbing with a feather's touch.

'I daren't!'

'I shall make a mould in my candleshop,' she said, ceasing her frottage, 'and bring it back, without her knowing it was gone, Jason.'

'Yes, yes, I'll do it! Anything! Just don't . . . stop . . . Oh, Oh, Oh . . .'

And with the loving pressure of her toes, Jana stroked the trembling cock until a glorious fountain of seed arched flashing in the sunlight, and spurted hot and creamy on Jana's writhing feet.

'Oh, thank you,' whimpered Jason, 'thank you, thank you . . .'

Jana started as she heard the door of the apartment open. Jason blinked, then rapidly donned his tunic. Man and woman both smoothed their skirts down and assumed decorous positions. But Jason could not hide his still-rigid penis under his frilly skirt, nor Jana the glistening sperm which formed soft rivulets between her bare toes.

'Well, well,' purred a warm contralto voice, 'and what does my slave have to be so thankful for?'

Jason and Jana bowed low. A pungent odour filled the air, and Jana recognised the oil and lemon juice lotion which Cassie had rubbed on her in faraway Mykonos, and which now made Leandra's splendid nudity shine like crystal.

'Barefoot,' said Leandra, flicking Jana's toes with her whip. 'I smell mischief. I think your feet have been busy, Jana.'

She flexed her muscles, suddenly, striking a body-builder's pose.

'It was my fault, Mistress,' blurted Jason.

'Ah! *What* was your fault, Jason?'

Blushing, Jason explained.

'You haven't had a lacing for a while, Jason,' said Leandra. 'Go and change into your punishment kit, boy, and bring me your phallus too.'

14

A Gift of Stockings

Jason went pale, but bowed and went to obey.

'Please, Mistress, it was as much my fault as Jason's,' said Jana. 'I should share equally in the punishment you choose.'

'You have spirit, little Jana.'

'I am not so little.'

'No ... and it took balls to challenge Kobo. I like a virgin with balls. You shall take your meals with me from now on. I want to build you for the contest. It is time young Kobo was taken down a peg. The diet in the refectory is all very well for English maidens, but we Germans are used to heartier fare. Jocasta agrees with me, of course.'

'So Jocasta is German,' said Jana, 'and you too, Mistress?'

Leandra flicked her whip lazily against Jana's breast.

'That sounded suspiciously like a question, little one,' she drawled. 'But, ah, here is our erring chevalier, and how pretty he looks.'

Jason was barefoot, and wore a pink silk peignoir with shoulder-straps and a deep cleavage that revealed his massive chest muscles, swelling like a woman's breasts; his mouth was rouged, his eyes darkened with kohl, and a barrette held his curly hair swept back off his forehead. Jana thought him curiously fetching. But Jason was embarrassed and did not return her sympathetic stare. Instead he held out a phallus to Leandra, a restrainer like that issued to virgins, but monstrously big, and covered in knots and striations eerily like those that adorned Leandra's bulging biceps.

197

'Why, the pretty boy isn't old enough to fasten his own restrainer,' cried Leandra with cruel mockery. '*You* fit her, Jana, while I watch. Go ahead, she is used to it. You love that big rough cock right up inside your bum-hole, don't you, Miss?'

'Y ... yes, Mistress,' mumbled Jason, crimson with shame.

Leandra handed the device to Jana and ordered Jason to lift his gown and bend over, with his bare buttocks well spread. Gingerly, Jana approached his exposed anus bud with the giant phallus. She looked at his bare bottom, so sweet and helpless and trembling, and longed to kiss it, not plunge this cruel engine inside the boy.

'It is so big,' she said doubtfully.

'Take some oil, to smooth its passage. Here.'

And Leandra placed Jana's hand on her naked breast, gleaming with oil. Jana scooped a palmful of oil from the skin of her mistress, noticing that the nipples hardened ever so slightly as her fingers brushed them, then applied the lubricant to the phallus, and a little to Jason's anus, working it inside his passage as far as she could. Jason sighed.

She pressed the heavy dildo into him about an inch, and he grunted and squirmed, his hands parting his cheeks to stretch his hole wide. Jana pushed with all her might, and Jason wriggled and squeezed, trying to take the phallus right inside him. At last his passage relaxed, and Jana pushed the phallus in right to the hilt. It slid easily, and Jason groaned in satisfaction. Jana saw that his cock had risen half-stiff, and hurried to snap the restraining harness shut before his penis became ungovernable. She stood back, satisfied with her work, but worried at the discomfort of that proud cock confined in its metal prison.

Leandra clapped her hands with glee, then handed Jana her whip.

'Now to make the girl dance!' she cried.

'I, Mistress?' said Jana.

'Of course. Don't tell me you've never laced a girl's naked arse before?'

'Why, yes, Mistress,' said Jana, taken aback at her crude words. 'But Jason is a boy.'

'Jana, under the lash, and under this roasting sun, an arse is an arse. Now, Jason, my girl, how many do you think your sweet fesses deserve? Three? Four?'

'A full seven, I think, Mistress, with all respect.'

Leandra shrugged and smiled at Jana.

'Seven it shall be, then. Go to it, girl.'

With a trembling hand, Jana lifted the heavy whip and brought it down with a frightening whistle on Jason's naked bottom, which flinched as the thong cracked, although the boy made no sound.

'Why, harder than that, Jana,' said Leandra, in mock outrage. 'Don't you agree, Jason?'

'Much harder, please,' murmured Jason.

'Right, then,' panted Jana, and whipped the naked boy with the force of every muscle in her body. Sweat blurred her vision as the strokes fell, hard and relentless on those juicy fesses that quivered so beautifully as the whip kissed them. Jana saw Leandra's hand stray to her quim, and gently stroke her own nympha, which slowly rose to an engorged stiffness. Jana's feelings of tenderness towards Jason had now turned to savagery. She wanted those fesses to jerk under the lash, wanted him to cry out. Her own sex was becoming wetter and wetter, and her body dripped with sweat. She no longer knew, or cared, if the flogged arse before her belonged to a boy or a girl!

Only at the seventh and final stroke did Jason let out a long, low moan, as his head sank down. The beating was accomplished. Jana was panting fiercely, the insides of her thighs sticky with the liquid that seeped from her soaking cunt, and when Leandra removed her hand from her own swollen nympha, pulled Jana to her and lifted her pleated skirt, Jana offered no resistance. Leandra lifted her hips and seated her on top of her, so that their founts and nymphae touched. The pressure of Leandra's engorged clit on her own made Jana giddy with delight, and she squirmed to rub the two tender limbs together in a dance of pleasure.

'Oh,' moaned Leandra. 'Quite nice. I think, now, the whip for me, here.'

Raising her thighs to clamp Jana's waist, she directed the handle of the whip towards her own anus. Jana responded to her mistress's desire by pushing it fiercely so that it sank all the way inside. Leandra moaned again, and eased her swollen nympha right inside Jana's wet slit. Jerking up and down, she fucked Jana like a man, while directing Jana, who needed little direction, to encule her with the rough handle of the whip. Leandra's nympha was hard and delicious, like a throbbing silky cock as Jana slapped against the Parfaite's squirming thighs, her mink rubbing the smooth, shaven mons as her love-juice flowed over Leandra's belly, making it a glistening, sticky lake into which Leandra dipped her fingers, then put them to her mouth and sucked the salty oil that had flowed from Jana's cunt.

'Mmmm,' she said, with a cat's smile.

'Yes, fuck me, mistress,' cried Jana, 'fuck me with your lovely cock! I'm helpless as you fuck me so hard and so beautifully. Please make me come, please . . .'

Leandra redoubled the vigour of her strokes.

'You shan't take pleasure where I have none,' she hissed, and suddenly her body went rigid and she gave one single howl as her belly shuddered, and that brought Jana over the edge, and Jana yelped as the sweetness of orgasm clutched her. Jason's eyes were wide with helpless envy as he viewed the women's pleasure, his cock standing clearly under his filmy pink dress.

'Well!' said Leandra cheerfully. 'I think you have the makings of a good disciplinarian, Jana. Jason's girly's bum looks nice and red. The question is, can you take punishment as well as deal it out?'

'I should scarcely be in Maldona otherwise, Mistress,' said Jana.

'Quite right. I shall put you to the test. But all this moral philosophy has made me hungry, and I think luncheon is called for. Jason, you may serve us.'

Jason curtseyed prettily, and retreated to his kitchen.

'I am sure moral philosophy will prove most rewarding, Mistress,' said Jana diplomatically.

'Why Jana, you must not forget you are a lady through and through. And for a lady, the most important lesson in moral philosophy is luncheon.'

'Protein,' said Leandra, her mouth insouciantly full, 'makes muscle. Muscle is protein. Have some more oysters.'

They sat at a table on the balcony, shaded by a parasol. Lunch was caviare, steak tartare, raw shellfish, raw everything, and washed down with a decent white wine.

'Wine, on the other hand,' added Leandra, 'is poetry.'

'Your body is poetry, Mistress,' said Jana.

'Thank you.'

Jana felt glorious. After a shower, she had been permitted to remain naked with Leandra, ostensibly so as to protect her uniform from spillage of the juices and oils that dribbled, unladylike, down her chin and breast, and now she looked out over the fragrant mountainside and felt ready to spread her arms and fly up into the air like a plumed bird. Noises of housework clinked from the shadows of the apartment, as Jason hovered back and forth with a frilly maid's apron over his restrainer, his crimson bottom glowing like two pretty beacons.

'Men are only happy when you treat them like girls,' said Leandra, her lips glistening with oyster-juice. 'That is moral philosophy.'

'I shall remember,' said Jana, 'as if I could ever forget!'

'Why do we like oysters, Jana?'

'They taste nice.'

'No, it is because they are salty and wet and squishy, and remind us of our juicy founts. Under this sun, everything sort of becomes like everything else, doesn't it? Boys are like girls, girls are like boys ... Wait till you see all the visitors at our Special Day. Lots of Arabs, gorgeous rich fellows with silky eyelashes, and wearing nothing under their djellabahs. You'll be well in trim, Jana, I'll see to that, and they'll look you over like a thoroughbred racehorse.'

'I find it exciting, Mistress,' said Jana. 'To fight naked, with all those men watching me, their pricks getting hard at the sight of my body.'

'Very keen on the body beautiful, our Arab friends,' said Leandra. 'They esteem body sculpting, the quest for moral perfection through physical perfection. Some of them believe that at his second coming, the Prophet will be born of a man, and they like to build breasts like a woman's, in the hope that they can give him suck. Their culture is very masculine, yet they strive to build bodies that are more than a male's.'

'How strange.'

'What is strange? It is the division into two sexes that is strange. But now, if you are to thrash young Kobo, we mustn't forget our carbohydrates. You do want to thrash Kobo, don't you? You are not softening?'

Jana thought of that unkind cut from Kobo's cane, on her first morning as a virgin.

'Yes, Mistress, I intend to thrash her.'

Leandra smiled and clapped her hands.

'Bring on the roly-poly pudding!' she cried. Jason appeared with the hot dish, and soon Jana was wolfing a huge stodgy plateful, slathered in cream. Leandra watched with approval.

'Energy,' she said, 'that is good,' and flexed her muscles in a sinuous ripple like an ocean wave. Jana looked at her ripe, curving body with envy.

'You would like to be me, wouldn't you?' said Leandra softly. 'I can tell.'

'I want to be you, Mistress.'

Jana cleared every morsel from her pudding plate, and Jason cleared the things away, then served coffee. Leandra invited Jana to join her at the balcony rail while she smoked a cigarette. She offered one to Jana, who, to her own surprise, refused. They stood looking over the mountains, Leandra lazily smoking, and her arm round Jana's bare waist. Jana thought herself in seventh heaven.

'Did you like it when I caressed you with my nympha?' asked Leandra suddenly.

'Mistress, you know I did,' said Jana. 'You made me come.'

Leandra allowed her hand to slip to Jana's mink, and then to her nympha, which she tickled with slow, gentle strokes, making it tingle and stiffen.

'What a sweet muscle of pleasure! Soon, she will be like mine,' said Leandra dreamily. 'Tell me, Jana, did your lovers whip you, before you came to us?'

'Yes, recently I have tasted the lash, Mistress. It was an awakening, that brought me to Maldona.'

'Oh, Jana, it was Maldona that brought you to her. She has agents outside, adepts who serve Maldona in the world, known only to each other, and constantly on the watch for potential perfection.'

Jana shivered slightly as she thought of Caspar and Netta Pennington. Were they adepts of Maldona? And had they enticed Henry? Again, she wished that she could find Cassie in this labyrinth, if she were indeed here, and ask her to explain everything.

'There are degrees of awakening, Jana. When the lash touches your naked skin with a high enough degree of loving cruelty, it induces an ecstasy that is almost religious. Have you yet felt such ecstasy?'

'There is no ecstasy comparable to feeling your nympha on my willing fount, Mistress,' said Jana, 'or your hand between my open thighs, stroking me to wetness.'

Leandra kissed Jana on the lips.

'When I whip you, you shall feel ecstasy, Jana. I knew the moment I saw you, a trembling little virgin, that ... that you were one of us. Born to be an adept. I won't ask, of course, how you came to Maldona. But I know that you must have felt the kiss of the whip on your naked skin and, like me, knew that henceforth life is no life unless the bottom shivers under a loving lash. Don't you feel that?'

'Yes, Mistress,' blurted Jana. 'Yes, I do, with all my heart!'

'I am a German, as you know, and the German soul longs for freedom, for the absolute, to live naked and fierce in lonely forests under the sky, or to swim like fishes in cruel, foaming oceans. Jana, the whip brings our souls closer to that elemental truth. The pain of building our bodies' muscles – which is the triumph of will over matter – makes us feel as goddesses, and then the greater pain of the lash chastises our impudence, reducing us to nothing but squirming, agonised flesh, and by taking punishment, our strength triumphs over it. The ecstasy of being trussed and gagged, of shuddering helpless as the whip bites our naked woman's flesh! And afterwards, we kiss the rod that chastised us, and thank our tormentor, and, as the delicious glowing in our flogged back and buttocks suffuses our whole reddened body, we know that we have taken it proudly. I am minded of a phrase of Goethe, the "*Drang nach Süden*." Do you know that?'

'It refers to the German longing for the south, for palm trees and sun and naked brown bodies, Mistress.'

'Just so,' laughed Leandra. 'We Germans are pale; we love dark people; their dusky skin seems to contain the elemental force of life that we can only achieve by aggression and other passions – including, I may say, the passion for physical culture. And, Jana, when a lady has her bottom flogged and reddened by a pitiless whip, and looks at herself in the glass, does she not wonder at the bright colour her pale body has become, as though her very soul is on fire? There is a legend of Maldona, that when the flesh is reduced by the whip to raw, quivering agony, the spirit is freed, and flies like a bird on golden wings.'

'I . . . I have felt this beauty touch me,' whispered Jana.

'Yes,' mused Leandra, 'we Germans are very basic people. We are harsh, and do nothing by halves. My first lover, Jana, was a black man, an American, a captain with the army. Such proud muscles, such vigour in his fucking! Well, I was not twenty years old, legally an adult, but in my father's eyes, still his little girl. When he found out about my liaison – a soldier, a foreigner, and a black man! – he whipped me until I agreed to give him up. Oh, he had punished me before, of course – I expect every girl's daddy has spanked her bare bottom – but nothing like this. He made me strip completely naked, with not even the shred of dignity afforded by shoes, or my bracelets or necklace, and strapped me with leather thongs to his workbench, then flogged me on the shoulders and fesses with a plaited dressage whip, like an animal.'

'And you agreed to give up your lover?'

'No! I took the whipping until it was my father who gave up, with the fatigue of whipping me! I took all of it, without a cry, and do you know, as he delivered the last savage and frustrated stroke to my burning buttocks, I secretly orgasmed.'

'Oh, Leandra, that is wonderful.'

'After that, I left home and my cruel father, and drifted in the cities: Berlin, Hamburg, Munich. I took many lovers, many black men and Turks, and with all of them I found myself sooner or later begging for the whip. My path, my *Drang nach Süden*, brought me south to Spain, to Africa, and to my rightful place, Maldona. Oh, Jana, how I wish there were time to give you a long, slow flogging this very moment! I see myself in you, Virgin! And I am jealous! When I caress you, I want you to come like a man, to drain you of your vital essence, and yet I know that it is impossible. Love between women is an enrichment of our vital essence, not a taking away of seed. We cannot do without men's seed to enrich us, Jana, but I think only a woman truly knows how to lace another woman's body. Don't expect me to trust you, Jana. I know you shall take pleasure in another's whip, and in lacing another's body. Oh, Jana . . .' She bit her lip, and silently squeezed Jana's naked body against her own.

'Mistress,' said Jana, 'to show my love, I have brought you a gift. I made it myself.'

From her bag, she took a gleaming new candle, shaped like the double phallus she had taken from Harry and Greta. One of the cocks was cream-coloured, the other dark brown, and perversely she had given the creamy cock brown balls, the brown cock balls of cream.

'How lovely!' cried Leandra. 'Such skill! Such impudence! I shall whip you for it, of course, long and hard and slow.'

'Oh, Mistress, you are making me so wet.'

'Well, wet you must stay, for I have business elsewhere.'

She gave Jana a final, chaste kiss on her cheek, picked up her whip, and, wearing only sandals, left her apartment. Jana dressed herself, except for her stockings, and joined Jason in the kitchen, where he was dolefully washing dishes. She put a friendly hand on his hot croup and stroked it.

'No hard feelings, Jason?' she said, and he rewarded her with a shy smile.

'I've a gift for you.'

And she held up her soiled stockings.

Jason's eyes gleamed, and he grabbed for the stockings, but Jana snatched them away.

'Not now. Tonight. You'll get my stockings, all ripe and smelly, when you get me Leandra's key. I'll go to the sauna after supper tonight. My uniform will be in the apodyterium, and you will leave the key in my breast pocket. Leave your own tunic there, or a spare, and when I've used the key, I'll return it to your pocket, with these.'

'Agreed,' said Jason, his eyes on the filmy soiled stockings.

She could not resist planting a tender kiss on his breasts, which, she thought, were rather soft and nice, like a girl's.

As she let herself out, Jason said, 'Curiosity killed the cat.'

'I am not a cat,' said Jana. 'I thought you might have noticed.'

Jana's work was quickly done, and she returned to the sauna to cleanse herself of the smuts of the candleshop. To her surprise, Jason was still there, sitting at the end of his bench with a towel prudishly round his waist, while the complement of virgins sprawled naked and unashamed as they chattered. Jana joined the knight, smiled and nodded to indicate that everything had gone satisfactorily.

'I wasn't expecting to find you here,' she said.

'I like the sauna,' Jason replied. 'It is carefree, like the womb. And I like you, Jana. I want to be sure of getting my . . . trophies.'

'My stockings are in the pocket of your robe,' she said, putting her hand on his thigh, and bending so that her lips were close to his ear. 'And they absolutely pong of me.'

She giggled, but Jason's face was grave.

'Let us shower,' he said.

'I've only just had one! Give me time to work up a sweat.'

Jason fastened his powerful hand on her arm.

'We shower,' he said, and pulled her roughly to her feet, then dragged her out of the sauna.

'Wait! What are you doing? Let go of me!' cried Jana, then yelped as he pushed her under the icy spray. Through the sauna door, they heard the giggles of the virgins.

Under the lash of the cold shower, Jason pulled her fiercely to him and kissed her on the lips, pressing her breasts and belly tightly against his. His cock was rigid against her wet mink, its bulb stroking her navel. At first Jana resisted, but then, as his hard body warmed her, and that stiff member stroked her belly, she weakened, feeling a flood of desire melt over her, and returned his kiss. Their tongues met and flicked together, and her arms snaked around Jason's massive back muscles, caressing him. His hands were on her fesses, firmly kneading them, squashing them towards his aroused manhood.

'Oh,' she moaned, shivering at the ferocity of his desire. No longer was he Jason the slave, pretty in girl's clothing; he was a savage, naked male animal, taking his prey, possessing her.

'I want more than your stockings, Jana,' he hissed, 'I want you. All of you. I want my manhood in you, in your sweet fount, fucking you, giving you my seed, my essence.'

'Take me,' panted Jana. 'Take me, Jason. Fuck my cunt, fuck me, sweet lord, I am wet for you.'

Jana's surprise had given way to fierce, delighted desire, the wish to surrender totally to this predator whose steel gaze signalled that he wanted her, not as a companion, not to admire or flirt or play with, but to take her and use her as his possession, to fuck her like a raging brute, and then probably to spurn her with contempt as a thing that he had conquered and used. He wanted her.

207

Jana parted her thighs, and with a swift motion, Jason grasped her hips and lifted her up so that her cunt was above his naked red penis. She felt his bulb tickle her engorged cunt-lips as she locked her calves around his back, and then he thrust her down on to his shaft, filling her slit to the hilt of his manhood and making her cry out softly. His thighs bucked as his strong arms pumped Jana's body up and down on his cock, with each stroke removing his cock from her fount all the way to the swollen bulb, before plunging fiercely back to the very neck of her womb. She leaned back, her heavy breasts bouncing with each thrust, and clasped her hands around his neck. 'Yes, Jason, yes,' she heard herself moan. She had never experienced such turmoil before. No cuddling, no sweetness and nice caresses, just this animal plunging into her, raping her, and yet she was close to exploding, maddened by the sheer ferocity of his lust which, with the fusion of their bucking bodies, had become her lust. She felt she could scarcely wait to come, and when she felt him shudder and moan as his cock washed her womb with its creamy fountain, she cried out in her own spasm, wailing like a baby.

The force of her orgasm, the release of the pent-up tension of her illegal adventure, made her go weak and slump to the wet floor of the shower. She squatted there, panting, her legs awkwardly under her as the cold water raised sprays of steam from her sweating body.

'Oh, Jason,' she moaned, reaching for him.

She looked up, pleading for an embrace, and saw him smiling cruelly, as he soaped his raw cock, as though to wash away the stain of her.

'It is true,' he said, 'you are a fine slut.'

'Oh.'

She folded her arms around his bare legs, but he shucked her off with a laugh.

'Kiss me, sweet Jason,' she pleaded.

'You thought me a woman,' he sneered. 'Our mistress treats me so, makes me dress as a girl, humiliates me.'

'You are so pretty.'

'I am a man.'

'Yes! Woman or man, you are Jason, you are the prettiest boy in Maldona!'

He slapped her naked breasts, and she wailed, clasping his buttocks and opening her mouth to take his limp penis inside.

'With the prettiest cock,' she blurted out, 'the sweetest croup, the hardest balls of any man. Please let me suck you until are you hard again, Jason. Please come inside me once more. I am hot for you, my gorgeous knight.'

Jana's body glowed at the embrace of a man, an embrace she realised she had been too long without. She wanted Jason's stiff raw cock to fill her fount, never to leave her.

'Make me whole,' she begged. 'Oh, Jason, I wanted you the moment I saw you. Take me, I am yours.'

He laughed cruelly.

'What foolishness!' he said. 'You know it is against the rules.'

'We can go down! Together! I have friends in Marbella, we can stay there, and find somewhere of our own to live!'

Roughly, he hoisted her to her feet by her armpits, then slapped her breasts very hard, with four strokes that echoed wetly in the water-slopped chamber. Jana was dimly aware of an audience: the other virgins had crept from their sauna and stood pink and giggling by the doorway. She flung her arms round Jason's proud body, longing for him to fuck her again. All the certainties of her last months seemed to have dissolved. She did not care any more about Maldona and her rules, nor even about finding Cassie. She was consumed with raw animal desire, not just for the caress of a man's flesh, but for the aura of a male beast, to embrace her, protect her, to kiss her and beat her and . . .

'Jason, be my owner,' she cried. 'I will be your thing, your slave, to care for you and open my thighs for you and bare my body to your whip. Let me come with you, away from here. To Marbella . . . to my house in London. Just let me be your slave.'

'You are Maldona's property,' said Jason, 'and what you say is quite unladylike. It is imperfect, and I shall beat you for it.'

209

'Anything you want!'

Jason slammed Jana against the wall, pressing her breasts against the cold tiles, and raised his hand. She felt his palm crack on her bare, wet buttocks with astonishing force, and cried out in surprise. Then, rapidly, came a second smack, and a third, each seeming harder than the last, until she could not help squirming as she bit back the cry in her throat. Jason spanked her bare bottom fiercely and methodically.

'It hurts more when you're wet, doesn't it?' he hissed.

'God, yes!'

'Had enough?'

Jana's sex was hot with wet love-juice as her bare fesses glowed deliciously under his cruel spanking.

'No! No! Punish me,' she wailed.

Jana could feel her acorn stiff and throbbing, and could not help herself; she freed her hand and with feverish fingers found the hard nympha, then, in rhythm with Jason's spanking, dealt herself slow, firm strokes that made her spine and nipples tingle with electric pleasure.

'In her early days,' said Jason, 'Maldona taught that a woman's soul resided literally in her fount, and was nourished by male seed. When a woman went without fucking, her soul went in search of food, and found the nearest thing to the male sperm, which was the glutinous tissue of the brain, which it proceeded to eat, causing hysteria and madness of the type you are now exhibiting, Jana. Maldona in her wisdom saw that sound and regular whipping was and is the only remedy for such disorder, if women were to live free of man's domination, no longer slaves to his phallus.'

Jana had lost count of the strokes her naked bottom had taken; as she rubbed her swollen clit, she felt on fire, ready to explode once again in sweet orgasm.

'Don't stop,' she begged. 'Spank me harder, Jason. I am so wicked, yes, I need it. I wish you could whip me, lace me till I squirm and beg for mercy, but show me none as my naked flesh writhes before you.'

'I am a man,' said Jason, 'but like all true men, my

loyalty is to women. To love them when they are good, and chastise them when they are naughty.'

'I am very naughty!' cried Jana, trembling on the brink of her climax.

The spanking stopped, and she felt Jason's hands part the cheeks of her arse, to the delighted gasps of the audience of girls. Then the tip of his erect penis nuzzled her anus bud.

'Yes, yes, fuck me in my hole,' cried Jana. 'Hard, Jason, hard. Make me beg for mercy!'

Without a word, he thrust his stiff cock all the way inside her anus and she redoubled the force of her masturbation as he pumped hard into her, filling her with the exquisite hot tickling of his swollen cock.

'This time, you shall not make me spurt, little virgin,' he hissed, 'so our audience may have a pretty spectacle.'

15

Whipped by Leandra

The spray of cold water was delicious on her reddened buttocks as she took his ruthless thrusts deep into her anus, squeezing the tender bulb of his cock with rhythmic pulses of her tight sphincter. Jason laughed.

'Sweet, Jana, but you won't fool me this time. I am ready for you, and I shall fuck you until you are raw as my manhood.'

'Yes, please, please, *please*. Oh! God! Yes!' gasped Jana, her fingers busy on her stiff clit.

Gradually, the first frenzy of Jason's thrust became slower, gentler. Jana's buttocks moved sinuously in time with his lips as he slid delicately into her, his bulb pushing right to her core, and withdrawing just as slowly until his cock was fully outside her, tickling her bud before plunging in to ravish her squirming bottom anew. Jana trembled in ecstasy. The giggling audience, the spray of water on her hot skin, seemed to belong to another world, far away. There was only the monstrous throbbing of her tingling clit as she rubbed her, and the sweet tickling ache in her anus as the man's cock dealt her the fierce pleasure of submission. She knew she had reached her plateau, and found to her delight that she could remain there, riding the wave of ecstasy that transfused her body. Her breath calmed; the heights of pleasure were not hers to command, as though she were a bird soaring in the cool clear air. Her fingers played gently on her nympha, not rushing her to climax, but teasing her, not allowing herself to cross the threshold of relief.

'You fuck beautifully, sir knight,' she murmured.

'Yes.'

'I am curious. You must have had good teachers.'

'Mmmm,' sang the girls as they watched.

Without ceasing to thrust in her anus, Jason reached up and turned off the shower.

'You wished to work up a sweat,' he said. 'And we must allow our audience an unclouded view.'

Jana twisted to look, and saw the naked girls shyly caressing each other, their faces flushed with heat and desires: hands stroked nipples and open, eager founts whose lips gleamed red and swollen with excitement as the girls cooed at the spectacle of knight and virgin fucking.

'Your croup is satisfying,' said Jason dreamily. 'It is tight, and well-firmed with muscle, now that you are of Maldona.'

'Don't tell me you're a Greek,' said Jana, mischievously.

'Say I am Mediterranean,' said Jason, not seeing her malicious joke.

'Part Greek, and part northern too, for my mother was Swedish.'

'Then where were you raised?'

'An island. Mykonos. Have you heard of it?'

'Why, I know it. I have been there. Oh, yes, *yes*!' Jana gasped.

'Yes Mykonos, or yes, fuck me?'

'Both, you ... Oh, mmm ... you silly. Talk to me, Jason, while you screw me so beautifully in my tight little arse that satisfies you so much.'

It was thrilling to talk so casually, as though they were taking tea, and not arse-fucking in front of an audience of naked girls caressing each other's clits and breasts, their bodies shining like slippery bare eels. And the thought that they might be discovered at any moment, and incur a lacing, added the excitement of danger. Jana sensed that Jason, for all his outward cool, felt the same.

'My father was rich,' said Jason. 'He owned ships; but I grew up with the children of goatherds and fishermen. Over the hills of our beloved island, and in the foaming sea, we would play naked under the godlike sun, and thought ourselves gods too. Out of season, beaches, were not full of tourists: we could play and no one disturbed us. Sometimes my mother would play with us on the sand, for, like her countryfolk, she liked to bathe naked.'

'Boys and girls together? And your mother?'

'And my older sister. Yes, we were very happy, Oh!'

Jana gave a hard, playful squeeze with her sphincter.

'And?' she said. 'Go on, Jason. I know you want to tell me, to confess.'

'There is nothing to confess.'

Jana squeezed again.

'Oh! How lovely, Jana!'

'Nothing? Naked with all those boys and girls, under the Greek sun, and nothing to confess?'

'My mother was with us!'

'Not all the time. And even so?'

Jason sighed, though the strength of his caress did not falter.

'Send these giggling virgins away, if you like,' said Jana.

'No. It is proper to be observed. It excites me, as it does you, Jana. As it excited me all those years ago on the gentle island Mykonos. We grew older, and so did our games. There was one boy, older by a few years, whose hairs were already sprouting round his cock. An Arab boy, very dark and handsome, and the son of my father's business rival.'

'You are dark and handsome, Jason,' purred Jana. 'Was he like you?'

'So my mother said. And on his sixteenth birthday, we had a party, high on the hill overlooking the beach and the town; we were gaily clothed, but the Arab boy's present was this: while we sang, my mother stripped him and herself, and, naked in our midst, they fucked. That was his birthday present, and he was no longer a virgin.'

'Well, it sounds so sweet and innocent. Pastoral, like a fairy tale.'

The murmurs of the watching girls had turned to fluttering sharp cries, as, excited by Jason's words, they brought themselves to sighing climax.

'Yes, I have always longed to recapture that innocence.

214

We boys played our games, of course, and many's the brown young bottom I've had squirming under me, or had pumping a stiff prick into my willing hole. But when these things were past, and my own hairs sprouted, I wanted more.'

'Not your mother!' cried Jana in horror.

'No, she gently spurned me, told me that it was not right. But there was one who would relieve me from my fevered curiosity, the ripening fruit of my balls, longing to spurt their seed. A young, female friend took me to an empty hut at the top of the island, and showed me how to fuck her. We were naked, wrestling in lust, my cock inside her wet fount; I pierced her, and she lost her hymen, but as I was about to spurt into her, my mother surprised us. She told me that she was sad rather than angry, and that I must leave home until the colours of my aura were calm and healthy again. First she tied me, naked as I was, in the doorframe of the hut, and flogged me with a rattan cane, so severely that I remember every moment of my lacing. And ... and at the last stroke of the cane on my bare bottom, I felt a sweet pleasure, and my seed flowed from my balls! So, Jana, you see why I belong to Maldona.'

'Was that the first time she whipped you?'

'Why, yes, though I was beaten often enough at my English boarding school. The matron loved to cane our naked bottom, mine in particular.'

'You liked it?'

'Yes. Yes, of course. She laced me most cruelly, but I loved her for it. I loved her, when she made me spurt with her hard lacing.'

'It is unusual for a female to beat boys at an English school.'

'She is an unusual matron,' said Jason, 'and that is why I followed her here.'

'You mean –?'

'She is the Matron of Maldona,' said Jason, crying as his seed spurted into Jana's quivering anus, and toppling her into a headlong rush of orgasm.

Not for the first time, Jana reflected that there was more

to Maldona than met the eye, when suddenly there was the crack of a whip, and squeals from the watching virgins, who promptly scampered back to their sauna. Before the naked lovers, magnificent in bird's plumage and robe of rainbow colours, stood Leandra.

'Mistress!' cried Jana, and bent in a clumsy bow. Leandra cracked her whip in the air.

'Well!' she said, a cruel smile playing on her lips. 'I said you could take pleasure, Jason, but it seems that you may have taken a little too much.'

'No, Mistress,' he said stiffly, 'I did it to tame the wicked girl, nothing more, I assure you. There was no pleasure.'

Jana could not believe her ears.

'You bastard!' she cried, lunging at Jason with outstretched claws, but then yelped and drew back as Leandra's thong cracked smartly on her hands.

'He lies, Mistress,' sobbed Jana. 'He fucked me – he took me, with force. I admit that I took pleasure, but the approach was Jason's.'

'Jason is a loyal slave, and I take his word,' snapped Leandra. She held up the key which Jana had made in the candleshop, and the stockings which she had placed in Jason's pocket as his reward. Jason smirked.

Leandra threw Jana's stockings at him, and he caught them.

'You may keep your reward for your pretended treachery,' purred Leandra. 'They will do nicely as a *strophium* and a *zona* to bind your exhausted little *nympha*, which the slut has made all red and raw. Yes, fashion yourself a nice bikini, for your pleasure and my amusement.'

'Thank you, Mistress.'

'As for you, Jana, what did you think to do with this key you have made improperly? Open my closet and take one of my bird masks?'

Jana was silent; her thoughts whirled as she realised she had been betrayed by Jason, trapped by his wicked game.

She looked bitterly at the boy, who was busy binding her stockings round his breasts and loins. He grinned cheerfully as he slipped the makeshift bikini on to his man's body.

'You see, Jana? I was a man a moment ago, but now I am the woman of my mistress again. And you know what they say, *cherchez la femme*. It's always a woman that betrays you.'

'Answer, Jana!' rapped Leandra. 'What was your purpose? You must tell the truth!'

'I wanted to open the locked door,' said Jana. 'I was ... curious.'

Leandra laughed, her voice a cascade of petals.

'Well, the key Jason brought you was not the key to the steel door, you poor thing, it was the key to the closet where I keep old toys and papers and odds and ends. Jason told me everything, you see.'

'That's obvious,' said Jana, sneering at the simpering boy.

'Oh, you have a voice, now,' said Leandra. 'Well, it won't save you from whipping, my girl, and no ordinary whipping, though I daresay you'll find that voice hoarse from overwork as you beg me for mercy.'

'I shan't beg you for anything, Leandra,' said Jana evenly, and was rewarded with a cut of the whip across her bare breasts. She bit her lip to stop herself crying out.

'Mmm, I'm impressed,' said Leandra. 'But you'll squeal when I lace you, make no mistake. They always do.'

'Not me,' said Jana fiercely. 'I'll take your punishment, Mistress, and I'll be proud to brave you.'

'Good,' cried Leandra. 'I knew you had it in you, Jana. You have my spunk, I can tell.'

'Don't try to stroke me, Mistress!' cried Jana. 'I've done wrong, I admit it, and shall take punishment. But I was betrayed, and that too is a wrong.'

'How perceptive of you, Jana. Your betrayer must be punished, too, for he "sneaked" – isn't that what you English say? How absolutely beastly of you, Jason. But I'll attend to you in good time.'

'I was obedient to you, Mistress!' Jason blurted out.

'Ah! *Cherchez la femme*, eh, boy? Never trust a woman, not even a perfect one. But it's late; no time to punish you now, Jana, because I require daylight for you to appreciate things to the full. We shall go back to my apartment and enjoy a light supper before retiring. Come, Jana. Dress, and attend me.'

When Jana had donned her uniform, Leandra courteously gave her an arm, and they walked thus in stately file, followed by the glowering Jason. Jana was puzzled by this unexpected show of friendship, the more so as the two women sat on Leandra's balcony to enjoy a cosy meal served with ill-disguised pique by the sullen young knight, sheathed once more in a pretty girl's robe of filmy blue chiffon.

'Stop sulking, Jason,' said Leandra. 'What do you expect, a medal? You did your duty by informing on Jana, but a sneak gets no respect. Jana, on the other hand, is guilty of deceit and curiosity and all sorts of wicked things, but a girl with no curiosity is a girl with no red blood in her veins. And we'll see what you're made of, Jana, when I give you your special lacing at dawn tomorrow morning. It is so pretty! I know you'll enjoy it.'

'Do not mock, Mistress.'

'I'm not mocking, you sweet. I knew you would find out. After all, *I* did. But you were foolish, dear Jana, and that is a terrible crime here; foolish, because all good girls get to see the finishing school when it is time.'

Leandra's tone did not invite further questioning on this point. Instead, Jana said, between mouthfuls of pudding, 'My punishment will be severe?'

'I promise.'

'Hurt me as you will, Mistress, I shall not cry out.'

Leandra smiled, and put her fingers to Jana's lips.

'I think you are wrong. I shall break you, Jana, and you shall love me for it.'

Jana seized her mistress's hand and kissed it, her face blushing with her secret truth.

'I love you already, Mistress. Yes . . . I want to be you!'

'And your friend Erato?'

'She . . . she was imperfect, and is gone.' Jana's voice trembled as she said it, for she knew that her words were a kind of betrayal.

'So you think,' murmured Leandra enigmatically. 'But

tell me, sweet Jana, are you not capable of crying out as she did? Of speaking the words "I go down" which will release you from this place?'

Jana smiled.

'Never,' she replied coolly. 'And even if I did, Mistress, you would not release me, would you?'

'You are right,' said Leandra.

That night, Jana shared Leandra's bed. Her mistress had made her vow to keep total silence until her punishment had been completed the following morning, and so fevered were Leandra's caresses during that sleepless night that it took all her strength to obey. She lost count of the times her thighs opened and her wet, swollen cunt-lips parted to receive Leandra's rigid clit; or the delight she felt as Leandra lay beneath her and guided her own rigid nympha into the tender folds of her own pink fount. Her nipples and neck were sore from Leandra's fervent bites, and her fesses smarted from the playful, gentle spankings they received from the Parfaite's hard palms.

'A spanking is nothing,' whispered Leandra. 'Just wait till the dawn, sweet thing.' And Jana could not reply, though she was bursting to do so.

While Jana had to keep silent, except for her rasping hot breath as her mistress tongued her again and again to climax, Leandra did not stint herself in enjoying the sounds of her vigorous pleasure, which, she said, was made more piquant by the knowledge that Jason was obliged to listen from his post on the balcony. As punishment for 'sneaking', Jason had been chained by his neck and forced to spend the night naked in the freezing air. This caused Jana a glow of malicious satisfaction, making up for whatever her own punishment might be.

'I expect you are afraid of heights,' whispered Leandra, as the two women, in each other's arms, drifted off into a doze as the first birds sang. Jana did not answer, as it was forbidden, but her body tensed in apprehension.

'I thought so,' said Leandra, kissing her. 'Good.'

* * *

The dawn over the sierra was bloody fire, its crisp air fragrant with the freshness of the new day. Jana rubbed the sleep from her eyes and breathed deeply as she watched the orange sun spread its love over the mountaintop of Maldona. She wore one of Leandra's robes; the Parfaite unlocked Jason's chain and kicked the boy's shivering, dimpled bottom, with a curt instruction to prepare breakfast.

The meal was taken in silence. Leandra's manner was neither friendly nor unfriendly: brisk, rather. When it was over, she gave Jason whispered instructions, then doffed her robe, and invited Jana to do the same. Jana shivered; she hoped for an embrace, but received only a chaste peck on the cheek, as though the night of caresses belonged already to her imagination. Reality was the strange whipping frame which dangled from the ceiling, where it was fixed to a kind of gibbet, whose purpose Jana could not see. The frame was a lattice of stout ropes, criss-crossed to the height of a person, and secured at top and bottom by polished wooden poles carved into hand-grips. It looked like a device from a children's schoolyard.

'A swing is so nice, isn't it?' said Leandra, politely gesturing that Jana should take her place on the rope frame. 'There is something so erotic about the up-and-down motion, the leaping in our bellies which is just like . . . well, you know. Hold on tight, Jana.'

Puzzled, Jana did as she was told, and grasped the wooden handles. Her arms and legs were splayed for her whipping, and that was familiar, but she could not see anything special about this particular beating.

Jason gravely handed Leandra her whip; it was white, with four vicious thongs, and Leandra stroked Jana's bare skin with loving gentleness, allowing the thongs to caress her fount, breasts, and linger in the crack of her fesses. Jana was glad she was forbidden to speak, for she wanted to cry out that Leandra shouldn't have a white whip like hers, surely? The whip felt lovely as it touched her, but she knew that it would take all her resistance not to whimper as it lashed her in earnest.

'Nice now, not so nice when I raise my arm,' said Leandra, as though reading her mind. 'But the swing will cheer you up.'

Jason was at work with a pulley system, which creaked as he turned the wheels. The ropes quivered, and the gibbet from which the whipping frame was suspended turned slowly outwards, swivelling, to Jana's horror, until her frail rope lattice was lifted over the parapet, and she hovered on the brink of a giddying drop. Her heart raced, and she fought to keep her eyes from blurring as terror froze her. God, she thought, I must say it. I must be released; I can't take it, I'll fall down, screaming, it must be a thousand feet. Oh yes, say it now . . .

Deftly, Leandra slapped a cold metal gag on Jana's mouth and clamped it tight. Jana's mouth was filled with a hard ball that pinioned her tongue, so that she could make no sound except an anguished grunt.

'There!' she cried cheerfully. 'That should stop you saying anything you don't really mean, Jana.'

And slowly the gibbet was winched out into the cold bright air until Jana hung swaying and fearful above the glittering green valley that stretched so far below. Desperately, she clung to the wooden handles, her only support. The whipping frame dangled at arm's length from the parapet, an arm's length that might have been a hundred miles. The sun was already fierce on Jana's bare body, but the breeze was thankfully cool. She faced away from the apartment, and as her nerves steadied, she began to feel a strange excitement at her predicament. She was naked, high over the earth, and free, not strapped or chained. She was a bird, flying as the whip sang . . .

And sing it did. Jana shuddered at the first stroke, which took her fiercely on the buttocks, and the momentum of the blow caused her swing to move forward. The second stroke, and the third, still on her smarting bare globes, and Jana held on tight, her teeth grinding against the metal ball of her gag, for she thought she had never, ever endured such a beating. The swing moved easily now, each blow of the whip on Jana's naked flesh sending it higher and higher

221

into the cool bright air, and despite the burning of her croup, and her shoulders now, as Leandra worked with devilish skill on the hard slabs of Jana's back muscle, Jana felt an elation, a sense of freedom and excitement. She *did* feel like a bird, swooping over the far canyon.

The whip crackled across Jana's naked skin, each stroke like molten gold, and she lost count of their numbers. She concentrated on holding on to her perch, clutching the wooden grips as the whip sailed her through the air. Her thighs were spread, her ankles lodged firmly against the rope wall and, to her surprise, she felt a trickle of moisture on her soft inner skin. Her fount was becoming wet; the smarting of the vicious whip was sweetened by a melting, liquid thrill deep in her belly, and she moaned in excitement.

Her heart leapt with joy, not just the physical joy of the white leather's caress on her back and buttocks, but joy at the knowledge that her body's pain was her heart's pleasure, and that the harsher Leandra's whipstrokes fell, the more Jana's elation grew, and the wetter and wetter her tingling cunt gushed. She was panting now, not wanting the whipping to stop, urging the swing to rise higher and higher as the sweetness filled her belly and sex. It was as though she were making love to the whole world, flying over it to anoint it with the drops of her love-juice which flowed from her fount and were sprinkled in little glistening droplets far below into the thirsty earth. Her whole body was on fire; Leandra had viciously and expertly flogged her on back, buttocks and thighs, and Jana glowed with pleasure. Her wrists were locked around the grips, and she wanted to sing as the beauty welled up inside her belly, and the hot oil flowed so thickly from her dripping sex, and her clit and nipples shivered hard and trembling in the wind's caress; suddenly, without warning, she felt herself give way. A flood of orgasm washed her, stunning her with its unexpected, uncontrolled force. She roared in her throat, a roar that turned to a high squealing scream as the whip's stroke, falling in the midst of her molten pleasure, seemed the sweetest, final kiss, as though a huge pair of moist lips had taken hold of her cunt and belly and were sucking every last drop of pleasure from her.

She twisted her head, to look at the woman who had flogged her to such ecstasy, and saw Leandra's head encased in her gaudy bird-mask. Her head spun, and the force of her climax made her faint, just for a split second, but enough to loosen her grip on the swing. And Jana fell, silently screaming, down towards the earth.

16

The Finishing School

The only thing Jana did as she fell headlong was to rip off her gag so that she could scream. She did not see her life pass in front of her eyes, she did not even know, or think, she was going to die. She did not think at all. Her body was a glowing node of pure terror, and she screamed, a long wail at the agony of falling, out of all control. The scented air grew warmer and warmer as her naked body twisted like a fish towards the deep earth, her proud muscles writhing in their final, useless spasm, seeking contact where there was none, reaching out to touch the fleeing rock face that sped past her eyes, utterly alone with the howling in her throat. Seeing the earth grow vaster, she involuntarily shut her eyes, then, terrified of the darkness, forced them open for a final glimpse of life.

The ground that had looked greyish-green from the heights of Maldona now took on a greyish-blue colour. It was not grass; it rippled, and Jana realised she was falling towards water. What had seemed like a field from above, through the heat haze, was a lake that lapped the skirts of Maldona. She stopped screaming, and took a deep breath, just as the surface of the water struck her body with the force of a giant whip, and she was plummeting down through the crystal depths of the lake, brushed by shoals of glittering fish that shone with a strange misty light that emanated from the rock face itself, the mountain on top of which Maldona sat. She arched her body to slow her descent, and kicked and wriggled to make her body level out from its fall and begin to climb. Her lungs bursting, she swam frantically upwards, past the smoky light, which seemed to come from a thick glass or crystal window, like the porthole of some giant submarine. After an age, she kicked out into the fresh air, and, with choking, grateful sobs, gulped for breath. The valley was serene, as though her passage had gone unnoticed. No one looked down from Leandra's parapet, but Jana was too busy relishing her life and breath to feel righteous rage. She trod water for a while, blissful in the sun, and wriggling like a happy sea urchin as the shoals of slippery fish tickled her naked body. Her thoughts swirled like the fishes: Leandra must know she would fall into the lake, and come looking for her. Naturally, she had hidden the fact that a fall would not be lethal, the terror of the falling girl no doubt adding a cruel frisson to the pleasure of flogging her. What would her relation with Leandra in future? It could only be that of mistress and slave, and there could be no going back. Jana would be the mistress. She would have Leandra.

For the moment, she was content to paddle in the warm water and let the joy of life wash over her. But her thoughts turned to the gleaming window under the lake, and thus obviously under Maldona herself. She turned to look at the fortress above, and tried to imagine where that window should be in the network of underground passages where the candleshop was. It was like a mental jigsaw puzzle, and she knew the answer before she reached it. The light was coming from the chamber beyond the secret locked door: from the finishing school. Gulping air, she dived and swam down towards it.

She floated naked as a fish in the water, and her mind raced with awful fantasies. The finishing school ... some kind of sinister pun. But what could it mean? Then she thought of Harry and his cameras, and Caspar with his film-making business, and the ready tribe of girls available at Maldona, accustomed to the sweetest caresses and the harshest punishments. Were they making erotic films here, the kind with brutal chastisements, because only in Maldona could they find actresses prepared to bare their bodies to the lash? But surely even hard movies like that could be made openly these days? Why, she herself would be flattered to appear in such a work, as she had been glad to pose nude for Harry and Greta. Unless it was more than chastisement. She had heard that there was a kind of film which went as far as it was possible to go. Jocasta the surgeon was involved, there was a clinic of some kind. Oh God, she thought. The finishing school . . .

She pressed her face to the thick glass, surrounded by bright darting fish, and she hoped that her blurred likeness would merge with the fish in the viewscreen of this giant natural aquarium. Her lips were tightly shut, or she would have gasped at what she saw.

She looked into a room similar to Harry's studio, but decorated like a film set. Well, it was a film set, rich with sensuous furniture. She saw whipping posts, pillories, various arrangements of wall-cuffs and leg-irons, such as old Elias Ardenne must have made. Some of them were heartily in use. And a camera was whirring. Jana had to break for air, and repeated the operation half a dozen times before her awed curiosity had been satisfied.

The room, or studio, was crowded, and Jana realised she was witnessing a cinematic orgy. There were virgins dressed in impossibly glamorous outfits of silk and lace, smoking cigarettes and brandishing champagne glasses. Some of them managed to do this while kneeling, with their filmy robes raised above their bare bottoms to receive a vigorous buggery or flogging from one of the many African or Arab men present.

Most virgins were nude, sucking the cocks of black men while their own quims were licked by their sisters. Threesomes and foursomes were common: a girl fucked in anus and cunt by different men, while her mouth was busy on the cock of a third, and even her armpits squeezed two bulging stiff penises. The groups swirled and merged, to the background of powerful floggings being administered to the chained and nude virgins, or to the sweating men's bodies, naked except for dazzling golden necklaces, nipple clamps and chains, cock harnesses and slave bracelets. There was every combination of lustful chastisement, and every face wore a scream of ecstasy. All was under the direction, it seemed, of a statuesque grey-haired woman. She was nude but for a network of tight chains that, apart from her bare buttocks, enclosed her body like armour, and she sang commands from her position trussed to a whipping post garlanded with roses. Her bare back and buttocks were receiving a hard birching from an African, who wore a gold chain fastened tightly round his balls, its other end clipped to her cunt-lips. The woman was Netta.

Jana thought that Caspar must also be there, and she saw him. He wore a black leather zona and strophium, and as his wife took her flogging from her African, so with a willow cane he whipped the bare bottom of the girl whose mink was shaped like a butterfly – Sarah Pennington. Well, thought Jana, she has made her finishing school.

But her greatest amazement was at another flagellant scene: wearing only a leather zona studded with bright silver nails, Henry Gordon Playste, wielding a four-thonged whip, administered a savage lacing to the jerking naked body of a tethered and strapped female. His penis bulged under the g-string, and Jana wondered if the nails were very sharp on his manhood, and if he enjoyed it. But it was the female who interested her most.

She dangled from chains fixed to the ceiling, her wrists tightly cuffed and her nude body on tiptoe, bouncing with the force of the blows Henry dealt. She wore a shiny steel gag; as her back and buttocks trembled under the lash, a black man fucked her from the front, standing, her body slamming on to his rigid glistening cock at every blow from the whip, while his hands squeezed her nipples almost white as he bit her breasts. Her face was dark red, streaming with joyful tears, and she wore a beatific smile as she quivered under her chastisement. It was Erato.

First bell rang, and Jana realised that she had better decide, now, what to do. Everybody would soon be at breakfast; it was the time to sneak back to her cell and retrieve her belongings. She knew that to reappear, as though back from the dead, would do her no good. It would perhaps be a few hours before she was noted as missing, and in that time she could find a hiding place. But

227

where? And how to gain entrance back to Maldona? Leandra, faithless Leandra, would say she had 'gone down', and if she were found, she had a good idea that she would end up like Erato.

Slowly, she swam to the edge of the lake and crawled out on to the grass. Above her towered the impregnable fortress, and the only way in she knew was all the way round to the other side, and Matron's little door.

There must be a main entrance, and she set out, grim and naked in that hot summer morning, to find it. She skirted the mountain face, shielding herself from any watcher on the battlements above, and still clutching the bird mask she had worn for her flogging with, somewhat absurdly, she realised, the gag Leandra had made her wear.

On and on she walked, and began to despair of ever finding an entrance, or a path up which she might climb. But gradually she became aware that the ground beneath her feet was not still. From time to time it hummed, vibrating as though at the passage of some vehicle underground. Underground? She looked back and saw that in her meanderings, she had not come far from the subterranean chamber, and cursed. The sun was starting to burn her skin, and there was no shade.

Suddenly the wall of Maldona curved sharply, and around the curve she saw a metal door, set into the surface of the meadow, with railings on either side and two steps protruding, as though the door shielded a staircase. She tugged open the door, reflecting that it would have been impossible to do so without her new, strong muscles, and, panting, laid it open. Into the depths of the earth a metal staircase weaved in a spiral, and from below came a faint smell of engines. Gingerly, she descended, carefully pulling the door shut behind her, though this left her in darkness. But there were lights far beneath, and she headed for them.

She emerged at last into a tunnel, whose floor was concrete, and lit by sodium lamps at ten metre intervals. Away from Maldona, the strip led into gloom, but in the other direction, a huge maw led into the fortress's bowels. A sound disturbed her; it was a low growl of a motor, and she ducked back into the stairwell as it approached.

228

It whooshed past, and it was the same vehicle she had seen so long ago at Harry and Greta's, disgorging its cargo of naked humans. Greta was at the wheel.

Breathlessly, she made her way to the loading bay from which the truck had emerged. Two doors led out, one into the finishing school, the other to a grimy staircase ascending back towards the safety of Maldona. She paused and shook her head. Erato was in the finishing school, evidently enjoying the morning's filming, if morning and night had any meaning for those orgiasts. But what would be the terrifying conclusion of the filming? She had to do something.

There was another truck waiting. Feverishly, she imagined hotwiring it and escaping with Erato down that mysterious roadway. Grimly, she entered, and found herself in paradise.

Concealed lighting made the place seem washed by bright sun. She was in a white corridor strewn with rose petals, and all along it little fountains splashed, set into the walls beside vidid murals which depicted naked men and women at every form of pleasure that two, or more, human bodies can devise. The corridor led to a courtyard, in which girls reclined by a larger fountain, laughing and sipping drinks, while male slaves in bright silks waited on them. The place was crowded, and Jana's nudity aroused no comment other than envious glances at the beauty of her muscled body.

'She'll fetch a good price,' she heard from one group of staring virgins, happily scurrying to their assigned studios. Jana was able to peek in, and she saw film sets like the one she had observed through the viewscreen, all well equipped with devices of pleasure and chastisement. Some were full of girls eagerly trying on gorgeous dresses, or having their faces and bodies painted, their long hair styled, or their nails manicured. Everywhere was a heady mixture of musky scents, flowers, perfumes, sherbet and sweetmeats, and Jana thought this must be like a harem of old Arabia. As she penetrated the labyrinth of the finishing school, in the direction of the room where Erato was, she heard more often the crack of leather stroking naked skin, and occasionally the high shriek of a flogged girl.

She came to a courtyard, with girls sitting by a fountain. They fussed happily with each other's long hair, or their lovely silk dresses, and there were cooing birds, uncaged, and bright with colour. A girl played sweetly on a lute: but there was no music in Maldona!

Erato was among them. She wore a filmy purple robe, like a Roman toga, with a garland of flowers, and white sandals. She glowed with happiness, and rose to greet her friend.

'Jana! I am so glad you have joined us! And so soon! I knew you had perfection in you!' The other girls smiled in welcome.

'Erato, I've come to get you out of here!' hissed Jana, and told her of her plan to steal the truck.

'Why, what foolishness!' laughed Erato. 'Greta will come for me in the truck, when my hair is grown and I am perfect. The road leads to her house, and that is where our owners come to take delivery of us. It will be so lovely to be perfect, to be the slave of a man, to bare myself to his whip, and wear his gold!'

'Erato, it's not what you think! Those films of Caspar's . . .'

'Oh, but it is! How else may our owners far afield know the beauty and willingness of the slaves that await them?'

'Come with me, Erato. Now!'

'No, Jana, you must stay here. You will fetch a good price; I'm so envious of those fine breasts, those rippling muscles! I think you can be a prized slave-mistress: wield the lash as well as receive it!'

'Slave! Erato, what are you saying?'

'It is a cruel and beautiful word. Do we not all dream of being a slave, Jana? Of freeing ourselves from all will, and all selfhood! The bliss of obeying the whim of our master or mistress! Of feeling their cane on our naked croup, flogging us into total submission! Do not forget that our master too must be chained and whipped until his naked buttocks glow sweet crimson, and in treating him thus, we are even more divinely his slave! What else does Maldona teach us?'

'Erato! I have seen the book ... I know the secret of Maldona,' cried Jana. 'There is a way for us to triumph!'

'I have triumphed, Jana. I have obeyed the will of Maldona, the training ground of our bodies and souls.'

Suddenly, the crowd of girls parted, and Jocasta was beside them. She wore her surgeon's tunic, breasts tied by her strophium that peeped enticingly from her unbuttoned cleavage. She was followed by Matron, in her severe black uniform.

'You are impetuous, Jana,' said Jocasta pleasantly. 'You have balls.'

'My, girl, how you've swelled!' cried Matron. 'And so beautifully! How glad I am you've been sent to us so soon!'

'She is here unlawfully,' said Jocasta gravely. 'She has committed imperfection, and must therefore be punished.'

'I agree, Surgeon Mistress,' said Matron, gazing with loving cruelty at Jana's naked body. 'How ripe she is for a taste of my cane on those firm fesses! How I long to see you, Jana, strapped to the flogging post and whimpering for mercy!'

Jana stepped away from Erato, and bowed low to the two adepts.

'I agree, Mistresses,' she said humbly. 'I obey. If I have committed imperfection, punish me.'

'Why, no,' said Matron, 'Leandra has already marked your body most prettily. How well you danced for us! No, now is the time for your flowering, dear.'

'Thank you, Matron,' cried Jana joyfully, and took off in a leap which cannoned her into Jocasta, knocking her into the others. They fell like lopped branches, and Jana delivered a savage kick to Jocasta's groin, which caused her to jerk and shudder, pinioning the other women in a struggling heap on the floor. The girls looked uncertainly, in mild alarm.

'Jana! Don't be a fool!' cried Erato, as Jana raced away down the corridor, towards the loading bay. She crashed through the doors and opened one of the trucks. There were no keys, and she realised that she did not have time to rip out the ignition and hotwire the contraption, for already there were cries and footsteps rushing on her tracks. Cursing, she got down from the van and made for the gateway that led to the road, then stopped. That way, they would find her easily. The road led only to Greta's; if she climbed out of the staircase by which she had entered, she would be back in the open valley, as defenceless as before, except that they knew where to find her. Sighing, she slammed through the door to the service stairs and began to climb once more, this time at a furious scampering pace.

Below, she heard the roar of an engine as the van started off to look for her, then a confused throng of voices:

'The lake . . . can't hide . . . no point checking the stairs, she'll find out soon enough if she's gone up there . . .'

Full of foreboding, Jana continued to climb. She managed to secure her mask so as to leave her hands free for the rails, but to her dismay, the staircase abruptly came to an end, as though it had been severed by a huge scythe, leaving jagged stumps of metal.

The passage upwards had been blocked, as though by some earth tremor, which had opened up a shaft below, now filled with debris of brick and plaster and tile. Opposite, Jana saw that the only exit from this dead end was a narrow channel scooped into the rock wall, about the size of a sewage pipe, and its mouth strangely encrusted with drooping stalactites. The inside of the passage was shiny, as though it had been waxed, and Jana realised that the stalactities *were* wax. A glimmer of hope shone: it was the refuse chute from the candleshop above her.

It was just possible for her to swing from the ruined staircase across the gap, and lock her fists inside the waste tunnel. She dangled, terrified, for giddy seconds before she got a firm hold and painfully levered herself up until her shoulders filled the chute's mouth. Below her was a drop on to jagged shards of stone which might be fatal.

The layer of wax was thick enough for her to gouge fingerholds and, when she had done so, she was able to

232

wriggle all of her body inside the narrow passage. It squeezed her like a glove, and the more she struggled to ascend, the more slippery her body became as the sweat moistened her.

Suddenly she gasped as she felt a burning sensation on her hand, and almost lost her hold on the gouged slit which supported her weight. Ahead she could see a flickering light, which was the furnace of the candleshop, but it blurred and darkened for a moment, and then she felt another spasm of scalding liquid which stung her bare nipples and brought tears to her eyes. Up above, they were ladling the *cire perdue*, the wasted wax, into the disposal chute! She did not dare cry out; all she could do was to hold on tight and grit her teeth, as the molten wax formed little rivulets of burning lava between her breasts and thighs, like the explorations of a burning lover. It seemed an age before the hot flow stopped, and she felt the wax congeal and harden all over her stinging flesh. Satisfied that she was safe once more, she wriggled on and, at last, not caring what her reception would be, she thrust her head out of the entrance to the waste chute. Beside her roared the friendly furnace; all round the candleshop stood astonished virgins, watched over by Miriam, who almost dropped her whip in surprise.

'Ah! Ah!' Jana moaned as she struggled to free herself, and when she had finally got her whole body out of the tube, and stood giddily on the floor of the shop, she saw that the whole company bowed to her.

'Leandra! We are honoured!' said Miriam.

Jana had to stop herself laughing. Of course! She had on Leandra's bird-mask.

She nodded curtly.

'You have not seen me, virgins,' she commanded, doing her best to imitate Leandra's voice. 'It is a wager between me and Circe.'

'Of course, Parfaite Leandra,' cooed Miriam unctuously, and Jana wished she could shove the vicious little corporal down the chute, and pour boiling wax over *her*. She hurried to the door, and was gone, out into the corridor, then ran as fast as she could through the empty bowels of Maldona. She was alone, and after a while she felt it safe to stop, secure in her unwanted disguise. She squatted and leaned against the wall of the corridor, panting. In a few minutes she could be at her cell; the company of Maldona at breakfast, the auberge would be deserted, and even if she met Hera or anyone else, her disguise as Leandra would, she thought, carry her through. Would have to! As she took to her feet again, she realised she was smiling, and her heart was swelling with joy, for she had passed for the beautiful goddess Leandra!

She broke off the crusts of wax which coated her, finding especially awkward the shiny carapace which had sheathed her mink, and silently thanking whoever had poured the fluid, for the covering of her mink had hidden the fact that her mons was unshaven. Little stalactites of the wax had drooped from her nipples, and, impishly, she let them remain, feeling them dance against her breasts like exotic jewels as she ran towards her cell.

Once there, she quickly gathered her bag, and as much of her kit as she could easily carry. A plan had formed, and she would need her things, but she would also need somewhere to hide until the Special Day, when, armed with her powerful knowledge, she would reappear, and take the greatest risk of her life. She paused in the corridor by Miriam's empty cell, suddenly riven with despair. She had nowhere to go. She could not remain Leandra, and she could not reappear as Jana, until the Special Day . . . and then she knew that there was one place she could go, that it was the only place where she might, hoping against hope, find refuge.

'Harriet!' exclaimed Jana, as she pushed open the door to the library.

'Hello!' said Harriet brightly, putting down the stack of books she was carrying. 'How nice to see you, Jana, dear.'

'I didn't expect to find you here.'

'Well, where did you expect to find me? I am the librarian.'

'I mean . . . breakfast . . .'

'Oh, I make my own breakfast when I want. There's some roly-poly pudding left. Would you like some?'

Jana realised she was ravenously hungry.

'Yes, please,' she said, and soon was sitting with a glutinous plateful, which she wolfed, raisin things and all.

'You can take your mask off,' said Harriet. 'You are awfully sweet as Leandra, but I think I prefer you as Jana. And you'd better put your uniform on, it wouldn't do to be caught naked without permission.'

'It won't do to be caught at all,' said Jana cautiously.

'I suppose not,' said Harriet, 'after all you've been through. How exciting! You'll want to stay here until the Special Day, I expect, when you are going to rise like the phoenix, and wow everybody.'

'How do you know?' said Jana, wiping custard from her lips.

'Oh, librarians know all sorts of things,' said Harriet airily. 'Now, why don't you shower, for you're a right mess, aren't you? And I'll lay out a nice clean uniform for you.'

She put her finger to Jana's breast, and flicked the little wax stalactite.

'How cute!' she cried. 'I'm ever so slightly hot, just looking at you, Jana. I hope you aren't too tired, later, for . . . you know.'

'You're insatiable!' said Jana, smiling despite her confusion.

'I am rather, aren't I? Comes of being a librarian.'

Harriet licked her lips, and her eyes gleamed.

'And,' she said, 'since you're here with all your kit and caboodle, you won't mind giving me a lacing with your white whip, will you?'

'What!'

'You have got it, haven't you?' said Harriet, frowning.

'Yes, but how did you know?'

'It is my *job* to know, Jana,' said Harriet, as if explaining to a simpleton. 'Now take your shower.'

'Well,' said Jana nervously, 'where is the nearest fountain? It might be too risky to show myself.'

'Oh, I have my own fountain,' said Harriet. 'Come.'

Harriet opened a drawer, and took out a key. Jana was too tired to ask what a key was doing in Maldona, and followed her to the back of the cavernous library, where Harriet deftly swivelled a tall bookshelf, to reveal a doorway set in the wall. She opened the door with her key, and waved Jana inside.

'How lovely!' cried Jana. She found herself in an apartment like Leandra's, cool and shady, and hung with tapestries and rugs in the Moroccan style. The floor was of painted tiles, and on the balcony a small fountain played, its jets sparkling in the sun that beamed down from the hazy mountain. Down below shone the lake into which Jana had fallen; its surface was near enough to appear as water, and she could make out the staircase which had led her underground. There was the sound of cooing, as turtle-doves twittered round a little bird-table.

'Lovely,' said Harriet, 'but the devil to keep clean. All this work in the library – so little space, you know – and this place as well, and since I am just a humble whipping girl, the lowest of the blasted low, I don't get a nice boy for my slave. Not me. But do I complain? Oh, no. A librarian's lot is not a happy one, dear Jana,' she added with an exaggerated sigh.

'I'll gladly be your slave, if I can stay here, Harriet,' cried Jana. 'I'll keep everything clean as a new pin, I promise.'

'And feed the birds?'

'I adore feeding birds! Please say yes.'

'Of course, after the Special Day, you'll forget about your loyal friend Harriet,' said the girl glumly. 'You'll be so high and mighty, and I'll still be a wretched whipping girl.'

'Never! I swear! When I have . . .'

Harriet grinned.

'Smart. You don't want to give your game away. Never mind, tra la la, I already know the game, ha ha! What else is a library for, what what?'

And Harriet burst into peals of laughter.

'Oh, Harriet, don't play with me. Please let me stay. I'll

lace you so beautifully with my white whip . . . please say
yes.'

Harriet broke off the two wax icicles from Jana's
nipples, and blew them at Jana's lips.

'Yes,' she said.

17

Arena

In the days that followed, Harriet proved to be a harsher, more efficient, and more loving mistress than Leandra had ever been. More efficient, because under a punishing regime of exercise and diet, Jana's muscles grew beyond her dreams; more loving, because every caress from Jana whetted her appetite for more; harsher, because as Harriet had promised, the housework was *never* done.

Blissfully, she could be naked all day long, save for a pair of woolly sheepskin slippers with curled toes, in which she glided, humming, on the smooth floor, making it gleam like a mirror. Jana especially enjoyed feeding the turtle-doves, tame creatures that let her hold them to her breast; she loved to feel their wings beat aginst her nipples, like a lover caressing her.

'You are as pretty as a picture,' said Harriet one day, as Jana held a brace of doves to her body. 'Perhaps the Mistress of Art will take a photo set of you.'

'I look forward to meeting the Mistress of Art,' said Jana.

'Oh, on the Special Day, you shall meet everyone,' said Harriet, 'But you shall have to make your own entrance, and in your own way, which I am sure shall be suitably dramatic. My help is of no use to you in your – tra la la, da da! – moment of destiny!'

Jana laughed at Harriet's mock-heroic declamation.

'Don't worry,' she said. 'I have been thinking.'

'Penny for your thoughts, then.'

'No.'

'Smart girl. But you're chatting, and that floor should be polished until I can see my mink in it! Get to work!'

Jana was already beaded in sweat from a hearty session of housework.

'Harriet, you beast! I've just polished it, as you know very well!'

Harriet grinned.

'Insolence, eh, virgin? Bend over and touch your toes!'

Jana loved these little games, which were repeated every day.

'Oh, no, not a spanking!' she cried.

'Yes! I'll give that bare bottom a lacing she shan't forget!'

'Not bare . . . please, oh cruel mistress! Let me wear my panties, for modesty!'

'Naked as the day you were born, hussy! Now spread your cheeks, so that I can see your pretty little bud wriggle as I spank you.'

'Oooh . . .' cried Jana, and obeyed, then sighed and clenched her naked fesses as the tough Harriet rained hearty slaps with her palm, until Jana felt her buttocks flaming and pink.

'Enough!' she cried at last.

'Never enough,' hissed Harriet, and had her fingers inside Jana's wet fount, to rub her clit with delicious soft strokes as she laced the squirming buttocks. The scene ended as it always did, with the two girls writhing in a tight embrace on the newly polished floor, their juices flowing and mingling on to the tiles, while the turtle-doves flapped their wings and cooed in loving appreciation. Jana knew just how to touch Harriet, deep inside her fount above her pelvis bone, to bring her to a shuddering orgasm, accompanied by a wonderful flood of copious love-juice, as though Harriet's very heart had melted over Jana's tender fingers.

'I certainly deserved a spanking,' said Jana, nuzzling, 'for the floor is a mess!'

'But I take the blame, silly, and you must whip me for it,' said Harriet quite seriously. 'A spanking is for girlies, pooh! I want some stronger meat.'

'The white whip?'

Harriet paused.

'I'd love it,' she said, 'but no . . .'

'Why ever not?'

'You know something of its story,' said Harriet slowly.

'Of course. You *know* I have read the secret book, and don't tell me you chose it at random, minx!'

'Of course I chose it at random. How should I know anything about anything, a mere whipping slut that I am? But I do know that the white whip is only for Maldona herself!'

'That's crazy! Who would dare whip Maldona? And anyway, I've . . .'

'You've what?'

'Oh, nothing. Tell me, sweet Harriet, how shall I lace you?'

'The evening before the Special Day. It shall bring you luck; your muscles will be as strong as mountains, and you shall be near perfection. Oh, how I wish I could be like you! But some of us are born to serve in other ways.'

Jana nodded her head, and was released.

'Come, then,' said Harriet, taking her hand. 'I must go back to the library in a moment, for they are coming out of luncheon, but I'll show you my Chamber of Delights.'

In the bedroom which the two girls now shared, Harriet pushed aside the heavy Spanish closet, and revealed a door, which she opened. It led to a dank cell, windowless, and in the dim light that filtered from the bedroom, Jana saw that it contained a glittering array of implements that had no kind purpose.

'These are the instruments of correction,' said Harriet proudly. 'In the old days, the regime of Maldona was less merciful, and this is where errant virgins received chastisement. Of course it dates from the time before Maldona, the days of the Amir, when there was no mercy at all.'

The centre of the chamber was occupied by a magnificent frame of gleaming, oily teak, accoutred with straps, cuffs and bracelets.

'That is the pride of my collection,' said Harriet. 'Actually it is a relatively late acquisition, a gift from one of our

240

adepts outside, from England, I believe, in the eighteenth century.'

Jana looked down and saw a brass maker's plaque, and her heart raced as she read: ARDENNE & CO., ENGLAND.

She said nothing; Harriet's cheerful smile could not invite suspicion, surely? The girl could know nothing of this awful coincidence, that the teak flogging-frame upon which she was to be chastised came from Jana's own forefather.

'It is lovely, isn't it?' said Harriet dreamily. 'That is where I have always longed to be chastised, by my chosen one. You'll strap me in tight, Jana, won't you, and give me the lacing of my life, until I explode with pleasure?'

'Yes, Harriet, I'll do it,' said Jana, 'but only if you promise to give me as good as you get, for that seems only fair. It will limber me up for my day's work in the bullring.'

'Agreed, then,' said Harriet. 'And now, back to your housework, slut! And I want a really garlicky gazpacho for my supper tonight, do you hear?'

That night in bed, Jana whispered, as she was about to drift into sleep, 'Harriet, did you mean what you said, about the white whip?'

'That only Maldona herself should taste it?'

'Yes.'

'Of course I meant it. I'll have to make do with something gentler.'

'Aren't you curious to know how I got it?'

'It is forbidden to be curious. Anyway, I know how you got it.'

'*How* do you know? Oh, I don't understand.'

'I told you, it is forbidden to be curious! And how many times do I have to repeat – never believe anything a whipped girl tells you. They're all liars.'

'But you are the librarian!'

'Librarians are even worse, Jana dear.'

Harriet's indifference, her lack of curiosity as to Jana's plans, could be infuriating. Jana longed to tell her everything, what she had learned, and what she intended to do. But she held her peace; subtly, with constant hints and compliments, Harriet raised her morale to its highest peak, readying her for battle, goading her to new efforts in the training of her body. Harriet would oil her for exercise, cooing praises of her bulging muscles, and Jana glowed with pride at the strong woman she had become, a woman she would not have recognised only months before.

'This sounds silly,' she said, 'but I feel that this is really me, that I have become myself at last. Before, I was just ... I don't know, a shadow.'

'It doesn't sound silly, for it is the truth,' said Harriet. 'Before, you were a lovely possibility, and now you are loveliness herself.'

Her fingers stroked Jana's swelling clitoris.

'You are almost perfect, Mistress,' said Harriet shyly.

'Mistress!' Not yet. The Special Day is tomorrow!'

Jana found that she had unconsciously adopted a regal tone, more imperious even than Leandra's contemptuous lilt. And she realised why she forbade herself the pleasure of confessing to Harriet, realised that she had always been aware: Harriet knew everything already. Her body thrilled as Harriet's hands passed over the breasts and belly she caressed each time with new tenderness, new subtlety, and she looked at her gleaming reflection, swelling with fierce pride. Yes, she was to be addressed as Mistress!

Third bell sounded.

'After my exercises, which will be my last, I shall serve supper, Harriet,' she said coolly, 'and then I shall lace you in the Chamber of Delights.'

'Thank you, Mistress,' said Harriet, bowing.

'But first, you shall shave my mink shiny and smooth; then I shall be ready for my Special Day.'

Harriet's tethered body, encased tightly in Jana's black rubber catsuit, gleamed in the light of the single candle that gave the Chamber of Delights the air of a romantic boudoir. The girl was strapped and cuffed to the flogging-frame, legs and arms stretched to their widest, and a taut chain held her high from its anchoring bolt in the ceiling. Leandra's gag was clamped firmly on her mouth. She could neither move nor speak; she rolled her eyes in pleasure and gratitude.

Jana raised the vicious flagrum, or quirt, which Harriet had fetched from its hiding-place, and brought the thongs savagely down on Harriet's buttocks. The stroke drew a moan of satisfaction from the girl, and at each further stroke, on her croup, the backs of her thighs, and round her squirming shoulders, her moaning grew louder and her sighs more feverish. The leather quirt cracked wetly on the straining rubber. Harriet – of course – had known of its existence, had begged to be imprisoned in it, and Jana willingly granted the favour, worried only that the ferocious lacing demanded by her prisoner would split the smooth rubber. But no, it was made for such tender attentions, and Jana flogged the writhing body of Harriet with all her strength without causing more than a sinuous ripple to mar the sheen of the black fabric. She beat her slowly, in silence, save for the hoarse breath that rasped in her throat, and the keenings of the flogged girl. Sweat ran in torrents down her bare skin, dripping from the taut peaks of her nipples like the icicles of wax she had worn a few days before. Jana revelled in the proud strength of her rippling muscles; she felt at one with her whip, and at one with her victim, a trinity of pain and pleasure. And soon, much too soon, Harriet's moan became a choked scream, and, as the whipstrokes rained on her squirming buttocks, she howled in the ecstasy of her orgasm.

Gasping, Jana put down the whip. Her sex was as drenched with love-oil as her body with sweat. Quickly, panting, she released Harriet from her bonds and, after rubbing her neck, the girl fell into her arms and smothered her lips and breasts with kisses. Harriet's eyes were moist.

'Thank you, Mistress, thank you,' she sobbed.

She took the catsuit, folded it reverently, and kissed it.

'It is all wet from my love-juice,' she murmured.

'Then I shall treasure it, and your essence shall give me strength when I wear it tomorrow,' said Jana. 'But you are forgetting that I must receive the same as you. Strap me as I strapped you, Harriet, but I shall take my beating naked,

if you please, for I want you to see my bare bottom grow
crimson as you lace me, grow crimson for *you*, my sweet,
my bottom as red for love as the lips of my fount and my
blushing cheeks.'

'Naked, then, Mistress,' said Harriet gravely, and proceeded to fasten the gag, pulling the chain tight so that
Jana's head was jerked stiffly erect, then snapping the cuffs
on her spread wrists and ankles. Jana felt blissfully helpless. Her sex was gushing with moisture, and every pore of
her skin tingled as she waited for the whip to kiss her, a
kiss which she knew would bring her all on her own to the
sweetest of orgasms.

The whip touched her skin in a delicate caress; Harriet
let it play over her buttocks and belly, its thongs soft and
cool and tickling, then stroked her hard nipples and
brought the instrument to her face. The tips of the quirt
dangled on Jana's eyelids, and she saw that it was not the
flagrum she had used on Harriet.

'Yes,' said Harriet. 'I am going to kiss you with your
white whip, Mistress. I shall give you no more than seven
strokes, but on the seventh stroke I promise that you will
come for me . . . Come for Maldona!'

The lashes streaked Jana's naked body like a thousand
fiery roses, caressing her skin with molten fire into a shuddering intensity of pleasure. Jana jerked and danced like a
maddened puppet, her eyes brimming with tears of joy at
the savage intensity of feeling to which the white whip
raised her. Her belly and sex swarmed with sweet sucking
bees and her bottom stung with their furry hot needles . . .
She lost all control, bucking and writhing and snarling in
the ecstasy of her submission to the whip, until, as Harriet
spoke 'seven' she felt white lightning transfix her and she
dissolved in a fury, as pain and ecstasy melted together in
the white glow of her orgasm.

'I promised you would come for me, on the seventh
stroke,' said Harriet, as she released her quivering prisoner.
'And you did come for me. More important, you came for
all of us.'

* * *

244

Jana waited until the sun was high before she decided to show herself. From dawn, she had watched the festivities of the Special Day, secluded in an eyrie overlooking the bullring of Maldona. A sprinkling of visitors chose to sit in the shade of the terraced seats, but most thronged the sandy arena, where a glittering company swirled in a kaleidoscope of fantastic costume and show. Jana saw the adepts in their finest uniforms festooned with ribbons, chains, and flowers; the Parfaites, nude and resplendent in birds' plumage and golden chains, their whips oiled and gleaming and flicking like the tentacles of sea-beasts as they walked; the company of virgins, twittering with excitement in their best kit, proud to be permitted the wearing of their gaudy panties, and carrying their skirts as tightly as they could to show the line! The rhythm of drums throbbed hypnotically and bodies swayed unconsciously to their beat, especially those of the Arab and African gentlemen, who paraded magnificently in flowing robes, followed by courtiers and veiled slaves. It was more like a gigantic *souk*, an oriental bazaar, than the prim 'open days' Jana remembered from her draughty boarding school. She saw the Deputy Superior, Matron, Jocasta the surgeon, mingling daintily with their regal guests, like dutiful salesmen at a show of merchandise. And, of course, it was a show of merchandise: the powerful men passed through the multitude of girls, eyeing, smiling, touching, appraising them as a rancher would appraise his steers, and smiling as they jangled purses of gold or jewels.

The events were well organised, naturally, since the Deputy Superior was an American of the can-do philosophy, so that they did not seem to be organised at all, but rather to take place naturally and spontaneously. There was a ring at the centre of the arena, in which the wrestling contests were held in the shadow of a gaunt flogging-frame where the ceremonious punishments were prettily dispensed by the Deputy Superior, or one of the Parfaites, to the great glee and applause of the distinguished guests. When the ring was not busy, their attention was distracted by numerous sideshows: dancers, jugglers, conjurors and acrobats, all virgins who had trained for this day, and all performing nude, their bodies oiled and scented to present the polished aspect of ripe fruits.

From her vantage point, Jana could see the subtle skein of deals made, nods exchanged, purses tapped and fingers raised in quiet haggling, the Parfaites mingling with the customers and smiling as bargains were struck. And, above it all, high in on a shaded dais at the end of the arena, sat Maldona herself, flanked by Parfaites, with Leandra at her side. Her costume and mask were the most sumptuous of all, her plumage the gaudiest, her jewels the shiniest. Only her eyes were visible, impassive as they surveyed her domain. Jana decided that it was time for her to mingle, and made her way down to the arena, slipping in amongst a crowd of virgins and Africans who were watching one of the wrestling contests between the auberges; she noted that Ragusa was fighting a girl from Allemagne, and doing rather well, so she joined in the cheers and clapping. Eventually, Ragusa won, having pinned her opponent in a stranglehold, and was carried in triumph from the arena, the fighters' place being taken by a virgin who had merited a Grand Beating.

This too Jana watched, unable to help herself from becoming excited like the other onlookers, who slithered and twitched in their tight uniforms at the bewitching spectacle of the flogged girl's silent dance under the lash. The Arab gentlemen were particularly appreciative in their applause, and it was impossible to tell whether they were more impressed by the skill of the flogging Parfaite, and the grace of her rippling harmony of muscle, or by the fortitude of her victim, who took her lacing without a murmur through her heavy gag. Another wrestling contest followed, and Jana wandered through the crowd, unrecognised by the girls she knew, her garb unnoticed in the motley finery which filled the arena.

Jana wore her black rubber catsuit; around her neck, the pouch containing her diamonds. For a belt, she had the white whip knotted casually around her waist, its thongs brushing her black thigh, hanging to her like a trophy of war. She saw Miriam passing among the guests, presenting them with gifts of candles, and feigning shy blushes. The candles were of Jana's own design, the two-pronged phalli, and Jana felt a surge of anger that, after such a short absence, her works had been so shamelessly purloined. She avoided eye contact with the excited girls, but knew she was the object of curious chatter, some of which, to her satisfaction, she overheard.

'A princess from the south ... fabulous wealth ... look at her jewel purse ... the desert tribe of women warriors ...'

It was the feverish stuff of schoolgirls' imaginations, but to be categorised thus gave her a useful cover. Except that she knew she would be recognised by those who would need to know her.

Steadily, she made her way through the crowd, towards the dais where Maldona sat in regal aloofness, with her retinue. Their faces were blurred in the shimmer of the heat haze; Jana could easily recognise Leandra, and Jason beside her, but the other faces were indistinct, and mostly swathed in princely robes. Opposite Leandra sat Circe, the Parfaite she was to fight, and her slave, whose face was indistinct yet vaguely familiar. She could see that his body was magnificent, stronger than Jason's, and wondered if Circe too had approached such perfection, making her more than a match for Leandra. Her curiosity was now to be satisfied, for directly after a light whipping of two virgins, which proceeded as gracefully as a ballet, and seemed artfully placed as a sorbet in the middle of a heavy meal, the Deputy Superior cried that Leandra would now fight Circe. There were tumultuous cheers, tempered by clucks of disappointment as she added that the contest between Prefect Kobo and 'a nameless virgin, who has shamefully gone down' would no longer take place.

Jana passed within an arm's length of Kobo and Hera, who were talking animatedly, and she thought that their rapid glances betrayed no recognition, although Kobo did frown briefly as though puzzled. But soon all eyes were on the wrestling ring, and there was wild applause as the two

Parfaites doffed their robes into the hands of their slaves, and stood proudly naked, their superb bodies glistening with oil. Leandra flexed her muscles, and nodded in acknowledgement of the crowd's cheers, which redoubled. Circe did the same, but got lesser applause, and Jana could see a flurry of betting amongst the virgins, the odds favouring Leandra.

The odds were right. There were no holds barred: true hatred animated the wrestlers, and many whispered that desires for the succulent body of Circe's slave Aelfric was the reason. After a frenzied bout of kicking, biting and gouging that was *pankration* wrestling at its most naked, Leandra extracted a strangled submission from her rival, whom she had pinned to the ground in an invincible backbreak hold.

When Circe had piteously begged for mercy, Leandra lifted the jerking body of her victim and slung her with contempt over her shoulder, then strode to the whipping-post, where she strapped Circe in tight thongs to hang bare and helpless for her punishment.

Leandra picked up her many-thonged whip, and began to flog Circe on the buttocks, making her shudder at each vicious stroke. Her shoulders, and the tender backs of her thighs, were whipped hard; there was no love in this punishment. Circe's silence was broken as her skin began to glow fiery red under the pitiless strokes, and she squealed softly in her throat, then louder and louder, her writhing more frantic, until at last, with a tormented scream, she cried, 'I go down! Please stop! Please! I go down! Oh, please!

Leandra delivered one final cut, right in the cleft of Circe's quivering bare buttocks, before turning contemptuously away.

Groaning in despair, Circe was carried from the arena. The Deputy Superior proclaimed all her goods and chattels, including the slave Aelfric, to be the prize of Leandra, who triumphantly led her new slave back to the dais. There, she knelt before Maldona and was permitted to kiss her fingertips. Seeing Aelfric in the middle distance, Jana thought him very pretty, and wanted him. And then she realised that she had seen him before, in the finishing school, flogging the naked body of Erato. Aelfric was her own lover, Henry.

18

To Wrestle Naked

She found it difficult to get easily through the jostling, excited crowd – necklaces were being ruefully removed, in payment of ill-advised bets on Circe – and decided to await a suitably dramatic hush before making her challenge. Now, an interval of relaxation was provided by a beauty pageant. A troop of nude girls, some of whom Jana recognised from the finishing school, paraded on to the sand still damp from the oil of the wrestlers' bodies, to the coos of appreciation from the excited spectators. There was a glint from Maldona's dais, and Jana saw the sumptuously robed figure of the Mistress of Arts busy with her telephoto lens. Jana wondered briefly why she was robed as an African, and did not wear the plumage of an adept.

Erato was in the parade of naked virgins, and wore a smile of blissful happiness. This, then, was the perfection to which they aspired: to be paraded naked, like animals, for the lustful satisfaction of their jealous peers, and their potential buyers. They stood in a line, breasts held high and buttocks thrust pertly outward, while a nurse passed along them with a jewelled bag, from which she took and handed something to each girl. At a curt signal from the Deputy Superior, there was a smooth flurry of movement and, with trained speed, each girl strapped round her waist a double dildo, one prong being inserted to the hilt inside her sex, while the other jutted monstrously erect before her shaven pubis.

A knight descended from Maldona's side and was escorted by whip-swinging corporals through the crowd to the parade of girls. His hair was braded in golden ringlets, and he wore a long silk dress that billowed round his thighs, with a deep cleavage hugging his massive breast muscles. He was very pretty; Jana's quim moistened softly.

Solemnly, the boy bowed to each of the virgins, then knelt and delicately lifted his dress to expose his naked buttocks. Jana found herself excited, her quim moist with hot liquid, as she watched the boy spread his muscled cheeks and take the cocks of every virgin deep into his anus. The show was brief, a play to show that these girls could fuck, and they fucked the trembling boy with every sign of vigorous enthusiasm, their loins pumping as they thrust their stiff cocks into his body, and their faces masks of triumphant strength. Erato drew the most applause, and to Jana's surprise, she finished her buggery of the helpless boy with a passionate show of orgasm that drove the audience wild, and had the African guests beside themselves in a frenzy of haggling and bidding. The Deputy Superior kept some kind of order in this chaos, for after the display of prowess, which had Jana soaking wet between her thighs – she had never seen Erato so strong and beautiful before – each virgin seemed to have found a buyer, and paraded in happy triumph back to their quarters. Erato passed directly in front of Jana but, in her glazed happiness, did not even notice her.

Jana knew she had to make her move. She looked round for Harriet, as if for encouragement, and could not see her, although she must be present somewhere. Already, the next girl to be flogged was approaching the ring, glum in the arms of her escorts, two grinning corporals. It was a prefect from the Auberge de France, who was due for a Noble Beating by two Parfaites at once, armed with scourge and birch. Before she could be fastened to the flogging frame, Jana forced her way through the mêlée and stood at the steps of Maldona's dais.

Swiftly, she untied the white whip from her waist and raised it before Maldona's eyes. The occupants of the dais reacted with varying degrees of alarm, all except Leandra, the Mistress of Arts, and Maldona herself. Jana took Leandra's mask from her waist, and threw

251

it contemptuously at Leandra's feet, then cracked her whip loudly in the air.

'What the hell's going on?' shouted the Deputy Superior, but Maldona lifted her hand, and motioned her to be silent.

'In the name of the Amir Akbar, whose princess I am, I issue the threefold challenge!' cried Jana. 'I have the white whip, and none may refuse me.'

'This is crazy,' cried the Deputy Superior. 'Whoever she is, take her away, corporals!'

Again, Maldona raised her hand. The entire arena was silent, watching the drama with bated breath. The voice that filled the stadium was soft and firm, a voice with the sad, fluting serenity of power.

'It is in order. She is Akbar's Princess, for she has the white whip, and she may issue the threefold challenge.'

'What the hell is the threefold challenge?' cried the Deputy Superior.

Maldona turned her head a fraction towards her.

'It is permitted. We may not ask questions. The threefold challenge has been issued. It is time.'

'I don't understand!' wailed The Deputy Superior, with the fury of one whose delicate arrangements have been spoiled.

'You shall see then, and understand. Maldona has spoken. Name your first challenge, Princess of the Whip.'

Jana bowed low to Maldona.

'My friend was to fight the prefect Kobo, before she was dishonoured,' she said coolly. 'I wish to restore her honour and fight Kobo.'

'Granted,' said Maldona, and turned to the Deputy Superior. 'You will make the arrangements, Mistress.'

The Deputy Superior bowed. Maldona had spoken.

'You insist on fighting in your costume?' drawled the Deputy Superior. Jana wiped a bead of sweat from her eyes, and faced the smirking Leandra across the ring of hot sand. Kobo was cool and naked, while Jana was bathed in sweat, her rubber catsuit a furnace.

'It is my right,' said Jana. 'It is in the rules.'

'Very well, Princess. But to nullify the advantage of your slippery suit, you must do combat with canes. That too is in the rules.'

'Agreed,' said Jana.

'Hand me your whip, then. The sacred whip must not touch the flesh of any but Maldona herself. That rule applies throughout our precinct, whatever you may be used to outside.'

'Agreed also,' said Jana, handing over her white whip. 'I wish Maldona to hold it for me.'

The Deputy Superior looked up for guidance, and Maldona nodded assent. Jana watched as the Deputy Superior mounted the dais and gave the whip to Maldona, returning with two short, supple yew canes splayed at the tip. These she handed to Kobo and Jana.

'You know that the rules are the same, in a threefold challenge, as in any contest between adepts,' she said. The girls nodded.

'Then you may –'

Before the words were out of her mouth, Kobo leapt forward with her teeth bared in a ferocious snarl, and lashed Jana hard across the breasts. The shock made Jana stumble, and that cut was followed by another, across the belly, then a third on the shoulders, narrowly missing her face. Tears filled Jana's eyes as her skin smarted, and she struggled to raise her own flail. Kobo paused to draw breath, and Jana was able to stumble forward and cut her on the left arm. Kobo sneered, and with a lightning stroke, lashed Jana's thigh; as Jana raised her arm, aiming for Kobo's face, she was cut right in the armpit, and almost cried out. The struggle was unequal; if only she had dared to be naked, and reveal her identity! This regret was made the more bitter when Kobo suddenly threw herself across Jana's body, ignoring the cane cut that striped her bare breast, and toppled Jana to the dust, where, pinioning her, she whispered in her ear, 'So you've come back, you foolish, faithless slut. Stupid not to have stayed and become a beauty queen like your slut friend Erato!'

With that, she fastened her hands around Jana's throat

and began to squeeze. Wildly, Jana flailed her arms and
legs, and got a thumb in Kobo's eye, at the same time
thrusting a vicious knee against her sex. She felt Kobo's
nympha half-stiff, and squashed under the force of the
powerful kick, and Kobo moaned in pain, jumping off the
spreadeagled body of Jana and groping once more for her
cane. Her foot clamped Jana's throat, pinning her helplessly to the ground, and with her other arm she brought the
cane down, knocking Jana's own weapon out of her hand,
to fall uselessly beyond her reach. Jana tried to gouge
Kobo's foot to release the iron grip, but Kobo began to
flog her so mercilessly that she was obliged to use her fore-
arms to shield her tender places. Kobo shifted her attention to Jana's sex, and got a few accurate strokes directly
on the lips, before Jana, writhing in torment, could close
her thighs against the deadly onslaught. Her rubber suit
seemed as thin as gossamer against Kobo's cane-strokes.
Through a blur of tears, she saw that the black girl's
nympha was standing rigid in the excitement of her power.

Jana's body burned as each stroke of Kobo's cane jerked
her like a puppet. Bitter rage rose in her throat, rage that
her plan was not going to work, and then she told herself
that it had to work, and *now*; grimly, she let Kobo whip
her, feigning submission and defeat, pretending to be sapped of all energy, and uttering little wails of torment. Kobo
grinned, the pressure on Jana's neck relaxed ever so little,
but enough for her to rise and grab Kobo's leg.

Kobo was strong enough to check her fall, but she was
brought down on one knee, and that was enough for Jana
to subdue her. She nipped at Kobo's stiff clitoris, feeling
its swollen excitment, and squeezed it hard, her thumb
flicking feverishly over the tip. Kobo dropped her cane and
howled; her whole body went rigid, then began to jerk as
she wriggled her pelvis in the rhythm of Jana's fierce clit-
stroking, and her eyes showed white in the intensity of her
orgasm. It was the work of an instant to flip the helpless,
squirming girl over and pinion her in a backbreak.

'Submit, Kobo?' taunted Jana grimly.

'No! Ah! Ah! God, yes, I submit.'

'Louder.'

'I submit!' screamed Kobo, sobbing bitterly, and the audience applauded and hooted with glee.

Jana released the shamed prefect and raised her arms in victory.

'It'll do you no good, slut,' whimpered Kobo. 'I know who you are, there was no mistaking you, and Hera knows too. We just wanted to see if you would reveal yourself before we unmasked you. But we didn't dream you would stoop this low.'

'Stoop low? Why, I am only following the rules, Kobo, and you must address me as Miss from now on, for I am your prefect.'

'You won by a trick!'

'No trick, Virgin Kobo, just know thine enemy. A word of advice – be careful whom you choose to shower with.'

Kobo crept out of the ring, head bowed, to the jeers of the assembled virgins, while Jana, panting from her ordeal, approached Maldona's dais and bowed low.

'Maldona,' she said, 'it seems that my identity is known here, so with your permission, I shall henceforth fight naked.'

'Permission is granted,' answered Maldona.

All eyes were on Jana as she stripped off her rubber suit and revealed her shaven gleaming body, shorn of its lush mink. She saw Leandra start in astonishment, but Maldona herself was immobile.

'So it is you, Jana,' she said, with a hint of wry amusement. 'And whom do you challenge second?'

'I challenge the Parfaite Leandra,' cried Jana.

Leandra sprang to her feet and removed her plumed mask and chains, placing them carefully on her seat.

'Watch my things, for I shall be back soon to reclaim my post,' she said cockily, 'and make way for one extra slave.'

Grimly, the two naked girls squared off in the sunbaked ring.

'You are a fool, Jana,' hissed Leandra. 'This secret knowledge of yours will get you nowhere. You tricked me, kept secrets from me – I'll wrestle you till you drop, and

255

thrash the daylights out of you, and this time I won't show mercy.'

'You call falling into the lake showing mercy?'

'It is a necessary ritual, a purgation. You could have become perfect, like Erato, you stupid slut. But when you are really my slave, there will be no fun and games for you, and the beatings you get will be cruel as can be, with not a jot of love behind my lash. Do you want to go through with this, you –'

This time it was Jana who seized the initiative, flinging herself at Leandra and toppling her with a mighty kick to the sex, which had the Parfaite groaning on the ground. But she was able to wriggle aside when Jana's body fell to pinion her, and grabbed her by the foot, swinging her round to dash her head hard on the sand, again and again, until Jana was blinded by tears and dust.

'Oh, I like this, I like this very much,' crooned Leandra, raking her nails across Jana's bare breasts with the force of sickles, then clutching her open sex-lips and gouging fiercely until it was all Jana could do not to cry out. The battle continued in this fashion, merciless and cruel, and Jana's newfound strength, and the training she had received from Leandra herself, enabled her to hold her own in the fierce succession of crushing grips.

'Give in,' hissed Leandra. 'I am the stronger, and shall break you.'

'I am stronger,' groaned Jana, fending her opponent's fingers from her eyes, and smashing her knee with massive force into Leandra's groin, where she felt that nympha, to her astonishment, just as hard as Kobo's had been.

'Yes,' grinned Leandra through misted eyes, 'it thrills me to hurt you, Jana, and my secret is that it thrills me to be hurt! I can take any punishment, for any time, because my nympha swells at every blow. Can you take it thus? And don't think the same trick will work on me as on Kobo. I saw what you did. My nympha is steel, little virgin.'

Their breasts were squashed together, Leandra's fingers groping for Jana's throat and eyes.

'Fuck your stupid nympha, you fucking hag,' gasped

Jana, and, leaving her throat dangerously unprotected, her hand dived between Leandra's legs, and found her swollen cunt-lips, bathed in her gushing wetness. Leandra cried savagely as she found Jana's throat and began to squeeze. Frantically, Jana got her hand, three fingers, then four, then a full five, inside Leandra's wet oily slit, and forced them upward, searching, exploring the hot oily cunt, praying silently – Harriet, please please don't you be the only one – and found the bone, inching forward, here, no here, oh God, please, it must be *here* . . .

Abruptly, Leandra's body arched and she cried out in a great shuddering wail as Jana's fingers found the strange spot into whose mystery Harriet had initiated her. The fingers relaxed and left her choked throat, and her own hand rubbed madly on Leandra's G-spot as the Parfaite writhed helplessly in a tortured orgasm.

Leandra writhed and trembled as though she had ceased to be human, and the roars from her throat were those of a yelping wolf.

It was almost with kindness that Jana gently turned Leandra and ground her face to the dust, pinioning her in the inescapable backhold as the yelps of her orgasm subsided to a sobbing whimper.

'I think it is time for you to submit, Leandra,' she whispered, twisting the arms high. 'You know you can't get out of this, so don't be stupid.' There was an anguished pause, and dead silence in the arena.

'I submit,' sobbed Leandra.

'Say it out loud, bitch Mistress.'

'I . . .'

Jana twisted her head to be level with Leandra's trembling breast, and took the nipple into her mouth, where she bit savagely. Leandra screamed.

'Say it,' hissed Jana. 'Out loud, whore.'

Leandra wailed loudly, in despair, and cried in a broken voice:

'I submit!'

Jana gave her nipple a last, playful bite and released it, as the crowd gasped in astonishment at the completeness of Leandra's humiliation. And, like Kobo, Leandra slunk from the scene, head bowed and sobbing. Once more Jana approached the dais of Maldona, and bowed.

The Deputy Superior announced Leandra's forfeiture of her possessions and post to the new Parfaite, the virgin once known as Jana, who had gone down but returned according to the rules and in seemly manner befitting a lady.

Maldona stretched out her hand.

'You may kiss my hand, Parfaite Jana,' she said, and the crowd cheered. 'And please take your seat beside me. The things on it are yours, and you should find it pleasantly warm from Leandra's big bottom.'

'I must make my third challenge.'

'But it is permitted to rest. You may sit and make your choice of Parfaites to fight; perhaps one of the adepts, perhaps even the Deputy Superior herself.' Her tone was slightly mocking, and the Deputy Superior glowered.

'I am unbeaten,' she snarled.

Jana reached out and took her whip from Maldona's arms. Holding it high, she said, 'I wish to challenge no Parfaite, nor the Deputy Superior.' Then, raising her voice to a proud cry, she said, 'I challenge Maldona!'

The silence was total, broken only when the Deputy Superior blurted out, 'She's out of her mind!'

'I have read the secret rules!' shouted Jana. 'It is permitted for any virgin to challenge Maldona!'

There was a collective gasp of shock from the assembly.

'But you are no longer a virgin!' snarled the Deputy Superior. 'No longer even of Maldona!'

'She comes from outside, carrying the white whip, and wearing black,' said Maldona calmly. 'You are not the only one to have read the secret rules, Jana dear. No doubt you fulfil the third condition also.'

Jana turned and, grimacing, spread the cheeks of her croup. Slowly, from the depths of her fount and her anus, emerged the twin black cocks of the eunuchs of Akbar, separated by her knife, but each whole, and in its appointed place. She handed the twin penises to Maldona, who took them reverently, raised her plumed mask a fraction, and pressed her lips to them. Then Maldona rose.

'It is time,' she said. 'The challenger has come, according to the rules, and I shall follow her to the ring of combat, and make myself naked as I once was.'

Silently, Jana returned to the ring, followed by Maldona at a stately pace, and reading the fear and awe on the faces of the nervous girls. Even the Africans sensed that these events were not part of the planned festivities.

When they reached the ring, Maldona nodded to her Parfaites, who removed her robe and mask, and unwound the golden chains that encased her body, then withdrew with lowered hands, leaving the two women nude, facing each other with impassive eyes. Jana looked at Maldona's body, and saw that it was perfect. Between her legs, the smooth swelling of the shaven mons, the olive skin shiny in the sun, with the perfect breasts now thrust forward by powerful muscles. Maldona's body was stronger and harder even than Leandra's the muscles gleaming like the crests and valleys of a mountain range.

'I knew you would challenge me, Jana, sweet,' she said, as Jana gaped in awe. 'I do hope the Mistress of Arts can get some good shots of our contest.'

'Cassie!' blurted out Jana.

'I have heard that name, but you should call me Maldona, until our combat is over at any rate. Shall we begin?' said Cassie Osorio.

'I . . . I cannot fight *you*, sweet Cassie!' cried Jana.

'But you must. You have come this far, properly accoutred, Jana. It is in the rules.'

'But how . . . why . . .?'

Cassie put a finger to her lips.

'Haven't you learned not to ask questions?' she said, with a lovely smile playing cruelly on her lips. 'I see I shall have to punish you . . . *slut*!'

'Oh, don't,' wailed Jana, 'it is not fair.'

Cassie, without warning, lunged at Jana, striking her with the flat of her hand hard across her breasts. Jana recoiled in dismay at the vicious attack, and groaned as

Cassie got a strong arm around her neck, bending her with a knee in the small of her back until she was twisted, choking, in an arch of pain. Tears sprung to her eyes, and she did not want to fight. If this was what her friend wanted to do, if Cassie wanted to hurt her, to break her, then so be it. At least then, she would have the satisfaction of being Cassie's, which was what she wanted more than anything. But she couldn't speak, though she desperately wanted to tell her these things. It *was* unfair! Why didn't Cassie realise that they didn't have to fight, that she would happily submit?

Cassie grunted harshly as she forced Jana to the ground. In a frenzy of rage and pain, Jana tried to grab her by her lush mink, only to be reminded that Cassie was as shaven as herself. In the midst of her pain, the comic aspect struck her, and she emitted a choked chuckle, which had the effect of putting Cassie momentarily off guard. Cassie frowned, puzzled, and then Jana kicked hard at that shiny mons, hating herself for doing so. But it worked; Cassie grunted in dismay and her grip slackened, and now it was Jana who had the upper hand. She slammed into Cassie with all the weight of her body, knocking her over, and then leapt to pinion her with a shoulder-hold, her thighs locked on Cassie's neck.

'This is crazy, Cassie,' she panted. 'We don't have to fight!'

'I'm not Cassie, I am Maldona, and you will fight me, slut, till you submit!'

'I don't want to fight you, I want to obey you, Cassie!'

Jana shuddered as she spoke.

'Do not be a plonker, you silly thing,' said Cassie, gasping at the pressure of Jana's hard thighs on her neck. 'We must fight to a submission.'

'All right, then, I submit!' laughed Jana through her tears.

'Not accepted. An imperfect submission is no submission.'

'I don't want to hurt you . . . It makes me feel awful.'

'Enough talk, slut!' cried Cassie, and suddenly her legs

scissored up and locked on Jana's throat, pulling her back, and flipping her over until Cassie's own heavy body straddled Jana's breast to breast.

'You can submit now, if you like, slut,' said Cassie through gritted teeth.

'No! That was sneaky, you bitch!' protested Jana.

Cassie responded by slamming her knee hard into Jana's sex.

'Pity you haven't any balls,' she hissed.

'Oh! Oh! Stop!' cried Jana, writhing helplessly, her breasts squashed unkindly against Cassie's in a cruel parody of their former embraces.

Cassie locked her hand over Jana's and began to squeeze, crushing the joints of her fingers. Blinded by tears of pain, Jana savagely butted Cassie full in the face, her forehead meeting her unprotected nose. Cassie yelped and drew back, her hands clutching her face, and Jana was able to throw her.

The two girls stood now and circled each other warily, Cassie grinning with a fierce grimace.

'Got your goat, eh, slut?' she taunted.

Jana threw herself at Cassie and they grappled silently, their naked bodies slippery with sweat, seeking to gain a submission hold. Jana was wary now, and no longer trusted herself to make dramatic moves; she decided to wear Cassie down, figuring that despite her stunning musculature, Cassie must be less fit than herself.

But as the contest wore on, and their bodies became streaked with dust, she was not so sure. Cassie was powerful, more powerful even than Leandra, and she saw that, like Leandra, she was excited by the naked wrestling. Her clit stood, and Jana tried not to let her eyes dwell on the mesmerising potency of the strong nympha between Cassie's thighs, for she could feel her own sex moisten with excitement. They parted from a particularly vicious embrace, involving much gouging and twisting of tender breasts, and faced each other, panting. Cassie saw that Jana's eyes were on her stiff clit. The older girl's eyes glittered maliciously.

'Like what you see, slut?' she sneered.

Jana's belly was fluttering and she could not answer. She wiped the sweat from her eyes; her fount was wet.

'Look at yourself, Miss,' taunted Cassie. 'Look down *there* . . .'

Jana's eyes fixed on her own loins, and there she saw that her own nympha stood proud and erect from the folds of her cunt-lips, and at that moment Cassie sprang on her, taking advantage of her surprise, and felled her to the sand, locking her in an embrace so tight that she could not rise, however she struggled.

'Submit?' she cried.

'Never! Break me, Cassie, if that's what you want!'

Their eyes met; Jana felt the full weight of Cassie's body crushing her, and suddenly the fight went out of her. Her cunt swam with liquid, and her belly was giddy and glowing, and she wanted to be washed away in the power of Cassie's will.

'I'll never submit,' she whimpered. 'Oh, Cassie . . .'

Cassie stared at Jana's face, and suddenly her body arched and her face was on Jana's, and their lips and tongues met in a kiss. And then, as though in a dream, Jana opened her thighs, felt the petals of her sex swell and part, and Cassie's stiff clit was brushing her own, sending tingles of joy along her spine. She could feel the shivering sweetness harden her bruised nipples, and then she moaned with joy as Cassie entered her fount. Jana's hands crept to Cassie's pumping buttocks as Cassie fucked her, stroking the smooth taut globes as they pumped in vigorous strokes, the stiff pink clit squeezed by Jana's trembling wet cunt.

'Do you submit?' panted Cassie.

'Never,' sighed Jana. 'Oh, Cassie, rub me, rub me with your lovely hard clit, please fuck me as I've always wanted you to.'

'Oh, yes, Jana, I'm fucking you, how I've longed to fuck you in your sweet wet cunt.'

'It's wet for you, Cassie – Maldona dear – don't stop, you are going to make me come. Oh, do what you like to me, I am your slave, Maldona, yes, *yes!*'

'Jana!' howled Cassie, 'I'm coming, God, it's so sweet. Oh, the honey, I'm melting all over you. Oh! Oh! Oh!'

Both girls bucked in frantic spasms as their orgams convulsed them, and all around the crowd watched in awe under the merciless sun as the two fighters cried out in their pleasure.

Jana felt the strong arms enfold her, lift her up, and then she was squatting on top of Maldona, her hands placed round her neck. Smiling and through tears of joy, she stroked Cassie's throat, cooing, 'Oh, Maldona, oh, Cassie.'

Cassie stretched her arms dramatically on the sand in a gesture of defeat.

'*You* are Maldona now, Jana that was,' she whispered, and then cried for all the world to hear, 'I submit! I am beaten, and submit! Maldona has crushed me, and I am her slave!'

And the wild cheering all around seemed to split the sky.

Footsteps pattered on the sand towards them, and Jana thought it must be the Deputy Superior; but she was still on the dais, cheering with the ecstatic crowd. Jana looked round, dazed, and saw the figure of the Mistress of Arts, pointing an excited camera at the entwined women.

'Superb!' she cried, pulling aside her mask and pressing the viewfinder to her eye. 'What a shot for my archives! May I be the first to congratulate you, Maldona?'

The voice was deep, vaguely Germanic. Jana squinted into the sun and made out the smiling, painted, pretty face.

'Why, hello, Harry,' she said. 'Nothing surprises me any more.'

19

Maldona Adored

High on her dais, Maldona acknowledged the jubilant
cheers of the crowd, chanting, 'Adore Maldona!' She was
surrounded by her friends: Netta and Caspar were there,
and Harry and Greta, and Henry, who was the slave Aelfric; and of course Cassie. When Maldona took her throne,
the whole assembly, men and women, prostrated themselves in the dust, then, at Maldona's signal, recommenced
the proceedings of the special day.

'We tried to dissuade you from seeking Maldona, Mistress,' said Greta, 'for it is in the rules. The imperfect are
dissuaded.'

'You didn't try very hard, I'm glad to say.'

'No, for we knew you were Maldona. That is why I gave
you the white whip, and the diamonds you had caused to
fall from her. They are Maldona's by right: of other girls
flogged with that whip, not one could dislodge a single
gem. You had to be Maldona.'

'I intend to make some changes,' said Jana. 'Maldona
must move with the times.'

Cassie laughed politely.

'You laugh, slave?' cried Jana. 'You have earned yourself a whipping, I think.'

'Gladly, Mistress,' said Cassie, her eyes glittering. 'It is
just that Maldona always wishes to make changes, to leave
her imprint in our tribe, and finds it impossible and un-
desirable. I, for example, wished to liberalise the rules, to
let the virgins shave their minks and wear their hair long,
if they liked. But they pleaded to keep the rules as they
were for, without rules, privileges mean nothing. The same

264

with the finishing school; those virgins, Erato and now Kobo amongst them, have passed out of Maldona on their way to positions of undreamt of power and luxury in the outside world.'

'And I suppose Leandra too,' said Jana sadly.

'Yes, for what greater power can a woman have over a man than to be his slave, binding his will to hers? True dominance lies in true submission! Mistress Jana, the most revolutionary change that can be made in Maldona is to keep her exactly as she is, a law unto herself that subverts and conquers all men's laws, because the law of Maldona is truth: the truth of pleasure unbounded, and submission unmerciful. Maldona is not just here in Spain, Maldona is everywhere, and when we go outside, as you yourself may, Mistress, we know each other, and adore Maldona.'

Jana thought of London, her flat waiting. Cassie and Henry, her two lovers, were both bound to her as slaves . . .

'Would you follow me to London?' she said abruptly. 'Cassandra? Aelfric?'

'We must, Mistress. We are your slaves.'

'Maldona may go down, and still be Maldona,' said Netta. 'It is in the rules. In past centuries, there have been outside Maldonas, with a princess regent left in Spain to rule in her place.'

'Some of us serve Maldona effectively on the outside,' said Greta. 'Harry and I help organise the recruitment, sale and delivery of slaves, as you saw at our house. Netta and Caspar too serve loyally.'

'I see,' said Jana. 'Meanwhile, the white whip has returned to Maldona, and the circle has been completed. My ancestor, Jana Ardenne, was flogged to death as a witch, as I learned. But she did not die, for it was not her they flogged, at the whipping-post was a model of wax, filled with feathers. She was helped to flee the county of Northumberland by her adepts, and came to Spain, where, on the site of the Amir's castle, she founded Maldona. She came dressed in black, and carrying the white whip, and it is thus that I have come. I am Maldona!'

'Adore Maldona!' murmured the adepts reverently.

'I, too, discovered the secret rules, Mistress, that any virgin may challenge Maldona for her throne!' said Cassie. And, thus, I too came to rule. But I knew that the true Maldona would come, that you would come . . .

'I think you all conspired to bring me here,' said Jana. 'Cassandra, my lover Henry known as Aelfric, Caspar and Netta, and, of course, Greta and Harry, our proud Mistress of Arts.'

'Maldona brought you here, Mistress,' said Greta softly.

'One thing puzzles me,' said Jana. 'Who may chastise Maldona if she commits imperfection?'

'Maldona cannot commit imperfection, for she is perfect. She may break the rules, and that is different. In that case, the Mistress Superior takes charge of the matter,' said Cassie.

Jana shivered pleasurably. She looked down and saw that little Sylvie was at that moment writhing under the furry birch, wielded energetically by Miriam the corporal, and she felt a pang of jealous sympathy.

'Poor little Sylvie,' she said, 'her fesses smarting from that cruellest of whips.'

'Mistress,' said the Deputy Superior, 'little Sylvie begs for the *betula pubescens*.'

At the sight of that bare bottom squirming under the pitiless birch strokes, Jana felt her quim grow moist and tingly, and she said playfully, 'I am sure I have broken some rules already, and merit my own thrashing . . .'

'Do not smile too soon, Maldona, my Mistress Jana,' said Cassie with a sigh. 'For it is my duty, as Maldona-that-was, to explain to you, that to properly become Maldona, it is necessary . . .' She broke off.

'What is necessary?' demanded Jana. 'Continue, slave Cassandra. Maldona must do what is necessary.'

'Oh, you will hate me, for it was I that brought you here, sweet Mistress.'

'Hate you, goose? Never. Speak.'

Cassie breathed in deeply, and said, 'To prove herself, Maldona who has won by conquest must take a Perfect Beating, in front of all assembled.'

'Well,' said Jana with forced gaiety, 'I knew my bum was tingling for a good lacing. This excitement has made me hot to feel the whip on my bare fesses! Let us begin! I shall take my Perfect Beating proudly – I look forward to it. You, Cassandra, must have submitted in your turn.'

'Yes, Mistress. And it is a beating I shall never in my life forget.'

'Well, then! I, too, must submit. But who is permitted to whip the naked flesh of Maldona?'

'The first stroke is delivered by the Superior, Mistress. That is the signal for the beating to commence.'

'I do not fully understand.'

'The recipient of a Perfect Beating must accept a lash, or lashes, from each and every Parfaite, knight, and adept of Maldona who so desires. And there is no limit to the strokes given, nor to the severity of the whipping tools used, nor to the time that may elapse.'

Jana nodded gravely.

'Very well,' she said. Then, turning to the slave Jason, she whispered instructions to him, and he left at a run. He returned a few moments later with Jana's bag, fetched from her cell.

Jana stood up, and the crowd, as though sensing what had been said, hushed expectantly. Sylvie's birching drew to a close, and, scorning assistance, the red-headed girl stood beside Miriam and watched Maldona with awe. Her voice rang out proudly in the still air.

'Maldona shall receive her perfect beating,' she cried. 'Let the Superior take me, and chastise me according to the rules.'

The crowd parted, and a small, brightly-robed figure emerged. She stood and bowed low before Maldona's dais. Her head was masked with plumage more dazzling than any Parfaite's, and in her hand was the six-thonged flagrum.

'Come down, Maldona, naked as a virgin, and take your beating,' she cried.

Jana stripped herself of her newly won robes and slowly descended the stairs, feeling the sun hot once more on her nude body. In her right hand she carried the wrapped package she had taken from her bag. When she reached the Superior, the Superior bowed again and beckoned Maldona to position herself on the flogging-frame, which had been tilted to lie almost horizontal, like a bed, so that its occupant would feel the full downward force of every lash, without the dignity of standing upright. Jana would be flogged like a tethered beast.

She handed the package to the Superior, and stretched herself on the flogging frame, where she felt cruel metal bands fasten her wrists, ankles, and, especially tight, her waist. She could not move; she was helpless, knowing her naked body would be whipped without mercy or respite, and as the bonds were given their final twist, she experienced a thrilling rush of utter pleasure.

'You may denude yourself for your hot work, Superior,' she said calmly, 'and throw away your scourge. I, Maldona, order it. You may don the flogging costume of Cecilia herself, and flog me with the white whip of Akbar, according to the rules.'

The Superior bowed, and obediently doffed her robes and plumage, and put on the golden chains of Jana's fan harness. When she had loosed the fans, and stood shining like a rainbow, the crowd applauded, and Jana turned to smile at the Superior.

'Yes,' she said. 'I had an idea ... Well, begin the flogging, Mistress Superior. Lace my naked body with your whip until my spirit soars like a bird. Whip me, sweet Harriet.'

The white whip scalded her naked flesh as no whip had ever done before. Each cut stroked her bare buttocks like molten gold, and when Harriet began to whip her shoulders and back – Harriet the whipping girl, Harriet the librarian, Harriet the Superior! – Jana felt herself twist in a sinuous dance of pure, white-hot pain.

'You suspected, Mistress?' gasped Harriet, panting with the effort of her flogging.

'Oh, yes,' said Jana. 'You are too intelligent for a mere whipping slut, Harriet.'

'It is because you are wise, Mistress. You saw that only the very fortunate are blessed with being slave and mistress at the same time.'

Silently, Harriet concentrated on the harsh rhythm of the flogging, each lash on Jana's defenceless body seeming harder than the last.

'There!' she cried, delivering a last, ferocious cut to Jana's squirming bare bottom. 'You have taken a full seven times seven strokes with the white whip, and I call the Perfect Beating at an end. I am too wet in my lady's place to continue, Mistress, for the sight of your lovely body dancing under the whip, and the horns of Cecilia in my cunt and bumhole excite me too much. My whipping would be imperfect, and I must not continue.'

'But the beating is not yet perfect, then,' groaned Jana, her eyes blurred with tears. 'Let others continue, according to the rules.'

'It is my prerogative,' said Harriet simply. 'I am Superior.' She raised her voice, and cried, 'I, Superior of Maldona, declare this beating perfect. Any adept who defies my edict shall incur my wrath and punishment for her imperfection.'

The crowd was still: no one moved, until, suddenly, Jana heard the pad of footsteps, and a familiar, loved voice rang out, 'Give me your whip, Harriet. I, Leandra, shall beat this woman.'

'What!' cried Harriet. 'You are no longer Parfaite, Leandra! Jana is Parfaite in your stead, and now Maldona herself! You are imperfect!'

'It is according to the rules, Harriet,' said Jana. 'Do as Leandra bids. I am Maldona, and order you thus.'

Harriet handed over the whip, and slid the glistening prongs of the fan harness from her quim and anus, offering them grudgingly to Leandra, but Leandra scorned her.

'I have no need,' she said. 'I shall whip my lady as naked as she is.'

Jana looked round at Leandra's face, and saw it a mask of icy, expressionless cruelty.

'Whip me, then, Leandra,' she said softly. 'But, as hard

269

and as long as you whip me, I shall still be Maldona, and you still my virgin.'

Leandra grinned a tiger's grin.

'Oh, I shall lace your sweet body, Mistress, until you beg me to stop,' she said, and Jana shut her eyes as she felt the tips of the four thongs caress her shoulders, then tickle her gently all the way down her spine, and dangle in the cleft of her buttocks, making her clitoris tingle and her quim, already wet from Harriet's cruel flogging, begin to gush with hot moisture.

'You are pleased to torment me, Leandra?' she hissed. The whip stroked her like a lover's tongue all across her reddened, glowing fesses, down the backs of her tensed thighs and calves, to the tips of her toes.

'I shall torment you well, Mistress,' said Leandra. 'A Perfect Beating has no time, no end.' She threw the white whip to Harriet, who caught it in astonishment. 'I shall flog your helpless body with the harshest whips Maldona knows . . .'

Jana felt her toes suddenly enclosed by Leandra's mouth, and tickled by her hot, wet tongue. She gasped in mingled fear and pleasure, then sighed as Leandra's tongue passed across her calves, to the taut muscles of her thighs. Tenderly, Leandra licked every inch of her mistresses' lower body, pausing long on the soft inner thighs, just below Jana's swelling red cunt-lips, now flowing with hot love-juice.

Then her whole body slithered with serpentine grace on to Jana, and her stiff nipples caressed the small of Jana's back, swaying back and forth in a lovely soft stroking that made Jana moan with pleasure.

'Oh, Leandra,' she sighed, 'what do you do?'

'I whip you, Mistress, with my tongue and with my breasts,' said Leandra, kissing the nape of her neck as her teats nuzzled her spine. 'Can you not feel how cruelly I lash your sweet bare flesh?'

The tips of Leandra's engorged nipples rubbed gently over all Jana's body, and now and again she pressed her full weight on thigh or bottom, so that Jana felt the magnificent naked teats of the ex-Parfaite silky and hard against her skin. Her cunt was gushing with love now, and her nympha was stiff and erect and sending tingling shocks from her own stiff nipples all the way along her quivering spine.

Then, the nipples lingered on her glowing buttocks, rubbing round and round in the caress of a circle, and Jana prayed that – yes, the flickering tongue found the cleft of her buttocks and darted there, licking full up the valley of taut skin and coming to rest at the base of the spine, to tickle and kiss with eager lips. Leandra gently bit Jana's fesses, licking the red skin with her wet tongue, and then her tongue was on the anus bud, tickling, pushing inside, and now going deep, across the tender causeway to the sex herself. Leandra's face pressed hard now into the soft fold of Jana's arse and thigh, her nose parting the fesses by her anus bud, as the tongue crept all the way round and found, at last, the sweet hard bud of her nympha.

'Oh!' cried Jana. 'This is cruel, Leandra! Stop, stop, I beg you!'

Leandra removed her tongue for a second, and said harshly, 'Make me your slave, Mistress!'

'You . . . you may not make conditions thus! Oh, God, Leandra, whip me, whip me according to the rules, I beg you!'

That vicious tongue continued her implacable caress of Jana's throbbing clit, until she felt herself on the very brink of orgasm.

'Make me your slave! I love you, Jana! I love you!'

Jana's body was a glowing firebrand of desire and tormented pleasure, and she felt the hot wet shiver of her climax well up. She was powerless, her mind and body whirling, and she heard herself cry out, 'Leandra is my slave!'

And then she convulsed in a climax that washed her in pure, searing beauty, and Leandra cried to the throng of ecstatic virgins, 'Adore Maldona! The beating is perfect!'

20

Slaves and Lovers

'This is not a democracy,' said Maldona. 'There is no need for the hoi-polloi to see what does not concern them. All they need to know is that there is Maldona to rule over them, that there is always Maldona. Therefore, the contest between Harriet and Leandra for the Regency, shall take place privately, here in my apartments.'

The Superior, Harriet, and the slave, Leandra, nodded in agreement.

'Yes, Mistress,' they said, curtseying.

'I am to leave for a while,' continued Jana, 'and be Maldona Outside, to pursue our aims in the world. As it is necessary to appoint a Regent to rule in my place, I want the matter settled definitely before my departure: there must be a clear submission. I do not want to think that there are intrigues and rancour poisoning the polity of Maldona while I am away. It would be simplest, of course, to appoint Harriet the Superior, as befits her rank.'

'Her rank!' snorted Leandra, 'why, her rank is nothing but a whipping slut!'

Jana gave a savage tug on the golden chain which tethered Leandra's breasts, and, lazily, reached over to lash her twice on her back. Leandra's eyes glowed, with pain and pleasure that her mistress should see fit to chastise her in view of others.

'However, Leandra has challenged, as is her right according to the rules, so the two shall wrestle. I am glad for you both, because true honour should be won, not bestowed. I know that my slave Leandra –' Mischievously, she gave the kneeling Leandra another lash with her whip, this time on the buttocks, which made her jump. '– has always longed to be Maldona: not true, slave?' Leandra nodded agreement. 'So it is right that she should have the chance to be my Regent. If she fights, and is defeated, then there shall be honour in her defeat. I wonder, Harriet, if you will defeat Leandra?'

Harriet's face was an expressionless mask.

'This I do decree,' continued Jana, stretching herself in her bath, 'the victor shall take Jason to be her slave, and the vanquished shall become Superior. Which, Leandra, includes the most important post of librarian! I know how you love books!'

'You mock me, Mistress,' said Leandra, blushing. How sweet, Jana thought, to see a true blush of modesty on that proud face! 'But my love accepts your mockery as an honour. I shall fight to take your place, Mistress, and I shall win, for if you are not here, then ... I must be you!' And her blushed turned to fire.

'Very well,' said Jana. 'The contest shall take place tomorrow morning at dawn. You are ready, Harriet?'

'I am a creature of duty, Mistress,' said Harriet inscrutably. 'I would only say: is it necessary for you to go down?' Her face showed a fleeting anxiety.

'Don't tell me you are getting sentimental, Harriet! I feel that my work, like that of Netta and Caspar, yes, and cunning young Sarah, shall benefit Maldona in the world, from which I am not long departed. How sweetly Sarah enticed me unawares to the joys of freedom, all those months ago! It is right that I should do the same. I have questioned my motives in returning to the world, and they are not from desire for home, since Maldona is my home. Simply, I must best serve her. There are so many females and males in the world to be taught the beauty of submission to Maldona!'

'Mistress,' said Netta, smiling, 'you are no submissive virgin like Sarah, who shall be a submissive virgin to the end of her days!'

'Indeed not,' said Jana, with a sigh of pleasure as Aelfric rubbed fragrant oil on her back. My slaves can testify to

273

that; two of them shall accompany me, Cassandra and Aelfric, and we shall live together in London.' Cassandra and
Aelfric glowed with pleasure. 'It will be exciting, slaves, to
submit to bright Maldona, to be bound by her thongs and
caressed by her whip, in the midst of the dark city: we shall
be an island of beauty and light in the world's confusion.'

'Yes, Mistress,' murmured her slaves, as Jana rose from
her bath and offered them her body to be towelled and
anointed.

'If you must go,' cried Greta, 'we shall send you off in
fine style, Mistress. Please come to our house, through the
tunnel that has carried so many slaves to their pleasant
destinies, and there shall be a great gathering of honour.'

'No. Maldona shall leave the way she came,' said Jana
thoughtfully, 'as is fitting. I shall appear to no crowd, but
depart naked and a virgin, through the mountain pass
which first welcomed me. There! No questions, it is my
word. And yes, I must go. I have a lifetime's task, a task
of beauty, the seduction of those who must be awakened
to themselves. Time must not be wasted. I shan't live for
ever, after all.'

There was a loud wail from Leandra, who darted forward, ignoring the savage pull of her breast-chain, and
prostrated herself at Maldona's feet, to cover them with
fervent kisses.

'Yes, Mistress! Yes, you shall live for ever!' she sobbed.

That night, Jana took Leandra to her bed. The slaves Aelfric and Cassandra were chained naked on opposite walls
of her chamber, to watch as Jana lovingly beat Leandra
with the white whip, leaving no portion of her naked back
and fesses unblushed; then the two women passed the night
in an embrace sweet with the desperation of parting, for
Jana was to leave as soon as the Regency had been decided.

The contest took place in a bright, crisply cold dawn, the
peaks of the mountains that cupped Maldona shining
purple and gold in the rising sun. The naked bodies of
Harriet and Leandra were oiled, and, gleaming, they set to
their combat.

Jana had never seen, nor imagined, wrestling so full of savagery. Leandra's muscles swelled more proudly than Harriet's, and she carried more weight. But in her arrogance was her downfall. The wiry little Superior clawed and bit with a tiger's grace, and delivered the fiercest blows with fist and forearm, until Leandra, in confusion, was a mass of livid bruises. It was as though Harriet did not wish simply to force a submission from the proud Leandra, but to annihilate her, grind her into the dust of utter humiliation.

Between rounds, it was almost impossible to separate the snarling fighters. Leandra slumped sobbing in her corner, feeling the bruises that marked her noble body, while Harriet prowled and spat like a tigress on heat. Round followed round; Leandra struggled to gain the upper hand, but the ferocity of Harriet sapped her spirit. The smaller woman used Leandra's size as a weapon against her, pulling her hair and swinging her to crash painfully on the bare stone floor.

At length, both women were lathered in sweat and panting harshly in genuine hatred. Harriet managed to flip Leandra on to her back and pinion her, then lifted herself as fast as lightning, and dropped on to Leandra with a sickening thud, her naked buttocks crashing with her full weight squarely on to Leandra's face.

Dazed, Leandra writhed helplessly on the floor, like a fish, and Harriet supported herself her knees while her arse and groin slammed again and again with vicious force on Leandra's helpless face, in a cruel parody of a loving caress. Leandra fought to restrain her squeals of pain, trying desperately to throw Harriet as her face took the shattering impact of that vicious drop-cut from Harriet's rump, and Harriet cruelly pummelled Leandra's defenceless naked breasts and arms with her balled fists.

Jana's heart was in her mouth, stunned at Harriet's cruelty. Those breasts that only hours ago she had kissed and sucked so lovingly, now treated so brutally! She could not, did not, wish to stop the fight, for under the rules of *pankration*, no holds were barred, and the fight could only end by a submission. Harriet's body moved like a piston as she tormented the erstwhile Parfaite, her pride now brought low by the Superior's savage pounding.

Leandra moaned deep in her throat, and Jana thought a submission could not be far off. Desperately, Leandra tried for a grip on Harriet's oily, jumping body, but her fingers slid from those pumping muscles. Jana could not understand how the brave Leandra could take such punishment, and her heart swelled with love and admiration: Leandra was taking that beating for her!

Suddenly, just when it seemed that Leandra's tortured body could take no more, Harriet slammed her cunt and anus square on to Leandra's face and, momentarily, held her there, without bouncing up for a further savage drop. The moment was enough; Leandra's jaw snapped in a cruel bite on Harriet's nether lips.

Harriet squealed, and jumped off Leandra in a somersault, which left her rather oddly flat on her back, without any sign of a move to right herself. Groaning, Leandra raised her body, and now it was her turn to crash with her full weight on top of Harriet, pinning her. Leandra's weight now counted in her favour; the smaller woman was pinioned and helpless.

'Oh,' cried Harriet in a voice of unexpected gaiety, 'I'm quite helpless! I suppose I had better submit!' Leandra kneed her brutally between her spread thighs, which she made no move to close.

'Ouch!' cried Harriet. 'I submit, then! You win, Leandra!'

Jana rose, then, proud and happy for her slave, and pronounced Leandra Regent of Maldona, while the beaten Harriet lay on the floor, making a fine show of her gasping. Jana wondered if anyone else had seen Harriet wink at her, with a brief but enormous grin.

And so it was that Maldona went outside. Jana was naked, in Matron's house, to receive her watch (the receipt duly surrendered) and the bag containing her belongings, including her Parfaite's harness and her white whip. No one knew that the diamonds were elsewhere. The door was open; beyond stretched the plain, and the mountain pass through which Jana had to retrace the steps to the outside world. The adepts lined up to pay farewell homage. They knelt for naked Maldona to kiss her bare feet, then her shaven cunt, her naked breasts, and her lips.

Leandra was last and, of all of them, she was the only one Jana had permitted to be naked. Silently, she knelt, presenting her fesses, and Jana took from her bag the white whip, and tenderly whipped the Regent Leandra for the last time, with seven hard cuts on her bare, proud buttocks. Then she dressed her lover in her parting gift: the harness of gold and plumage.

Leandra gave her kisses on feet, cunt, and breasts and, when she came to kiss Jana's mouth, Jana put her arms round her and locked her in a tender embrace. Both women's eyes glistened. Jana stopped in the doorway and faced her adepts.

'I shall return,' she said simply, and stepped out of the door. The door abruptly slammed shut behind her, as she had ordered, and Jana was naked and alone, a virgin in the wide world.

Her step was gay as she came out of the pass through which she had climbed to reach Maldona. The landscape was not forbidding now; it was an old friend. There, far below, twinkled the waters of the lake where she had bathed. The sun was high in the bright sky, and she thought another bathe would be nice. She could see Henry and Cassie waiting for her; maybe they could all bathe together. Humming happily, she set off down the rocky hillside.

'Gosh,' said Henry, 'this reminds me of Mykonos, all that time ago, you know, with the nudists.'

They splashed and giggled in the little lake, like babies. Beside them stood the shining bulk of Jana's new car: a silver-grey Mercedes with Gibraltar plates.

'I'm glad you remember, Henry,' said Jana, showering him with water and making him laugh. 'I'm pleased with you. That is a nice car. Maldona must ride in splendour.'

'I didn't have to sell many diamonds, either – got a good price for them. But am I no longer Aelfric?' he said, a little sadly.

'In the outside, you are Henry – my sweet loving Henry and still my slave.' She grasped his balls and held them rather tightly, and he purred with pleasure. 'And you, girl –' She fastened her other hand firmly on Cassie's cunt. '– can drop this Cassandra. You're Cassie, also my slave. I am still Jana.'

'Why?' Henry blurted out, and then said, 'Sorry, Mistress!' as she gave his balls a playful squeeze.

'Because I say so,' she said, 'for I am Maldona, here and everywhere. You shall take turns at driving me on my progress back to London and when we get there, you shall move your belongings to my home, and attend me there. Now, bathing naked like little children, we are happy. But when we begin our journey, you shall know once more that you are slaves. You shall be whipped regularly and severely, if you displease me you shall be trussed, and you shall sleep in chains.'

'And we shall still be happy, Mistress,' beamed Cassie. 'Won't we, Henry?' He smiled in agreement.

'Very well. Let us go now, to our home, where you shall be my slaves, now and for ever!'

'Yes, Mistress!' chorused Maldona's two lovers.

NEXUS NEW BOOKS

To be published in December

PROPERTY
Lisette Ashton

John and Cassie are partners in a property development business, and pervertedly intimate lovers too. When Brandon MacPherson, a business rival possessed of a darkly dominant sexuality, begins to chase a lucrative contract involving the conversion of an old stately home into an adult theme park and retreat, Cassie puts her wiles to work. But even if she can distract Brandon for long enough for Adam to get the contract, the torments and tribulations she endures at his imaginative hands have her wondering whether she wouldn't be better off switching sides after all.

ISBN 0 352 33744 3

CORPORATION OF CANES
Lindsay Gordon

Set in the bizarre corporate world of a company town, where sex and power are irrevocably intertwined, *Corporation of Canes* explores the vices of a group of its employees: from the female PA of a cruel, dominatrix sales director, to an incompetent, submissive male executive, and a female accountant who's a natural for the environment of sexual manipulation and deception. Powerful prose from one of Nexus's most talented and original authors.

ISBN 0 352 33745 1

THE ISLAND OF MALDONA
Yolanda Celbridge

The women of Maldona are an ancient order devoted to Sapphic love and strict discipline. Unfulfilled by her mundane London existence, their leader, Jana, selects the most nubile and obedient of her slaves and sets out on a quest for adventure. In an ancient castle on a deserted Aegean island, Jana and her dedicated followers set about recreating their passionate rituals of punishment and reward. But her reign as Supreme Mistress comes under threat from a flagellant girl goddess who calls herself Aphrodite. In the scorching heat of the Med, it is only a matter of time before their rivalry comes to a head in the most physical of battles.

ISBN 0 352 33746 X

To be published in January

DEMONIC CONGRESS
Aishling Morgan

Eighteenth-century Devon. Old Noah Pargade is a wealthy yet cur-mudgeonly miser who marries the nubile and game Alice Eden. As anxious to avoid sharing his wife as he is his wealth, he makes sure she is enmured in his desolate old house on the moors. Fortunately for young Alice, there are enough young bucks in the vicinity whose advantage it is in to take pity on her. Noah's fears are well-founded, as Alice is able to continue her cheerfully sluttish goings-on. Especially when the swash-buckling John Truscott returns from his foreign travels, and quack doctor Cyriack Coke, replete with a cartload of bizarre colonic devices, visits the county. When the truth becomes plain, old Coke is forced to take drastic measures.

ISBN 0 352 33762 1

CHALLENGED TO SERVE
Jacqueline Bellevois

Known simply as 'The Club', a group of the rich and influential meet every month in a Cotswold mansion to slake their perverted sexual appetites. Within its walls, social norms are forgotten and fantasy becomes reality. The Club's members are known to each other by the names of pagan gods and goddesses, or those of characters from the darker side of history. Two of them – Astra and Kali – undertake to resolve a feud once and for all by each training a novice member. After one month, the one who's deemed by the other members to have done the best job will be allowed to enslave the other, finally and totally, for the duration of the Club's activities and beyond.

ISBN 0 352 33748 6

PRIVATE MEMOIRS OF A KENTISH HEADMISTRESS
Yolanda Celbridge

Graceful young heiress Miss Abigail Swift founds a new academy to teach Kentish maidens discipline and ladylike manners. She meets the stern, lovely matron, already adept at the art of a young lady's correction; the untamed Walter, longing to become a lady; and the surly beauty Miss Rummer, who keeps the local gentlemen on their toes. Visiting Paris, Abigail learns from the voluptuous Comtesse de Clignancourt that English discipline makes for French pleasure, and triumphs at the masked ball in Dover Castle by introducing her perverse but well-tested methods to royalty.

ISBN 0 352 33763 X

If you would like more information about Nexus titles, please visit our website at www.nexus-books.co.uk, or send a stamped addressed envelope to:

Nexus, Thames Wharf Studios,
Rainville Road, London W6 9HA

------ ✂ ----------------------------

Please send me the books I have ticked above.

Name   ....

Address   ....

            ....

            ....

            .... Post code...................

Send to: **Cash Sales, Nexus Books, Thames Wharf Studios, Rainville Road, London W6 9HA**

US customers: for prices and details of how to order books for delivery by mail, call 1-800-343-4499.

Please enclose a cheque or postal order, made payable to **Nexus Books Ltd**, to the value of the books you have ordered plus postage and packing costs as follows:
    UK and BFPO – £1.00 for the first book, 50p for each subsequent book.
    Overseas (including Republic of Ireland) – £2.00 for the first book, £1.00 for each subsequent book.

If you would prefer to pay by VISA, ACCESS/MASTERCARD, AMEX, DINERS CLUB or SWITCH, please write your card number and expiry date here:

....

Please allow up to 28 days for delivery.

Signature ....

Our privacy policy.

We will not disclose information you supply us to any other parties. We will not disclose any information which identifies you personally to any person without your express consent.

From time to time we may send out information about Nexus books and special offers. Please tick here if you do *not* wish to receive Nexus information.   ☐

------ ✂ ----------------------------